ARMAGEDDON: 2155 AD

Against the sweeping backdrop of a world fanned by the flames of destruction, a handful of players battle for the fate of humanity:

Faisel: Self-proclaimed King of the World, tormented by his desire for the one thing he cannot have—his brother's wife.

Abdullah: Faisel's brother, the only man on earth who could challenge Faisel's rule. His strength lay in his kinship with the peoples of the desert and the love of his wife, Nura.

Olson: The outsider. A ruthless warrior in the battle for the city of Orleans, driven by the vision of a world to come to save its people.

Elwood: An aging executive who saw in Olson the last, desperate hope to save the people and redeem his own dreams.

Gret: A Houris, a woman raised from birth to give men pleasure, fighting for her freedom, learning from Olson the true meaning of love.

Milander: The Hand of God. Cult leader of the Jits, prophet of a new age of destruction, ready to sacrifice a million lives to bring the millennium.

Rennie Du'Camp: Olson's only true rival for control of Orleans. A cunning, ruthless executive who would use or destroy anything or anyone to satisfy his lust for power.

JITTERBUG

"A startling example of the "what if" novel. JITTERBUG takes the reader to a frighteningly vivid world of an all-too possible near future.

—David Brin, author of *The Practice Effect* and *Startide Rising*

"McQuay's books are always fast-paced, explicit and ingeniously plotted; but the double-length novel JITTERBUG... gives scope for even greater inventiveness and exhuberance."

—R.A. Lafferty, author of *Annals of Klepsis*

JITTERBUG

Mike McQuay

BANTAM BOOKS
TORONTO • NEW YORK • LONDON • SYDNEY • AUCKLAND

JITTERBUG
A Bantam Book / August 1984

Caricature of Mike McQuay by Mel White.

ISBN 0-553-24266-0

Published simultaneously in the United States and Canada

Bantam Books are published by Bantam Books, Inc. Its trade-
mark, consisting of the words ''Bantam Books'' and the por-
trayal of a rooster, is Registered in U.S. Patent and Trademark
Office and in other countries. Marca Registrada. Bantam
Books, Inc., 666 Fifth Avenue, New York, New York 10103.

PRINTED IN THE UNITED STATES OF AMERICA

O   0 9 8 7 6 5 4 3 2 1

Acknowledgment

There is no way in such a short space to properly give thanks for the help I had in every aspect of the production of this book. From the outset my wife, Sandy, took in hand the prodigious task of obtaining the medical and cultural research I needed to complete the project. It was only through her knowledge and talent that I was able to undertake the work at all; and in its completion, whatever good there is to be found here is the sunlight of her goodness shining through. Mere thanks cannot begin to compensate her invaluable contribution, both artistically and emotionally.

I'd also like to thank Lou Aronica and Tappan King of Bantam Books for their faith and enthusiasm in the project, and also for their Freud-like skill in dealing with fragile egos.

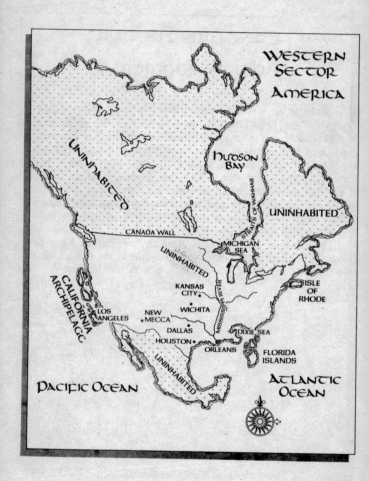

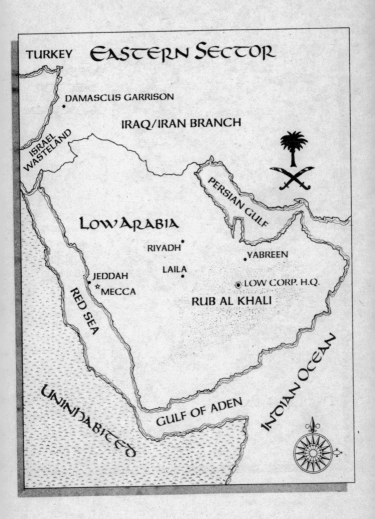

EASTERN SECTOR

TURKEY

DAMASCUS GARRISON

IRAQ/IRAN BRANCH

ISRAEL
WASTELAND

PERSIAN GULF

LOW ARABIA

RIYADH

LAILA

YABREEN

JEDDAH
MECCA

LOW CORP. H.Q.

RUB AL KHALI

RED SEA

UNINHABITED

GULF OF ADEN

INDIAN OCEAN

PART ONE

Prescribed for you is fighting, though it be
*   hateful to you.*
Yet it may happen that you will hate a thing
which is better for you; and it may happen
that you will love a thing which is worse for
*   you; God knows, and you know not.*
                                    —The Koran
                                    II. The Cow

*O believers, expend of that wherewith
We have provided you, before there comes a day
wherein shall be neither traffick, nor
friendship, nor intercession; and the
unbelievers—they are the evildoers.*

—The Koran
II. The Cow

*Whoso obeys me, obeys God; and whoso rebels
against me, rebels against God, and whoso
obeys a governor, obeys me, and whoso rebels
against a governor, rebels against me.*

—The Prophet Mohammed

I

Saudi Arabia
Rub Al Khali—The Empty Quarter
Light of the World,
International Headquarters

The pulley creaked like a snake charmer's song as it hefted the bulk of the huge computer high above the bloodstained mosaic floor of the Hall of Justice. The ceiling of the majestic room rose over twenty meters and would reverberate in thunderous ovation when the workers answered the Allahu akbar, the daily call to prayer.

3

Faisel ibn Faisel Al Sa'ud watched through twelve centimeters of the bulletproof glass wall of his private box as some twenty of his black-robed Elite strained on the ropes that inched the heavy machine ever higher. The Hall was marble, pure white, cold and unornamented. The only decoration on the walls was the small niche that faced Mecca. And the Hall of Justice was like a tomb, a place of death buried deeply under the bleak lunar landscape of the shifting Sahara.

The Hall was beginning to fill with people, the workers in the underground complex, their shuffling feet loud as an army in the hollow room. And even as they pushed their way for a better view around the yellow restraining line, the television camera cranes stiffened their necks to bring the event to the world. The audience would be large, perhaps a billion, since viewing was mandatory.

Faisel sat in the darkness of the booth, exterior light sifting in from the Hall. The booth was safe, secure. Bombproof, its exterior walls were thick steel, its life support self-contained. Within, it was comfortable with rich tapestries covering the walls and thick wafting waves of sandalwood smoke hanging heavy in the air. A large hooka sat in the corner, curling its own brand of haze and the brazier of cardamom coffee heated on the thick carpeted floor near at hand. Faisel occupied the only chair; the rest of the floor was covered with cushions. With a world in his grasp, he spent much time in the booth, the only place he felt truly safe.

In one hand he held a tiny handleless cup of steaming coffee, in the other, a small microphone. He was intent, for he was meting out the justice of Allah. His mishla was brilliant white, trimmed with gold thread, his ghutra was pale blue like the evening sky and tied loosely around his neck. He wore fire opals on all of his fingers, and had a beard trimmed to perfect precision. His eyes were dark, dark like velvet, or like a pit, and they smoldered within lean, coarse brown skin. He was a severe, determined man, and he held the power of life and death over every creature on the face of the planet.

"Tie it up," he said into the mike and his voice boomed through the speakers in the room.

Below, two of the Elite hurried to secure the ropes that held the machine as it swayed in easy, hypnotic rhythm high above the floor. And still the crowd poured in, their voices crashing like a thunderstorm.

Leaning back into the cushions of his black leather chair, a gift from the Western regions, Faisel sipped the greenish coffee and awaited the start of the trial. His Elites had circled the place of judgment, holding back the now pulsating mob, and the black eunuch with the Sword of God was taking his place nearby.

A red buzzer began flashing within the booth and Faisel turned to peer at the Elite who guarded the door. Without a word, the man turned and toggled the security tv screen to life.

"It is your brother, Abdullah," the man said, the dull sheen of his eyes the only thing visible above the black veil that covered his face. Elites lived in total secrecy, complete anonymity from all, including others of their kind. It was a matter of trust, or distrust, depending upon one's disposition.

Faisel smiled slightly, a hard glint just touching his eyes. He nodded. Now he would see.

"Is he alone?"

The Elite shook his head. "He has one of his wives with him."

Faisel waved the hand with the mike. "Bring them to me."

The guard disappeared for only a matter of seconds before returning with the party of four. Abdullah was flanked on either side by bodyguards, though their arms had been taken before entering the booth. Faisel smiled when he saw his brother's tattered thobe and red-and-white-checked ghutra. He stood, extending his arms.

"Man of no enemies," he said, smiling broadly. "Let me embrace you."

Abdullah ibn Faisel Al Sa'ud hurried across the cubicle, taking his brother in his arms. He smelled of camel urine and sweat. He nuzzled Faisel's collarbone, then took his face in his hands.

"God is good," he said loudly, "to keep you in such fine health."

The two rubbed noses, their eyes fixed. "You have been too long absent from my house," Faisel said, and he kept his gaze steady, their faces nearly touching. "I worry about my brother."

Abdullah took his shoulders, shook him. "You worry too much," he said. "Your brother fares well."

"You travel a great deal."

Abdullah felt trapped, uneasy in the confined space. The smells of civilization set poorly in his nose. "Is that not the duty of the Minister of the Interior?"

There was a commotion from the Hall below. The crowd cheered wildly as a man was brought in, shackled in heavy iron. Two of the Elite clamped his chains to the rungs set within the great floor.

Faisel turned to look quickly through the window, then turned back. When he did he was not looking at Abdullah.

"Nura," he said, and the woman in the veil lowered her eyes. He knew that she understood what this was all about and that excited him. Moving past his brother, he took the woman gently under the chin and raised her eyes to him. When they came up, he fixed those eyes with his own eyes of command. And he saw the fear response and was glad. He turned from her.

"I am pleased that you both have come to share my humble hospitality."

Abdullah inclined his head slightly. "I am in turn pleased that you saw fit to honor me so by calling for me over all the television boxes in the world."

Making an expansive gesture, Faisel twirled his hands at the wrists. "What good are the television boxes if one cannot use them to find one's brother?"

"And such a reward!"

Faisel clasped his hands. "It was nothing, a pittance." He pointed to the dusty bodyguards who had taken places by the tapestry that pictured Wahhab stoning the adulteress. "You travel with protection now?"

Abdullah spoke quickly, his large, happy face settling into something graver. "There have been attempts on my life," he said.

Faisel took his seat, motioned for them to occupy cushions on the floor. "And why have you not come to me about these things?"

"You are a busy man," Abdullah answered. "You have a kingdom to run."

Leaning down, Faisel poured a cup of coffee from the brazier. He handed it to Abdullah. "We have business of a private nature."

Abdullah pursed his lips, and Faisel knew that he was weighing the situation. He spoke to his bodyguards. "Wait outside," he said, and they left immediately.

"Bedouin," Faisel said.

"I'm safer on the move."

"Safer with them than with . . . your brother?"

Abdullah tried the coffee; it was too hot. He shared a look with Nura. "The desert people are simpler," he said, choosing the words carefully. "It . . . pleases me to spend time with them."

Faisel looked out the window. Everyone below was staring up. "I must send you on a mission," he said.

"There's nothing you could need me for," Abdullah returned flatly.

Faisel smiled at him. "You underestimate yourself," he returned. "This is very important. I trust you. I trust your judgment. Besides, if you leave for a time, perhaps you will be leaving the source of your trouble here."

Abdullah drank the hot coffee anyway, its harsh aroma cutting the sickly sweetness of the incense. "I am unaware of the 'source' of my trouble, my brother. Do you know something that I do not?"

Faisel looked at Nura. "We are having a problem in the Western Sector."

"Across the ocean?" Abdullah put his cup down. "The Nasrani?"

"You must go there for a time."

"I think you are mistaken."

Faisel noticed Nura's hand come out and gently flick her husband's leg. His eyes met hers only briefly before coming back.

"It is God's will," Faisel said, "that you do this thing for me."

Abdullah's jaw was set, and his eyes were the only thing to give vent to his feelings. "Are you making refusal impossible?" He spoke loudly, for the noises outside the booth were beginning to drown them out.

Showing him empty palms, Faisel said, "There is no one else." He then spoke into the microphone. "Prisoner," he said, and the chamber immediately hushed to a deafening silence, a frightening silence.

The man was kneeling on the floor, his head darting madly. He tried to stand, but the length of the chains would only let him crouch. "I've done nothing!" he yelled, his voice static through a tiny speaker in the wall.

"The work machine was left in your care," Faisel said. "And now it is no more."

"I did my best," the man called up. "The power train was

messed up; there was nothing I could do. Sometimes computers just wear out . . . that's all.''

"You had a sacred duty to keep the machine alive. You have failed all of us. You have failed yourself."

"I did my best!"

"Then I commiserate the shame that you now must feel. As an example to yourself and others, you will share the fate of the machine that you could not keep alive. You must taste the justice of Allah and the wrath of the House of Sa'ud." He paused for a moment, while the television cameras slithered closer like cobras with a rodent, then he raised his voice high. "There is no god but God, and his prophet is Mohammed!"

With the words, the eunuch quickly raised the sword and brought it down on the ropes that held the dead computer aloft. The pulley wheels creaked slightly. The machine seemed to sit poised in the air for a second before plummeting quickly to bring justice to the repairman below.

A piercing scream distorted coming through the speaker, then cut off cold. After a second of silence, the cheers of the crowd shook the building. Faisel turned to Abdullah, yelling to be heard. "We were discussing the Western region."

Slowly, deliberately, Abdullah leaned over and poured himself another cup of the bitter coffee. Faisel leaned down and held his cup near his brother's. They shared a look and Abdullah filled the cup. They waited until the clamor died down.

"What is wrong with the Nasrani?" Abdullah sighed.

"Not all the Nasrani. Just one city." Faisel studied the man, the only one of his sixty-three brothers whom he feared. The only one of his brothers who had the wisdom and following to take his kingdom away if he chose. The fact that Abdullah lived the life of the Bedouin did not mean he didn't have plans.

Faisel sipped his coffee, his eyes wandering once more to Nura, sleek and uncommonly wise—a wife who was able to make Abdullah forget his other wives. She wouldn't return his gaze. "The Port of Orleans," he said. "On the Gulf they call Mexico. The city is not paying its tribute properly."

"Send in your army," was the reply. "They will give in under force of arms."

Faisel shook his head, watched them dragging away the amalgam of man and machine, both broken. "It's not that simple. They pay, but it's not as much as before. The machine people tell me that everything looks all right—but the tribute is less. I want you to go in with the machine people and see that it is set right.''

Abdullah didn't move, but the strain was evident on his face. "You could send anyone to do this.''

"But, my brother, I trust you.''

Abdullah felt himself tightening up. He was caught by duty. His honor demanded he serve his brother. "I know nothing of the machines.''

"You will oversee, that's all. A simple thing to ask.''

"I will not live there.''

"You may make your tent at the garrison at New Mecca, in the desert. The troops there will serve you well.'' He reached into his robes, pulling out a gold chain that hung around his neck. A series of keys was looped through the chain. "You will need one of these.''

"A dome key? I thought this was going to be simple.''

Faisel unhooked one of the keys and handed it to him. "The greater the power, the louder the voice,'' he said. "Go to the Nasrani and make them hear the word of Allah.''

The crowd was filing out now, returning to their work stations, as several of the Elite hosed down the floor.

"I fear this will take a long time,'' Abdullah said.

Faisel opened his mouth to smile and his teeth glinted gold. "I will look after your camels while you are away,'' he said. "And I will take good care of Nura for you.''

Abdullah stood, and a small cloud of dust rose with him. He moved to Faisel, kissing him on the lips. "It is a Bedouin belief,'' he said, "that if a man cannot kill his enemy, he should kiss him.'' He paused a moment, staring. "Wish me good journey, and that I meet no enemies.''

Faisel stood also, and his movements were smooth and fluid. "Destiny,'' he replied, "is the enemy of us all.''

*　　*　　*

The best part of faith is to say, "There is no god but God,'' and the least of it is to remove all injurious things from the road.
　　　　　　　　　　　　—The Prophet Mohammed

The house praises the carpenter.
—Old World Wisdom

II

The Highway
Western Region 14-C—
East Texas America

Gret'amaine crouched monkeylike on the big front seat, listening to Junex Catanine talk his Junex talk, and watching the big, deserted highway rush past her in the labia-pink light of the early early morning.

The tv screen set in the dash showed a satellite picture of one of Faisel's famous theme executions, but Gret was tired, too soon awake, and even that wasn't of interest to her.

"Promotion," Cat said to her for the seventy-fifth time, "is the stew meat of life. The little tasty bits that slosh around in the muck of existence."

"I'm hungry," she returned. She twirled a delicate finger through ass-long honey tresses, and wished that he'd stop comparing his life to food.

He looked at her, dark eyes molding through the heavy leather face harness he wore on the road. "You're always hungry."

"For one thing or another," she said, and snaked a red-nailed finger across the expanse of seat toward him.

He slapped her away, bright stringers of pain washing out the other feeling. He turned from her without a word, watching the road jump at them. She slumped back in the seat, letting the dull light bathe her, letting it creep up her body to heat her brain.

The aut was a big one, Company Exec model. She'd only been in one other like it in her life. It was pre-set for the transfer to Regional and was heavily armored. Cat acted as if they let him ride it out of respect, but Gret figured they were just delivering it to Regional for someone else's use.

Narrowing her eyes to slits, she glanced sidelong at the man who had drawn her name. He was lying stretched out on the seat, boots up on the upholstery, though she knew he had cleaned the heels and soles thoroughly before he had gotten in. She noticed that, always noticed such things, but never, ever let on that she noticed anything. The big control panel wrapped around him in layers, but he only knew how to operate the stop and start switches and a few simple commands. His hands played with the dials, but she knew they were Junex-proof, knew that only a VeePee had the knowledge to use them properly.

"I've got potential," he said, not necessarily to her. "Kicking me up to Orleans." He turned and winked her way. "You should be proud of me. You'll get to move right up with me."

"Right to the top," she offered, and she was also talking to herself. She got stuck out of the Houris pool with Catanine when he got promoted to Junex, and she knew him, knew that his transfer to Regional came through because they had quicker, more efficient means of dealing with the dull and mirthless than the Dallas Branch. If Gret got to the top, it would be over Cat's dead body.

She smiled and sank deeper into the quasi-foam seat cushion. She had the hornies, but that would have to wait. She was just floating off, ordering cocktails in the dream lounge, when Cat's strangled gurgles woke her up.

Opening her eyes reluctantly, she turned her head to him. He was sitting up straight, zipping into his maced gloves.

"Please don't stop," she said. "I want to get there for breakfast."

He smiled wide, and tapped the radar screen with a gloved finger.

She followed the movement. The pale blue screen was bleeping bogies several miles ahead. By their proximity to the road, they had to either be Jits or Bandits.

"Do we really have to do this?" she asked, blinking her blue-lidded eyes to clear them.

"I'm bored," he returned. "I want to kill something. It gets my blood working in the morning."

"I know something better than that to get your blood working."

He licked dry lips, his upper lip glistening. "How many coffee breaks we had?" he asked, rasping up the final zipper tabs on the deadly gloves.

She sighed, resigned herself to it. "Two," she answered.

He smiled. "Good. Contract calls for three on the road. Set the timer."

While he reached out and bullseyed the radar on the blips, she started the twenty-minute Junex coffee-break timer.

"Count 'em," he said, as he flipped the stop switch that slowed the aut gradually to the proximity of the bogies.

Gret dutifully counted. "Seven in all," she said, but through her sleep haze failed to notice an eighth dot just at the top of the small round screen. Maybe she missed it intentionally. Such is the nature of Karma.

Olson sat at the top of the small hill and stared down the road ribbon that could have stretched all the way to forever. The roadways were Corporate territory, jealously patrolled, but they held a fascination for him. The roads drew him, drew on his soul. They were freedom of movement, straight-line movement in a serpentine world.

The sky was overcast, the Texas ground flat and hardpacked and altogether lazy and uninvolving. Olson's hill was a high point in more than one respect, the roadway an exercise in brain magic.

He was young, but old enough, and strong because survival required strength. He was a Transie, a drifter of importance only to himself. Most especially, he was a sitter by the side of the road—an action requiring mental carelessness and great courage.

At that exact instant, he was watching a family of road bandits huddled below him. They were dressed like bushes and had strung nail-laden boards across the highway, hoping to catch a Corporate aut going full speed. They wanted to roll it over and crack it like a nut to get the sweet meat within.

From his vantage point, he saw the slowing aut long before they did and knew, even before they were aware of its existence, that they were going to die. Standing slowly, he dusted off his canvas overalls and sauntered down the hill for a better look. As with most everything else in his life, it was an action to which he gave very little thought, and its ultimate outcome would prove astounding to many, not the least of whom would be Olson himself.

Gret could feel herself tensing and knew, instinctively knew, that all was not going to be well. "Something's wrong," she said, and the aut was beginning to slow down almost to a crawl.

Cat was up, vibrating in his seat, lips twitching in anticipation. "Look," he said, pointing through the windshield at the nail barricade stretched out before them. "Bandits. We'd have never made it past them." His lips stretched across bright white teeth in a nasty smile. "I'm gonna love this."

"Something's wrong," Gret said again, and she found herself mentally memorizing Cat's features, as if she were trying to burn his image into the drippings of her brain pan. Brain lithography.

Slapping his wrists one at a time, Cat engaged the power packs on his wrist burners. The aut had slowed nearly to a stop, rolling hills and meadows stretching out uninterrupted in either direction of the knife blade of the highway. Gret found herself looking for escape routes.

They stopped just before they reached the barricade. Cat was checking his exo that was barely covered by the traveling leathers. Everything seemed calm around them, and they sat, the silence getting louder by the second.

"On the hill," Gret said, pointing. And Cat squinted into the ever-brightening light at the lone figure that stood thirty meters from them with his hands on his hips.

"May be a Jit," he said. "Keep your eyes on him." Then, all at once, he punched up the door security releases and kicked his way out of the aut.

They were on him in seconds—running, screaming bushes, thorny bushes. Gret watched through the windshield as Cat pinwheeled into the human forest on the shoulder of the road.

Their weapons were simple ones: clubs and knives. One of them seemed to have a gun of some sort, but couldn't use it in the close fighting. Cat moved through them easily. Trained in combat from birth, it was his passion in life; and suited in his armor, he could withstand almost any attack from those less well equipped.

His gloved fist slashed into them, rising and falling, the razor's edge of his gauntlet raining red all over the hood and windshield. Gret turned on the wipers just so she could watch the man on the hill.

* * *

*Hell is veiled in delights, and heaven in
hardships and miseries.*
> —The Prophet Mohammed

*The unbelievers say, "Thou art not an Envoy."
Say: "God suffices as a witness between me and
you, and whosoever possesses knowledge of
the Book."*
> —The Koran
> XIII. Thunder

III

The Elevator
Light of the World, Headquarters

The elevator was plush. Hung with heavy purple drapes
with yellow sashes, it was large enough to stable a small herd of
camel. Ringed with heavy, overstuffed couches and tables piled
high with dates and mutton, it could almost be mistaken for a
café left behind by the Ottoman—were it not for the continual
creaking and vibrating that accompanied the hour-long journey to
the surface. Small screens were inset in all the tabletops, twenty in
all, and featured the usual television fare: Faisel reading passages
from the Koran while musak trilled gently in the background.

Abdullah and Nura made the journey in silence, afraid that
private conversation was impossible anywhere within Faisel's
direct grasp. They ate, and listened to the bodyguards make small
talk, their voices strained and nasal due to the rags they had
stuffed up them as protection from civilized smells.

Festering with rage, Abdullah controlled it because he had
to. He didn't want to go to the Nasrani, didn't care about their
tribute or their machines. He wanted confrontation, direct and

14

final, between himself and the man who wanted him dead, the man who feared his power with the Bedouin.

As if feeling his anger, Nura reached over and laid a hand on his arm. And his frustration grew. Not content with a whole world, his brother wanted his wife, too.

It had always been that way. From the time they were children, Faisel had feared Abdullah's closeness and magnetism. The power was a precious gem to Faisel, one that he felt anyone would steal away if given the chance; and so he feared his brother, and his fear turned to hatred because it is the other side of the same rock.

"You will prevail," she whispered, and he marveled at the depth and feeling in her pale brown eyes.

He nodded, feeling his lips curl into a dusty smile beneath his drooping mustache. She was truly a prize, a jewel more valuable than anything Faisel could ever have or offer. And in such, lay his understanding of the nature of happiness and of life.

A bell rang, distant and soporific, and Abdullah found himself on his feet without thinking. It was distance he wanted, as much distance as he could possibly put between himself and his brother. Every moment he spent within Faisel's reach was another moment spent making love with death.

They all stood as the room jerked to a stop, Nura dutifully behind her husband, Ahmad and Bandar in front, tensed and ready.

There was the sound of a door sliding, then light and warmth beating against the thick curtains from without. They stood for a second, waiting, then Bandar reached out and jerked the curtain aside with a loud rasp.

They were looking at desert, a vast expanse of sand sculpted by the winds of God—peaks and valleys, shimmering like a rolling ocean under the glare of the sun. And the sky was bright blue, nearly translucent, a canvas as large as eternity on which to build the sand castles of Heaven.

Ahmad turned to them, his weathered brown face grinning childlike, his eyes bright and glowing.

"If the wind chases us," he said, "we will be chasing our wives before nightfall."

Abdullah laughed, then pushed him through the opening. "If you thought about the Koran as much as you think about your pleasures, you would be as holy as Wahhab."

"Wahhab," Bandar said. "He would be as Mohammed himself."

Looking around, Abdullah once more felt the bile rise in his throat. "Let's be quit of this place," he said, and started to walk through the door.

"Wait," came a voice behind him. He turned to see twenty television boxes staring at him with Faisel's face.

"You will return tomorrow," his brother said, dark eyes boring deeply, burning themselves into the cathode. "We will go over the details of your journey."

"I will do what I must do," Abdullah returned, and walked out into the sunshine. The door slid closed behind him, its thick steel clanging loudly into place. Their rifles and bandoliers lay on a carpet on the ground. They quickly retrieved them and slung them on their shoulders.

The camels were still in their places by the elevator. Bandar retrieved them, leading them by the reins. The elevator door was encased in thick concrete, and a series of identical bunkers, evenly spaced, stretched out behind as far as Abdullah could see. There was also a large, flat parking area, enclosed in a huge plastic bubble that was half buried in sand about a hundred meters distant and, behind that, the mammoth runway filled with jets and copters, its control tower stretching solitary and forlorn into the afternoon sky. Several miles distant was the army base whose job it was to protect all this, but Abdullah didn't look in that direction. He was going North, farther into the desolation.

He helped Nura onto her camel, then mounted himself, slapping the animal into a running gait. He didn't look back until the complex was totally out of sight. He slowed then, letting Ahmad and Bandar go ahead to bring word of their arrival to camp. He and Nura rode side by side.

"He's not content to leave us alone," she said.

"No."

"Do you fear the Nasrani?"

"No. The Nasrani are not our problem." And then he remembered the key in the pouch tied around his neck, and his stomach knotted up. Death was a personal thing to him. Death was something that happened face to face with the bringer of Death.

It was not keys, and it was not an obscene dance that ended with an exhausted giving over of life. The key felt hot through the pouch.

Later that night, he and Nura made love in their tent, love as she had taught him, face to face, eyes to eyes, soul to soul. He moved in and out of her easily, yet there was a desperation to it that neither one of them would acknowledge.

"Will you not take me with you?" she asked, as the sensations took her emotional control away.

Abdullah pushed against her, the fire in his brain. "Faisel sends me away to die," he said through clenched teeth. "You will not be there to witness that."

"If you die, I wish to die with you."

The fire pushed from his brain to his body and he cried out, shuddering against her. "Life is the precious gift," he said, and kissed the sweet softness of her neck. "Do not call upon Death. He will find you soon enough."

And he thought about the key.

* * *

Rules of the Road

1. Avoid strangers when possible.
2. Watch for Jit contamination in speech and actions.
3. Do not touch strangers, disease is passed through touch.
4. Avoid close proximity, disease is passed through the breath.
5. If you suspect a Jit, or are uncertain, best to err on the side of order. Destroy the suspected carrier from a distance.
6. Burn the body.
7. Take no souvenirs.

—Daily TV Message

Be in the world like a traveler, or like a passerby, and reckon yourself as of the dead.
—The Prophet Mohammed

IV
Deep Six on the Highway

Olson had seen the results of combat with Corporate officials many times, but had never had the good fortune to witness it firsthand. The man in black was a killing machine, laughing as he mangled his attackers—a lumberjack enjoying his work.

And the trees fell, one after another. It was a family affair: mamas, papas, and little baby bandits—and they all crumbled together. Olson came down the hill a little farther, picked himself a rock to sit on to watch.

The Exec toppled six of them, the seventh, a girl of about ten, making a screaming run for it. He let her get a good start, then pointed a bloody finger in her direction. His arm hummed and a line of pink light slid from his fingertips. The girl stopped screaming, fell heavily on her face and didn't move. Olson noticed a small wisp of smoke curling gently from the back of her head. The show was over.

Grunting, he stood, and started moving back up the hill.

"You!" bellowed a voice from behind him.

He turned to see the dark figure pointing at him. He looked once at the still figure of the little girl and froze in place. He raised his hands high over his head. "I was only watching!" he yelled back to the man.

"You punched the time clock when you walked down here," the man returned, and his voice was as dead as the little girl.

A woman got out of the passenger side of the aut. She had long hair and was scrubbed clean like Olson didn't know people got, and she wore a dress that looked soft as the clouds.

Gret stared hard at the man on the hill and realized that he was the source of her concern. "Kill him," she said to Cat. "Hurry. We need to be back on the road."

He turned to her, his face and chest splattered with blood, his plasteel exo oozing it. "Our coffee break's not over yet," he replied.

Olson knew that the woman had said something, but he

18

couldn't hear what it was. The dark man snapped at her, then turned back to him.

"Come here," he ordered. "Slowly. And let me see your hands."

Olson started moving. "I'm kinda in a hurry," he said. "Got some things I need to be doing."

The man didn't say a word, he just watched—intent, careful. And Olson knew that if he didn't think of something pretty fast, he'd probably be joining the bandits on the Hellbound road.

He got down the hill, then crossed a small expanse of Johnson grass and dead bodies to reach the shiny silver aut with the red splatters all over it.

"I know what you're thinking," the dark man told him when he got up close.

Olson was genuinely surprised. "You do?"

"You're hoping that I'll let you go."

"The thought had crossed my mind."

"Forget it."

"Okay."

The woman spoke up. "Stop playing, Cat," she said.

"Shut up," the man told her.

"Cat sure is a strange name," Olson said.

The man turned back to him. He was encased in leather, but it was ripped in several places where he had been gashed by the bandits. Underneath was something slick-shiny, something hard. "I know what else you're thinking," the man said. "You're thinking that maybe you can fight me and win 'cause you're a clever country boy, or a Jit—huh? That right?"

"No sir," Olson said, as sincerely as possible. But the man named Cat was right, that was exactly what he was thinking; but he was still thinking of the first thing, too, and thinking that if he was nice enough that maybe the Cat-man and the woman dressed in clouds would let him go.

"Well, forget all of it, boy," Cat said. " 'Cause I'm better than you, and I hate you, and I'm gonna kill you just like the others. Now tell me how that feels?"

Olson got a little bit mad at that. After all, he was only watching, and if the man wanted to kill him, that was his right, but he didn't need to be an asshole about it. "You thinking about burning me with that finger stuff?" he asked. "Or are you going to do it like a man?"

The man dredged up a hocker, spit it on the ground.

"Depends on whether or not you plan on trying to run away," he answered.

"I won't run," Olson said. "If you promise to make it quick and not make me suffer."

"What makes you think you deserve a man's death, country boy?"

Olson looked him dead in the eye. "I guess the same thing that makes you think you can dish one out," he said, and with that, he threw the handful of dirt in the man's face that he had been saving since the hillside.

It wasn't much, but it bought Olson a couple of seconds. He sprang at the man, pushed him back against the hood of the aut, but then he was stumped. The man was a fortress, the only vulnerable part of him his exposed eyes, nose and mouth, and the man's hands were protecting that.

Swinging out wildly, Cat caught Olson a glancing blow with a gloved fist. Olson fell back, white light shooting through his head, his face immediately sticky with his own blood.

Cat sprang upright from the hood, blinking dust out of his eyes. He swung again, Olson moving back out of the way.

"Kill him!" the woman screamed, and Olson could almost have sworn that she was talking to him.

He stumbled around the front of the aut, Cat right behind. The man couldn't wipe out his eyes without taking off his gloves, so he just kept yelling, shaking his head.

He swung again, crazily, then lost his footing on a patch of bandit blood on the roadway. Staggering forward, Olson let him get by, then shoved him from the back, tumbling him headfirst on the road.

Right on top of the nailed boards.

There was a squish as his head took the long nails. His voice choked and his body tried to heave itself up in disbelief, but that only lasted for a second. When he went down for good, there was no doubt but that he was the one walking the road bound for Hell.

Olson looked down at him, neither surprised nor relieved. That was his nature. The woman walked up beside him.

"He was no prize," she said. "But I figured he'd at least make it to the new job."

Olson turned sheepishly to her. "Sorry," he said. "I really was only watching."

He felt the woman's eyes on him, felt her studying him up

and down. He didn't know what to make of that, and found himself shifting his weight uneasily from one foot to the other.

"So what am I supposed to do now?" she asked him at last.

He turned to her then, wanting to stare, but afraid to. "What do you mean?" he asked her.

She was a vision to him. She had a rugged look, but feminine—masculinely feminine. A pattern of freckles was splattered across her nose like paint drippings. And she had pale blue eyes, crystal cold like a thin skim of ice on a clear blue lake, and a mouth that knew everything and told it with its movements.

"I mean that you killed my meal ticket, country boy, and now what am I supposed to do?"

He stuffed his hands into his pockets, feeling through the pocketholes with his fingertips. He hunched up his shoulders. "Well, I guess that you go on doing what you were doing before."

She frowned deeply, hitched up her skirt, and hoisted herself up onto the shiny fender of the aut, on the side away from the bloodstains. "Can't," she said. "He drew me out of the Houris pool to take with him to Regional. I can't show up without a Junex."

He took a look at the dead man under his feet, then moved to sit with her on the hood. "Go back where you came from then."

She slid away from him, for fear he was a Jit, then shook her head, her hair fanning out around her shoulders. "Once you're gone, you're gone. They give your place to somebody else. You've lost your seniority."

"I'm sure they . . ."

She held up a hand to stop him. "That's the way the system works," she said. And he knew then that it was all there was to it.

That didn't make any sense to Olson, but then, very little in life made any sense to him. "What do they expect you to do?"

She nodded toward the earthly remains of Junex Catanine. "I think they'd like me to die with him."

His eyes widened and he stared at her. "Are you going to?"

She made a very unbecoming face. "How the hell do you survive out here?"

He made the same face back to her. "Same as you do, I guess. I eat and sleep and count off the days one at a time."

"What do you eat?"

"It depends."

She rolled her eyes heavenward, and Olson liked that gesture a lot better than the other one. "Depends on what?"

"Depends on if I'm on the road or holed up someplace. My family got the Jits from the Kansas City plague when I was just a kid, so I ran away and have been on the road ever since. I drift around, doing odd jobs. I find farms hidden away sometimes, and usually talk my way into a job or something. When I do, I eat what they eat. Other times, I hunt."

"What do you hunt?"

"Dog and cat mostly. Ground squirrels when I can't find anything else."

"Are there many freebooters out there?" she asked, and Olson had never heard the term before.

"Free . . . what?"

She looked impatient. "Farms that don't work for Corporate."

He narrowed his gaze, realizing that maybe he couldn't trust her. "There's some," he said.

She looked hard at him, and he could tell that she knew what he was thinking. "Do you like it?"

"Like what?"

She made a gesture with her arm. "All this. Living out here."

He shrugged, not for the first time. "Nothing to compare it to."

The eyes were on him again, and he could almost feel them burrowing inside of him, turning him inside out, studying. He shivered. "That's crazy," she whispered low, then smiled a cat smile. "What the hell. It's better than eating dog."

Suddenly she jumped down off the aut hood and began looking him over. "How do I know you're not a Jit?"

He slid down off the hood, a lump caught in his throat as if embarrassment were a physical thing and he was choking on it. "You can check," he said.

She smiled, her tongue coming out to dart quickly over her lips, then disappear. Moving cautiously up to him, she knelt down, her hand sliding slowly up his leg. And her own brain juices started to bubble. She fought them back.

She found what she was looking for, felt it grow under her soft caresses and felt the air go out of her in relief. He was no Jit, not by a long shot.

A Jit could never get it up; it was always the first thing to go. Everything else went quickly after, but that was always first.

Always. She felt him jump and pulsate under her hand. It was contact that spread it—close, touching contact. She looked up and caught his eyes. She didn't look long before she knew she had him.

Reluctantly letting go of him, she stood. "How tall are you?"

"I don't know."

Pulling him away from the aut, she walked around him, checked him over as if she were buying a horse: teeth, ears, hair. "You obviously get a lot of exercise."

"Not by choice."

She stood back away from him, hands on hips, admiring. "My name's Gret'amaine," she said. "Most people call me Gret."

"Olson," he returned.

"That's all?"

"I had another one, but I forgot it back there someplace."

"Wonderful. Can you read?"

"A little."

She nodded. "It'll be a little bit tight a fit, but I think you can get into Cat's exo just fine."

"Why would I want to do that?"

"Because you're going to the Port of Orleans with me, the showplace of the Mississippi. You're going to take Cat's place."

She moved to the man, tried to roll him off the bloody spikes. "Let's get these clothes off him, and get him into the ditch."

Olson bent down and helped her lift him off the nails and roll him to the side of the road. "What makes you think I'd do something crazy like that?"

She pulled the leather helmet off the dead hulk, then spit on it, trying to wipe the bloodstains away. "Because you don't have anything to lose," she said.

He looked at Cat, looked at the ugly black-and-red hole in the middle of his forehead that formed a perfect equilateral triangle with his wide, staring eyes. "How about my head?" he replied. "I may not have much, but at least I'm alive to not have it."

She was zipping him out of his gloves, pulling at a finger at a time. "It won't be as tough as you think," she said. "If this dumb shit can do it, any dumb shit can do it."

Olson straightened, started walking away. "Well, this dumb shit's got other things to do."

She stood also. "Olson," she called, and her voice was like a song.

He turned back to her.

She began to unfasten the clasps of her cloud dress. "When I was born," she said, "they gave me an operation." She pointed to her head. "Up here. They found the nerves that connected to my sexual organs and put a power boost on my brain. So, when I get horny, the juices heat up and the electric booster powers me up to the sky. I've been raised as a Houris, raised to give and accept pleasure in unlimited doses, and I not only like to do it all the time, but I know tricks that you haven't even dreamed of. And, as Cat's replacement, I belong to you."

The clasps came loose and the dress fluttered to the asphalt like a covey of tiny sparrows fluttering out of their nest for the first time. Olson just stared, entranced.

Bending down, Gret picked up the dress and laid it carefully on the hood of the aut; then she spread herself out on it. "So, don't ask any more stupid questions and come here," she said.

Olson took one faltering step after another. He was a man who had never turned down anything free in his life, and he wasn't about to start now.

*   *   *

Live together like brothers and do business like strangers.

—Arabic Proverb

The commerce of the world is conducted by the strong, and usually it operates against the weak.

—Old World Wisdom

V

Port of Orleans
Western Sector America
Regional Office,
Light of the World

The graves were all built above ground because the soggy earth and flooding that brought the dead to the surface was a culturally atavistic method of conducting business in a civilized society. So, the dead were entombed with the living and the ground was like a sponge bloated full of Mississippi water that came charging past to the tune of three and one half million gallons per second on its headlong rush to the Gulf of Mexico just one hundred and ten miles away.

Forty percent of the city was below sea level and all of that seemed to be graveyards. It was founded by a Frenchman in the year 1718, which probably explains why it was built at all, the French never being noted for their understanding of natural laws. It flooded in the spring, had hurricanes in the summer, and was a hotbed of Yellow Fever all the rest of the time. But, it was a good port, second best on the Continent; so it attracted people, the living and the dead, who dwelled together and probably shared similiar philosophies of life.

The citizens worked for the Company, producing goods given as tribute to the House of Sa'ud. In return, they were given a minimum subsistence of food and the right to live on the good side of the wall. They dealt in barter and poverty and filth and disease and that was just the way of things.

The House of Sa'ud had the citizens in a double bind. Energy production was illegal, so all energy flowed back from Arabia. And the walls were the only protection against the Jits, something the Arabs created themselves. Faisel had the people coming and going. Mostly going.

The river was the city's life and its curse. The river flowed through Orleans in uncontrollable measure and the lives of the people flowed from the river in measure that was somewhat more controlled. The streets were like carnivals by day, choked with people selling and buying, bartering for subsistence among the sickly sweet odors of spice and decay that roiled through the twisting alleys on the coattails of the South wind, the Gulf wind that at least kept it warm there all year long.

Boats continually flushed through the harbor, Sa'ud freighters come to trade or just to take, and a smattering of Yid Liners, acceptably illegal trader families who bartered exotic goods from the boats on which they had spent generations, because they had been ordered by law to be given asylum in no country.

The town was old and getting older. New construction hadn't taken place in any living person's memory. It was a hand-me-down city, a city getting by on the merits of the past. It was a city that was rotting like the smells of the carnival days and the corpses that didn't want to get flooded out. But it was a good port and Faisel was doing quite well with it.

Dirigibles floated above all else, balloons swollen large on helium gas and manned by Arabs who never entered the city, but kept watch on it at all times. There were hundreds of them. The balloons hung low and pregnant, and at midday could blot out the sun, and plunge the city into darkness. They were like God.

There were two main architectural features in Orleans, two points of interest to even the most casual of observers. First was the wall, the hundred feet of concrete that ringed all of the city except for on the river. It was Jit protection, and the reason why everyone stayed there. Second, was the LOW tower, Light of the World Regional offices. The building was ninety stories tall, far larger than anything else within a thousand miles. It was constructed of prefab concrete with steel reinforcement and windows double sealed to withstand hurricanes and earthquakes up to 8.4 on the Richter scale. It was painted flat black, and was unornamented. A pole was set on the very top of the building. Atop the pole was a mammoth gold sphere that glittered in the sun by day and was lit by searchlights at night. It was the focus of the city, the matrix.

It was Jitterbug.

On the fiftieth floor of the LOW building were the main conference rooms. In counterpoint to the rest of the city, LOW kept itself in good repair. The offices were completely redone every three months without fail, and looked and smelled brand new. Everything was done in natural woods and leathers, like a stable.

A Houris moved hurriedly through the outer offices to the conference room. Her name was Jerianna. She had red hair and was, at that moment, very concerned about the excess baggage under her right eye, a swelling that seemed connected with too much self-abuse on too little sleep. She worried about getting old, and that worry led to more self-abuse. She was on her last leg and knew it. Like a moth caught on a spiderweb, she was furiously beating her wings against inevitability. In her hands she carried a stack of papers, papers still wet with printout ink, papers with edges sharp as swords.

Moving through the small outer offices, Jerianna quietly entered the big conference room with the floor-to-ceiling holo of Faisel staring darkly at all who sat in there.

There were about twenty in all. Strictly male, it was young men and old, sitting tensed at the big round table. They were survivors, scarred by countless battles, dressed in velvet suits with brocaded ties that looked like things that crawled out of the primal sea. Their ghutras were of the prescribed red and white check, offset by black aghals. They were all shaved clean with short cropped hair, facial hair being reserved by law for purebred Arabs.

They awaited the day's action.

Jerianna began walking around the table, handing out papers to the men seated there. Mr. Elwood watched her as she made her way. He was seated apart from the others, and higher, on a stiff-backed seat of ornate, flowing design. He was of regal bearing, majestic. His eyes were brown and his skin was as dark as the thoughts that usually occupied his mind. He was leaning on one elbow and stared through eyes that had seen it all before. He watched Jerianna carefully, relating to her fears. He shared her concern about things terminal, for he had a bug eating away at his gut, a bug made out of alcohol and amphetamine and ulcers and pancreatitis, and it threatened to eat through his stomach at any second and drag his guts out with it. He did not have a great deal of time left to live, and though he was no psychic, he was well aware of that fact. It hounded him every moment he was awake, and most of the time when he slept.

And if that wasn't bad enough, he had Corporate on his neck, too. They said the tribute was too small, that it had dropped nearly twenty-eight percent behind last year's totals. He had checked and double-checked the figures enough to know that everything was as it should be, but that didn't matter. What mattered was the fact that they wouldn't let him go on this way much longer—they would be coming down hard on him. Soon.

Rennie Du'camp sat at the table with the others, watching their eyes. He was getting ready to make a move, and watched to see if anybody else could recognize that in him. His features were dark, although he didn't know why, for his parents were fair-skinned. The reason is the simplest in the universe, and one that nearly caused his father to kill his mother. But that was before he was born, so he couldn't be expected to know it. His eyes were gray, and his dark hair slicked back naturally. He was almost handsome, but there was a hard edge there, an inner darkness that crept to the outside and made him look the least bit odd. He made people feel self-conscious just to look at him.

"Thanks," he said, as he took the papers from the aging Houris. He laid them in front of him, stacking them into a neat, smooth-edged pile.

Of the group of men around the table, none but him seemed to have that cranked-up look of somebody ready to make a move. That was just fine by Rennie. When he had the stage, he didn't like to share it with anyone.

He had spent the last several weeks searching for weakness in any of the work records of senior VeePees, and finally thought he had found something the night before. The story would soon be told.

They talked low, filling the somber room with a nasal buzzing. Everyone smiled uneasily, tried to remain calm, but there wasn't a soul in the room who wasn't worried about coming under fire.

Du'camp turned to the Junex on his right so as not to give anything away. He met the man's eyes and saw fear in them, as if someone below him had anything to worry about. Rennie was the youngest Junior VeePee in LOW's history. A Junex was beneath his contempt.

"How goes the West side, Hermie?"

Hermie cleared his throat, answered cautiously. "Business as usual."

Du'camp nodded. "Making any money over there?"

"Can't complain. How about you?"

"Could be better, could be worse."

Hermie nodded and rubbed a small mole that sat beside his little rat nose. "I hear that Mr. Elwood has been sick lately."

Rennie narrowed his eyes, but only for a second. "He's tough," he answered, wondering why Hermie said that to him. "He'll be all right."

"No doubt about that," Hermie replied. "No doubt at all."

Mr. Elwood watched the hungry tigers and wondered who would be the one to take his place when he cashed it in. He had ideas on that subject, but wanted to think about it a little longer.

When Jerianna gave him his papers, he motioned her down closer to his mouth. "You don't look well," he said.

She smiled quickly, tried to put something extra into her voice. "No, not at all. I'm fine. Just stayed up a little too late last night, that's all."

Mr. Elwood nodded, almost feeling a touch of nostalgia for her. "I think you need some rest," he said. "Everybody can use a little vacation from time to time. You take some time off and we'll get someone from the pool to fill in."

The woman straightened. "H-how long?" she stammered.

Mr. Elwood winked. "I'll let you know," he said, and turned away from her for the last time. He didn't even hear her leave. In two days' time she would be breathing water for air and looking through eyes that didn't see—just part of the flotsam following the rushing river to the wide sea.

He glanced quickly at the papers, saw that everything was approximately as it should be, and leaned back in the chair, clenching his teeth against the slow pain that climbed up his back.

"Good afternoon, gentlemen," he said, and the room immediately became as quiet as a morgue.

Olson could barely breathe in the tight exo. He felt crammed into it, like stuffing in a goose, and had to take his air in small, quick gulps.

The aut was charging along the wide, empty road, flat Texas plains turning to thick, impenetrable forest the farther they went.

He had never gone so fast before, never knew it was possible. It all rushed past him in a dreamlike blur. He was scared and excited, but never once thought any more about his decision to go to Orleans once he had made it. It was going to be an adventure, and he would take it as it came to him.

Gret was kneeling next to him, rummaging around in her

belongings in the backseat. He watched her perfect buttocks and thin legs as she leaned way over. He reached out a tentative hand to touch her.

"Don't start anything you can't finish," she said without turning around, and, startled, he jerked his hand away. She turned around and sat again, her wide face smiling at him. In her hands was a pair of scissors. "Once you get me started," she said, "I'm out of control. We're fresh out of coffee breaks and late already. We can't afford the stop."

He was looking at her, eyes wide. "How did you . . . know?" he whispered.

"That you were going to play grabby-ass with me?" She wiggled her eyebrows, then got a serious look on her face. "I work on a totally emotional level," she said, answering his question. "The operation saw to that. I guess you could say I'm a slave to my weakness for sex."

"That sounds terrible."

She turned to stare out her side window for a few seconds, then came back around to dwell on his eyes. "What did you say before . . . nothing to compare it to? I've always been this way. The drawbacks are obvious, but it has its advantages. I operate on such an emotional level that I feel things intuitively. I pick up . . . messages, feelings. I can tell lots about people, about what they're thinking and feeling."

He suddenly felt exposed, and it embarrassed him. "What do you pick up about me?" he asked quietly.

She reached over and touched his leg. "That you really don't want to know what I pick up about you."

They passed a checkpoint, a small metal hut. The Arab within waved to them as they went by. They were out of Texas by then, Olson was sure of it. Gone completely were the flat plains, replaced by the thick trees that could, and did, hide many things.

The inside of the aut was large and fancy. It smelled of exotic incense to Olson, and its soft, quilted seats and scalloped instrument panels seemed obscenely luxurious. There was a small screen set in the panel. A bearded man was talking, but the sound was turned down so that he couldn't hear him.

"Who's that?" he asked, pointing.

Gret flinched. "The first thing you're going to have to do is stop asking questions. Don't ever ask, just pretend that you know everything. All right?"

"But . . ."

"Don't say it," she replied, and opened and closed the blades of the scissors. "For starters, that man on the screen is Faisel ibn Faisel, the man who runs everything."

"Everything?"

"King of the World, honey. Secondly, the beauty of the business system is that you don't ever have to ask about anything. There's always going to be somebody or some . . . thing or some memo that will tell you exactly what to do and when and how to do it, and the more you keep your mouth shut, the better off you are."

Olson thought about that for a second. "It doesn't make sense," he said.

Gret slid down in the seat and sighed. "It's not supposed to," she returned.

"Oh."

"Now." She got up on her knees on the seat and turned to him. "We're going to have to cut some of your hair."

"Why?"

She was pulling the face mask up over his head. "Don't ask questions," she said, and started snipping away, sun-bleached tresses sliding down the leather-covered exo. Then she used a wet finger to wipe away the dried blood from his forehead where Cat had slashed him.

"How is it?" he asked.

"Superficial," she said, then kissed the place. "There. All better."

She smelled good up close, and his mind turned back to the hood of the aut with Cat, whose name he now had, lying in the ditch and seven bandits scattered around the countryside and the sun beating down on them.

"Stop!" she said.

"What?"

"You know what."

"I can't help it, Gret," he said. "You give me the Jits in my pants."

She felt his desire wash over her like a boiling wave, and felt herself responding helplessly. "Damn," she cursed low and tried to force her mind in other directions.

"I'll stick close to you as much as I can at first," she said. "We'll have to keep it casual, though. Execs don't treat their Houris very well."

"Will we live together?"

She leaned back to examine her work, then returned to cutting. "They'll issue you an apartment in the LOW building and send me to the dorms, but I can stay with you as much as you want. That's what I'm here for. The rough part's going to be the first day."

"Why?"

Leaning back again, she brushed all the hair off his exo, then began scooping it into her hand from where it had fallen on the seat. "It's customary on the first night at a new office to offer your Houris to the boss of that office. So, you'll be on your own that first night."

He watched her working, watched the curve of her back as she bent down picking up hair. "You'll be with somebody else?"

"Yep."

"But I don't want you to."

Punching through the security locks on the panel, she then pushed a window release and threw the hair out to scatter in the wind. "That's the stupidest thing I've ever heard," she replied.

That made him angry, and this time he didn't stop himself. Reaching out, he grabbed her around the waist and pulled her close. Before she could react, he had her breasts in his hands, tugging on the erect nipples.

Her eyes got wide. "You bastard," she rasped through clenched teeth, then her eyes rolled back and her head followed and she began moaning, and he realized that they didn't need to stop the aut to do what they were going to do.

He slid her quickly out of the cloud dress as she writhed on the seat cushions. And as he began to undo the hooks on his exo, he decided that it wasn't fair to take advantage of her weakness that way. Although that was a moot point, since he didn't intend to stop anyhow.

Rennie Du'camp quietly waited for his chance. While Mr. Elwood read the status reports of the various branches in his sonorous, lullaby voice, Rennie took even breaths, concentrated on the breathing, and psyched himself up.

He was going to do it today. He was going to make senior VeePee. He was going to take the offensive and not let up. The whole city could be his if he just handled himself right. In a world of company men, chosen for their ability to take orders without thought, he was a creative entity, a free spirit who lied his way through the testing just to get the job. He could think, while everyone else could only wonder—and that not very often.

He was smart, smarter than the system, but not smart enough to rise above it. He used the system, not creatively, but with selfishness and contempt. He was the oyster with the pearl, but still an oyster.

Mr. Elwood read through the printouts, trying to keep his mind on what he was saying, failing miserably. He didn't much care anymore. He had it all and it wasn't going to keep him alive. Everyone in the room knew it. He pictured them all drooling over his carcass. When Elwood died, it meant that everyone moved up a notch. He had heard that there was even an office pool to pick the month and day of his death.

"The freighter with our oil rations for the month will be here next week sometime," he was saying. "In the name of Allah, Jerry Joe, make sure that you keep it away from any Yid boats that might come in."

Junex Jerry Joe stood up quickly. "We've already made arrangements to keep everything out the day the freighter docks," he said.

Mr. Elwood nodded. "Make sure you do," he said. "Last month, the Arabs blew three Yids out of the water when they came in, and as most of you know, one of them had a booze consignment. We nearly ran out because of that."

"We'll meet them at the mouth of the harbor," Jerry Joe said.

Mr. Elwood nodded again. "That seems to cover the field," he said, and felt a small charge of excitement rush through him. "I'm open to new business."

Rennie gave it about ten seconds before he opened his mouth. Everyone kept still and steady, but their eyes bounced back and forth like they were strung up with rubber bands. He stood slowly, theatrically, straightening his suit coat for quite a long time before looking to Mr. Elwood.

Elwood smiled to himself. He had made quite a study of Rennie Du'camp and had been expecting this. "We recognize Mr. Du'camp," he said quietly.

Rennie drew his lean frame up full and put a hand on his hip. He knew that he cut quite a figure, for he had practiced this pose in front of the mirror many times.

"I have something of a sad duty to perform here," he said with drawn-out sincerity. "And it breaks my heart to have to do it. But I have a duty, a duty to my God, and the House of Sa'ud. I have a duty to Light of the World and to its regional representative, Mr. Elwood."

He turned and gestured with his free hand to Mr. Elwood, who bowed his head in acknowledgment. He felt the atmosphere of the room charge with tension, as if the molecules of the air had somehow inflamed with electricity. He gazed around at the questioning faces, but didn't stop at any of them.

He continued, speaking low, making everyone lean closer to hear his words. "One of our number is guilty of treason, foul and disgusting."

A buzz went around the table, but Rennie silenced it quickly with an upraised hand. "Oh, there's been no flagrant sellout, no meditation of treasonous acts; but sins of omission are sins nonetheless, and an overwhelming bundle of such sins presents a danger to all of us and the lives we hold dear."

"Treason is a serious charge," Mr. Elwood said. "We hope that you have evidence to support such a statement."

Rennie let his voice pick up a bit. "I not only can support the charge, I intend to prove it absolutely." He walked slowly around the table, tasting the fear that was hanging in the air. He stopped beside the chair of his immediate supervisor. Reaching out, he suddenly spun the chair around to face him. He pointed an accusing finger right into the man's face. "VeePee Marden, I accuse you of treason against the Light of the World and the people of Orleans!"

Marden's mouth fell open. He was an older man, early sixties, small and withered, with staring snake eyes. He came to his feet, mouth working soundlessly. Finally the words came. "Rennie, what are you doing?"

"You," Rennie said loudly, and jammed his finger into the man's chest, "through incompetence and calculation, have cheated this Company out of a fortune."

"Rennie!" the man shouted.

"Shut up!"

"I've been like a father to you!"

He was pleading already. Good. Rennie had played up to Marden for so long that the old man couldn't even muster the desire to defend himself.

"This man will be silenced while I make the charges!" Rennie said.

Several of Marden's allies came to their feet, Junexes

mostly, who had thrown in their lot with him and curried his favor.

"This is an insult," Junex Willard with the pockmarked face said. "VeePee Marden is above reproach."

"Will you then share in his fate once proven?" Rennie shot back.

The man stared hard at him, said nothing.

"I've spent months going over the records in Agri-disbursement," Rennie said. "And what I've uncovered made me sick to my stomach."

He stomped quickly back to his seat, while Marden's supporters at the table remained standing in support. For his part, Marden sank heavily to his seat, continually shaking his head. Getting into his briefcase, Rennie pulled out a stack of papers. He threw them on the table, where they slid on the polished surface, fanned out within everyone's sight.

"The incompetence is monumental," Rennie said, as those around the table began picking up pieces of paper. "Grain, harvested grain, left out to mold in the weather for five years running. An incalculable loss."

Marden narrowed his eyes and stared up at Rennie. "There's always grain loss," he said. "We harvest more than we have space to store. That's ridiculous."

Hooking his fingers in his waistband, Rennie began pacing the length of the table. "So, you're saying that loss is built into the system and there's nothing you can do about it."

Marden's lips were moving again. He wiped his brow. "I didn't say that exactly. I suppose that it's possible . . ."

Rennie folded his arms. "That the system could be designed for maximum yield and maxiumum storage?"

"I suppose."

"Why haven't you done it? You could have saved us a ton of plastic."

"I talked to Mr. Herman about it many times," Marden answered. "He always said that we could never get the authorization from Finance for more silos."

Everyone turned to the head of the table and looked to Mr. Herman, a tall man with bright blue eyes and a harelip. He stood up quickly. "No," he said. "We never talked about anything like that."

Marden's mouth was open again. "Freddie . . ."

"Why are you trying to drag me into this?" Herman

demanded, eyes darting around the room. "I don't know anything. This is the first I've ever heard of this. Why didn't you come to me?"

Marden ran his hands through his hair. He was blanched white, and shaking. "I did, Freddie . . . I did," he mumbled.

Several of his supporters sat down, looking around. Du'camp walked up to Mr. Elwood and handed him a sheet of paper. "I have here a plan I worked out that transfers excess grain to one of the Eastern Regions in exchange for the materials to build new silos. I've already cleared it through them. The plan took me about two hours to work out."

Mr. Elwood read the paper, nodding as he went. Murmurs were passing around the room, as more of Marden's supporters took their seats.

"There's more," Rennie told the group. "Much more." He walked back to Marden, got down in his face. "Why don't you work your fieldhands during all the daylight hours?"

"They get tired," Marden returned. "I found that they turned out more work with shorter hours."

"Do you have figures to back that up?"

"No. It was personal observation."

Rennie straightened. "Well, I did a little personal observation of my own. A routine part of my training in Agri was to run the fields for a month. Under my supervision, I eliminated rest periods and worked the hands as long as there was light. As a result, I got three percent more work done per day."

The murmurs got louder, and the rest of Marden's support melted away.

"You had more sick call, too." Marden yelled, to get above the noise.

"Fire the candyasses and replace them with folks willing to put in a day's work. We don't need dead weight!"

There was applause for that.

"I could go on and on," Rennie said loudly. He bent to Marden again, grabbed him by the lapels. "Holidays off," he spat. "Overpaid tribute, rotted fruit, barren fields, low yield, theft loss . . ."

Marden was pleading now, shaking uncontrollably. "Those things happen. You can't control everything."

Rennie dragged him out of his chair, shaking him. "Why not?" he demanded through clenched teeth. "That's no answer.

This is your company we're talking about. Your company! Don't you have any sense of shame, of decency?''

He slapped him repeatedly, drawing blood from the corner of his mouth. "Rennie," the man sobbed. "How could you do this to me?"

"It was easy," Rennie returned. "I love the company. I care about it."

He walked Marden up to the table, threw him down on it. "That's not all," he said. "You've stolen from us yourself."

The voices were loud now, angry. Rennie was flush with it, excited. "Bring them in," he said. "Bring them in!"

The door opened and uniformed LOW security entered, along with Marden's wife, Jerlyn, and his daughters, Sunmaid and Daisy, both pre-marriage age. Behind them, a burden Engy seven feet tall was pushing a two-wheeler loaded down with sacks of potatoes.

"We found these in your apartment, VeePee, in transport bags marked 'Rochester'."

Marden turned his face on the table, smearing it in his own blood. "I don't know what those are!" he screamed.

"Tell him, girl," Rennie said, not even looking at her.

The one named Sunmaid stepped forward. She hesitated, looked once at her mother, then turned back around. "He brings them home sometimes," she said in a tiny voice. "Says they're extras."

"Extras!" Rennie yelled, looking around the room. "He says they're extras!"

"Thief! Thief!" The word came from everywhere.

Marden was crying. "Everybody does it!" he yelled. "Tell them, Freddie. You do it too."

Freddie was up again, his face twisted with rage. "Liar. You're a thief and a liar." He turned to Mr. Elwood, who sat motionless on his high-backed chair. "Mr. Elwood, I demand that this man be fired immediately and Rennie Du'camp put in his place!"

The room reverberated with affirmation. Rennie smiled around the group. "My only wish is to serve my brothers," he said, and walked over to the only window in the room, the window that had but one purpose.

Throwing the latch, he pushed it open easily, looking down the fifty stories to the miniature world below. He turned abruptly and looked at Marden.

"Will you not be a man even once in your life?" he asked.

Marden sat up slowly on the table, turned to his wife and children. They were silent, their faces frozen in terror.

The little man got up slowly. Firing meant expulsion for him and his family. Death meant a stipend for them and a place within the city. It was no choice at all.

He moved to the window, looking once at Du'camp. Rennie smiled at him. "You weren't like a father to me," he said. "I was like a son to you."

Nodding, Marden climbed up on the sill and jumped without fanfare.

Several Junexes joined Rennie at the window, craning their necks to get a good look at the end of Marden. It was a happy time for everyone of lesser seniority, since a link removal from the chain of command meant that everyone got to move up a rung. Advancement without involvement.

"I've just been handed two messages," Mr. Elwood said. "The first is that stray Jits from the Houston kill have entered our parameters. The second is that Abdullah ibn Faisel, esteemed brother of Faisel ibn Faisel, will be coming to the city within the week to inspect our records."

Mr. Elwood looked around the suddenly quiet room and tried to keep the tension out of his voice. "Gentlemen," he said. "We're going to be audited by the second most powerful man in the world. Allah help us all."

* * *

Not even a collapsing world looks dark to a man who is about to make his fortune.
                    —From the Introduction
                      to Standard Operating
                      Procedure Manual, LOW
                      Branches

Whatever mishap may befall you, it is on account of something which your hands have done.
                    —The Prophet Mohammed

VI
The Orleans Gate

The thunderheads built up high, moving fast, and pastelled the sky in thirty different hues of gray and blue. The cracks of lightning were sharp and crisp, nearby, and flashing the landscape from bright light to thick cloud blackness and back again as Olson and Gret had to slow the aut to a crawl to make it through the streaming mobs of people who filled the highway.

Olson sat up straight, craning his neck this way and that to get a look at more people in one place than he knew even existed. People carrying children and belongings crammed the roadway and the surrounding countryside, all of them grim and determined, all moving in the direction of Orleans, several miles distant. And the lightning flashed again, and cracked the whip, herding the citizens forward, jamming them tighter together.

"Speed it up some," Gret said, looking around. "They'll get out of the way."

"What are they all doing?" Olson asked, as a woman carrying a squalling baby tripped and nearly fell under their wheels.

"They're all seeking harbor in the city," she said, reaching out to knob up the speed a bit. And as if that were some sort of signal, rain began sheeting down, falling out of the clouds as if it were all coming at the same time.

The noise of the driving rain was loud on the aut hood, forcing Olson to speak up. "Why?" he asked.

She shook her head. "Might be Houston," she replied. "They had a big kill a month ago, accidental I think, and the Jits have probably been spotted heading this way. That's the only reason why all the farmhands and factories would try to get inside the wall."

Olson looked down the road, at Orleans shining way off in the distance. The wall was massive, unignorable. It was covered with red and green lights that shone brightly in the cloud-darkened morning. Beyond the wall, the city proper was also lit, windows and signs, and with the dirigibles hanging overhead like

39

so many toy balloons in a traveling show, Olson couldn't help but feel that he was walking into the circus. He had seen a circus once, at least part of one, when a band of jugglers lost a wheel on their wagon and had to park for the night in a forest near where he was staying. He had sneaked down and watched them practice, huge Engies juggling five or six tiny ones, then throwing them back and forth. He determined once and for all that he would really see a circus sometime.

"Should we let some of the children ride on the hood?" he asked loudly.

She shook her head. "Don't ever mix with the citizens," she returned. "An Exec is not in their class; they wouldn't know what to do with a friendly gesture from one." She winked quickly at him. "Just keep your place and let them keep theirs."

She drew her lips tight, irritation showing on her face, her freckles flushing red. Unsecuring the window, she leaned her head out. "Come on!" she yelled, and lay on the blaring horn. "You got a Junex coming through!"

He put a hand over an ear, and used the free one to pry hers off the horn. "Give it a rest," he said. "What else we got to do?"

She pulled her head back in, her hair stringing water that ran in tracks down her face. "I'm hungry," she said indignantly. "All that fucking gave me an appetite."

"I said I was sorry."

"Yeah . . . after the third time." She stuck her head out the window again. "Get out of the damned road!"

And the deluge was turning the farmland that surrounded them into mud rivers as the citizens got soaked through their clothes and skin all the way down to where it hurts to even think about it.

The bottleneck got even tighter the closer they got to the gates, since the human river had to funnel down to a narrow passage.

Exasperated, Gret pulled back in and slammed the window shut, folding her arms across her chest.

"You look kind of cute all wet," Olson said quietly.

She pointed a dripping finger at him. "Don't even think about it," she said.

He put up his hands. "I couldn't, even if I wanted to."

Just to be on the safe side, Gret kept her arms folded, where the wet material of her thin dress showed the jutting outline of her nipples. "What do you do about Jits on the outside?" she asked.

He shrugged with his face. "Not much," he said. "First off, we don't see too many of them, since they head for the cities. Second, we leave them alone because they're holy people."

"You don't kill them?"

Olson shook his head, horrified. "Oh no," he said. "You don't kill them that are holy. They see the visions. Oh, no. I'd never kill one of them."

Rennie Du'camp stood on the top of the wall near the front gate, watching the crowds pouring into the city. The rain was sheeting down, but he could barely feel any of it through the body-hugging exo that covered him from head to foot. His exo was red, bright red, and he wore it without leather harness, preferring the garish highlights to the somber downplay that went along with the leathers. He did wear the leather helmet, though, in pure white that he set off with a bright red plume that drooped off the top nearly down to his waist.

The news from Houston had set off a minor panic, bringing the hordes of country dwellers into the city faster and in greater initial numbers than the circumstances demanded. It would be days, weeks perhaps, before the Houston Jits would be a problem; but it was impossible to tell that to the single-minded mob that was crowding the gates. In the course of time, everyone had lost friends or relatives to the Jitterbug. In the course of time, everyone might lose himself to it. Nobody wanted to take the chance. And for that, Rennie could scarcely blame them.

The wall itself was a beehive of activity. The defenses were all being bolstered, in preparation for the siege that would surely come. Citizens and Execs flowed around him as he leaned against the rusty iron railing that ran around both sides of the ten-mile stretch of wall. They were carrying .50-caliber machine guns and crates of ammo to the pillboxes that jutted out from the top of the wall every twenty feet or so. All the Execs had been pulled off other duty to help with the defense of Orleans.

It was a massive job, and all coming at the wrong time. There was no way to house the extra thousands who were moving in for an unspecified amount of time. They'd most likely be sleeping on the streets, increasing the chances of epidemic Yellow Fever from the wet spring and marshy flooding that Orleans had been experiencing for months.

And so it was loud, even from a hundred feet up, and by next week the city would smell like an open sewer and worse. There would be other problems, dysentery and looting and the violence that goes with overcrowding. If there were a lot of deaths, the bodies would have to be burned. If the Jits kept them locked in through harvest, there'd be nothing to eat next year.

Rennie turned and walked to the pillbox nearest him, his plasteel boots clanking loudly on the cement pathway that was just wide enough for two people to pass one another going in opposite directions. The traffic was heavy and confused, with single-file lines of citizens carrying crates squeezing by one another. One of his Junexes, Marty Jerny, stood inside the pillbox, taking a smoke. His exo was flat black, partly leathered, and his chubby face was red within his mask from too much sun.

Taking the cigarette from him, Rennie dragged deeply on it. "I'd forgotten how many there were," he said, handing it back to Jerny.

"Where the hell are we going to put them?" the man returned.

"It's a big city," Rennie answered, but he didn't know where to put them either.

The box was large enough for four men standing upright. There were window slots cut through the cement for viewing and firing the guns. The machine gun stood on a tripod in the center of the room, with much of the wall space filled with ammo crates. The rain was coming down hard, some of it dripping through the window slots to make small puddles on the floor.

Jerny puffed, then handed the cigarette over to Rennie again. "Congratulations on your promotion today."

Rennie nodded, took the cigarette. "I worked on that one for a while," he said. "But when it came down to it, old Marden wasn't as tough as I thought he'd be."

Jerny nodded. "Well, you made it look easy. I wish I had your talent."

Rennie dragged on the smoke. "I don't," he replied. "The competition's bad enough as it is."

He tried to hand the cigarette back to Jerny.

"Keep it," the man said.

Rennie shrugged, dropped it on the floor to sizzle to death in one of the puddles. Going over to the gun, he got behind it, sighting down at the crowd on the roadway below.

"Wish the rag heads would let us use something bigger than this," he said, as he raked the crowd with imaginary bullets.

"Don't say that too loud," the man answered, looking around. "I wouldn't put it past them to bug these places."

Rennie spit loudly. "Too much trouble for them, Marty my boy. Our Arab friends are just too lazy to bother."

"I don't know..."

Rennie swung the gun around, trained it on Jerny. "You getting soft on me, Marty?"

The man jumped, then his dough face settled into a grin. "Don't you worry about me," he returned. "I've never let you down yet, have I?" He reached out a tentative finger, pushing the wide mouth of the barrel a few inches away from him.

"No, you never have let me down," Rennie said. "And I think I'm going to be needing you again soon."

"The air's pretty rarefied up where you're breathing it now. Promotion doesn't come so fast."

Rennie swung the gun back to the window, sighting the crowd again. He hadn't shot one of these in years. He briefly considered cranking it up and emptying a few hundred rounds into the mob, then rejected the idea as more trouble than it was worth.

"Promotion comes at whatever rate you can handle it," he said. "No guts, no glory."

"You sure got big ideas."

"What's wrong with that?"

Jerny sat down on a stack of ammo crates. "Nothing," he said, "if you can back them up."

Rennie smiled over at him. "That's why I've got smart boys like you working with me."

Jerny slapped the crate next to him, then pointed at Rennie. "I just figured it out," he said. "You want it all, don't you?"

Rennie's face got grave. "I'd better not hear any talk like that getting back to me," he said low.

Jerny stood up. "You know my loyalty."

"I know that talk's cheap, and cheaply given."

"You can depend on me."

"Yeah," Rennie said, and didn't even look at him. "You probably have work to do."

Jerny moved to the open doorspace. "Matter of fact...guess I'll see you later."

"There's a party tonight, a promotion celebration. I'd like to see you there."

Jerny brightened. "Sure. Thanks."

"And, Marty. You've always liked my Houris; I've seen you watching her."

"Yeah."

"She's yours tonight."

Jerny came over and slapped him on the back, the blades in his gloves clicking on the exo like tiny castanets. "You've just made my life complete, Rennie old pal. I can now die a happy man."

Rennie looked into the man's eyes—locked on them. "I probably don't need you to die, Marty. I just need you to be willing to."

Jerny gulped audibly and backed out of the doorway. "See you tonight," he said, and clanked hurriedly away, losing himself in the flow as it moved past.

Turning back to the window cutout, Rennie shook his head and watched what looked to be a never-ending parade. The ground around the road, already soaked with months of rain, was ankle-deep mud being carried into the city one shoe at a time. It would clog even more the antiquated sewers and back up the water, flooding the streets. And if the rain itself didn't stop soon, the river would rise past the sandbags and bury them all.

He saw something cutting through the road crowds. It was an aut, a silver one, horn blaring, moving steadily. Pushing the crowd, always pushing.

Rennie knew that it was the new Junex from the Dallas Depot, because Rennie made it a point to know everything that was going on. He was to train on the river with Jerry Joe, which was a good place for him if he knew how to keep that place.

He worried over new blood, over anything he didn't have direct control over. Slapping the gun once, he walked out of the pillbox and toward the long steps down. There was only one way of finding out anything.

Mr. Elwood's office was totally secured, as was his attached apartment. A detailed nomenclature of his defensive systems would be repetitious and tedious; suffice it to say that if a bird got within twenty yards of the ninetieth floor of the LOW building, it wouldn't be bringing any worms home for the baby birds that night. In a world that was proud of its security, Mr. Elwood had more to be proud of than almost everybody else.

He was on the top floor, overlooking everything else. He had windows floor to ceiling that gave him a panoramic view of his domain. There was even a skylight that gave him a totally unobstructed view of the Jitterbug dome at all times.

He had the whole floor, and spread himself wide to fill it. He liked softness, considering himself basically sensitive. His furniture was sparse and slung low. It was done in pastels and creams—thick white carpets, fat down pillows in pale greens and blues, wide-open spaces and all soft curves with no hard angles. It was a jelly doughnut of an apartment with powdered sugar so thick that it dusted off and filled the air with sweetness that you could breathe.

He sat naked in the lotus position on his creamy carpet, the rain-sheeting world outside his windows a pale, dark vision lost in a dreamlike haze as the humidity steamed up the incredibly thick glass. He sat naked, dark like a raisin in contrast to the white carpet. Still trim at fifty-three, he marveled that such an attractive package could hold so much dissipation and disease. He felt bad deep inside, felt like he wanted to split open, and that he would empty himself on that white carpet and it would be all smoking, festering sickness that could eat like acid right through the floor and kill those below him. It wasn't a question of it, it was simply a matter of timing.

He sat, alone, in front of a small tv screen. He was talking to the King of the World.

"You will treat my brother with all the respect that you would treat me with," Faisel was saying.

"I will do that," Mr. Elwood answered.

"You have this one more chance to pay us the tribute that you owe us."

Mr. Elwood sighed deeply, painfully. "We have paid you your due," he said.

The response came quickly and simply. "No."

They stared at one another through the screens, and there was a long desperate silence. Finally, Faisel ibn Faisel Al Sa'ud reached into his thobe and came out with the necklace of keys. "Do you know what these are?" he asked.

Mr. Elwood's eyes drifted up to rest on the dome, gold flashing brightly in the lightning. Pandora's egg. "Yes, I know."

Faisel shook his head. "And still you refuse us what is our
God-given right?"

"My books are in order."

"My brother has one of these keys in his possession,"
Faisel said, still holding them up. "He will use it if we are not
satisfied."

"That is his prerogative."

"Is your life, the life of your city, so unimportant to you,
Nasrani?"

Mr. Elwood nearly laughed at that, but he didn't. "No."

"You have nothing more to say to me?"

"Wish your brother a pleasant journey," Mr. Elwood said.

Faisel's eyes flashed and he blanked the screen. Almost
immediately, Mr. Elwood doubled over at the waist, an incredible pain grabbing his spine like a cold hand. He lay there,
moaning quietly, crying softly, until it subsided, then straightened. Pulling the tiny keyboard up near him, he punched up the
listing for Accounting. A Houris with blond hair and overlarge
breasts floated onto the screen. Her eyes widened when she saw
the face on the other end.

"Mr. Elwood . . ."

"Get Gritchem for me," he said. "Right now."

She opened her mouth to say something, but made the
wisest decision she'd ever make in her life by not saying it.
Without a word, she stood and moved away from the screen.

Mr. Elwood reached for the decanter that stood by the
screen on the same low, long table. He poured himself a drink
and hurried it down. Then he poured another and waited.
Gritchem appeared seconds later.

"Don't say anything," Mr. Elwood said. "Just listen." He
took a breath. "You and everybody else who works for you have
got yourselves a job. You get into the computer, tear it down
program by program, and find out what the hell's going on with
our tribute payment. Faisel's brother will be here to inspect the
installation in three days. If you haven't found the problem by
then, you, and all the Junexes under your control, will be
executed. That's all."

With that he reached out and shut down the screen, then
finished the second drink. It didn't help the pain, not any of the pain.

They were caught behind a large group of mongoloid giant
plow-pullers right in front of the big wooden gates. They were

trying to search the giants, but the members of the gate guild, who tended to be small by nature, couldn't reach past their waists to pat them down.

Gret, the edge sharpened on her emotional sword, was leaning fully half her body out of the window space.

"Come on, you idiots!" she screamed, beating her palms against the side of the aut. "Let's move it!"

Olson was in a daze, attacked on all sides by sights and sounds and smells like he had never known before, could only gawk at the insane world that surrounded him.

"Lay them down!" Gret screamed. "Search them that way."

Not content with the simple solution, the green-jumpsuited gaters were trying to climb up on one another's shoulders to reach higher; but the rain-slick clothing that they wore wouldn't hold their shoes, so they kept falling to splash in the monstrous mud puddles that now dominated the roadway.

Meanwhile, the area outside the gate was becoming more and more clogged with people, all pushing to get through to the other side before the Houston Jits, who were weeks away, could come and scare them to death.

Gret pulled back in, her face twisted with rage. "Dumb sons of bitches," she spat, and sat, arms folded, vibrating in her seat.

"Take it easy," Olson said. "We'll get in soon enough."

"Easy for you to say," she returned. "You probably had breakfast."

She had splatters of mud on her face that mixed with her freckles, and her hair was stringing, plastered all over her face. Reaching out, she viciously poked the door release.

"Let's get out of here," she said. "Somebody else can drive this thing in."

Olson narrowed his gaze. "You sure that's all right?"

"You're an Exec, buddy. You can do anything you want." She put a leg out of the door, then twisted to look back in. "Remember, your name is Joey Catanine, but everybody calls you Cat. Other than that, keep your mouth shut and do what they tell you. And, in the name of Allah, don't be nice to the citizens. That's about the last thing you need to do."

"What about—"

"You've got it," she said curtly, and disappeared out the door.

Olson took a deep breath. "Oh well," he muttered, and punched out of his door.

The crowds were thick all around, pressing. Workers in overalls and their families behind carrying gunnysacks full of clothes. Wagons loaded full of half-ripe melons and cabbages, creaking past, slinging mud, pulled by genetic beastmen who growled and grunted with the strain, the powers of speech beyond their limited scope. And the thunder crashed loudly, and the voices were a constant thunder. Olson felt lost in the confusion as smells at once sweet and pungent assailed him from all sides, and the old ladies cawed like crows, their severe black sack dresses heavy with dripping water. The dirigibles hung like fat sausages overhead, the tiny forms of Arabs on their decks laughing and pointing at the carnival below, as the gatekeepers shouted through cupped hands to keep it moving as they continued to slip and slide off the shoulders of the giants who were too stupid to understand how to use weapons, much less hide them. And there were sick people, weak with Yellow Fever, their energy gone, being carried by their fellows or just left to crawl through the fecal slime and slush of the roadway.

"Come on!" Gret called to him, and he saw her waving arms and the bright blue of her cloud dress through the somber earthen colors of the citizens.

He moved toward her, bumping his knee on the head of a tiny man who cursed in a low, guttural voice until he saw Olson's leathers, at which time he scurried away through a forest of knobby knees.

And the crowd parted for him. An avenue opened before him as he walked, and they all averted their eyes and mumbled apologies for having the gall to be standing at that place in time. And the wall was thick stone running trails of water that shone with reflections of the red and green blinkers and sparkled like diamonds with the sharp-as-razors glass embedded in its surface.

He got through them, made it up to Gret. The rain had gotten inside his leather mask, feeling good, cool. The gatekeepers were six deep, holding back the unruly crowd, while local constables kept a close watch in the distance, their fuzzy top hats done up in black with bright gold bands.

"Here he is," Gret was telling one of the Guild members.

The man looked up at him, dull eyes shining wetly. "Identify yourself," he yelled up.

Olson looked at Gret, she winked quickly at him as if she

did this every day. "Junex Catanine," he said quickly. "Transfer from Dallas."

The man squinted up, rain getting in those dull eyes. "Just a minute," he yelled again, and moved to a small computer screen that was inset in the stone of the wall.

He was shaking a shaggy head, drops of water spewing in all directions. "Don't see you here at all, Junex. Not at all."

"You'd better let us in," Gret said. "Or the Junex will take your lousy head off!"

"Gret," Olson said low, his eyes darting around.

"All due respect," the man said. "He's not on the list."

Gret looked up at Olson. "Kick his fucking ass," she said.

Olson rolled his eyes, then looked at the sea of gatekeeper faces that was staring at him.

"Maybe we could come back later," he offered.

"Kick his ass!" Gret screamed.

Olson looked at the ground. The mud completely buried the tops of his boots. "Guess I'm just not in the mood," he said.

Her eyes flashed. "Well, if you don't, I will." With that she flung herself on the poor gatekeeper, both of them going to the ground, sending a mud gusher into the dark sky.

And everyone converged on the spot, pressing in close.

"Just a little disagreement here," Olson said, holding his hands up. "Nothing to be concerned about."

"Bastard!" Gret screamed. "Rotten bastard!"

Olson tried to bend down to stop them, but he lost his footing in the mud and went down too. He tried to get up, but someone pushed him from behind and he fell again, his slick exo sliding him a distance across the ground.

Then hands were lifting him, pulling him up. He turned to thank his rescuer, only to see five men dressed in exos just like his.

"Brother Catanine," a man in a bright red one said, and embraced him, their armor clanging loudly together.

"Call him Cat," Gret said from the ground. And she was covered completely in a thick skin of oozing brown.

"Call me Cat," Olson said, and he still thought that was a silly name.

"I'm Rennie Du'camp," the man in red said, "and these are some of my friends." He turned and indicated other nodding Execs. "Welcome to Fun City."

All at once, a mammoth wagon drawn by twelve giants

rumbled through the gateway. It was piled high with television sets, the most useless commodity on the face of the planet, gifts from Faisel ibn Faisel. The wagon's wheels were as large as a man, and the thing filled the entire gateway, forcing the Guild aside. Behind it, the crowd suddenly pushed up to the back of the wagon and began flowing in unrestricted.

It was a trickle, then a flood that couldn't be stopped, as gatekeepers and constables were pushed aside like dried brush.

The Execs were off to the side, watching.

"Assholes!" Rennie yelled at the crowd, then turned to the others. "What do you think?" he said.

"I think we'd better do something," a man in green said.

"It's our duty," someone replied.

"That's absolutely correct," Rennie said. "It's our duty." He looked at Cat, clapped him on the shoulder. "Let's whip up on them, Junex. That is, if you can keep your feet."

Everybody laughed then, but in a second they were checking the locks on their suits.

"Ready!" Rennie shouted.

Olson looked at Gret. She was shrugging, spitting mud out of her mouth.

"Let's go!" Rennie yelled, and they charged into the middle of the crowd.

Olson looked at Gret again. She was shouting silently. "Go! Go!" Then she flashed him those nasty eyes again, and he chose the lesser of two evils and charged into the flow.

People were thudding against him, but he didn't feel them. Putting his arms up to defend himself, he was coming away with the blood of others all over himself, and the path was parting somewhat. He swung more deliberately then, putting his weight behind it, and people were falling all around. He was a fortress. Someone swung a large stick at him, and it glanced harmlessly off his chest. He felt nothing.

All around, he could see the other Execs flailing their arms like pinwheels, as moaning humanity piled up around their feet.

And all at once it was over, before it had even started. The mob had retreated outside the gate, and the Guild members had assumed their former positions.

Du'camp was strutting through the thirty or so who lay around him in various stages of disability. "Those who can walk, get up and do it now. Free medical aid at the old armory. Those that can't walk but can hear me, try to get someone to

help you out of the road or you'll get trampled. Those of you
who can't walk or hear me are a bunch of dumb fucks and
deserved everything you got."

They all laughed then, all the Execs, and people were
slapping him on the back, telling him what a good time they all
had together.

Olson looked over at Gret again. She had her hands on her
hips and was giving verbal hell to the gatekeeper whose ass she
kicked, who was sitting up with his back against the wall and
holding his head.

He realized that he hadn't had breakfast yet, either.

*   *   *

> *The path of duty lies in the thing that is*
> *nearby, but men seek it in things far off.*
> —Eastern Proverb

> *A covetous man's penny is a stone.*
> —Ali ibn Abi Talib

> *Ye followers of Mohammed! I swear by God,*
> *there is not anything which God so abhors, as*
> *His male and female servants committing*
> *adultery.*
> —The Prophet Mohammed

VII

The Desert
Somewhere Near Yabreen

Abdullah lay on his back, watching the gray morning seep
through the cracks in the folds of his tent. It was the time when a
black thread laid on the back of the hand could be distinguished
from a white one, the Moslem time for morning prayer. Outside

he could already hear the gentle murmurings of his Murrah
clansmen as they bowed and prostrated themselves before Mecca, and it was somehow firm and reassuring—an oasis in a dust
storm.

He was hot, sweat glistening on his naked form, soaking his
sleeping linens with a cold, stale odor. He hadn't slept at all, had
simply lain in place all night, staring at the tent cracks, waiting
for the gray morning.

Nura stirred beside him, shifting position, her breath coming easily, innocently. He could just make her out in the unstable
light. Her hair was sleek, black, and long, falling across her face
as she curled on her side toward him. Her breasts were small, the
nipples dark brown. Reaching out, he lightly flicked a dark
nipple, watching it rise of its own accord, and he became
aroused again.

Sliding over to her, he kissed her softly, and her lips parted
in a tiny smile, though her eyes hadn't opened yet. He pushed
himself against her, and her hands came up to cup his erection,
then stroke. She rolled onto her back, spreading her legs.

"Nura," he rasped.

"Say nothing," she whispered quickly, and her eyes opened
to meet his. "I am your field," she said, and pulled him on top
of her.

He entered her quickly, pent-up anger and frustration trans-
lating to excitement, and she rose to meet him measure for
measure. Her passion was the equal to his, and she moaned low
and then louder, until she was nearly as loud as the day he had
taken her for his wife and chased her, as prescribed by custom,
around the tents, finally taking her virginity, to the delight of the
entire clan. Later, the old women carried the bloodstained sheet
around camp, proudly displaying it to every woman they chanced
upon.

And their voices rose together, cried, until they collapsed
into a pool of sweat and fantasy and unspoken fear. Nura rolled
onto her stomach and wailed softly into her arm, and Abdullah
pretended not to notice as he dressed hurriedly.

"My brother's people will be here with the sun," he said.
"We do not have much time."

She looked up, her face a mask. "I will be ready," she said
simply.

He nodded, grunting, and turned to the tent flap. Reaching
for it, he turned and took one more look at his home. Large

enough to move around in and eat, but not a burden to move. Abdullah couldn't think of a place where he'd rather live. The tent was quick and easy, and it kept him from overburdening himself with the useless material possessions that were the source of human greed.

He moved through the flap and into the camp proper. To the East, the sky was already crowning blue atop a kingdom of pink, fiery sun. Their tents, bright bands of loud voiced color, numbered over fifty, spilling out of the small oasis that presently gave them water, onto the eternal carpet of sand that reached out all around them.

The sand didn't reach out to eternity, though. Abdullah ibn Faisel Al Sa'ud realized that all too well. His ocean of sand, his eternal sea, was smaller, more accessible, every second. The world threatened to reach out and crush him under its impossible weight.

It was hot already, close, and people shambled sleepily all around him, their plain white ghutras already thick with dust. The community fire was close by, a majlis circle of dark, bearded men already in place around it. Abdullah joined them.

A little boy sat on a carpet in front of one of the black goat-hair tents making coffee. As he called for water and beans they were passed silently to him over the embroidered hanging that separated the women's section of the tent.

Taking his place in the circle, Abdullah reached into the bowl that sat beside him and removed a small quantity of the bread dough it contained. Rolling it into a small ball, he tossed it into the flames.

An old man named Thamir sat beside him, his beard white straggles, his face dry and brittle as palm bark.

"You leave us today," he said, not taking his eyes off his own scone that burned black in the fire.

"Only for a time," Abdullah responded.

"For a time," the man repeated. "Is this not Jaluwa—exile?"

"I will be back."

As the water boiled in the blackened brass pot, the boy roasted the dry green beans in a shallow pan, and Abdullah was just beginning to smell their delicate aroma when the boy tossed them into a heavy brass mortar and began pounding them.

A man named Musa'id, who owned the third largest camel herd in the clan, spoke up from across the fire. "We fear that harm will befall you among the Nasrani. We fear that perhaps it is already written that harm will befall you.''

"We all live from one breath to the next," Abdullah responded. "Beyond that, only Allah knows what is written.''

"You say then," replied Thamir, "that our suspicions are created as the dunes from the wind?''

The boy called for cardamom seeds, which he put into the boiling water along with the crushed, now brownish, beans.

Abdullah stood slowly, looking around the majlis, which now numbered about forty, the number that the Bedouin use to describe large amounts. He spoke loudly, so that all could hear.

"You accepted me into your camp many years ago, accepted me as one of your own without question. You are all as brothers to me, perhaps more so than those who would use that name too loosely.''

Everything became still and quiet as he spoke, only the smell of the brewed coffee disturbing the glasslike atmosphere.

"And now I must leave. I will tell you from my heart that I am being forced to do this thing . . .''

There was much muttering around the fire, and Abdullah raised up his hands to stop it. "Please. I did not ask for this thing, but I do not shun it either. My life, my love, is here with you. But I go willingly, out of respect and honor for my brother Faisel.''

Bandar spoke from outside the circle. "Give respect only to those who deserve it.''

"No!" Abdullah shouted. "I will not hear such talk. Faisel is our ruler; we will honor him.''

The boy was walking around the majlis, pouring coffee into tiny cups and giving it to the men.

Abdullah lowered his eyes. "But I fear that my venture will be a perilous one. I fear not for myself, but for my family . . . for Nura, my wife.''

Bandar moved up closer, pushing through the inner ring of men to stand close to the fire. "You have been a protector to us," he said, and there were mumbled affirmations. "Not just to us, but to all who make this place our home. It is a debt that needs repaying.''

Abdullah turned his eyes to his friend's, held their darkness within his own. "Do you know what it is you are saying?''

Men were grabbing their bread out of the fire, prying the

blackened crust from the sweet inner dough with callused fingers, and eating the steaming scones.

Bandar nodded slowly. "I pledge myself to you, and there are others who will do the same. When Faisel wanted to disband the clans and make us move to the cities, it was you who were our eyes and mouth, it was you who saved us from the wall he wanted us to become. I pledge my life to the defense of your family while you are among the Nasrani."

Old Thamir stood up, opening his toothless mouth. "And I, my feeble bones, will to you."

Others stood, adding their voices. And still others, raising a cheer.

Abdullah shouted to get above the din. "You do not know what you are saying!" he screamed. "My brother is the wrath of Allah; he is the pestilence on the land!"

"And we are the pure white fire of justice!"

"You don't understand!" Abdullah shouted again, and all at once the air was choking with sound, hollow reverberating sound that seemed to originate within his skull. Looking up, he watched the large black forms that were filling the skies in front of the rising sun. Helicopters, hundreds of them, beating their props in a frenzy against the crisp morning air. They came closer, creating their own kind of wind, blowing smoke and sand and tents in mammoth swirling confusion.

Men began backing away, moving off, some running, and the women wailed invisibly from within the tents. They were everywhere, surrounding the oasis, coming down, huge flags rippling madly from the gear.

The flags were green, the color of the cloak that the prophet wore. The flags bore the legend: "There is no god but God. Mohammed is the messenger of God." Beneath the words was the likeness of a gleaming sword.

The copters began touching down, stirring up a maelstrom of sand. It was fog, a dirty, gritty fog of blowing sand. And tents were falling all around, houses flying away from their owners as the fire blew out, its embers crackling into the dirty sky, dying in pops and sizzles.

Black-robed Elite were disgorging from the bellies of the mechanical beasts, rifles slung on their shoulders, hollow eyes shining darkly through the fog. They moved silently toward him, like an army of the dead.

Turning, Abdullah looked toward his tent. Nura had come

outside, her delicate robes whipping around her in the horrible
wind. She reached her arms out to Abdullah, and to him she
looked like nothing so much as a specter, an apparition there in
the blowing dust, and then the curtain got thicker and she
disappeared behind it.

When Abdullah turned back around, he was nose to nose
with an Elite.

"You will come with us," the man said.

Faisel sat amidst a thick incense haze in the soothsayer's
private quarters. Not known for his extravagance, Misha'al ibn
Abdul slept on the floor of the small room, with only his Koran
and computer to keep him company. That, and the mandatory
television, of course. And the computer was programmed with
the Koran, as was the television, so they really added nothing to
the general sum of Misha'al's fund of knowledge. He did have a
bank account, though, somewhere far away; and someday, some
way he was going to go to it and never sleep on the floor again.
But right now, it was business.

The room was dark except for two white candles that
flickered under the constant stream of life-support air coming
through the vents. A small wooden table with two chairs sat
pushed up against one of the bare walls, but neither Faisel nor
Misha'al was interested in the chairs. They sat on the cold
cement floor across the length of room from one another, legs
folded, arms at their sides. Several Elite stood just outside the
locked door; several layers of soundproofing kept them from
listening in.

The tv was set into the wall, its sound turned down. It ran
all the time, as was prescribed, but the sound did come under
direct control of the watcher, and it was a control that Misha'al
exercised now—while he had the real Faisel in front of him.

"I had a dream last night," the Ruler of the World said,
and watched carefully the candle-jumping eyes of the man before
him. "The dream awakened me in the middle of the night."

"And you wish for me to interpret it?"

"Is that not your function?"

Misha'al smiled then, with a knowledge so secret that to
even hint of its fact would cost him his head in a matter of
minutes. "My function," he said, "is to eat and sleep and
excrete waste and pray to Allah. Anything else that you may
expect is a foolish exercise in wish fulfillment."

Faisel tightened his jaw. "Why do I let you treat me the way you do?"

Picking a stick of jasmine out of the burner beside him, Misha'al brought the end ember up to his nose as if it were a rose. He didn't sniff it, though. He hated the smell of incense. "It seems that you are greater qualified to answer that question than I," he said softly.

Faisel tightened again, relaxed. In a world that bowed and scraped, Misha'al did neither. He was a man totally free, who told the King things because he wanted to, not through loyalty, or even gain, since all he ever gave the soothsayer was a roof over his head and minimum food. That's why he let the man act the way he did. He trusted his information, trusted it absolutely.

Misha'al realized this also, which is the reason he acted the way he did. He never really concerned himself with whether the information he gave to Faisel was real or not. He mostly operated on what he knew Faisel wanted to hear. And as for personal gain, he needed nothing from Faisel—why should the man who is the King's personal confidant? Faisel was his passkey to the world.

And it was a key he had used and would use again and again, for Misha'al's cleverness was exceeded only by his overpowering greed. It was a greed grounded in cleverness and steeped in patience. He had waited long, and could wait longer.

"Will you help me?" Faisel asked sheepishly. "I meant no disrespect."

"I am your humble servant," Misha'al said, bowing from the waist. "I make no promises, except to serve you well."

Faisel nodded, satisfied, for everyone needs someone to confide in. "It concerns my brother's wife," he said.

"Nura," the man said, and smiled again, for his path was very clear as regards this particular problem.

"I was in a tent," he said, "a strange tent that was unfamiliar to me. It was small on the outside, but huge inside, the walls far away and shining with something slick . . . wet."

Misha'al stood quietly and moved to the computer, which was inset in the wall and covered most of it.

"She was naked, the most beautiful woman I'd ever seen. But I was encased in a shell of some kind, a hard shell that kept me from moving around much. Still, I came to her, tried to express my love for her, but the words wouldn't come out right. I reached for her, but just as my fingers touched her, she burst into flame. I screamed for her, but she began laughing through the fire. Laughing, laughing as the flames spread throughout the room and surrounded me. The last thing I remember is the flames creeping toward me, closer and closer."

He looked at Misha'al. "That's when I woke up."

The soothsayer lightly flicked on the computer. Its name was Insh'allah, meaning "as God Wills." It lit up in brilliant, flashing strobes and fire belched out of it in three or four different places, squirting black smoke through the room. It rumbled loudly, volcanolike, and Faisel could feel the wall behind him vibrating.

Misha'al ibn Abdul backed against the machine that he had programmed with the Koran, his arms outstretched, and the machine whined when he came in contact with it, a noise that he duplicated in his own throat until the two sounded almost as one.

"Fire," he said loudly. "I can feel the fire!"

The machine began clattering loudly, a printout slowly feeding from its innards.

Misha'al looked, wide-eyed, at Faisel. "The tent is Islam," he said in a husky voice. "Small to the outsider, but large and rich to the sons of the Koran. You two are enclosed by the tent of the Law. But it's broad, all-encompassing. The woman is the object of your desire, of all desire."

The printer clattered on, as the fire tongued out again, on either side of the prophet's outstretched arms.

"But you have encased yourself in a shell of righteousness that keeps you away from that which you desire, and you speak to yourself in the false language of lies."

"The fire," Faisel hissed, his heart pounding in his chest.

"Yessss," Misha'al returned, and ripped the printout out of the machine. He carried it to the place where Faisel sat, handing it to him. "Read."

Faisel stood, moving to the candles on the wooden table so he could have enough light.

The words from the Koran flickered at him: " 'This is your Paradise; you have been given it as your inheritance for what you did.' The inhabitants of Paradise will call to the inhabitants of the fire: 'We have found that which our Lord promised us true; have you found what your Lord promised you true?' "

Misha'al sat across from him at the table, the candles between them. "The fires are the hellfires that you have created within yourself through your false righteousness."

"Why did she laugh?" Faisel asked.

Misha'al slammed a hand down hard on the tabletop and leaned up close. "She laughs at your stupidity," he spat. "In a world full of denial, why deny that which you may have?"

Faisel nodded slowly. "You're right," he said.

Reaching out, Misha'al snuffed out one of the candles with thumb and forefinger. "The fires extinguish easily," he rasped. "Very easily."

The flame coughed from the machine again and both men looked at it. "You will speak of this to no one," Faisel said.

Misha'al rubbed a hand across his smooth face. "I will do as I please," he answered.

"Wallahi!" Faisel said, and pointed a slender finger. "Someday you will push me too far, Ulema. My patience with you is not eternal."

Getting up, the soothsayer went over and shut down his machine. "Nor mine with you . . . Caliph."

Faisel spat loudly. "Don't call me that," he growled.

"I serve you in everything you desire," Misha'al said as he came back to the table. "And my thanks amounts to a very generous portion of abuse from you. If I offend you, send me away. I could do no worse than what you have to offer. We'll see who pushes whom too far."

There was a knock on the door. "Leave me alone!" Faisel screamed.

A muffled tiny voice drifted back through the soundproofing. "Your brother has arrived," the voice said.

Faisel was staring at Misha'al and the man was actually fearless in his return of the stare. "We will continue this discussion later," he said.

"Is that a command?"

Faisel stood and moved to the door, unlocking it. "A faithful servant doesn't need a command."

He opened the door and left without a backward look. Misha'al listened to them leaving outside the door and waited until he was sure they were gone before getting out the small directional transmitter.

Flipping it on, he listened to the static for a moment. Then a familiar voice came on low. "Yes," it said simply.

"I have need of your services," Misha'al said, glancing around.

* * *

The scooters charged madly down the hallway, careening off sidewalls and knocking over pedestrian traffic that was unfortunate enough to be walking there. Faisel loved the sensation of speed, loved to get the heavily padded low-riding things cranked up so far that it would be impossible to deal with an unforeseen threat. There were four of them, all except one manned by Elites. The fourth was driven by Faisel himself, and he was going so fast that the hall lights were rushing past as one long streamer.

"Where'd you put him?" he asked the Elite sitting beside him in the tiny machine.

The man's eyes were huge above the line of his veil, his hands gripping the sidebars as if his very life depended on them. "In the room of televisions," he said, and pointed. "That turn! That turn!"

Faisel slammed down on the brakes, sliding into the hallway turn to the sound of screeching echoes. They banged the wall hard, then bounced back and started on their way again, the other scooters screeching up behind them.

Abdullah walked slowly through the room of televisions, hands behind his back, his mind settling itself into control. The rooms were huge and wide, and there were many of them, stretching out one from the other like a monstrous maze that worked its way over many acres. It was, indeed, possible to become lost in the room of televisions if one did not know the way.

The walls were filled with screens floor to ceiling. There may have been a million screens. There may have been more. They were lined up in neat, military rows, and every third vertical row, a catwalk cut between them, so that the Watchers could walk up and down, checking whatever it was that they were checking on at any given time. Faisel liked to watch his subjects; it gave him a fatherly feeling.

Abdullah walked and looked at the uncountable windows that only worked one way. He stopped before the harem section in amazement. There were hundreds of screens, manned by eunuchs, all filled with pictures inside the underground hotel where Faisel housed his wives and slaves. So many women, and very few Arab. They were from everywhere, like a random sampling of all the women in the world.

He shook his head. Why did his brother desire Nura so

much? And he knew the answer to that without asking, and the answer had very little to do with Nura herself, although Faisel would be the last to admit any of that.

Screeching tires. He turned to the sound, and saw Faisel, yelling and whooping as he careened through the rooms on his scooter, his Elite trying to keep up.

The machines cried loudly as they skidded to a stop beside Abdullah. The Elite who was in the car with Faisel jumped out immediately and began kissing the ground.

Heaving himself up and out of the open-topped car, Faisel walked right up to Abdullah.

"Salaam, my brother," he said, smiling broadly.

Abdullah hugged him quickly. "Wa alaykum as Salaam," he replied, as tradition demanded.

The two backed away from one another. "You do not look happy," Faisel said with overdone seriousness. "Has someone treated you wrongly?"

Abdullah avoided his gaze, turned instead to a tv screen that showed a picture of a drawn and haggard man sitting in a dingy jail cell. "Was it necessary to send your Elite in force to take me from my people?"

"I am your people," Faisel said quickly. "The blood of the same mother runs through our veins. You should remember that son. times."

Abdullah turned to him then. "My brother, I very seldom forget."

Faisel grunted. "I did not order a force to bring you here. If you wish, I will take the Elite commander's head as an apology."

Abdullah shook his head, and couldn't help but feel that the man in the cell was familiar to him. "Who's that?" he asked.

Faisel shrugged. "This is a family wall," he said, indicating a block of several hundred sets. "He's probably one of our brothers." Putting a hand on Abdullah's back, he gently led him away from that particular wall. "You know, the Elite probably went out in force because they fear the Bedouin. The blood between them has not always been good."

"Because it was their job to push the nomads from the desert, to make hadhar of them."

"It was only out of love for me that they did that," Faisel said, and began leading Abdullah quickly along the walls to the place he wanted him to see. "Though I had nothing to do with it, of course."

"Of course."

"The wandering tribes interfere with my defensive radar here. The Elite only wanted to please me." He stopped before a metal staircase that led up to one of the higher catwalks. "Ah, here we are. Come with me if it pleases you."

"It pleases me to return to my camp and stay there."

Faisel smiled. "They say that traveling is a very worthwhile and broadening experience," he said. "It will be good for you." And he began climbing the stairs.

Abdullah sighed and followed behind. They climbed a double tier of stairs, the Watchers always avoiding them, giving them a wide berth. When they reached the second catwalk, they were up near the ceiling of the high room.

"I'm going to show you where your travels will lead you," Faisel said, and moved down the catwalk. Abdullah followed.

"Why is it," Faisel asked, "that you settle for so little in life when you could have so much?"

"I have a good herd of camel," Abdullah answered, "many good and true friends, and a wife like none other. I worship God and love our country. How could anyone be richer than that?"

"You are a man of small expectations," Faisel returned.

"As far as I know, that is not yet against the law."

Faisel stopped walking, and tapped a screen with an index finger. "Here, my brother. This is your destination."

Abdullah moved to the screen and looked. It showed a walled city, that city's main gate. It was a scene of mass confusion, of people in incredible numbers pouring into the city, fighting one another, scrabbling for a chance to enter the filth of that closed-in place. Abdullah felt himself shiver.

"A big responsibility," Faisel said. "That's why I need my brother to handle it."

"What's going on down there?" Abdullah asked.

"Some sort of mass movement of people," Faisel answered matter-of-factly. "It is of no importance. What is important, is that the Nasrani be made to understand that we will not tolerate their behavior. We lose respect with the rest of our people if these heathens are allowed to cheat us openly."

"What if they are not cheating us?"

"They are."

Faisel moved to the next screen. It showed a tall black building with one of the Jitterbug domes on top.

"Light of the World Regional Headquarters," he said. "The key slot is in the base of the dome." He moved to the next screen, which showed a close-up of the dome base. "There's a hidden panel on the base. Remove it and you will find the key slot. Put in the key and turn it and the dome opens one hour later."

"You're so sure that I'll need to use the key?"

Faisel moved to the next screen. It was the inside of a richly done apartment inside the building. A naked black man was sitting on a sofa with a fully dressed woman. He was putting a hypodermic syringe into his arm and emptying its contents.

"His name is Elwood," Faisel said. "He is our Regional Director. You will deal directly with him."

"What is he doing to himself?"

"The Nasrani are pigs, my brother. They realize very little of the Shariah, the Law. Discount them. Their lives are worthless."

"I am to look at their books?"

"I am sending people with you who know what to do. After they have had ample time to examine the machines, you will determine the use of the key."

"Do they know that I have the key?"

"Of course."

"What is to stop them from trying to take it from me?"

Faisel smiled gold again, made an expansive gesture. "Harm my brother? They wouldn't dare. Besides, you have the whole garrison at New Mecca to protect you, and for extra measure, I am sending a squad of Elite as your personal bodyguards."

"I do not want the Elite."

Faisel shook his hands around. "No, no. I insist. I know that you fear for me to lower my protection, but it is the least I can do for my brother."

Abdullah turned and leaned on the metal rail of the walkway. His entire vision was filled with screens, Faisel's eyes and ears. "Is the key really necessary?"

Faisel spun him around, his face dark and angry. "Has the sun addled your brain? Of course it's necessary. We rule by fear, by force, and by the word of God. The ungodly must be taught harsh lessons in order to be kept under control. We've destroyed before, and will again. The heathens bring it upon themselves."

He grabbed Abdullah's arms tightly, squeezing. "You will swear a bay'ah to me."

"Faisel, I . . ."

"You will do it right now! An oath, an oath before God that you will obey me in these things."

"Why are you doing this?"

"Swear! Now!"

Abdullah stared darkly at Faisel. Culture and tradition made direct discussion nearly impossible. Talk was an opportunistic dance. "My brother," he said, breathing heavily. "I am no threat to you, I . . ."

"Of course you're not!" Faisel snapped. "Do you insult me?"

Abdullah felt his jaw tighten. "No, I . . . just want you to know that all this is not necessary."

"Don't tell me how to conduct my business."

"It has become my business too," Abdullah returned, and knew it was the wrong thing to say as soon as it came out.

Faisel was shaking. "You will swear the bay'ah!"

Abdullah looked at him for a long time, fire burning in his eyes. Jerking his arms from Faisel's grasp, he took his face in his hands. "I swear two oaths," he said slowly. "One is an oath of allegiance to my King. The other an oath of vengeance to anyone who would do harm to my family. Before God, I swear these things."

Faisel turned his face and kissed the palm of the hand that held it. "God is the qadi of us all," he said. "His Will be done."

*   *   *

If You Suspect Self-Contamination:

1. Isolate yourself immediately.
2. Look for telltale signs (severe stomach-
      ache, nausea, impotence, fever).
3. Inform the proper authorities about
      yourself and all who came in contact with you
      by shouting from a distance or leaving a
      note.
4. Beg Allah for forgiveness.
5. Destroy yourself, preferably by immolation,
      for the good of the Company and your loved
      ones.

—Daily TV
Message

VIII
The LOW Building
Seventeenth Floor

"Ouch!" Olson yelled, as Gret tried to stuff the washcloth in his ear.

"Would you stop fidgeting," she said angrily, and looked down at the water all over herself and the floor. "Honestly. You'd think that you've never had a bath before."

"I haven't," he returned. "Not like this anyway. And if it's this bad all the time, I don't think I want another."

He sat in the warm tub, perfumed bubbles piled high like hot snow, while Gret scrubbed his back and ears.

"I've never seen anybody so ungrateful in all my life," she said, and wrung a ragful of water down his back to slick away the soap.

"Ungrateful!" he said, turning to her quickly, which sloshed another wave of water onto her. "I'm ungrateful?"

"Look at all I've done for you. I've taken you off the frontier, given you a decent job with a future and the best sex you've ever had in your life."

"Who's doing who the favor?" he returned. "Whose rear got saved because I stuffed myself into that dumb suit? Who was going to have to stay back there on the road because her boyfriend got killed?"

"Yeah," she returned. "But who got him killed?"

"I was just minding my own business, and now, all of a sudden, I'm dressed up in this turtle shell beating up on people. And I want to tell you right now, I didn't much care for any of that."

She threw her head back and looked at the ceiling. "Tell me you've never beat up on people before."

"Not without a reason," he said. "You got to have a reason."

She threw the sponge at him, bouncing it off his head. "The reason is that you're a Junex, and they're just citizens."

He stood up, sweating soap bubbles. "That's not a reason."

She stood also, wiping her hands on a towel. "It's the only reason that makes any sense, and don't forget it."

He stepped out of the tub, taking the towel from her. He did feel good, really clean and relaxed, but he'd never tell her that.

The room was handsome, all tiled in black and white check, sparkling clean. He'd heard of bathrooms before, with running water and pipes that carried the nasty stuff away somewhere, but he never thought he'd actually see one, much less have one to use all the time.

It could almost make him believe he was special.

Gret had walked through the door and into the bedroom. He followed her, toweling himself as he went. Wexler, his servant, stood in the bedroom with his hands outstretched. He was a small man, about half Olson's size, and his head was all lopsided, as if it had been run over by a wagon and pushed out of shape. He was what Gret called an Engy, a person they had specially made for some purpose, like the giants. But Wexler hadn't come out right; something was wrong with his brain. So they used him as a servant, and as nearly as Olson could figure, the little man belonged to him body and soul.

The room was large and well lit through the thick glass windows that were tinted on the outside. It had a canopied bed that Olson had tried out with Gret no sooner than they had come into the place, and massive wooden furniture that was built to take all manner of beating. Past the bedroom was a large living room and a kitchen where Wexler could prepare his meals. That was of some excitement to Olson. A large part of his day-to-day life was taken up with looking for food. Suddenly, that was no longer a consideration.

Gret was by the closet, slipping her wet shift up over her head. "I'm glad I had enough sense to not wear my good clothes. You were worse than bathing a dog."

"Who would do a thing like that?" he asked, then looked over to Wexler, who was smiling up at him. "Why's he got his arms out like that?"

Gret pulled off the dress and threw it on the floor. "He's waiting for the towel," she said.

"Oh." He walked over and gave Wexler the towel, even though he wasn't finished using it yet. The little man smiled, and Olson patted him on the head. "What do you think, partner?"

Wexler's face suddenly got serious. "Well, I think that it's beginning to get dark and that there are an awful lot of people out on the streets and that you certainly act strange for a Junex and that your Houris is quite beautiful and that you may need to hurry or you'll be late for the party and you are not important enough yet to be late for parties and that I'm not sure if you want dinner before or after the party because if you want it before I'm certain you'll be late and if you want it after I'll lose some sleep because I like to sleep early and need a great deal of sleep to keep myself at my peak during the day and I hope you'll be with me for a long time because you don't treat me like the others have and—''

"Enough!" Gret said, and looked at Olson with raised eyebrows. "Stick to simple commands, would you?"

Olson shrugged. "I didn't know," he replied, and stared at Gret for a minute. "You sure you want to be . . . you know, naked in front of him?"

Gret had been going through the closet and stopped abruptly, turning to look at him. "You're really strange," she said. Pulling a black velvet suit out of the closet, she threw it on the bed. "Put this on."

He turned his nose up. "It looks tight."

"Put it on!"

Forcing himself over to the suit, he began struggling into the purple cotton shirt. If only Cat had been just a little bigger. "Is your place as nice as this?" he asked.

"Hardly," she returned. "The women live in open dorms with built-in beauty parlors. They don't want us to like it too much or we wouldn't have as much incentive to do you people a good job."

"I see," Olson said, but he really didn't. "What about this party we're going to?"

Gret pulled a white, nearly transparent dress out of the closet and began to step into it, using the wall for support. "I checked it out with some of the other Houris while I was moving in. It's some kind of promotion party for Rennie Du'camp, who just got bumped up to senior VeePee. He's apparently a real Mover, somebody to watch."

"I met him out at the gate today," Olson said. "Seemed like a nice enough fella."

She slipped her arms through the straps and backed up to Wexler, who immediately began zipping her into the dress.

"Watch out for him," she told Olson. "Bad feelings roll off him like gas off the swamp."

"How come we got invited?"

He was struggling into the pants, hating the confinement.

She pulled a brush out of a small bag that sat on the floor and began combing her long hair before a full-length mirror that occupied the whole wall facing the foot of the bed.

"You're the new blood," she said. "Everybody scopes out the new blood to see how tough the competition's going to be. My guess is that Mr. Du'camp arranged your invitation so that he could smell you out."

He sucked in his gut and barely got the waistband closed on the pants. The first chance he had, he was going to have to get some other clothes. "Well, I'm really worried about this. What if I mess up?"

She was checking her makeup in the mirror, leaning up close to daub at eyeliner with a long-nailed finger. "Just keep your mouth shut," she said. "Strong and silent—they're used to the type. Play dumb . . ." She stopped, shifted her eyes to take in his reflection behind her. "Just be yourself. I'll try to stick close in case you get into trouble."

He was winding the tie around his neck, trying to figure out what do do with it. "Like you did at the gate today?"

Smiling, she turned around and came over to him, winding the tie with practiced hands. "I got a little carried away," she said.

He looked at her, horrified. "I can see right through your dress," he said.

She jiggled her eyebrows. "Like what you see?"

"All those men are going to be looking at you."

"I certainly hope so," she said, and started struggling with his top button.

"But they'll be thinking about . . . about . . ."

"I'll bet that Wexler likes the way I look, don't you?"

Wexler had folded the towel neatly in quarters and dropped it in the middle of the floor. Such was the nature of his evolution. He walked right up to her, staring at her breasts, which were at the level of his eyes.

"I think you are wonderful, a goddess, a sensation, a cause célèbre. From the delicate curve of your neck to the very tip of your painted toenails, I think you are a vision, the essence of womanhood. Your hair is rich as spun gold and soft as the first downy snow of fall. Your eyes are the finest crystal, your mouth ripe berries bursting sweetness, your teeth precious pearls. Your breasts are like—''

"Stop!" Olson said, and turned Wexler's back to them. "Don't ever describe her...body parts again. That's disgusting."

Gret pushed the tie's knot up full against his throat, gagging him. "So, I'm disgusting, am I? Well, you should be overjoyed to remember that I won't be spending tonight with you anyway, so you won't have to be disgusted anymore."

He choked, working the knot away from his throat. "I didn't say you were disgusting, I said that Wexler was."

The little man broke down crying, then threw himself to the ground, hugging Olson's legs. "Oh, please, don't send me away. I don't mean to be disgusting; I won't be disgusting anymore. Disgusting as a word or an activity is no longer in my vocabulary. I don't think that the lady's breasts are like proud twin mountains topped with gardens of bright red roses; I think they are sagging, wrinkled bundles of loose flesh that—''

"Stop!" Olson yelled, and wriggled free of Wexler's deathgrip, only to lose his balance and fall to the carpeted floor. He lay there for a second, feeling an extreme metaphysical closeness to that piece of carpet.

Wexler scurried around to his face, squatting beside it. In his hands was the folded towel, which he tried to shove under Olson's head. "Oh, Mr. Cat, I hope that you're not hurt. The injuries that one could sustain in a fall such as that are numerous..."

"No," Olson said, muffled, into the carpet. "I'm fine. Really. I just want to...rest here for a while, that's all."

Gret squatted down on the other side of his face. "We need to be going, really. It doesn't do for a Junex to be late to something like this. For the people who are supposed to arrive late, there needs to be somebody already there for them to arrive late to."

"Of course," he mumbled. "I understand perfectly."

"Of course you do," Gret said.

"Of course you do," Wexler added.

*　　*　　*

How many a Prophet We sent among the ancients,
but not a Prophet came to them, without they
  mocked at him;
so We destroyed men stronger in
valor than they, and the example
of the ancients passed away.

—The Koran
XLIII. Ornaments

A man came to the Prophet, and said, "O
Prophet! enjoin upon me a duty, but do not
demand much of me, lest I forget." The Prophet
said, "Do not thou be angry."
—The Prophet Mohammed

IX

College Station, Texas
South/Central Region
America

The dirigible drifted lazily through the moonless night over the remnants of the old stadium where the city's Execs had held their Engy tournaments. Ted Milander sat in the gondola of the balloon that he had been crafty enough to liberate and watched the fires, the brilliant ecclesiastical fires, that stretched out magnificently below him as far as he could see, leveling the city, heralding in the New Age.

The stadium was filled with several thousand of his followers who were cheering the Glory of the New World. Beside him, his brother Maury lay quietly dying.

He looked at Maury's eyes, saw the fear and the happiness

70

there. The Jitterbug had dealt him a double blow. Decimating his spinal cord, it had left him totally paralyzed, but still subject to grand mal seizures that accompanied the disease. The result was that he was being torn apart from the inside while remaining inert outwardly. It only showed in his eyes—the fear and the happiness.

"We share the visions," Ted said, and took Maury's face in his hands, not even feeling the ravages of the fever since he had it too. "You will pass from this plane very soon and move into the matrix of creation where all will be one."

Leaning down, he kissed him on the lips. "I will miss you, but your work here is over, while mine is not. Someday soon, we will be once more together."

He smoothed Maury's sweaty hair and stood. A tall, lean man, Ted Milander had a face lined with character and eyes like a whirlpool that sucked all that he viewed into his personal domain. He was a born leader of men, a man of compassion and understanding, a man spared temporarily the end results of the Jitterbug because he had a duty to perform.

He looked at the instruments, blinking ghostly blue through the darkness before him. The motors that propelled the dirigible would run out of fuel eventually and they'd have to abandon the airship, but for now they were still in good shape.

Ex-Junex Thirdle, still dressed in his blue exo, came in from the next compartment. His ability to walk was impaired severely, and he was using a rifle for a cane. His neck had stiffened up and was tilted at a severe angle, nearly resting on his shoulder.

"Radio message," he slurred, his speech nearly unintelligible.

Milander turned to him. "Who from?"

"From . . . from . . . from . . ."

Milander watched the man's eyes glaze over, recognized a petit mal seizure. He waited for a moment while it passed, noticing that Maury was foaming from his lips.

"From . . . from . . . from the commander of the garrison at New Mecca to the leader of the Houston balloons."

A cheer went up in the stadium below. Milander looked down in time to see the citizens being brought into the stadium, into the middle of the field. "I've been expecting it," he said. "What were the orders?"

Thirdle's hair was blond, and was tousled all over his face like a giant fuzz ball. His face was strained, partially paralyzed. "They said to . . . to . . . to chase us and shoot down the b-balloon."

Milander nodded. "They've got to find us first," he returned. He nodded toward the window. "Tell the others to get ready; we're taking it down."

Thirdle started to turn and leave, but his already ragged breath became even more labored. He strained for a moment, hands coming up to clutch his throat. Milander watched quietly as the man choked, finally to fall to the floor, dead.

Moving toward the door, Milander stepped over the body and called through the compartment door, "Get ready! We're going to be taking it down."

He walked back to the controls and sat down heavily before them. While the Jitterbug was a frightening mystery to most of his people, it wasn't to him. Milander had been in charge of the Houston Clinic, the largest medical facility in the Region. Being a doctor was the most frustrating of professions since there existed a huge body of medical knowledge that had to go untapped, for the want of medication and instrumentation that hadn't been produced in centuries.

Barely a month before, an Arab dirigible had accidentally crashed into the Houston dome, scattering the Jitterbug virus over the whole city, and in the midst of the panic that followed, Milander had learned a good deal about the disease.

It was a very lethal form of encephalomyelitis, an inflammation of both the brain and spinal cord. The viral agent responsible for the disease process was known as Herpes Medeaii. It was first isolated in the late twentieth century by Jean Thorgeson, a virologist who named it after her pet cat, Medea. It was a particularly nasty strain of a virus that had plagued man through the centuries, causing everything from chickenpox to shingles. It was an adaptation of the Herpes simplex virus, the agent causing oral fever blisters and venereal disease.

The disease was spread via droplets through the air like the common cold, and was extremely contagious. It circumvented the human's normal immunological mechanisms, leaving very few victims able to produce any amount of antibodies against it. There was no cure, and it was always fatal. It just took some longer than others to die.

It was a neurotropic virus, having a special affinity for damaging nervous tissue, causing cerebral edema and petechial hemorrhages, destroying the brain in stages. As the brain and spinal cord went, several things occurred: grand mal seizures of a classically epileptic nature gave the disease its common name,

Jitterbug. There were other kinds of seizures, from petit mal to psychomotor to Jacksonian to myoclonic. Males invariably became impotent, which was always the quick test to check for the disease. Those with the Jitterbug showed alterations in the level of consciousness through progressive dementia and disorientation—hallucinations of a visual and auditory nature occurred. Brainstem damage resulted in respiratory depression that, as in Thirdle's case, resulted in death.

Death was slow or fast, the disease sometimes lingering on for years. But those cases were rare. Eighty percent of those exposed died within weeks of infection. The rest were usually gone within six months.

Below, the citizens were being formed in a wide spiral that turned gradually inward there on the field. Milander toggled off his helium feed lines to let the balloon gradually settle down.

He knew that what he saw in his visions was supposed to be caused by hallucinations, but that didn't matter. He saw God, at least his perception of God, and to him that was all that mattered. When he saw God, he realized that there was some purpose to all of this. He realized that he and the others left alive were there to use the Jitterbug to purify the Earth. Things were bad; he could set them right. He could raise an army of walking wounded to spread the New Age throughout the land. He could use purifying fire to remake the World, and never, ever, was there a higher calling.

He turned to look at Maury, and the next thing he knew he was squatting beside him, zipping and unzipping the front of his jumper. He shook his head and smiled.

"We're almost finished here," he said. "Then it's on to Orleans to spread the word there."

Maury looked proudly up at him from the floor, the muscles in his eyes the only part of him that worked. He was on fire inside; he was liquid, molten lava and he knew that it was burning him up. The colors in the room were bright, throbbing in syncopation to the pounding of his enlarged overworked heart. Ted was smiling down at him, and he was surrounded by an aura of pale blue. When he moved he was a blur of beautifully colored streamers and Maury knew, really knew, that Ted was the salvation of the Earth. He felt the end coming and wanted to reach out and touch his brother, to say good-bye to him; but he couldn't, so he closed his eyes and died alone.

Ted Milander cradled Maury in his arms and cried lightly.

But the cries weren't in sadness, but rather in happiness in the knowledge that, for Maury at least, things would be better.

Several of his people had come in and were dragging Thirdle away. He laid Maury back lightly on the floor so they could get him, too.

They had settled gently into the stadium, fifty feet from the ground. Going to the controls, Milander stabilized the helium and walked out of the control room.

The passageway was narrow and dark, with doors leading off from it that were all closed. Milander's walk was affected, making him limp badly, but he was still able to get around on his own power.

Coming to the end of the hallway, he opened the last door. It led into the way out.

Jory and Helen Cabal had shoved open the double doors that opened into midair, and were throwing the long coil of rope ladder through it.

The small empty room was flickering orange light from the fires that raged in the countryside around them.

Helen's left arm was shaking uncontrollably. He grabbed it steady, then raised it to his lips to kiss. She smiled crookedly through half paralysis.

"God bless you," she slurred. "It's a great thing you're doing."

"We are all doing the great thing," he answered. "We just play different roles."

He shook Jory's hand, and by his looks, it didn't seem as if the man could last out the night. "Thanks for everything," he said lightly, and sat with his legs dangling through the opening.

Turning around, he began climbing down the ladder. The fire was all around him, everything but the stadium ablaze, and he was blasted by gusts of hot wind.

The crowd cheered when they saw him, and he waved at them as he clung to the swaying ladder. Beneath him, the citizens of College Station snaked around the grass field, weaving in and out of his vision. He was becoming extremely disoriented and hurried his descent before he got too dizzy.

He got to the field and began walking slowly, steadily, trying not to show his limp. The citizens were lined up side by side by side, and many of the Jits were rolling on the ground, lost in seizures as the fire lit up the sky all around them. And the noise of the cheering was like a gigantic ocean crashing against the shore of Heaven.

The citizens were frightened, many of them crying, and Milander wanted to hurry through this as quickly as he could to ease their pain.

The first person in line was a young woman, a teenager, and Milander remembered that he had been a father, and had a teenage daughter a million years ago. Her eyes were wide with fear, and she cried openly, tears rolling down her face. Her hair was long and he reached out and stroked it gently. "Calm down, little one."

"P-please," she sobbed. "Don't hurt me."

"You poor child," he said. "You misunderstand."

He took her face in his hands, forced her eyes to look at his. "I'm not going to hurt you."

"Y-you're not?"

"I'm here to bring you peace, and happiness. I want to give your life purpose."

He kissed her on the lips, parting hers with his tongue. He came away from her, smiling. "I love you," he said, and moved to the man next to her in line.

The people who were watching her motioned her away, and she ran, excited and happy that she had been set free.

Her name was LuAnne, and she would run for two days trying to find her relatives in Euliss before the fever and chills could overtake her. She would infect thirty-seven people before being shot dead at the gates of a small village whose name she'd never know.

*   *   *

One tames a people as one tames a lion—by masturbation.
                                        —Turkish Parable

When thou dost follow up the vices of thy people, thou wilt bring ruin upon them.
                                        —The Prophet Mohammed

X
The Party

No one wore exos, and weapons were off-limits anywhere in the LOW Building. It didn't take long for Olson to understand why.

The party was uncontrollable; it raged like a brushfire in the middle of a drought. It filled Mr. Elwood's apartment like pus fills a boil, and Olson kept waiting, waiting for the pressure to build up so much that the whole thing would pop and spew like so much confetti over the black, rainy city.

There must have been a hundred people in there, and all of them thought they could be louder than the other ninety-nine. They stood in clusters, like bananas, arguing and jabbing one another with index fingers, their free hands pivoting constantly to bring their glasses to their mouths.

It was dark like pitch, but lightning flashes jabbed the rooms in and out, and the campfires that the transient population built on the wet streets provided a reverse star pattern to make up for the cloud-infested sky. And still the rain poured outside, threatening to flood the city at any moment.

The musak was loud, throbbing its godforsaken violins to the distortion range, and a thick layer of smoke hung ominously over the entire room. The smoke was of different consistencies and smells, and wafted casually around like one of the invited guests.

And Olson was drunk.

He hadn't meant to get drunk; it was the last thing in the world he wanted to do; but it was impossible not to get drunk when people kept filling your glass and acting hurt if you wouldn't drink with them.

He was drinking something clear that they poured out of large pitchers and called martinis. These were, apparently, the official drink of the upper classes. The first one tasted vile and the second one didn't taste like anything at all, so he kept at it. When they asked him how it all was, he kept repeating the one phrase he had picked up. "Dry," he would say. "Very dry."

So, he got drunk and got loose and began to have a very good time with the Junexes who were standing there with him, who he knew, just knew, were the best friends he had ever had. One was dressed in a bright yellow tweed suit with a fat blue tie. He wore glasses and his name was Billy something-or-other. He had his arm around his Houris, who apparently didn't have a name. She did, however, have long red hair and a pair of yellow tweed short pants—and nothing else. Billy kept fondling her breasts while he talked and she must have been like Gret because it was all having quite an effect on her. The other man was Marty Jerny, who was dressed in red satin to match his face. Jerny was Rennie Du'camp's man and was feeling Olson out. But, of course, Olson had no way of knowing that.

Jerny didn't have a Houris or a wife with him, but he kept looking around as if he were waiting for someone. Olson thought about mentioning this to him, but decided not to pursue it.

Gret was on Olson's arm, clinging to him. She had no idea that he would get as drunk as early as he did, and the more his tongue loosened, the madder and the more frightened she became. A lot of serious politics took place at these parties, and she was going to have to keep a tight rein on her Junex's mouth.

"Well, I like to fuck about three times a day," Billy said loudly, and he was as drunk as Olson, so it seemed a perfectly natural thing to say out of the blue. "It keeps my bowels regular." He squeezed his Houris's breast like he was squeezing the juice out of a prune. She responded by gluing herself to him and moaning.

"How long you been a Junex?" Jerny asked Olson, putting a hand on his arm.

"He's just been promoted," Gret said. "Natural rotation."

"She's a great one, don't you think?" Billy said, and kissed his Houris on the temple.

Olson could only nod dumbly. "Looks fine to me."

Another Houris, this one wearing long hair and nothing else, came up with another pitcher and began sloshing more booze in their glasses. Billy grabbed that one in his other arm, and her pitcher spilled all down his front.

"Shit," Billy said.

"You can drink your suit," Olson said, his eyes traveling from one pair of breasts to another.

"How quick do promotions come in Dallas?" Jerny asked. "Got any Movers down there?"

Billy had Olson's hand and was putting it on his Houris's breast. "Firmest suckers you ever got hold of," he said, as Olson bent down to study it clinically.

His eyes traveled up to Billy's. "Wonderful," he said. "Very nice."

"How'd you get the transfer?" Jerny asked. "You got connections here?"

"How about yours?" Billy said, reaching for Gret.

Olson stiffened, just as a shouting match broke out on the other side of the living room. He called the man something extremely uncomplimentary, but it got swallowed up in all the excitement.

Gret quickly put herself between Olson and Billy, and put the man's hand on her breast.

"Hmmm," the man said, and Gret clenched her teeth. She fought it, needing to keep a rein on Olson.

A group of partyers had formed a single line, one behind the other, and were dancing through the room, hands on the hips of the one in front. As they passed, Gret broke away from Billy's grasp and pulled Olson to the back of the line.

"Here," she said. "Keep your hands occupied." She took away his drink and put his hands on the hips of a woman who had been spray-painted gold. Olson dutifully joined the parade, his eyes glued to the gold woman's buttocks.

"I'm having a wonderful time," Olson said loudly.

"Could have fooled me," Gret responded. "How about sobering up a little?"

Olson kicked out his foot when the line did, and Gret had to move fast to keep up with them. He leaned his head back to stare at her.

"Say, who's the man around here?" he asked, voice laced with sarcasm.

Her eyes flashed at him. "These people find out who you are, and you'll never live to see adulthood, sonny."

With that, she turned to stalk away.

"Where you going?" he called to her.

"To get you something to eat."

"What are we having?"

"Hot dogs," she responded. "And sushi."

Olson brightened. "Sounds *wonderful*!" he yelled to the ceiling, and the line turned, Olson almost slipping off the back as the whip cracked.

He followed the line as it snaked through the living room, around sofas full of people copulating and men arguing, jabbing with the lightning flashes. His mind was stuffed full of cotton, and it was the first time he had a chance to reflect on that. The men in the room were all the same, cut from the same sausage. The women were of two types: the Houris, whose purpose was out front and obvious, and the wives, who dressed with extreme modesty and were treated with respect without exception.

There was a pair of hands on Olson's hips. He turned quickly to see Jerny smiling up at him.

"Marty, my friend," he said. "I've been taking a little exercise. Good of you to join me."

"Never miss my evening constitutional," Jerny yelled back.

"That's the spirit," Olson returned, and kicked out with the line again, as they moved through the hallway toward the bedrooms.

"Tell me the truth, Cat," Jerny said, and Olson nearly forgot that he had a new name. "How did you swing the transfer? Who do you know in Orleans?"

Olson broke from the line as it moved into the bedroom and put his arm around Jerny's shoulder, drawing him back down the hall. "I'll tell you the honest-to-goodness truth, Marty. Truth with a capital T because you're my friend and friends should tell one another the truth."

"Poetic words," Jerny said. "Wrapped in plastic."

The sky flashed brightly overhead, and Olson looked up in time to see a brilliant flash of lightning run down the long rod that was stuck atop the gold dome outside. They kept walking, staying close to the wall to make way for the steady stream of people who passed them going both directions.

"I just fell into the transfer, you know?" Olson said into Jerny's ear. "One minute I was just sitting there, minding my own, as they say, and the next, I was stuffed into one of them funny suits and was driving down the road."

"You don't say. It was that simple?"

"Would I lie to you?"

"Of course not."

"Of course not. And I'll tell you something else. I don't know anybody. Nobody there, nobody here." He shrugged with his free hand. "Nobody." He looked around. "You seen my drink?"

"We'll get you another." Jerny winked. "I look out for my friends."

Olson nodded, touched. "That's the way it should be."

"You know," Jerny said, stopping the walk and pushing Olson back against the wall, gently but firmly, "we all need friends."

"Hear, hear."

"Here in Orleans, friends are important to your career. The right friends will help you to make the right moves. You know what I mean?"

Olson nodded again. "Right friends," he said. "Right moves."

"Take Rennie for instance."

"Nice fella."

"Rennie looks out for his friends. He helps them and they help him. And, you know, the more friends someone has, the more everybody can do for everybody."

Olson nodded again. "Rennie's a nice fella."

Jerny pinched his cheek. "I'll tell you a secret," he whispered loudly. "Rennie likes you a lot. He thinks we can all be friends."

Olson pursed his lips thoughtfully and nodded for the third time. "It's good to have friends," he said.

"So here you are," Gret said, walking up to ease Olson away from Jerny. "I've been looking all over for you."

Olson straightened to his full height. "I've been doing just fine," he said. "Me and Marty have been having a nice little chat about friendship."

"I'll just bet you have," she said, and stuck something in his hand. "Here, eat."

His eyes brightened and he looked down, astonished to find a long, slender tube of some kind stuck in some bread. "What the hell is this?"

"A hot dog," Gret said.

Olson frowned deeply. "It doesn't look like any kind of dog I've ever eaten before."

Jerny started laughing, doubling over until it got lost in a cough.

Gret pinched Olson, hard. "Honestly," she said through clenched teeth. "Stuff the damned thing in your mouth and shut up."

Someone in the living room was banging a spoon on a metal pitcher. "Attention," he yelled. "Let's have your attention."

Gret took Olson's arm and led him back toward the living room. "Come on, let's get in there."

He went, dropping the breaded tube on the floor when she wasn't looking. Some lights had been turned on in a corner of the living room, near the television set where Faisel ibn Faisel talked continually. An Exec in a bright blue velvet suit was calling for everyone to group around.

"Come on up, everybody," the man was saying, and the crowd started jamming tightly together. Olson and Gret ended up somewhere in the middle of the throng, without Jerny.

Someone turned the musak down a bit and things got suddenly quiet. The Exec began talking.

"This is a wonderful party, don't you agree!" he said loudly.

A cheer went up, and the man put up his hands to quiet it again after a time.

"We don't all get up to the ninetieth floor that often," he said, and there were amens to that. "And some of us may never make it here again." There was nervous laughter. "But every one of us is proud and grateful to be here now, and I think it's time to express that gratitude to our boss, the man who gives us our plastic, Mr. Elwood!"

There was wild applause, and Olson found himself joining in. After it had gone on for a time, a black man in a kevlar tuxedo walked into the circle of light. He shook hands with the man who introduced him, then turned and waved to the crowd, which then increased the applause. He seemed like a nice man to Olson, somehow unassuming despite his position. He put up his hands for silence.

"I suppose you're all wondering why I called you here today," he said, and Olson joined in with the laughter even though he didn't know what was funny; although in his condition, everything seemed funny.

Mr. Elwood put his hands up again. "But seriously, I hope that you're all having a good time while you're killing my gin budget for the month."

More laughter, and Olson was beginning to feel really comfortable, really at home.

"I'll let you all get back to the party in a minute," he said.

"But I have a couple of announcements to make first. Let's start by talking about the audit."

A groan surged through the crowd, while Mr. Elwood nodded, waiting for it to die down.

"As you all have probably heard, the home office in Saudi Arabia is sending one of its officials to audit our books. I just want to go on the public record saying that I'm damned proud of all of you and the job you've done, and I'm sure that the audit will come out just fine. I'm behind you all one hundred percent."

Applause and cheers.

"I also have news. The streets are kind of a mess right now and it's getting worse. But all of you have done a fine job getting the citizens inside the gates. The Houston Jits are apparently moving this way; they've already reached some of our outlying branches. I want to assure all of you that their force is small and unorganized and will pose absolutely no threat to our security or well-being. We'll have to put up with a little inconvenience for a while, but nothing to worry about."

Mr. Elwood picked up a drink from the table beside him, toasting it in the direction of the television set. Tilting his head back, he drained it in one swallow, much to the excitement of the crowd. Olson noticed that a flash of pain seemed to skip across his face for just a second, but no one else seemed to notice, so he didn't think any more about it. Mr. Elwood wiped his mouth on the back of his sleeve and continued.

"There is a reason for this party," he said. "As you all know, we have in our midst what's affectionately known as a Mover, somebody who through constant hard work and vigilance is able to work through the system at an increased rate. You all know who I'm talking about, so let's get him up here." He was motioning with his arm. "Come on up here, Rennie."

Rennie feigned shyness until the applause reached a peak, then he walked up next to Mr. Elwood and they shook hands. He was dressed in red again, a three-piece patent-leather suit.

Rennie turned to the crowd. "I didn't do anything that any red-blooded, Light of the World genius Exec couldn't do."

The crowd roared, as Olson felt himself getting a headache. He knew he shouldn't have stopped drinking.

"Rennie," Mr. Elwood said loudly, "has just become the youngest senior VeePee in LOW's history. And to honor this occasion, we'd like to present him with a special gift."

He pulled a small box out of his pocket. "Too small to be a raise," someone yelled from the audience.

Mr. Elwood smiled. "I said a gift, not an endowment." Then he began looking around the room. "I am told that we have a new employee in our midst. Is Junex Catanine out there?"

Olson wasn't even listening, but he heard Gret's sharp intake of breath and looked up. She poked him in the ribs. "That's you, asshole," she said, and Olson stupidly put up his hand.

"There he is," Rennie said. "Clear the way for him."

All at once, there was a break in the crowd and Olson found himself walking up front to stand with Rennie and Mr. Elwood.

"Glad to see you got the mud out of your hair," Rennie said, and there was enough laughter that Olson knew that the story had gotten around.

"Good to make your acquaintance," Mr. Elwood said, shaking his hand.

"Call me Cat," Olson said loudly, and smiled giddily around the room.

"Well, Cat," Mr. Elwood said, handing him the box, "it's only appropriate that you give Rennie here the gift, since you were instrumental in his receiving it."

Olson's eyebrows went up. "Me?"

Mr. Elwood nodded, but Olson noticed that his eyes had narrowed somewhat.

Swallowing hard, he turned from Elwood and handed the box to Rennie. "Eat it in good health," he said, and was surprised to find that he, also, had gotten a laugh.

Rennie took the gift and pulled the top quickly off.

"All right!" he yelled, and held up a set of aut keys. It must have been the one that Olson had ridden in, and he wondered if they had washed all the blood off it.

There was loud applause and Mr. Elwood and Rennie embraced one another like long-lost relatives. Then Rennie turned and embraced Olson.

"Thanks," he said. "Thanks."

And Olson told him he was a nice fella and he was happy to do it.

"Congratulations," Mr. Elwood said loudly, and motioned for them to move away.

"Come on," Rennie said to Olson and led him into the crowd.

"And now," Mr. Elwood said, "I have an extra-special surprise for all of you. Professor Norwood is with us tonight with a whole new crop of fun Engies."

There was great excitement then, as a man wearing a white suit stepped into the light. He was smiling jovially.

"As you all know," Norwood said, and his voice was high and nasal, "in Engy Research, we develop a lot of worker mutants to help in the fields and factories. But, as you also know, we develop Engies just for fun sometimes, for the amusement of our LOW Execs. The models I want to show you today can be owned with a minimum down payment, and room and board your only expense when you take them home. They have a five-year guarantee, unconditional, and a limited wardrobe. They're great fun to keep, or to trade, or to give as gifts." He pointed to his left. "And here they are!"

A man walked into the light, an ordinary man dressed in overalls. "This is our new Allsee model II," Norwood said. "Amuse and astound your friends with him. Watch."

Norwood got deliberately behind the man and held up an open hand. "How many fingers?" he asked loudly.

The man closed his eyes. "Five," he answered immediately.

"Right!" said Norwood, who then grabbed Mr. Elwood's empty glass. "And what am I holding?"

"A glass," the man answered. "An empty glass. Would somebody get this man a drink?"

There was laughter and applause, and much confusion on Olson's part.

"How you liking the party?" Rennie asked.

Olson smiled wide. "Did you invite me?"

"Wanted a chance to talk to you . . . to get to know you."

Dr. Norwood turned the man's back toward the audience and pulled up his hair. "Eyes, ladies and gentlemen, in the back of his head."

Olson's mouth fell open. The man had a large, hideous eye glaring out at the audience.

"I see you sticking your tongue out," the Engy said, and everyone laughed.

Norwood directed him away. "And now, for the man who has everything . . ." He pulled a naked woman into the light. She had three perfectly formed breasts.

"Something to do with both your hands and your mouth," the good doctor said.

"Where have you been assigned?" Du'camp asked Olson, who was staring at the three breasts in disbelief.

"I don't know," he answered.

Rennie clucked his tongue. "The river, I'll bet. They need a Junex helping with the river traffic."

"Sounds . . . interesting," Olson said, but he wasn't really listening. Dr. Norwood had brought another naked woman up in front. This one's skin changed color to match her surroundings. Norwood held a red handkerchief up by her head, and her whole face changed to the color of the cloth. Olson wondered what the point was.

"Let's go get a drink and watch some matching," Rennie said. "We'll get acquainted. What do you say?"

"What's matching?" Olson asked.

Du'camp's eyes lit up. "You've never mind-matched?" he asked.

Olson shook his head. "Don't think so."

"Well," Rennie said. "We're going to have to further your education right now. Come on."

He turned, grabbing two glasses out of the hands of the people nearest him. They smiled quickly and backed away. He handed one to Olson, who turned and took one last look toward the lights. Norwood had brought on a man with a three-foot erect penis that had the women swooning.

As Rennie drew him through the crowd, he looked helplessly around for Gret. Then he saw her. Billy had her backed up against the wall and was thrusting himself against her. She leaned back, her head lolled to the side, her mouth open. Olson felt the anger flash through him, then forced himself to turn away, walking off with Du'camp.

They went into another room, a room filled with men smoking cigars. On the far wall, two men sat across a table from one another, metal bands stringing wires wrapped around their foreheads. There was a large screen on the wall beside them. On the screen was a scene of the same two men. They were circling one another with knives in their hands. Both men were covered with blood.

"What are they doing?" Olson asked.

Rennie took a big drink, then smacked his lips. "It's a competition that tests their intellect and their will," he said.

"Those wires connect to a machine that mixes their brain waves. Then they put themselves into direct mental conflict and see who's the strongest."

One of the men lunged with his knife, missed, and the other slashed him viciously on the arm. The man at the table flinched.

"Did he really feel that?" Olson asked.

"Sure," Rennie replied.

"Does anybody ever die on the machine?"

Du'camp nodded. "Sometimes the older ones with the weak hearts do. Most everybody else stops short of combat to the death unless it's a duel of honor."

Olson noticed that Mr. Elwood had slipped into the room and was watching them.

The wounded man lunged again, apparently desperate, looking for a lucky shot. The other one was ready for him and slashed his arm again, making him drop the knife. Then he fell upon him, knocking him to the ground. He came around with his knife, jammed it tight against his throat. "Do you yield?" the man at the table said, and his image on the screen said it too.

"Yes," he hissed, and toggled a switch on the table, making the screen go blank.

The men around the room applauded lightly, as two of the hurt man's friends helped him away from the table. They began loudly exchanging round plastic disks of various colors. Apparently the betting had been heavy.

"Like to try it?" Rennie asked. "Just to see what it feels like?"

Olson laughed. "No thanks," he said. "I wouldn't know what to do."

"You just think, Dallas boy," Du'camp said, and suddenly his face looked dark and unfriendly to Olson. "You do know how to think, don't you?"

"I tried it once, but it hurt my head," Olson joked, but this time, nobody was laughing. Everyone in the room was staring at him silently, with deadly intensity.

Rennie had gotten grave. "You don't have a hair on your ass if you don't try it," he said, low and menacing.

And, all at once, Olson realized that he was being challenged, and that he'd have to take the challenge seriously. His eyes drifted to Mr. Elwood. The man was nodding slowly up and down.

"Well, why not?" Olson said loudly. "I like television as much as the next fella."

"That's the spirit," Rennie said happily, and the atmosphere of the room eased up at once. "Since this is your first time, I promise to take it easy on you."

Olson drained his drink the way Mr. Elwood had done. "Fair enough," he said, and swaggered up to the table.

He sat down on a metal chair that was bolted to the floor, then picked up the ring, looking it up and down.

"Here," someone said, and opened it on a hinge.

He looked up to see Jerny smiling down at him.

"Hook it around your forehead," the man told him. Then he winked. "And good luck."

Olson locked the ring into place as Rennie was doing the same thing.

"Any bets?" Rennie said to the men, and everyone laughed loudly, and Olson began to think they were all making fun of him. He didn't much like that.

Reaching out, Du'camp flipped his toggle and motioned for Olson to do the same.

"I'll set the scene," Rennie said, and his smile was swallowing his face. "You just think your way through it."

"Sure," Olson replied, but he wasn't very happy anymore.

Olson flipped his toggle and immediately felt his brain slide into a different gear. It felt crowded now, like there was someone else's brain up there, too. And, all at once, his control slipped away totally. He closed his eyes and looked at the movie that was playing inside his skull.

He was lying on a bed, but he wasn't himself. He was in a farmhouse on the frontier. He was small and frail, a woman, and she was just waking up.

The moonlight slatted through the window blinds, casting oblong shadows across her covers. When she awoke, she knew that something was wrong. Fear was on her, fear like cold steel driven into her heart.

Turning her head slowly to the side, she looked at Jeremy, her husband. The first thing she noticed was the shaft of moonlight glinting hotly off the blade that protruded from his chest. His eyes were open wide, his mouth frozen in a silent scream.

She had a second for it all to focus in her consciousness,

then felt the hand on her throat, choking. The fear gripped her mind, controlled it.

A man stood over her, grinning, leering, pinning her to the bed by her throat. She thought she recognized his face, but somehow it was all far away, dreamlike. Outside, the dogs were barking, and it sounded like laughter.

The man got right down in her face, his breath putrid, smelling of death and decay.

"Pretty girl," he rasped, and with his free hand he stripped the cover from her naked body.

Releasing her neck, he began fondling her, rough, painful. Free from his pinioning grasp, she tried to wriggle away, kicking out.

"No!" she screamed. "Noooo!"

He laughed loudly, obscenely, and slapped her hand, knocking her back to the bed. His hands pulled roughly on her breasts as she tasted her own blood on her tongue.

He climbed on the bed, straddling her, and pulled his pants down. His erection was enormous, much too large.

"Please, God no!"

He was forcing her legs apart, and she fought him desperately, futilely. His breath was rotted potatoes as he lowered himself onto her and he was drooling on her chest.

The revulsion was total, absolute, and he was forcing himself into her.

And somewhere, from far away and deep within, a bell was ringing, a strand of pride and control was exercising itself.

"Yes," she heard herself say. "Come on. Hurry."

The leering face was looking at her, puzzled.

"Come on, let's have it," she said. "I haven't had it good for years."

He reached out and slapped her again, hard. "Yesss," she moaned again. "Hurt me. Kill me with sex."

He hit her again and she started to laugh. "Come on," she said. "What are you waiting for?"

He was trying to force himself into her, but he was losing his erection. He hit her again.

"What's the matter?" she demanded. "God, I've had it better from that jackass." She pointed to her dead husband. "I've had it better from hedgehogs. I've had it better from Jits!"

She heard a strangled cry and everything was fading away....

Olson shook his head and opened his eyes. Men were

crowded around him, applauding and slapping him on the back. He had won.

He pulled the ring off his head and looked across the table at Rennie. The man was staring at him, staring deadly hatred. His face was flushed with embarrassment and his breath came short.

Olson couldn't resist, though he tried mightily. "Thanks for taking it easy on me," he said.

Du'camp slammed a fist down on the table. "This is not the end of this," he said, and jumped up from the table, running out of the room, Marty Jerny close on his heels.

The headache was on Olson in earnest now. Getting up, he smiled at the well-wishers, then moved through them to find Gret.

Mr. Elwood stopped him at the door by grabbing him by the lapels. His face was smooth and hard, betraying no emotion. "Just who the hell are you?" he whispered low.

* * *

> *Life is strewn with so many dangers, and can be the source of so many misfortunes, that death is not the greatest of them.*
> —Napoleon I

> *Man eats the big fish*
> *the big fish eat the*
> *little fish*
> *the little fish*
> *eat insects*
> *in the water*
> *the water insects*
> *eat the water plants*
> *the water plants*
> *eat mud*
> *mud eats man.*
> —LOW Computer's Life
> Analog, 2053

XI

LOW Building
Night Games

Tonight it was the corn crop.

The man sat quietly in the dark room, the glow from the CRT screen casting a deathly blue pallor on his face and the backs of his hands. He typed quickly, fingers rhythmically clicking the keyboard that sat before him.

His name was Paul-Paul Baggins. He had a small head, like a cat, thin sweaty hair, and eyes that would never directly meet other eyes. He was that kind of man. He was simply a minor liaison who had access to some passkeys. He was a painfully shy man who took orders well, and who had enough sense to know that you grabbed opportunity when it came along and held on for dear life.

The computer room stretched out wide around him, clicking and whirring, running in the darkness, running whether anyone was there to watch it or not.

Baggins was there.

The words ACCESS CODE appeared on the screen.

He typed quickly: 2Q2-1719.

There was a tiny whir, followed by a faraway ping, and then the whole world opened up when the words CLEARED FOR ACCESS glowed red at him.

He typed: WICHITA PASSWORD.

He looked around quickly, hearing footsteps in one of the hallways outside the room. Sliding his chair quietly back, he prepared to make a run for it. Then the footsteps receded and he was alone again.

Baggins looked at the screen, perspiration beading his face, glistening in the blue light.

PASSWORD: SHARIAH

He typed in the password and Wichita was his. Bootlegging into Accounts Receivable, he was, within minutes, transferring corn futures from the Orleans account to the Wichita account, Password Shariah—the Law of God.

Rennie Du'camp rode the elevator down with Marty Jerny and Billy Fain. He was mad, as mad as he'd ever been, but he'd kept his exterior calm.

"Why didn't you warn me about him?" he asked Jerny matter-of-factly.

"There didn't seem to be that much there," Jerny answered.

Billy belched loudly from too many hot dogs on top of too many martinis. "He seemed like a dumb shit," he said.

Rennie fixed him with eyes hard as stones. "Well, you should be an expert on that subject," he told the man.

Billy flinched, but kept his mouth shut.

"It's not that big of a deal," Jerny said.

"The hell it's not," Du'camp answered. He remembered that he had promised Jerny his Houris for the night, but at this point in time, he wasn't willing to suffer alone. "He beat me. The son of a bitch beat me."

Jerny ran a hand through his red hair. "This was your big night," he said. "Why let that stupid game ruin it?"

The elevator shuddered to a halt, the doors sliding open after an amount of difficulty. Rennie stepped out, the other two following after.

They were standing in a large carpeted lobby. The room was ringed all around by floor-to-ceiling one-way glass that was barred on the inside. Weapons racks were set conspicuously in various parts of the room. Outside the glass, they could see the rain still sheeting down, the streets rushing ankle-deep water. A few people still walked those streets, looking for something better, while many who had already given up sat huddled against the building.

Rennie walked to the weapons rack, looking over a variety that included everything from maced gloves to laser pistols. "To begin with, it's not a stupid game. Matching is an intellectual battleground that is a perfect judge of contrasting abilities."

He picked up a nailed bludgeon and hefted it a couple of times. "Secondly, I haven't lost a match in five years. This bothers me a great deal." Frowning, he put the club back on the rack and continued looking.

"Maybe he just got lucky," Billy said.

"Maybe," Rennie answered, looking over a whole line of broadswords. "I was overconfident and didn't protect myself well enough." Picking up a sword, he slashed designs in the air before putting it back.

"That's all that happened," Jerny said. "Dumb luck."

Rennie snorted. "You'd say anything to quiet me down," he returned. "I can't afford to take the chance that this was a fluke. If this man's a serious threat, I need to know it. First thing in the morning, I want you to check him out. Get into the computers and check his background. I want to know everything there is to know about Mr. Junex Catanine."

Rennie picked up a long knife with a triangular blade. Smiling broadly, he stuck it in his belt, and turned to the men. "I want no more surprises, no more 'dumb luck.' You understand that?"

Both men nodded, and Rennie started for the exit to the outside. Reaching the double doors, he stuck a key in the lock and turned back around. "She's waiting in your apartment, Marty," he said, winking. "Don't wear her out too much."

With that, he pushed through the door, moving into the dark, pouring rain. It was humid rain, and a rancid odor drifted up from the streets. His hair matted quickly, water soaking through his suit.

Soft light sifted through the mirrored glass, glowing a small section of the sidewalk in front of the building. Six or eight people were huddled in the fog of light that brought no warmth. Rennie walked up to the closest one to him.

"You," he said, pointing. "Citizen. Come here."

A small man stood up reluctantly, huddling in burlap. He took faltering steps toward Du'camp.

"I ain't done nothing," he said.

"I know that," Rennie answered, and drew the knife from his belt. Working quickly, he plunged the blade in and out of the man, gutting him like an animal carcass. When he was finished he left the man lying in the gutter so that the water would wash the small rivers of blood down into the sewer.

After that, Rennie felt much better, much calmer inside. He took the elevator back up to his apartment, and knew that he would sleep well and not even think once about Junex Catanine.

One of Dr. Norwood's Engies was lying, drunk, facedown on the carpet, the eye in the back of his head staring listlessly at the ceiling. Olson watched as a couple of servants grabbed him under the arms and dragged him across the floor toward the front door.

The party was over, the last of the revelers being ushered out. He hadn't realized how noisy it had been in there until it got quiet again. There was a pile of passed-out citizens by the door, who were, one by one, being picked up and tossed into the outside hallway.

He and Gret sat at a small dining table, under the only real light in the whole place. Mr. Elwood sat silently staring at them from an easy chair pulled into semidarkness. He held a glass of white wine and was rolling it between the palms of his hands. He had asked them to stay, and Olson knew that they were in trouble.

Olson looked to Gret, and saw fear in her eyes. She reached out a tentative hand to lay on his arm, but he pulled away, still angry that she had allowed herself to be violated by that lush, Billy.

The atmosphere grew thick, oppressive, and when the last of the partyers and the last of the servants disappeared into the night, Mr. Elwood cleared his throat and spoke.

"Who are you?" he asked Olson.

Gret spoke up. "He's the man who—"

"Not you!" the man said, pointing at her. "We'll talk later."

He swung his gaze back to Olson. "You were saying?"

"I'm Junex Catanine," Olson answered. "A transfer from the Dallas Branch."

Mr. Elwood sighed deeply, painfully. Standing slowly, he moved to a small computer terminal set in the wall beside the dining table and began working his fingers on the typer. Olson just watched, not understanding, but when a picture of the real Cat flashed up on the man's screen, he knew for sure he'd been discovered.

"That's Junex Catanine," Mr. Elwood said.

"There must be some mistake," Gret said, but her voice was quaking.

"Let me make it easier for you," the man said, and began playing on the keys again. All at once, Cat's picture broke apart on the screen, then disappeared in a burst of static. The word EXPUNGED appeared on screen.

"Where'd he go?" Olson asked.

"That's my question," Mr. Elwood replied. "Where did he go?"

They stared at one another, and Olson knew the string had run out. "Dead," he answered. "On the road. I didn't mean to kill him, but he wanted to kill me."

"Why did you come here?"

Now, there was a question. Olson thought about it for quite a while, then said quietly, "I was curious. I was sick of the road. I was bored."

"Where does this one fit in?" he asked, indicating Gret.

Despite his anger, Olson saw no reason to take Gret down with him. "I forced her to take me instead," he replied. "Told her I'd kill her if she didn't."

"I don't believe you," Mr. Elwood said, and returned wearily to his seat in the darkness. He sat down with a groan, rubbing large hands across his face. "But it doesn't matter."

"It doesn't?" Gret said.

The man picked up his goblet from where it sat on the floor. He put it to his lips, then set it down without drinking. "I'm not going to do anything to you."

Olson loosened his tie and unbuttoned his too-tight jacket. He slouched down in his chair. "Why?" he asked.

"Why," Mr. Elwood repeated, but never answered the question. He seemed so old to Olson, so used up.

A large shaft of lightning branched across the sky, brightening the Director's face. There were tears in his eyes, tears that slipped quickly back into the cover of the night. "You made a formidable enemy tonight," he told Olson.

"I can take care of myself."

Mr. Elwood laughed without humor. "If we don't do something permanent about those computer records, you'll be discovered sometime tomorrow."

"We?" Gret said, and sat up straight in her chair. She was climbing out of her lethargy, reacting to new stimuli.

"I mean to help you survive here," the man said.

"Why?" Olson asked again.

Gret leaned forward, her face flushing. "Because he's dying," she whispered, and her eyes were also filled with tears.

"Break contact!" Mr. Elwood said angrily, then softened. "Please. Allow me this dignity."

"I can't help the feelings," Gret said, and she was crying.

"I know."

Olson stood up, looking down at Gret. "Will someone please tell me what's going on?"

Mr. Elwood stood also, walking into the circle of light. "The Houris feels what I feel," he said. "It comes with the territory."

He turned and walked farther off into the room. The place was a shambles. It looked as if it had been vandalized. "I've fought my whole life," he said. "Scrabbled for a handhold, pulled myself up. I took on life, gave it my own sense of values and learned to control it, learned to make it important and, consequently, make myself important. Does this make any sense to you?"

Olson followed him into the darkness, stood near him, touching near. "No," he answered honestly.

"It will," the man said, not looking at him. "Someday it will be clear as glass. You see, we give life meaning, define it. Then we control it and give ourselves meaning. And then we die, and know that we've been lying to ourselves. None of it means anything. It's all nonsense."

"We all have to live with death," Olson said.

Mr. Elwood turned to him, put a hand on his shoulder. "Living with it is not the same as accepting it," he returned. "Believe me."

"And you're dying," Olson said.

"And still not accepting it," Mr. Elwood replied. "I wake up every morning and know that second of sweet forgetfulness, of unknowing bliss. And then reality sinks in and I feel the pain, and I remember. It still tears me to pieces."

He moved right up to Olson, took him in his arms and hugged him close. "And then tonight, you beat Rennie on that stupid machine. You whipped his ass, and I knew in that instant who you were and what all this meant."

"I don't think I . . ."

"Just listen," Elwood rasped, and pulled away, walking to one of the rain-sheeting windows. Olson followed him, while Gret stayed at the table, her knees pulled up on her chair, her chin resting on her knees.

"The business has been my whole life, my whole reason for living," Mr. Elwood said to the window. "I worked hard to get the Branch Manager job, then worked hard to make Orleans the best branch in the LOW Kingdom. It takes guts to run an operation like this, and ingenuity. The trouble is that there is very little of either within the organization.''

''Why?''

The lightning flashed again, and Olson could look down and see the flooding streets.

''They test people for Exec jobs, and place them on their ability to follow orders. That's important because working according to S.O.P. is what allows the Company structure to stay intact. Unfortunately, people who follow orders aren't very creative, so they fail in the higher positions that require independent thought and action.''

''What has this got to do with anything?''

Mr. Elwood turned again, leaning his back against the window. ''I'm getting to that.''

And then he coughed, deep and loud, doubling over. He began gagging and Olson rushed to help him. The man waved him away, then fell to his knees, coughing and spitting blood. It passed after a moment, subsiding in ever-decreasing waves. Then he sat there on the floor, breathing heavily, hand still protectively clutching his stomach.

He smiled weakly up at Olson. ''Helluva way to make a living,'' he smiled. Then his face turned grave again. ''I'm not content with my life. I want to know that the business, the only thing I've ever cared about, will be able to continue after I'm gone. It's immortality to me; the only kind that makes any sense.''

''And there's no one to take over for you.''

''No one.''

''What about Rennie? He seems eager enough.''

Mr. Elwood spat on the floor. ''He's a mad dog. He's an animal masquerading as a human being. His own gratification is all that concerns him. The future means nothing.''

He stuck a thumb toward the window. ''If you think things out there are bad now,'' he said, ''you oughta see what a maniac like Rennie could do.'' He shook his head. ''I've been there. Mass executions, forced child labor, starvation . . . there has to be some limits.''

''Then, what . . .''

Mr. Elwood made a face. ''Haven't you figured it out yet, boy? I want you. I want you to take over for me when I die.''

''Me?''

"You're bright; you're quick; you're creative—beating Rennie proved that; and you're not a part of the system."

"But that doesn't mean that . . ."

"Figure it out, damnit!"

Olson looked down at him, so frail and pitiful there on the floor. Then he squatted slowly down, an inch at a time, until they were eye to eye. As he looked, the man began to smile, very slowly, and as he did, the light dawned in Olson's brain.

"You're from the outside, too," Olson said softly.

"It was many years ago, and my story's not worth dragging out," he replied. "I got in on a fluke, kept my nose clean and my eyes open. You learn a lot about survival on the outside."

The man crawled quickly across the floor and retrieved his glass of wine. Still on hands and knees, he finished it in one swallow, grimacing the whole time. Then he eased himself back up into his chair.

"Given enough years and enough pain, I made it." He gestured around the room. "Now, here I am, with all this and no way to share it, no way to pass it on. I have no wife, no . . . son."

Olson moved back to sit at the table with Gret. His head still hurt and he was getting very sleepy. "I'm not your son, Mr. Elwood."

"You could be," the man said quietly.

Olson slouched back again. "This is crazy, stupid crazy," he said after a moment. "It could never work."

"Allah," Mr. Elwood rasped. "Can't you just indulge me a little bit? I've got nothing else, don't you understand that?" He leaned forward, resting his elbows on his knees, his hands shaking up and down. "Think about yourself. If this works, you'll be one of the most powerful men in this country. Tell me that doesn't appeal to you."

"Staying alive appeals to me."

"I've been trying to tell you: it's not death that's the frightening thing; it's the emptiness. I'm offering you the means to fill your life any way you choose."

"What if I'm not interested?"

Mr. Elwood suddenly turned cold, and Olson realized how he had gotten to where he was sitting. "Don't give me that," he spat. "I've been where you are, remember? You're used to kicking to stay alive, and now you've got the chance to kick real high. You've already had enough of a taste of it that you could never go back. Tell me I'm lying. Go ahead, tell me."

Olson breathed deep, shaking his head. The logic was irrefutable. "What about Gret?" he asked, and the question came without his thinking about it.

"The Houris will stick with you a lot at first," he said, "to help you out when you need it. But we'll have to get you married off as quickly as possible. A good marriage will make you some good alliances. We'll need to groom you quickly, because I don't know how much time I have left. First thing I'll do is take care of those computer records..."

"Stop!" Olson said loudly, and stood up. "I'm beginning to get sick of people telling me what to do."

Mr. Elwood matched his fire. "Need I remind you that the penalty for impersonating an Exec is death?"

Olson walked up and stuck a finger in the man's face. "Need I remind you that you need me as much as I need you right now? The only way I'll approach this thing is as an equal partnership between me and you. It's time for me to start making my own decisions, and I intend to do that right now."

He began pacing back and forth. "You make suggestions. I'll decide if I want to take them or not."

"Fair enough," Mr. Elwood said without hesitation.

Olson looked at Gret. She seemed small and fragile to him, huddled on the rough wood chair. His anger at her melted away. She stared hard, no feeling seeping through the porthole of her eyes.

"I'll decide about this marriage business," he said. "I may not be ready for anything like that yet. When I know, I'll let you know."

Gret's face was quizzical, but Mr. Elwood was smiling. "What's your name?" he asked. "Your real name."

They locked eyes. "Olson."

"You're going to do okay, Olson. Son."

*   *   *

And when you are greeted with a greeting,
greet with a fairer greeting than it, or return it;
surely God keeps a watchful count
over everything.

—The Koran
IV. Women

*The fly that prefers sweetness to a long life
may drown in honey.*
—Bedouin Wisdom

XII

Holmes Air Base
Rub Al Khali

The hundred-piece orchestra played musak, as the Sun
shone down from the blinding blue sky and glinted off the silver
wings of the airplane like perpetual popping flashbulbs. Thousands of people crowded around the air strip and surrounding
buildings, most of them soldiers and employees of LOW. Faisel
ibn Faisel Al Sa'ud was putting on a show, and the world was
there to witness it.

Tables piled high with dates, mutton, rice, and sweetbreads
filled the compound, stringing out long lines of revelers around
them who stood impatiently, laughing and yelling on the carpet
of sand that stretched to the horizon in all directions. Bright-
colored mishlahs swirled like a carnival against the backdrop of
bright white, and the smells were sickly sweet, sweat mixed with
incense and the thick aroma of butter-cooking.

And the tv cameras watched it all from scaffoldings set outside
the action, broadcasting Faisel's generosity to the world. Camels
wandered freely through the crowds, and jugglers. There were bins
full of televisions for the taking, but there were very few takers.

A large platform had been erected at the end of the runway,
and Faisel sat atop it in his leather chair, surrounded on all sides
by thick sheets of protective glass.

His subjects lined the stairs leading up to the platform, and
he listened one by one to their grievances or to the poems of
praise they had written in his honor. He smiled always, but his
eyes searched the crowds for his brother.

Abdullah wandered a distance from Faisel's prying eyes. He
and Nura, along with a contingent of Bedouin, moved through
the fringes of the large crowd, watching the acrobats and tasting
the foods on the brightly colored tables. Several of his male

children wandered with them also, laughing and squealing, pointing into the pressing crowds when something amused them.

"You will supervise the children," he told Nura. "Malize will give you trouble in this regard, but I have already instructed her to place herself second to you."

Nura lowered her eyes. "Malize has always had that responsibility. Why do you take it from her?"

Abdullah grunted. "I've always been here before to supervise Malize," he answered. "You will do this thing for me."

"And when you come back?"

Abdullah took a breath, smiled absently. "We shall see."

Bandar came stumbling up, his mouth stuffed full of meat, old Thamir by his side. The old man sucked on a date, the best his toothless mouth could handle.

"Your brother honors you," Bandar said loudly. "Before the whole world, he honors you."

Abdullah smiled wide. "He, indeed, has witnesses to his act of generosity. I see that you enjoy this hospitality in large measure."

Bandar drew up his lizardskin pouch of weak tea and drank heavily, overfilling his mouth to spill into the sand at his feet. He brought down the pouch, wiping his mouth on the sleeve of his pale red mishlah. "We break him from within," he replied, then belched loudly.

The old man cackled. "That's right. We eat, but hate every mouthful."

"Father! Father!" a small voice called. Little Nasr was waving his arms from within a jam of people.

They hurried to the place, and watched with the children as two men juggled gleaming scimitars between them, the razor's edge of the blades glinting hotly in the Sun. Placing his hands on Nasr's shoulders, Abdullah pretended to enjoy the show; but what he really watched was the bus that had pulled up on the runway next to the jumbo jet that was to take him to the Western Sector. A squad of Elite, deadly and mysterious in their blank black robes, filed out of the bus and immediately climbed the gangway leading into the plane.

He feared the Elite more than anything else, for they were bound in physical slavery to Faisel's whims. They each had a small charge set in their brains, a charge that Faisel could detonate whenever he chose. To ensure their absolute loyalty, Faisel had a transmitter implanted in his own heart that would cause the detonation of the charges if anything happened to that heart. If Faisel ibn Faisel Al Sa'ud were to die, his Elite would die with him. So, even on the other side of the world, the loyalty of the Elite would never be in question. They belonged, body and soul, to the King of the World.

Faisel's voice boomed from loudspeakers set all over the grounds. "Where is he, where is the man whose praises we sing today?"

He felt Nura's hand tighten a grip on his upper arm. "So soon?" she said weakly.

He covered her hand with his own. "Stay with the clan," he told her. "Keep on the move with them."

"Where is my brother? Have him come forward so I may kiss him and wish him a good journey."

Abdullah turned to Bandar, hugging him close. "Be as my own eyes and ears," he said. "Watch over my camels, my wives and children."

Bandar pulled back, studied Abdullah's eyes for a long time. "My life and my love are yours," he said, and there was a catch in his voice. "All that I am, I give to you. That is my bay'ah."

"Bring me my brother!"

Abdullah hugged the man again, then noticed that uniformed military were wandering through the crowds, searching him out. Bending down, he quickly kissed Nasr, from behind, on the cheek. "You are the oldest," he whispered in the child's ear. "You are the man now that I am not here. You must look after what is ours." With that, he pressed a gold coin into the boy's hand, and he turned, eyes lit up.

"You will come back soon," Nasr said in a tiny voice.

"If I can."

The soldiers were moving closer; he needed to go. Looking at Nura, he shared her eyes one last time, and in them noted a strength born of fervor that made him feel strong in turn. They both felt it; there was no need for words.

Turning from her, he strode through the crowd, shunning the military. Reaching the runway, he moved onto it and walked toward the platform.

He passed the plane, window spaces filled with staring Elite, then strode to the steps of the platform.

The crowd was cheering, their sounds distant and unreal to him. The group on the steps parted, leaving a wide berth up the middle. He started up the steps, and watched his brother, flanked by his seer, Misha'al.

Faisel stared back at him, and his lips were stretched into a thin, bloodless smile, a smile chiseled from marble and just as cold.

Gret lay naked on the bed, watching the tv that was inset in the canopy looking down at her. The room was totally dark except for the light from the television, which flashed shadows in and out in the room according to the ever-changing picture.

Faisel was throwing some kind of celebration and beaming it to everyone, and it was daytime where the party was, bright daytime.

She could hear Olson in the bathroom, playing with the toilet. He would flush it, then laugh, and when the bowl refilled, he would flush it again. From the living room she could hear Wexler snoring lightly from the couch where he slept.

She felt strange tonight. She should have been happy; after all, things were going exceptionally well, but somehow there was a foreboding creeping up her spine. It was a feeling, dark like a culvert, and she always listened to her feelings.

Olson walked into the room, backlight from the bathroom highlighting his naked body. He looked good to her.

"Damnedest thing I ever saw," he said, nodding back toward the bathroom. "Where does the water go?"

She slid over, making room for him. "It travels through pipes to the river," she said. "Then I guess it goes into the Gulf, then the Ocean."

"Think of that," he said, and climbed under the sheets with her. "Just think of that."

He immediately rolled onto his side, facing her. Placing one arm across her chest, he brought a bent leg up to rest on her upper thighs.

She felt what there was to feel, but put it off for a moment. "Are you still mad at me?" she asked.

"No," he answered, and from his tone she knew to leave it alone.

His hand moved to rest on her breast, as he took the already distended nipple between thumb and index finger. Her breath caught in her throat and she felt her hips automatically begin to rise and fall.

"Why did you . . . say what you did?" she asked, and her voice was quaking.

"About what?"

"About . . . marriage."

He rose up on his elbow to stare down at her, and his face was filled with conflicting emotions. "I don't know, I . . ." Then his face solidified into something harder. "I don't know," he said with conviction, and moved partly on top of her.

She could feel his penis pushing insistently against her upper thigh. The thoughts began dissipating from her brain as the barrage of feelings built up a floodgate in her body.

He was moving on top of her, his lips on her ear, and the lips were like waves crashing in ever-increasing tempo as the sensations zipped along the electrical relays of her spine, exploding back from the power boosters, the mechanical short circuits that the surgeons had given her.

Waves.

Waves that built

like a hurricane.

Swirling and crashing.

And GROWING.

His lips moved to hers, his tongue a red-hot poker entering the cold clear water of her mouth, his hands roving her body, touching, pulling—and everywhere he pulled, it was a million tiny pinpricks connected to a generator that juiced the current, making her jump, and in her mind's eye the contacts kept arcing, lighting the dark room with showers of cascading sparks as he pushed her legs apart, exposing the volcano of her cunt.

She wanted to scream to him.

SCREAM TO HIM

that the heat would sear his flesh, would melt him into a bubbling puddle, but control was gone, language a lost art. She was a machine, an organic machine with but one function.

She reached, stretching her hand, closing over his burning cock. It was a living thing, writhing, pumping, pulsing—a live beating heart she held in her hand—and she pulled it into the heart of the volcano.

He was talking, saying words, but she couldn't understand words. There was only the volcano and the floating, tumbling images.

IMAGES.

She was bucking, thrashing, and she tumbled with him through a void where a small boy lived, crying, standing over the bodies of his parents, their flesh ripped to pieces, his mind filled to overflow with grief and fear of the future.

She cried with him. She was him.

And there was another feeling, a new feeling, ballooning into the picture as the volcano built pressure, sought release.

She saw the boy eating weeds, eating fruit when he could.
She felt the fear gradually give way to anger, the anger subside
to acceptance, and the boy was a man who taught himself to read
when he worked for an old couple on an old farm burned to the
ground by Jits.

But the new feeling inflated larger, the alien feeling threatening
to override the other images as the relays were popping now,
physically popping, so loud she couldn't hear anything else.

Somewhere far away, she felt her body rising and falling on
the bed, heard screaming far away, didn't know whether it was
her or the images.

He took her on the aut hood, took her like the child he was
inside. There was something different, different this time—but what?
What?

Orleans danced through her brain, flooding streets, Rennie
Du'camp floating the flooding on a raft made of a human body.
The water forged through her, trying to cool the volcano, the raft
body coming closer, the head huge in her vision—Mr. Elwood,
teeth clenched in agony. Dead. Floating death, death by water,
fire on the water, stoked by millions of Jits as she wrapped arms
and legs in a deathgrip to hold in the steel shaft that plunged in
and out, stoking the volcano.

And the force of it threatened to tear her apart.

The balloon grew, and it had Olson's face, and it popped
and flooded her with warmth and security and protection and she
was drawn and repulsed at the same time—a feeling she had
never known, was never supposed to know. It came from him,
and she knew why he put off the idea of marriage.

She vibrated totally, every nerve, every cell, and she saw
herself, drowning in the new feeling, tiring of the fight, and
drowning was death.

Death

  of

   self.

Another voice was mixing with hers far away, as the
volcano blew off the top of the mountain and in a single,
frightening image her brain stoked alive with a vision that would
haunt her the rest of her life.

A woman.

A woman.

A woman in veils and robes.

A woman on fire.

A woman laughing

    at the King of the World.

PART TWO

The duties of Moslems to each other are six.
It was asked, "What are they, O Messenger of
God?" He said, "When you meet a Moslem, Salaam
to him, and when he inviteth you to dinner,
accept; and when he asketh you for advice,
give it to him; and when he sneezeth and saith
'Praise be to God,' do you say, 'May God have
mercy upon thee'; and when he is sick, visit
him; and when he dieth, follow his bier."

—The Prophet
Mohammed

You never expected justice from the Company, did you? They have neither a soul to lose nor a body to kick.

> —Motto for Industrial
> Relations, LOW
> Corporate

XIII
The Streets

Mr. Elwood gently guided the aut through the early-morning streets, bumping the large, shuffling crowds aside as they went. Olson sat beside him, bewildered at the huge number of people now stuffing the city to bursting.

"Why do they come here?" he asked the Director. "Why do they live this way?"

"Profound questions." Mr. Elwood laughed, pulling a cigarette from somewhere within his gleaming gold exo. He put it between his lips and lit it on a lighter inset in the dash.

He took a drag, coughed it out. "They come here because they fear the Jits or the loneliness. You can understand that, I'll bet."

Olson swallowed and nodded without looking at the man.

Mr. Elwood grunted. "They stay because we can give them some juice—"

"Juice?"

"Electricity," the Director corrected. "And that's quite addicting. They stay because we let them feel safe inside the walls when there's a Jit scare. And they stay, basically, because most people prefer having someone tell them what to do instead of figuring it out themselves."

"I don't get it."

Mr. Elwood pulled on the cigarette again, coughed again. "We all need something to believe in, boy. And don't forget that if you forget everything else I tell you."

"So you put them to work?"

"Sure. We put them on the farms or in the factories. They give us a day's work and in return get a roof over their heads, a tv for their eyes, bread for their mouths and a safe harbor for their asses."

There was a disturbance ahead. A bird had miraculously fallen from the low-hanging sky onto the street, and a large crowd was fighting over it. There were hundreds of them, blocking the street, making driving impossible.

Mr. Elwood picked up a small microphone on the dash and spoke into it. "This is mobile L-1, that's Light-one. The street is jammed on the fourteen hundred block of Marlyn. A riot is in progress. Over."

He put back the mike and winked at Olson. "That'll take care of them."

Olson grimaced. "You know, I don't much care for the way you run your city."

"Can't blame you," the man returned.

"You treat your people like animals."

Mr. Elwood turned and stared at him without speaking, the cigarette locked between the fingers of his left hand, as if he were afraid of smoking it anymore for fear of the cough.

"You said we all need something to believe in," Olson continued. "Well, I believe that human beings have got to be worth a lot more than this. When I take over, things are going to be different."

The Director nodded, a slight cast to his brown eyes. "I hope you make it," he said quietly, then turned to stare out the windshield.

A squad of fuzztops came charging down the street armed with long clubs. Without hesitation, they rushed into the thick of the crowd, swinging at shins and heads.

"When I came here I was a lot like you," Mr. Elwood said, not taking his eyes off the riot. "I tried for years to change things." He chuckled slightly. "I've never been able to figure out whether the system beat me or if the citizens just really didn't want to change."

He leaned his head wearily back into the seat cushion.

"After a long time I got tired, worn out from fighting. I gave over, let the system run me. Even at that, Orleans treats its citizens a lot better than most places. You ought to go to Dallas sometime and see it there."

People were scattering, running in all directions. A man stumbled against the aut and fell, leaving a stream of blood on Olson's window where his head had been laid open by a truncheon. Olson reached for the door release.

"Don't go out there," Mr. Elwood said. "It's not safe right now."

Olson glared at him quickly and pounded the release. It stayed locked.

"Took care of it over here," the Director said.

"He needs help," Olson said.

"We all need help," Mr. Elwood said.

Olson drew his lips firm and tried to control his breathing. "I won't give over like you," he said.

Mr. Elwood nodded, his eyes sleepy-looking. "You're my hope for the future," was all he said, then sat up stiffly. "Road's clear."

Putting the aut back in gear, the old man eased them down the street. "Don't hate me too much," he said after a time. "Don't judge me until you've been in my place."

Olson nodded. "I owe you that much."

They inched along, past shuffling crowds and street vendors and lines of chained Engies being marched to the river by whip to help with sandbags. That's the direction they were heading— to the river.

"Jerry Joe will be your immediate boss," Mr. Elwood said. "He's the Junex in charge of River Ops. He's a good man who keeps his place. You'll like him."

"Won't he know I'm a phony?" Olson asked.

"Naw. Told him you worked in Manufacturing in Dallas and that you'd have to learn the river from scratch." The man glanced to his rearview, then reached up and straightened it out. "Besides, most Execs don't have the sense Allah gave a turnip."

"Then how did they get to be Execs?"

"Kind of a reverse evolution," Mr. Elwood responded. "They're smart enough to know an order when they hear one, and dumb enough to follow any order. That's the way LOW likes them because nothing ever changes that way. It's called maintaining the status quo, and it's the official rule around here. Hell, that's how come somebody like Rennie can move up so fast."

"What do you mean?"

Mr. Elwood looked at his cigarette. It had burned almost down to his fingers, filling the aut, but not his lungs, with white-gray smoke.

"All the citizens take a test when they get to be twelve or so," the man said. "The test decides if you're Exec material. If you do bad enough, they train you."

"You mean that people who fail the test get to be Execs?"

"Exactly. But in Rennie's case, I think he was smart enough to figure that out early on and screwed up the test on purpose. Watch that boy; he's a shark among minnows."

"Or maybe too smart for his own good," Olson added.

Mr. Elwood turned to him with cold eyes. "Don't count on it, Mr. Catanine."

Just then, the cigarette stub burned down to his fingers, making him jump, the cigarette dropping from his hand.

*   *   *

> *Every nation has its Messenger; then,*
> *when their Messenger comes, justly*
> *the issue is decided between them, and*
> *they are not wronged.*
>
> —The Koran
> X. Jonah

XIV

The Louisiana Forests
South/Central Region
America

The explosion showed up in Ted Milander's fieldglasses as nothing more than a tiny puff of smoke followed, several seconds later, by a distant rumble, like faraway thunder.

"That's got it," he told Danny Ford, his newest aide, and the man responded with a crooked, paralyzed smile.

Leaning out of the window space, he looked down from the creaky, wooden fire-spotting tower to his people below. Even knowing they were there, he could barely see them. The forest was thick like brambles, and the bush camouflage that the citizens wore made them nearly invisible.

"Success!" he screamed down, and thousands of bushes and shrubs cheered back to him.

"Will they go for it?" Ford asked him, his voice slurring, barely intelligible.

"Not forever," Milander answered, still looking out the window. "But we've bought some valuable time."

The distant, explosive puff had grown quite large, and was dissipating slowly in the wind. He had cleaned out the College Station armory, loading thousands of pounds of explosives into the gondola of his balloon. They had kept moving, staying ahead of the Houston search parties from LOW, and when the flat Texas plains turned into the thick carpet of Louisiana forest, he headed the balloon, empty except for the explosives, North, along with a thousand of his more infirmed Jits. The explosion was the signal, the sign that the Arabs had caught up to them. With any luck, when the Arabs killed off his splinter army, they would think they had gotten the main force and return home, giving them the valuable time they needed to get to Orleans and dig in, maybe even catch them off guard.

That was the plan anyway.

Milander watched the dynamite cloud drifting lazily across the green-brown patchwork of Nature that stretched to the horizon all around him. If he could take Orleans, they could use the boats in the harbor to command the whole Mississippi before pushing Eastward. If only he could hold together that long.

He smelled roses, sickly sweet, and knew a seizure was coming. He felt dizziness, and his next conscious memory was waking up on the floor of the tower, his body still vibrating slightly, the front of his shirt soaked with his own drool.

Ford was fiddling with the radio, and found the Houston balloons in time to hear that they were dropping napalm on the remains of the Jit army.

Milander sat up slowly, his leg now totally useless. He and Ford smiled at one another.

*   *   *

> *He is true who protecteth his brother both*
> *present and absent.*
>   —The Prophet Mohammed

> *Who draws his sword against the prince must*
> *throw away the scabbard.*
>   —Old World Wisdom

XV
The River

The river was up high, but, for the moment at least, wasn't getting any higher. The rain had stopped temporarily, allowing life to go on as usual. The Sun shone blinding gold overhead, but it was fool's gold, ready to hide behind a cloud layer at a moment's notice and drown worthlessly in a mother lode of silvery showers.

"Easy!" Olson yelled to the crane operator. "Bring it down easy!"

He stood on the deck of the huge schooner, its sails tightly furled, its anchor embedded in Mississippi mud. It was a big rusted metal ship that at one time ran on propeller-screwing engines, but now limped along under the power of its sails.

The large crate of wheat swung slowly from the pier to the open maw of the cargo hold, tons of tribute ready to make the long journey to the Gulf of Aden and Faisel's bulging coffers.

The crane operator looked to Olson, who began waving his arms slowly downward as soon as the crate swung uneasily over the hold. With a creak-jerk, the man started the box down.

The harbor was alive with activity. Everyone wanted to take advantage of the good weather while it held out. Boats of all shapes and sizes squeezed in and out of prebooked berths, trading crops and materials. Alcohol was popular in Orleans, and textiles, things that LOW didn't approve of. There were steamboats spouting gray and gray-white smoke, their whistle sounds shrill and pleasant. There were sailboats, small and large, with big colored sails that flapped like a bird migration across the sounding board of the rolling waters. There were even rowboats, some quite large with many slave rowers, and flat-bottomed barges that merely went with the current, to be abandoned after their business was done.

And people.

People crowded the docks, buyers and sellers. They smelled of sweat and sometimes disease. They traded what they could for the goods being hawked by loudmouthed pitchmen. And when they didn't have anything else to trade, they swapped out their children, knowing that at least the kids would be able to eat.

The crate thunked into the dark hold, and Olson watched men scurrying to unlatch it from the crane cable. When they were done, he turned and, holding out his clipboard, motioned the cable back up.

It was humid on the river, the mosquitoes nearly large enough to carry off unsupervised children. Olson was dressed somewhat comfortably in a white suit without tie that Mr. Elwood had gotten him, but he had a difficult time adjusting to the ghutra that they all wore on their heads. It just made his neck sweat a lot, and he couldn't appreciate the value of keeping that sweat in.

"Hey, Cat!" someone called, and he nearly didn't respond.

Turning, he saw Rennie Du'camp, dressed in a red jumper with white ghutra. Beside him was his constant appendage, Marty Jerny, dressed in dark brown. They were standing on the dock, clipboards in their hands also.

Moving to the rail, Olson waved them aboard, and they started immediately up the gangplank. He didn't want to deal with Du'camp, had managed to avoid him since the party, but he figured that he'd have to face up to the man sometime, and now, in public, was as good a time as any.

Du'camp had his hand stuck out even before he reached the deck. Olson took it, then Jerny's in turn. Du'camp's face was a lot friendlier than the last time he had seen it, but his eyes were still as nasty.

"Taking good care of my stuff?" Du'camp asked.

"What?"

"The grain all comes from my department," he said. "You getting it loaded up all right?"

The man walked over to the hold and stuck his head in. He left it there for a long time and Olson knew that if the man didn't like what he saw, that somebody would know about it.

Finally, Rennie pulled his head out of the hold. He looked disappointed. "Been trying to get you for the last couple of days," he said. "You're a tough man to catch up to."

"New city," Olson answered cautiously. "Lots to do."

Du'camp stared at him. "I'll bet. Getting settled in okay?"

"Sure."

The man fidgeted, looking at his feet as if there was something written on the toes. "I'd kind of like to apologize for the way I acted at the party . . ."

"Forget it."

"No . . . I . . . I'm not used to losing. Guess I just let the booze go to my head."

"Forget it," Olson said again, remembering that Du'camp had seemed perfectly sober at the party. "You were just going easy on me because I was new. I could never beat you again."

"Maybe we'll try again sometime."

"Yeah. Maybe," Olson returned. "I don't like to lose either."

They locked eyes, and Du'camp's were unreadable. "How about dinner tonight to show there's no hard feelings?" the man asked. "Maybe we could swap Houris or something."

Olson walked to the rail, watching the workers on the pier fit the cables around the next crate. "Can't," he said over his shoulder. "I'm having dinner with Mr. Elwood tonight."

Du'camp joined him, leaning his elbows on the rusty railing. "Mr. Elwood," he said flatly. "Sounds like you've got friends in high places."

"Everybody needs friends," Olson answered.

"I wouldn't know."

The group of men on the pier backed away from the crate after securing the cables.

"Got it?" Olson yelled, and the foreman gave him the thumbs-up sign.

Turning to the crane operator, Olson motioned him to lift the crate. The crane whined to activity, but no sooner had it begun hoisting the crate than one of the cables slipped off a corner, dumping the crate, to break, on the dock.

Du'camp went crazy.

"You son of a bitch!" he screamed, and ran to the gangway, taking it down in long strides. Jerny was right with him.

Olson watched over the rail as Du'camp charged the foreman, knocking the man violently back to fall into a huge pile of wheat.

The man sat there, stunned, for a second. Reaching into his belt, Du'camp pulled out a pair of razored exo gloves and slipped them on.

"We're going to have to teach you," he told the man, who was struggling to stand in the ever-shifting mound. "You have a position of responsibility with this Company. You'd best learn to respect that."

His voice was controlled, quiet. Olson had never seen such suppressed rage in his life.

The man was back on his feet again, trying to explain to Du'camp what had happened. Rennie stood there nodding for a moment, then said:

"I'm sorry. You'll just have to learn."

Then he swung out at the man, tearing a line of flesh from his face from jawbone to hairline. The man went down again, rolling fetally, trying to hold the blood back in his face.

Du'camp jumped on him, slashing, his arm rising and falling maniacally, and Olson could only think of Cat on the roadway hacking his way through the bandits.

"Stop it!" he yelled, and didn't even realize he was saying it.

Jerny looked up at him in puzzlement, but Du'camp kept flailing away.

His vision moving in skip-jumps, Olson was down the gangway, pulling Du'camp off the man. Jerny grabbed him by the shoulders, but Olson swung out, knocking the man to the dock.

A crowd had gathered, circling wide around them. Jumping on Du'camp again, Olson managed to jerk him back, away from his prey.

Du'camp flared around, his eyes on fire, blood dripping from the studs in his gloves to puddle at his feet. He was breathing shallowly, fists vibrating.

"What the hell do you think you're doing?" he spat.

Olson backed away, keeping a good distance between them. He held his arms up. "Take it easy," he said.

Du'camp took a deliberate step toward him. "How dare you interfere with me!"

"You would have killed him," Olson said.

"So what!" Du'camp yelled, and swung a wide fist not meant to connect up to anything. "I do what I want."

Jerny was on his feet again, but had backed away with the crowd. Being a lower Exec, he could do nothing but win in a confrontation between two majors.

"Not with my people," Olson replied.

Du'camp came out of his defensive crouch, stood upright to stare at Olson. "What difference does it make to you?" he asked, and Olson didn't like the edge to his voice.

Olson took a breath. "This is my territory," he said at last. "If anyone's going to beat up my citizens, it had better be me. Go fuck with your own people."

The question slipped out of Du'camp's eyes. "It gets harder and harder for us to be friends, doesn't it?" he said. "You have a lot to learn about how things run around here."

"Who made you boss... Mr. Du'camp?" Olson said coldly.

The man slowly removed his gloves. He turned his head to the crowd. "What are you looking at?" he demanded. "Move on!"

The people rumbled away, carting the injured foreman with them. Olson just stood, stuck to his place.

Du'camp threw his bloody gloves to Jerny, then put his hands on his hips, walking a circle around Olson. "What a funny man you are," he said casually. "Something odd about you, something... different. Wonder what it is?"

"I'm not scared of you, Rennie. That's all," Olson answered, but he could tell by Du'camp's face that the man didn't believe him.

*   *   *

We thought because we had power we had wisdom.
                                        —Ancient Proverb

Lord Mohammed said, "He is not Mu'mim who committeth adultery, or who stealeth, or who drinketh liquor, or who plundereth or who embezzleth—beware, beware."

—The Prophet Mohammed

XVI

New Mecca, Arizona
South/Central Region
America

Abdullah watched out the window of the jet as they made their approach to the garrison at New Mecca. It was desert here, that was a fact, but it was flat and hard-packed, nothing like the shifting sand sculptures of his homeland. It only made him miss Arabia that much more.

As they settled down lower and the ground stretched out wider around them, he could begin to make out the garrison itself: spiring minarets and high stone walls, a fortress built to withstand any attack. But more imposing than the fortress were the balloons. A thousand dirigibles, green and emblazoned with the sword of the House of Sa'ud, sat moored close to the ground. They stretched out for miles in all directions, the chief arm of God in the Western Sector.

Their wheels bumped the runway several times before screeching to a halt, and Abdullah found himself glad that he had arrived. He was ready to face what destiny had in store for him. He wanted to get it over with.

It had been a long and boring trip. They had overnighted twice on the way, staying at garrisons in the European and Eastern America sectors. It was the same in both places: gracious hospitality with an undercurrent of fear. It made him feel that he was being stuck in a category with his brother, and that didn't set well.

The Elite were all up and moving silently toward the exits. Not one of them had spoken the entire trip unless it was to answer questions. He had passed some of the time with the two computer experts sent along on the trip, but they were Nasrani and feared him more than the others.

When the Elite had all filed out, Abdullah stood and moved to the exit. Local dignitaries filled the space around the bottom of the exit ramp, all smiling, all done up in their finest thobes and mishlas—and those were very fine, indeed.

He walked down the ramp, waving to the crowd. A man in a pure white mishla and ghutra greeted him at the bottom. His beard was trimmed to a point and he had a wide smile that encompassed his entire face. A front tooth was missing, replaced by bright, shiny gold. He wore a bandolier and a rifle slung over his shoulder.

"Salaam! Salaam!" he called and pulled Abdullah to him, kissing him fiercely on the lips.

"Wa alaykum as Salaam," Abdullah said.

"Welcome to our humble outpost," the man said. "My name is Majid ibn Ghalib. I am Emir here."

"Ghalib ibn Nasr?" Abdullah asked.

"Your father's brother, yes," Majid replied. "I am of his pure blood. We are cousins, then."

"My firstborn son is named for your grandfather."

The man's face lit up. "We are honored. Come. Enjoy our hospitality."

The whole group of them moved away from the plane, constant introductions tumbling through Abdullah's mind to where he knew he would remember none of them. The Elite and the computer experts were led away to a bus where no one would have to deal with them. The reputation of Faisel's personal bodyguards was well known, though very few living eyes had ever seen them. Most people wanted to keep it that way.

Enough magne-carpets for the whole party were set out on the runway, even though it would have been a fairly short walk to the garrison which sat several hundred yards in the distance.

The carpets had been Abdullah's great-great-grandfather's folly many years before. Invented for a mammoth social event celebrating Arabia's history, they had proved unwieldy and dangerous. But rather than admit a mistake, Mishari ibn Sattam forced their usage at all state functions. After his death, the carpets were still used, since by then they represented a link to the past.

Everyone squatted on the rich Persian rugs, two to a flier, and Majid pointed to an overlarge one in the front. "We will share this one," he said.

Abdullah nodded and climbed into the rear position, Majid taking to the tiny control panel in the front. The man turned his head, smiling with his huge mouth.

"You'll enjoy your stay with us," he said. "Your brother will be proud. Perhaps we'll hunt Jit together when you have the time."

With that, he turned back around and spun the dial on the magnets, the carpet immediately rising quickly in the air. Abdullah felt as if his stomach had taken up permanent residence in his mouth when they finally leveled off at one hundred feet.

He sneaked a look over the side of the thing and saw the ground weaving distantly below him. He felt dizzy and grabbed for handholds where there were none. "Allah be merciful," he whispered, and closed his eyes tightly.

"Is it not wonderful?" Majid called over his shoulder.

Abdullah opened his eyes and stared at the man's back. "The earth is wonderful," he said. "The sky is for birds." He continued staring straight ahead, finding that he wouldn't get dizzy if he avoided looking down.

The other carpets rose with them, twenty in all, and they hovered there, barely more than a patch of fabric keeping them from instantaneous death on the ground below. Abdullah had never been on one of the carpets before, his fear of heights always keeping him more firmly grounded; and from the looks on the faces of the others, he knew why such things were usually reserved for ceremonial occasions.

Throttling forward, Majid guided the small wheel in the direction of the fortress and they were off—too fast for Abdullah's tastes.

They approached the walls of the garrison, troops in uniform lining those walls, waving and cheering. They skirted one of the large towers, Abdullah waving to the people who threw flowers to him from the window slots, almost near enough to reach out and touch.

The cheering rang out, disappearing quickly into the void of the desert; the air smelled clean; and the uniforms of the soldiers

were green like the balloons and tied around the middle with red
sashes that stood out boldly amidst the pale, drab colors that
surrounded them.

Majid slowed the carpet, hovering over the inner courtyard
of the garrison. The rest tried to follow suit, some with more
success than others. Since they were tightly packed together in
the air, there were several collisions marked by wailing and
shaking fists. One man was unfortunate enough to try to stop
abruptly, the resulting inertia sending him over the front of his
carpet to plunge to the courtyard below. His passenger could be
seen frantically trying to get to the controls as the carpet
continued its journey over the walls and back into the desert.
Abdullah laughed despite himself.

The carpets set down slowly then, Abdullah's stomach
settling with them, and they all reached the ground without
further mishap. The man who had fallen from his carpet was
killed going through the windshield of one of the many black
auts that were parked haphazardly around the brick courtyard.
The aut the man fell upon was his own, though, so the whole
incident ended happily.

Majid jumped up quickly, reaching out a hand to Abdullah
to help him rise.

Ignoring the solicitation, Abdullah stood on shaky legs. "A
man's feet belong on the ground," he said, and stamped just to
make the point. "No one should have to fall any farther than the
length of his legs."

Majid was smiling, always smiling. "A little danger helps
one to appreciate the simple things. Come. Eat with us."

The entourage walked briskly through the courtyard. Fan
palms were planted in uneven rows through the brick yard and
cast long, fingery shadows under the afternoon sun. In a few
hours, the great walls themselves would be able to cast the whole
yard into darkness.

They moved past the parked auts, one with a pair of legs
still sticking out of the black-tinted windshield. Several soldiers
stood around, arguing among themselves about just how to
remove the dead man.

The entrance to the hall was a wide arch, beautifully tiled in
pale blues and yellows, the arch supported by twisting, ornate
columns, like fat frozen rope.

"I pray you brought an appetite," Majid said.

"As large as your hospitality," Abdullah returned, though

the carpet ride had destroyed whatever hunger he may have possessed.

They kicked off their sandals and entered the majlis, many of the party already inside, sipping coffee. Loud talk and laughter filled the small sitting room, as the men embraced and exchanged greetings. These were dignitaries brought from all parts of the Western Sector, for this was an important event. A member of the ruling clan of Sa'ud had never honored the American branches before.

The small room was filled with the smells of boiled fat and woodsmoke, and Abdullah decided that he might be able to eat after all. In the majlis, he was greeted by more people, many of whom he recognized as relatives that had been sent away to the outer sectors by Faisel because he didn't like them. Nepotism was the rule with LOW: but there were jobs and there were jobs.

"They wonder what brings you here," Majid said, arching an eyebrow.

"I wonder that myself," Abdullah answered.

The smile was there again. "Speculation runs rampant."

This time Abdullah smiled, enjoying a little his role of god from the East. "Those anticipating will be disappointed," he said. "Those fearful will be relieved. My business is with the Nasrani, not with my brothers."

Majid cocked his head, the smile fading. "That could be one and the same here," he said seriously, and linked his fingers together. He held his bonded hands up in front of him. "All is intertwined. It is not like the old ways."

A small boy ran into the majlis, searching until he found Majid. He tugged on the man's robe, Majid bending to listen to him.

Majid's smile returned and he stood upright. "Nakull!" he shouted. "We eat!"

Abdullah moved with the others from the sitting room into the large banquet hall. The hall was open, with good ventilation and sunshine from the outside. There were no tables, but rather many serving areas set around on the floors, each able to accommodate twelve men.

Soldiers were carrying in the food to each area, huge dishes, four feet across.

Majid put his arm around Abdullah. "Sit with me, my cousin. We will show you the best that any world has to offer."

He picked a place somewhat in the middle of the large

chamber, and they squatted down, soon to be joined by others of similar station.

Two soldiers staggered toward them, weighted down by the huge plate. They set it on the floor in the middle of the circle of men. A large crater of white rice a foot thick fortified the rim of the plate, and rising within, a pyramid of steaming sheep limbs, ribs, and haunches, the whole thing crowned by the boiled head of the sheep itself. It faced Abdullah directly, its tongue curling between glistening white teeth and bared gums.

Reaching out, Majid grabbed at the sheep's head, pulling out some of the hard, pink crescent of gum. He handed some to Abdullah, pulling more out for some of the others.

"Is it honorable to ask what business you have with the Nasrani?" Majid asked, as he continued to hand out the gums.

Abdullah glanced at him in surprise. "You are a direct man," he responded.

Majid nodded, taking a bit of the gum for himself. "We have been around the Nasrani for a long time. It is their way."

"But it is not our way."

The man shrugged. "Perhaps. You have come from the desert. Things are different there."

Another soldier walked up with a huge brass pitcher that he had to carry with two hands, steam rising indolently from the gaping mouth. The man poured the contents over the sheep and rice: liver, kidneys, salted little knots of yellowed intestine for chewing like gum, and the thick white tail pad of fat that is the sign of the well-fed sheep—all this in a sauce of grease and juice and melted butter that slid down the pyramid and began soaking through the wall of rice at the bottom.

It was time to eat.

Abdullah began rolling up his sleeves. "What do you know about the City of Orleans?" he asked.

Majid was rolling some rice into a small ball. "We have had no trouble with them," he said, and popped the ball of rice into his mouth. "They are the regional offices and have always run smoothly."

He used a large knife to pull off a strip of the carcass, stuffing his mouth with it. When he had choked some of it down, he asked, "Are you here to visit Orleans?"

"There is a problem with the tribute," Abdullah said, stuffing his own mouth as the grease ran down his hands. The food was as good as Majid had promised.

He felt no duty to tell the man what he was doing, but decided there was no reason not to. "They have not satisfied my brother for quite some time."

Majid was up on his feet, moving around the circle of men, using his knife to cut everyone meat. "They are conscientious in the extreme," he said, shaking his head. "It makes no sense that they would cheat in an obvious manner. Is it bad?"

A fat man with a gray beard and purple mishla spoke. "He wouldn't have brought the angels of death with him if it weren't bad."

Abdullah stared hard at the man, recognized him as a stepbrother long removed. "Perhaps you should eat more and think less, Rajan," he said.

The man spit a bone out onto the floor. "So you remember me," he said.

"And why you're here." Abdullah smiled, and he and Majid shared a look.

Majid ran to Rajan and tore off a large piece of liver, shoving the knifeload near his mouth. "We are here to honor our guest," he said. "Eat. Enjoy."

The man nodded slowly and took the liver. "I am overwhelmed by your hospitality," he said, "and, of course, I honor my brother."

Majid gave food to everyone, then returned to sit by Abdullah. "You really don't need to tell me anything," he said.

"I know that."

"I am at your command. My whole garrison is. I would be less than truthful if I said that I felt good about not knowing what is expected of me and my men. This is my life here. I am the High General-Commander-Marshal-Emir of the Regional Garrison." He winked. "A title I picked for myself, by the way."

"I respect that," Abdullah said, and was surprised that Majid hadn't been told anything in advance. He ate for a moment, thinking. As he did, he noticed at other places in the room, many were drinking openly what looked to be alcohol. Things were different here.

He looked at Majid, then roved his eyes around the table to make sure no one else was watching him. Then he quickly pulled the cord out of his thobe and dangled the attached key for a second before putting it back.

Majid's eyes got wide, and he frowned as large as he had been smiling before. His voice went low and he leaned toward Abdullah.

"I'm sorry," he said, "but that's crazy. Orleans is the backbone of this region. You can't destroy it."

Abdullah nodded. "Believe me when I tell you that it is not my intention."

The man twisted his knife around in his hands, watching the blade reflect the afternoon Sun. "We are already fighting a Jitterbug army from the South," he said. "Believe *me* when I tell you that trouble like that in Orleans could be the beginning of the end of this entire country." He laid the knife down and sighed deeply. "There have been too many accidents, too much retribution. There are close to a million people in that city, and they have the river to take them wherever they want to go. Even if the tribute is wrong, that's no reason to do that."

Abdullah felt a flash of guilt. Majid's world was just as important to him as Abdullah's was to him. "These are my brother's wishes, not mine."

Majid looked him dead in the eye. "Tell him he's wrong."

"I have."

Majid stood up and went around the circle again. The rest of the meal passed in heavy silence. When they were finished, they washed and perfumed their hands, then returned to the majlis for tea, coffee, and conversation. Majid spoke no more to him, and he listened to the stories being told with half an ear, a dark worry sinking into him. Then several young boys moved around the room with braziers of incense to be smelled and fanned into beards, the signal that the feast was over. But the worry stayed with Abdullah, through the rest of that day and far into the sleepless night.

* * *

Pleasure is the object, the duty, and the goal of all rational creatures.

—Old World Heresy

Keep yourselves far from envy; because it eateth up and taketh away good actions as fire eateth up and burneth wood.

—The Prophet Mohammed

XVII
Orleans

The giant pulled the two-wheeled carriage quickly through the darkened streets. Though the street crowds were still thick, even at night, the carriage was fixed with the LOW insignia and given wide berth by the population. It clacked quickly along, the nearly naked giant drawing raspy breaths as he ran, bare feet slapping the cracked concrete and splashing the huge puddles that still filled the streets.

Olson, dressed in dark corduroy, occupied the passenger seat, his ghutra balanced on one knee, his servant, Wexler, balanced on the other. Gret sat, sulking, beside him, her simple blue shift surprisingly modest.

"You'd better put the damned thing on," she said, staring unfocused eyes on the crowd that flashed past them.

"I'll put it on when we get there," he returned, and smiling, clucked Wexler under the chin. "It makes my head sweat."

She fixed him with those eyes, *those* eyes. "What am I going to do with you?" she asked. "First you pick a fight with Rennie today and now you refuse to wear the hat."

Olson tousled Wexler's limp, dead hair. "What's she going to do with me, Wex?"

The little man pursed his lips. "Well, she has several choices. Let's deal with the major ones first. She can either kill you or let you stay alive. Either alternative leads to several more choices. If she kills you, the subsidiary question becomes, how. There are thousands of ways of ending a human life. We'll take them alphabetically. First, asphyxiation, which can itself be accomplished by several methods—"

"Would you stop it!" Gret said.

The little man gulped, eyes wide. Olson hugged him close. "Look," he said. "I didn't pick a fight with Rennie; I stopped him from killing my dock foreman, which isn't the same thing.

And I don't see what possible difference it makes whether or not I wear the stupid hat."

Gret sighed deeply. "It's a sign of your station," she said. "It's bad enough that you came out here without an exo, but not wearing your ghutra is like not wearing your pants."

Olson smiled wide. "Not quite the same."

"Would you be serious!"

"Why?"

She looked away from him, then looked back quickly. "I don't want anything to happen to you, okay?" She turned away again.

Reaching out his free hand, he took her by the chin and made her face him. "Okay," he said quietly, and put on the ghutra.

There was no Moon that night, and cook fires built along the pavements slashed the streets in and out of orange jumping light. As they rode, Olson could smell cooking meat and vegetables, and see the silhouettes of citizens backlighted by glowing white smoke as they huddled around the makeshift stoves.

The driver turned down a narrow alley, brick buildings rising on either side leaving just enough room for the carriage to creak past. Once through the alley, they entered a wide-open area of torn-down and cleared buildings. The area was well lit with electric spotlights on high poles, and in the center of it all, the coliseum. There were a great many auts and carriages parked by the entries, plus citizens milling around, their numbers controlled by a large force of the fuzzy-top-hatted police.

A fuzztop with a large mustache directed them to the VIP parking. Their driver pulled them up next to a line of carriages, and after helping Gret out, went over to join a group of other carriage pullers who were talking and smoking off to the side.

Carrying Wexler in his arms like a child, Olson got out of the carriage and joined Gret as she walked toward the gently sloping ramp that was the Exec entry.

"This is where Mr. Elwood wants to meet us?" he asked as they moved up the well-lit incline toward the huge, rounded building.

"We're playing Shreveport in bashball tonight," she said, as if that answered the question.

Olson shrugged and followed her up to the checkpoint. Two fuzztops greeted them at the entrance. Gret spoke up. "Junex Catanine and party for Mr. Elwood's box."

The men stepped aside immediately, one of them pointing to a flight of stairs that was set nearby.

They went in. The structure was all concrete, pillars and entries. People were milling around, and Olson could hear occasional cheers throb through the structure, only to reduce it to quiet again. The ceiling was way above them and edging downward like upside-down stairs, and Olson realized that they were beneath seating of some kind.

He followed Gret up the stairs.

"Ever seen bashball?" he asked Wexler.

The little man shook his head. "But I know all about it," he said. "Just ask me something."

"You do and I'll wring your neck," Gret said over her shoulder.

Olson and Wexler shrugged at each other.

They reached the top of the stairs, only to be confronted by another fuzztop, who reluctantly let them inside.

They entered a small plush room. It was heavily carpeted and done up with thick velvet hangings and overstuffed furniture. In the center of the room was a table occupied by Mr. Elwood and enough food to keep Olson happy for the rest of his life: a lot of fruits and vegetables, with the center occupied by a roast pig.

"Come in," he said. "Have a seat."

They shook hands, but Olson didn't sit. Instead, he walked past the table to the glassed-in wall. One whole wall of the room was open to the stadium's interior. Olson was looking down at the whole thing.

There was a large field of some kind at ground level. Then, surrounding it and rising upward, seating for thousands. And all the seats were filled.

"Our national pastime," Mr. Elwood said.

On the field, there was a huge portable screen set up and two men were mind-matching a violent confrontation. They were fighting with axes.

"This is just the pre-game show," Mr. Elwood said, and he was dressed all in slick shiny black. His aghal was lying unworn on the table. Olson threw his next to it.

"A couple of prisoners from our jail, dangerous types. We offered them a match to the death. The winner gets to go free."

The screen images were hacked and bloody, their real-life counterparts lying back weakly in their chairs. Every time one of them would swing the ax and connect, the crowd would cheer loudly.

"One way to take care of troublemakers," Olson said, and took a seat at the table.

One of the men on screen got himself together for a last savage attack, battering down the other man and finally burying the ax in his head. The man in the chair spasmed for a moment, the screen flickering as he did. Then he jerked out of the chair, falling to the ground dead.

The screen went blank as the crowd cheered. The other combatant stood up shakily, raising his fists in the air. He took a couple of faltering steps away from the machine before he, too, collapsed to the ground.

Everyone laughed loudly, including Mr. Elwood. "He was free for a minute there," he said, nearly choking on something in his mouth.

Maintenance people rushed onto the field, carrying away the equipment and carcasses. Loud march musak started playing through speakers set all around the stadium.

Olson looked and saw that Gret and Wexler were standing off to the side. He realized they were waiting for permission to sit.

He motioned with his finger. "Do you mind if they...uh..."

"'Course not," Mr. Elwood said, and pointed to the chairs. "Enjoy."

A carving knife was stuck in the pig. Olson slid it out and cut himself off a hunk, putting it on his plate. "I had a run-in with Rennie Du'camp today," he said.

Mr. Elwood sat back in his chair. "So I heard. He's your competition, so it's inevitable."

Olson cut off a hunk of cheese. "I'm afraid it's going to come down to a fight sometime."

"'Course it is. You're going to have to kill him."

"Or him me."

Mr. Elwood smiled. "It's a rough world." Then his eyes narrowed. "Speaking of that. You look like you're unarmed."

"I tried to make him take something, at least a wrist laser," Gret said, "but he just won't listen."

"Don't be stupid, Cat," the man said. "Most Execs won't even go out on the streets without exos."

"I've taken care of myself this long," Olson replied, but knew he would probably take the advice in the future.

There was cheering out on the field. The players were filing out. One team was in red, the other blue. It was a strange conglomeration. The players were all Engies, obviously designed solely for the game. Each team had one very tall, stiltlike man. They had to be fifteen feet tall if they were a foot. The human frame was obviously not meant to stretch to those ridiculous extremes, and the men looked like mammoth walking toothpicks. They hobbled, as if in pain, unable to move very fast. Along with the stilt men, each team had ten men who looked like human walls. Wide and low to the ground, each had to weigh over six hundred pounds. They wore helmets on the tiny heads, but were otherwise unprotected by anything other than the skintight uniforms they wore. Finally the cages were brought out, each cage containing a large, squirming number of small round creatures. They were fuzzy and had four tiny legs, but no other distinct features. Each was dressed in a little uniform that corresponded with its team colors.

Olson watched in fascination as the wildly cheering crowd urged the players out. The field itself was odd. Large and rectangular, it was made up totally of uneven ground: little rolling hills, small jagged cliffs, and moats of various shapes and sizes. At each end of the field was a basket set atop a large pole. The baskets stood a good thirty feet in the air and could obviously be reached by no one but the stilt men.

"Faisel's brother arrived in New Mecca today," Mr. Elwood said. "He'll be coming in here tomorrow."

"You're worried about that," Olson said, not taking his eyes from the field.

"Of course I'm worried about it," the man returned. "You should be, too."

"Hmmm."

A large holo of Faisel ibn Faisel Al Sa'ud appeared in the middle of the field, and the musak switched to the Arabian National Anthem, everyone in the bleachers standing and bowing his head.

"Is everything going all right on the docks?"

Olson gave him a quick look. "Guess so," he answered. "I've always been a pretty quick learner, and Jerry Joe is showing me everything I need to know. Pretty busy right now, though."

The crowd booed as the officials came onto the field. They took positions around the periphery. The stilt men lined up near

their baskets, the wall men forming a picket in front of them.
The cages were wheeled right up to the sidelines, as an official
with a gun ran to the middle of the field.

"Sometime in the next few days we're going to have to
begin teaching you the chain of command and the inside moves
of the business," Mr. Elwood said. "You'll find it mostly takes
jungle sense, but there's a lot of tricks I can pass on."

"He's going to need some protocol lessons, too," Gret
added.

Olson smiled over at her. She smirked back at him.

The official fired the gun, and the contest began. As the
man ran off the field, the cages holding the little creatures, called
clomers or rounders, were opened. The things scurried out of the
cages, charging off madly in every direction.

The wall men began charging downfield to meet in the
middle. Several stayed behind, apparently to guard the stilt men,
who still stood under their baskets.

"Are you listening to all this?" Mr. Elwood asked.

"Wait a minute," Olson said, holding up a hand. He was
wrapped up in the game.

The wall men met at mid-field, with a tremendous slapping
of flesh on flesh, snapping like whips. Several of them went
down, and the others started lumbering around the field, trying
to catch the little creatures, which were amazingly nimble and
fast.

Up and down the hills the fat men waddled, falling into
moats and crashing over the cliffs, while the clomers danced
happily around, perfectly at home in this atmosphere.

"You've got a lot to learn," Mr. Elwood said, "and not
much time to do it."

"Take it easy," Olson said.

"Easy!" Gret said.

"Easy," Wexler said. "Not difficult. A state of relaxation.
A . . ."

"Stop!" Gret yelled at the top of his little head, which
barely cleared the table.

When one of the wall men managed to grab hold of a
clomer, he would hold it up to his teammates, bellowing in a low
bass rumble. If the thing wore his colors, he would then toss it
for all he was worth off the field and into the stands, where
spectators would scramble for possession of it. If it wore the
opposing team's colors, his teammates would rally around him,

while the other team would go on the attack. A huge brawl would ensue for possession of the clomer.

Tossing the animal from one to the other, the team would try to move it downfield toward the goal, while the other team tried desperately to stop them. They rolled around on the field like some monstrous blob of living jelly. Everything seemed fair except for blows to the genitals, which would result in immediate expulsion from the game by the offending player. As far as Olson could see, this was the only reason for the officials.

A rounder would be fought for all the way downfield, the movement sometimes being measured in inches. When they got near the goal, the idea was to get it to the stilt man, who would try to deposit it, still living, into the basket. If the living creature was thrown into the basket, a horn would sound and a score marked on the board.

The scramble for more clomers would begin again immediately.

"Would you listen to me," Mr. Elwood said. "This is important."

Olson turned from the game to look at him. "Why?" he asked.

"Why?"

"Yeah. Why is it important?"

Mr. Elwood just stared at him. He looked at Gret. She was staring, too.

Olson took a quick look at the game, then turned his attention fully to them. "A few days ago I had nothing," he said. "Today you say I can control a city of a million people, plus all its commerce. You expect that to make any sense to me?"

"But I—" Mr. Elwood started.

Olson waved a large hand. "Don't worry about it. We're doing okay."

Gret spoke up. "We're doing okay because Mr. Elwood and I have broken our backs covering for you."

Olson turned his attention back to the game. "And a fine job you've done, too."

The blue team was making a concerted effort to gang the stilt man on the red squad. He had lost his defenders, and was hobbling around the field on his long, knobby legs, striding over hills and moats while the wall men moved like bread dough under a rolling pin, trying to cut him off.

"Rennie has been running computer checks on you," Mr. Elwood said.

Olson just touched him with his eyes. "I thought that was taken care of."

"It is, as long as he doesn't retrace back to the Dallas computers. I got our info changed, but can't touch theirs without someone knowing about it."

There was wine on the table. Olson poured himself a glass and drank half of it. "Good stuff," he said. "Where I come from, we make our booze out of potatoes."

"Yeech," Gret said.

Olson chuckled. "Listen, a good shot of tater juice and a roast dog is about the best combination in the world."

Gret sighed deeply. "He doesn't need a teacher, he needs a trainer," she said.

"Just keep watching yourself around Rennie," Mr. Elwood said. "If you're not careful, he'll eat you alive."

"I've seen his kind before," Olson said, suddenly serious. "Let him try."

"He will," Mr. Elwood replied.

Olson finished the wine and belched loudly. He poured another and winked at Gret. Maybe if he drank enough, his courage could be as big as his mouth.

"Hell of a game going on out there," he said, nodding toward the field. "What color is our side?"

"Red," Mr. Elwood replied.

"Go, red!" Olson yelled through cupped hands, and craned his neck to get a better look.

The Orleans shooter stumbled down a small ledge right in front of Rennie Du'camp on the fifty-yard line. He was immediately crunched under by several burly Shreveport wallers, the sound of snapping bones mixing with the Engies' pitiful cries. As the shooter's squad rallied to pull the wallers off him, Rennie was watching the movement in Mr. Elwood's box across the field.

"What could they be talking about up there?" he asked Jerny, whose interest was occupied on a more visceral level.

"We're done for," Jerny mumbled through a mouthful of popcorn. "They've broken him like a twig."

Orleans guards and wallers had managed to pull the Shrevies off their shooter and had formed a human cordon around him, all at the expense of several goals, as the Shrevies were now free to wallow around the field without interference, trapping rapidly tiring rounders and moving for quick baskets. By the time they had helped the mangled shooter to his feet, the score stood at 9 to 4, Shreveport.

"There's something really wrong here," Rennie said, and his mind was turning like a pinwheel. He was an expert on Company politics, and this communication between Mr. Elwood and the new Junex just didn't slot out.

"You told me to bet on this one," Jerny said, irritation showing in his voice. "There's a month's pay riding on this."

"Forget about it," Rennie told him.

"Forget!" Jerny shouted, gagging on a husk caught in his throat. "We're out of it. Our shooter can't even stand up."

"Are his arms all right?" Rennie asked, and slapped the man on the back to dislodge the husk. "Can he still shoot?"

"I . . . I guess so."

"Then we'll win."

Jerny gave him a long, slow look, his red face even redder after his ordeal with the popcorn.

Rennie smiled. "Just watch."

The shooter, with two broken legs and an obviously dislocated neck, was being bodily carried back to his station, moaning wretchedly the whole time. Most of the Shreveport squad was down their end of the field, still trying to rack up as many goals as they could before action got back to normal. A large number of rounders had already been thrown out of the field and the game, so the numbers were smaller, the competition hotter for the ones that were left.

Most of the Shrevies were playing defense now, simply trying to sweep their rounders off the field so that Orleans couldn't score with them. Their backs to the wall, Orleans did the only thing they could do—rushed the Shreveport shooter to make sure he scored no more goals.

The strategy was simple; the Orleans wallers met at midfield and charged. Rennie smiled. Now they'd see.

Jerny was on his feet. "No!" he was screaming, his popcorn bouncing up and down, raining on everyone around him. "Go for points! Go for points!" He was waving his arms wildly, as the rest of the stadium went crazy, their screaming rising in waves, like heat from a summer pavement.

Rennie looked up at the box, saw Cat standing at the

window, watching the game intently as Mr. Elwood talked to him. Cat almost seemed to be ignoring the man. It made no sense at all.

The Shreveport shooter had five guards, one more than was customary. He seemed invincible until the flux actually reached him. There was the slap of contact, and all at once the defense melted, guards rolling away, leaving the shooter exposed.

"Yes!" Jerny screamed. *"Yes!"*

"The arms," Rennie said quietly.

They pushed the shooter back against his own pole, wrapping his arms around it like bunting on a Maypole. They mangled both arms to uselessness, then charged off looking for points. The shooter knelt on the ground, crying, his bandy arms dangling uselessly beside him, and he wasn't even able to wipe away the tears. Nine was all the points Shreveport would be scoring today.

Jerny sat down, smiling sideways at Rennie. "Did you have something to do with that?"

"Maybe those guards ate something that didn't agree with them," he said cryptically, and, like any good magician, wasn't about to give away his secrets.

With the shooter out, Orleans had only to worry about acquiring points. The guards were still rolling around on the field, hurt, so Orleans now outnumbered them. They began a very physical game then, their trademark, manhandling Shreveport wallers at every opportunity, wearing them down in a long hard struggle, seeping out points in a slow but steady cadence.

Rennie was watching the window again. A woman had joined Cat at the window.

"Who's that?" he asked Jerny.

The man glanced up quickly. "That's her," he said, "Cat's Houris. The one I told you about. What's she doing up there?"

Rennie shook his head. "You checked out all his computer records?"

"He's ordinary," Jerny returned, then stopped talking for a minute as the crowd cheered an Orleans goal. "Nothing special. Fact is, it looked like they sent him here to get rid of him."

"I don't believe it. A nothing Junex and loudmouthed Houris sharing the Regional Director's private box. What's going on up there?"

Jerny put a hand on his shoulder and held the popcorn bag in front of him. "Maybe Mr. Elwood just took a liking to them."

Rennie pushed aside the popcorn. "You know the difference between me and you, Marty?" he asked. "You wouldn't recognize an alligator if it came up and bit you on the leg, and I'd be making shoes out of it."

"What's an alligator?"

"We got anybody free at the moment?"

"I could probably break a couple of guys loose if you needed."

There was a loud cheer, and a rounder came flying up into the Exec section, landing in Rennie's lap. Smiling, he held it up in the air, its little legs pumping, its fuzzy round body squeaking and rasping for air. It wore a red Orleans sweater.

"Who on the staff has got kids?" he asked Jerny.

"There's a junior VeePee in storage who's got a couple."

Rennie handed him the rounder, the little thing trying to squirm away during the transference. "See that he gets this for the kids," he said.

"Sure."

Rennie nodded his head toward the glassed box. "I want him followed, Marty. Get loose whoever it takes to do the job. Maybe we can figure out a way to wire his apartment, too. Something's up. It's up to you to find out what."

Jerny gulped, nodding slowly.

More cheers. The fans all around were up on their feet, jumping up and down. Orleans wallers had just passed a rounder down to their shooter. Unable to stand, he was totally supported by his guards, his frail body looking like nothing so much as a giant mantis. Painfully, he reached up, tossing the thing into the basket. There were several seconds of tension as the machine checked if the creature were alive, then a loud buzzer sounded and the scoreboard changed. It was 9 to 7, Shreveport.

Rennie stood up, shoving his way through the delirious crowd. The game was forgotten, its outcome already assured. He had bigger worries on his mind. Deeper worries.

* * *

I asked, "What is Islam?" The Prophet replied, "Purity of speech and hospitality."
                    —The Prophet Mohammed

*The rights of women are sacred. See that women
are maintained in the rights attributed to
them.*

— The Prophet Mohammed

XVIII

Rub Al Khali
South of Laila

Faisel ibn Faisel Al Sa'ud bumped slowly on his camel
toward the Bedouin campsite that lay in the distance, a brightly
striped tiger eye against the backdrop of white sand. Two full
mechanized divisions of his army rumbled behind, their motors
crying and coughing, the fumes from their fuel hanging in the
still air like the cheapest perfume.

He was sore and hot, his thobe, soaked through with sweat,
clinging tightly to him. It had been a long time since he had
ridden a camel; it would be a longer time until he would again.

But this was a special occasion.

As he drew nearer to the sea of tents, a crowd began to
gather. He could hear them talking, but couldn't make out the
words, their sounds no more than a distant buzzing. They were
gesturing wildly, not knowing whether to marvel or fear at the
might that confronted them.

He smiled. Good.

Stopping no more than fifty yards from the camp, he
gestured back to his force. A jeep broke away from the main
body and tracked up to him in a shower of sand. Colonel
Musa'id ibn Yazeed stood in the passenger seat, his hat cocked
to the side of his head, his dark wraparound sunglasses making
his face a blank. He chewed furiously on a toothpick.

"You will make camp here," Faisel said to him.

The man turned his blank face to Faisel. His sleeves were
rolled up to the elbows, his green uniform shirt soaked dark with
sweat. He took out the toothpick.

"You will make your camp with us, then?"

"No. I camp with my people."

Musa'id nearly smiled, masking the gesture by putting the

toothpick back in his mouth. "I must insist that you take an armed company in with you for protection."

Faisel grinned wide. "But, Colonel, this is my own brother's clan."

"Your brother isn't here, Great One."

"But you are."

"Someone could knife you in your sleep."

"Then you will avenge me."

Musa'id sighed deeply and sank into his seat. "Nirooh," he mumbled to the driver, and the man jammed it into reverse, jerking them quickly back.

Faisel listened to Musa'id curse the man all the way back to the convoy. Gently flicking his crop on the camel's rump, he moved again toward the camp.

He was looking for his brother's tent, but didn't have to look far. The crowd was forming up in double lines in front of a large tent with pale red and white stripes. He knew whose residence that was.

He clopped into camp, small dogs yapping around the camel's knobby legs. Lines of Bedouin were formed on either side of him, marking a human pathway to Abdullah's entry.

Their talk dropped to nothing as he rode into their midst. They were eyes, staring eyes, questioning. They bowed slightly as he passed, and he acknowledged with curt nods of his head.

Stopping in front of the tent, he twisted around to the large group. "I am a man of the people," he said loudly. "And I love my people of the desert most of all."

A man whom Faisel recognized as one of Abdullah's bodyguards stepped out of the crowd. "Had we word of your arrival," he said, "we would have prepared a feast."

Faisel smiled. "There will be time for that."

Bringing a leg over the camel's neck, he slid painfully to the ground. Walking deliberately around to the animal's head, he began to slowly adjust the harness, a ritual long prescribed by custom.

After a moment, Nura appeared at the opening of the tent. In her hands she carried a bowl of camel's milk. She looked beautiful and mysterious in her robes of soft blues and greens, the tail swirling gently around her face and head, leaving only her deep, probing eyes to assess the outside world.

She walked to him, holding the milk up. He took it from her slowly, letting his hands linger on hers when they exchanged the bowl. He suspected that she would turn away, but she didn't, preferring to meet his eyes dead on.

"Will you offer a poor traveler the hospitality of your camp?" he asked, and drank a long sip, pouring the rest on the ground.

"It is our custom," she said coldly, then gestured behind him. "But I fear we cannot accommodate the rest of your party."

He followed her hand, saw his army lined out along the nearby ridge, armored personnel carriers and tanks digging in a long line, nearly surrounding the camp.

"They're not there," he said, turning back to Nura. "They don't exist. Forget them."

"You have word of my husband?" she asked him.

"No," he answered simply.

"Why have you come?"

He turned a full circle, arms open wide. "Cannot a father come to visit his children?" he said, then moved closer to her. "Cannot a brother-in-law visit his sister-in-law in her hour of loneliness?"

"Will you be staying with your soldiers?" she asked, a slight catch in her voice.

He looked around at the crowd. They were all looking at him expectantly. He addressed them en masse. "I simply seek the hospitality demanded by custom. I have traveled far and seek the shelter of my brother's tent."

He looked at Nura and smiled. She would have to invite him in for three nights. It was Bedouin custom, and Bedouin lived by custom.

Taking the empty bowl from him, Nura moved wordlessly to the tent, pulling back the flap. Stepping aside, she held the flap so he could enter.

He waved to the crowd. "We will feast tonight," he said, and handed the reins of his camel to little Nasr, who stood nearby. "Take care of her, son," he said, patting him on the head, "and you can have her."

With that, he strode into the tent without a backward glance.

*   *   *

*Those unbelievers of the People of the Book
and the idolaters wish not that any good
should be sent down upon you from your Lord;
but God singles out for His mercy whom He
will; God is of bounty abounding.*
                                    —The Koran
                                    II. The Cow

*He is not of us who seduces a woman from her
husband, or a slave girl from her master.*
                          —The Prophet Mohammed

XIX

The Louisiana Forest

Ted Milander sat alone, listening to the sound of the night.
It was a low, pervasive moan, a moan of either pain or ecstasy. It
hung heavy in the air, like a dark cloud bursting full with rain,
ready to explode at any second into something fiercer, something
unstoppable.

The sound came from his people. They moaned, awake and
asleep; it was something inside of them that had to come out.
The sound was music to him, soothing.

The night was dark, a sliver of moonlight like a shard of
broken glass sending soft shivers of silvery light to warm the
rough barks of the thick stands of pine and maple trees. His
people slept fitfully all around him as far as he could see.
Occasionally, someone would jump up, charging wildly through
the soft light, caught in the throes of grand-mal euphoria. And
for a time, the soft moans would crescendo with their screams
before plunging back to the pianissimo of the main theme.

And many were dying in their sleep. He could gaze out over
them, almost sensing the death, almost able to see its cold hands

reach out to take a son or daughter to its rattling bosom. When the living awoke in the morning, those who didn't rise with them would be their food, their sustenance for the journey still ahead. Even in death, they served the cause.

He got up slowly, using the tree he had been leaning against for support to help him rise. The pain was excruciating all through his legs and lower back; he wouldn't be able to get around on his own power much longer. Taking hold of the crutches made from tree limbs, he fit them under his arms and hobbled through the piles of twisting, turning bodies—the unresting sleep of his brothers and sisters.

He moved slowly, carefully, not wanting to disturb anyone, not wanting anyone to see how bad he was getting. They hadn't seen any search balloons since his earlier ruse, and while he knew that he couldn't hide his army forever, he was satisfied with the time he had bought for them. Taking Orleans, and consequently the river, was of the utmost importance. For his mission to succeed, he had to have Orleans. He would have it; it was God's will.

The only way to save Mankind was to destroy it. Light of the World was a cancer that had to be surgically cut from the body of Man so as to free his spirit. And from that freedom of spirit could come rebirth, redemption into a pure land. It was a dream full of gleaming gold and celestial trumpets and he knew—*knew*—that he could accomplish it.

Getting through the thick of his people, he hobbled over twigs and pine needles to the armory. Plundering College Station, plus several smaller communities, had given him a fair-sized arsenal. Piles of guns and ammo lay scattered about a large area, the long barrels of cannon playing lines of dull moonlight along their lengths.

His army needed no guns. Their weapon was the message of love. But Orleans would not fall easily; they would have to lay siege to it, which meant the possibility of Arab attack from the air. The guns would ensure them at least equal footing.

He moved into the arsenal, looking for the baroque sculpted machine that he had retrieved from the gondola of his balloon before he sent it away to die. He found it easily, flowing ornate filigree amidst machined lines and angles.

Grunting, he sat down beside it, resting a hand on its bright red barrel. It had the look of a toy, a miniature cannon painted gaily in pristine candy colors—an Arab laser cannon. It wasn't a toy; it was a fire-spitting dragon breathing a pink symmetry of death from its gaping mouth. Its power was limited to the juice left in its batteries, so he'd have to use it just right; but it was a laser cannon and it was his.

"Just what am I going to do with you?" he whispered to the machine.

He leaned against it and closed his eyes. After a time, he fell into a shallow, fitful slumber. It was the only kind of rest he knew anymore.

He would awake in the morning to find both legs paralyzed and useless. He wouldn't dwell on his infirmity, but rather order that a litter be built so that he could continue his campaign without losing any time.

He watched Nura move gracefully around the tent, pretending to be straightening, actually avoiding him as much as possible. The light was beginning to go, the heat from late afternoon already sunk deeply into the interior of the dwelling. He sweat, felt stifled, drank sweet tea, longed for the woman.

There was a man's side to the tent, divided by hanging tapestries, but Faisel didn't want the wall and pulled it down upon entering. It was a breach of protocol that he tried to make up for by staying on his side of the now invisible barrier.

"Why does my brother live like this when he could have so much more?" he asked her.

She stopped what she was doing, turned slowly to him. "Your brother is not interested in the same things you are, that's all."

"What is my brother interested in?"

She cocked her head, putting her hands on her hips. "Abdullah is a simple man," she said. "He wants only the feel of the sand beneath his feet, the curtain of stars at night, and the companionship and love of his close friends."

"And a good wife," Faisel added.

She turned away from him, straightening up cushions on the ground for the third time. He watched her move and bend, watched the swirl of her robes around her hips as she swayed to some internal melody.

He didn't believe for a moment that Abdullah was a simple man. His brother was too close to the power not to want it. He would have killed him outright long ago had he not feared the many years that Abdullah had spent among the people. The world was in chaos and at a distance. The desert rolled right up to his feet. The only threat to Faisel's power was at home, and he meant to protect that power.

He watched her patiently for several minutes. Finally, she turned back around to him.

"Why are you here?" she asked.

"You already know the answer to that," he returned. "You've known it all along."

She lowered her eyes, but raised them again quickly. "You could have any woman in the world."

"But I want you."

It was getting dark rapidly, the light left in the tent no more than a haze. Nura struck a long match, and started lighting candles. In the distance Faisel could hear the loud voices of the clan as they laughed and joked, preparing the sheep for the night's feast.

She moved near Faisel, lit an orange candle on his side of the tent. "You will never have me," she said quietly.

He stood, walking right up to her. A kind of heat seemed to roll off her, a humidity that Faisel felt down in his stomach. He grabbed her wrist, jerked her hard against him. "I am the King of the World," he whispered. "I can have anything I want."

She struggled against him in vain. "Remember that Bandar camps outside my door. A word from me will bring him running."

"If anything happens to me, my colonel has orders to burn your camp, kill your men, and take your women for slaves."

Holding her wrist with one hand, he used the other to roam freely over her body. She stiffened, turned to stone.

"It is the honor of the clan you dirty with your talk," she spat. "For honor we would gladly die."

He hugged her close again, and it was like holding a tree trunk. His mind was jammed full with vague feelings that made it difficult to think clearly.

"You must want me," he whispered into her ear, as he bucked his hips against her. "I am greater than Abdullah. I will do everything for you."

She suddenly pushed out hard, breaking away from him. He took a few steps toward her. She matched them with backward steps toward the entry. "You shame me with your talk of adultery," she hissed.

He rolled his eyes. So, that was it. "Oh, Nura. You misunderstand. I am not suggesting . . . no, no. I wish to honor you, to make you my wife. No one would question your honor.

As my brother's widow, it would be my duty to make you one of my wives.''

Her eyes got wide. "Widow! What have you done to..."

Faisel quickly put a finger to his lips. "Shhh," he rasped, pointing to the front flap. "Nothing has happened yet, but it may soon. And then we will be free to have one another."

Her voice took on a strained timbre. "I don't want you," she said. "Ever."

"Of course you do," he answered.

"Not on pain of death," she said.

He shook his head. "You have the spirit of a wild colt," he said. "But you misunderstand. I mean to have you. I will have you. There are no other considerations."

She walked back to where he stood, his head nearly touching the sloping roof. Her eyes were on fire. Slowly, deliberately, she unwound the scarf from around her face, exposing it. Her hair was dark and full like a horse's mane, her face a lotus flower unfolding on a dew-filled morning.

"What you have," she said, "is three days of hospitality. Then you'll have a faceful of wind."

"We shall see."

"See this," she returned, and spat full in his face.

Bringing around the tail of his ghutra, he used it to slowly wipe his face. He kept his anger in, held it for the time being. He wanted her to come to him of her own free will. He wanted her to bend of her own accord, to reject her husband on her own. But if that was not to be, it would have to be another way, a more unpleasant way.

"You are more beautiful than the night," he said to her.

* * *

> Our Lord,
> take us not to task
> if we forget, or make mistake.
> Our Lord,
> charge us not with a load such
> as Thou didst lay upon those before us.
> Our Lord,
> do Thou not burden us
> beyond what we have the strength to bear.

> *And pardon us,*
> *and forgive us,*
> *and have mercy on us;*
> *Thou art our Protector.*
> *And help us against the people*
> *of the unbelievers.*
>
> —The Koran
> II. The Cow

XX
New Mecca

Abdullah was awake long before the morning call to prayer. Thoughts of Nura were crowding into his mind, thoughts of their last night together, of the fears they both shared. He thought about Majid also, and about the key that weighed heavier upon his neck each passing moment. He was bound by honor to do his brother's bidding, but even honor must have its limits.

He was lying on the floor of his small room, rejecting the bed that sat beside him. Naked except for the key, he sat there in the fuzzy gray light, feeling it upon his skin.

There was a knock on the door. Jumping up quickly, he answered it, opening it a crack to peek through. Majid was smiling at him, his gold tooth pressed almost to the door space.

"We go to prayer," he said. "Then to Orleans."

Abdullah swung open the door. "So soon?" he asked, and allowed Majid to walk past him.

The man turned to look, his eyes resting on the key. "Over the television box," he said, "came the news."

"News?"

"That you would go to Orleans today. You didn't know?"

Abdullah stared at him.

"Look," the man said, pointing.

Abdullah looked at the television that played soundlessly in the corner. It was showing his celebration and departure from LOW Headquarters.

"I don't understand," Majid said, "why you seem to know so little about what you're doing here."

Abdullah picked his thobe off the bed and slipped it over his head. "I think I know too much," he replied, reaching for his mishla. "Tell me more of your fears about this city."

Majid walked to the window that opened into the courtyard. The sky was brightening, although it would still be several hours before they would see the sun crest the high walls of the garrison. "You've never seen the Jitterbug," he said.

"No." He adjusted the mishla, then moved to the small sink to wash his face. He had seen running water before, but it had been only on infrequent visits to his brother at LOW.

"It's horrible," Majid said. "Not the death for a man. Jits must be killed on sight or they infect everyone they touch. Cities must defend their borders or risk taking the serpent to their bosoms."

Abdullah splashed water right from the tap onto his face, then dried it on the towel that hung on the wall beside it. "What has this to do with Orleans?"

Majid picked up Abdullah's ghutra from the windowsill and tossed it to him. "The Jitterbug is the way your brother keeps control of the world." He swung his arm back and forth. "It is the executioner's sword that hangs over everyone's head. Are you ready?"

Abdullah walked into his sandals. "Yes."

Majid grunted and moved to the still-open door. "Unfortunately, controlling it is like trying to control the whirlwind. The systems are old; they break down, or get broken down, or broken into."

He walked out the door with Abdullah, moving down the darkened stone hallway to the courtyard. "Every time a system breaks down, we have another outbreak. No outbreak is totally containable, because if one person slips through our fingers, he can start another outbreak. We spend most of our time hunting Jits in a country that is barely inhabitable because of them. We've lost huge segments of the Continent, and are trying desperately to hold on to what we have left."

"And if Orleans goes, so goes the country."

They shuffled across the cold stone floor, then down some stairs directly into the courtyard. There was a slight chill in the air, and the fan palms were rustling gently in the morning breeze. The courtyard was already filled with soldiers prostrating toward Mecca. They slipped out of their sandals and walked toward the throng.

"There's an army out there right now made up of Jits," Majid said.

"An army?"

The man's eyes got wide and he nodded slowly. "They're organized," he said. "And smart. They pulled a maneuver a few days ago, sacrificed thousands of their people, to make us think we had defeated them. Even now they march, only Allah knows where, and it will take all of our resources just to find them."

They reached the edge of the group, knelt down with them—and prayed.

When they were finished, the courtyard became a jumble of activity, of men and noise going in all directions. Majid and Abdullah walked slowly back to their sandals.

"From what I've seen, these Jits are different from others," Majid said, and got into his sandals. "They have purpose and direction. They spread the virus intentionally. To keep themselves going, they eat their own dead."

"Wallahi," Abdullah said, and his throat was dry.

"If Orleans goes, we won't be able to handle it," Majid said. "No one will."

"Does my brother know this?"

"We tell him often enough, but when you have everything, destroying part of it still means you have everything. What does he care?"

"How many garrisons in the country?"

Majid held up a hand. "Five. All understaffed and overworked. So, while we need to be hunting the Houston Jits, we are outfitting our balloons for a parade in Orleans."

"Why?"

Majid put an arm around him, led him through the courtyard and toward the front gate, the cool air waking Abdullah. "You are the brother of the King of the World. You must arrive according to your station. It will take us several hours to reach Orleans. We will eat on the way."

They moved through the giant archway of the main gate and into the balloon field. Men ran everywhere, untethering the monstrous green floaters to sluggishly rise and rumble against their last restraints. They were huge beasts trying to wake themselves. Their gondolas creaked loudly, crying into the morning sky, and men rode around on little carts, hurrying to the more distant balloons, crisscrossing paths at breakneck speed like army ants on a food foray. Propeller motors began revving up, and the crisp morning was filled with irritating noise as a thousand balloon creatures ached for the freedom of the air.

The command dirigible sat on the outskirts of the squadron, its gondola brightly colored and trimmed with real gold. Ornate metal latticework dripped from its edges like iron snowflakes. It wasn't until they reached it that Abdullah noticed the Elite.

Several uniformed soldiers were arguing with the Elite commander with the gold braid on his black sleeve. The large man stood silently, his arms folded across his chest.

"What goes on here?" Majid asked when they reached the scene.

Majid's man, a uniformed lieutenant with a twitch in his left eye, turned to them, frustration evident in his face. "This man tells me that we must vacate our posts to them."

The Elite looked hard at Majid, his dark eyes blank and unfeeling. "We must travel with Abdullah ibn Faisel for his protection."

"Not this time," Majid said amiably. "I need my own men to fly the balloon. I will take responsibility for the safety of our honored guest."

"My orders come directly from Faisel," the man responded. "They will be followed."

Abdullah flushed with embarrassment, moving between Majid and the Elite. "The Emir has told you that you will not make this trip. Now, I will tell you. Stay here. Await my return. I appreciate your concern for me, but I will be all right."

"I have no concern for you," the Elite said. "My devotion belongs solely to Faisel. And I will follow his orders."

"You're mistaken. I'm in charge here."

"My orders came last night. I was told to go with you to Orleans no matter what. That is what shall be done."

Abdullah and Majid shared a look, Majid's eyes narrowing as he stared, and Abdullah felt humiliation. "I want to talk to whoever gave you those orders," he said.

The Elite shook his head. "My apologies," he replied, "but no one but me has access to my radio."

"Suppose we just arrest you and your men and leave you here?" Majid said, anger shading his voice.

"Abdullah ibn Faisel Al Sa'ud would not dishonor himself

or his family that way," the Elite said. "Besides. We are all trained balloon pilots and will do a good job for you."

Abdullah looked at the other Elite who stood quietly around their leader. They would have their way; there could be no doubt about that. He decided to give in rather than cause a public scene. "When we return," he said, "you will use your radio to call my brother and tell him I would speak to him."

"As you wish," the man said, then took a breath. "I was told to inquire of you if you had your key on your person."

"Suppose I don't," Abdullah answered, his anger bubbling just under the surface. "Suppose I just threw the key away and never thought about it again. What would you think about that?"

The man shrugged. Reaching into his black mishla, he came out with a key identical to Abdullah's. He dangled it in front of his face, and Abdullah wondered if the man was smiling behind his veil.

"The King of the World thinks of everything," the Elite said.

*   *   *

Helpful Hints for Immolators:

1. Wear several layers of dry clothing.
2. Wait for proper authorities to provide fuel (if feasible).
3. Immolate in groups for mutual support.
4. Avoid congested areas, lest the fire spread.
5. Bind and secure yourself against last-minute cowardice.
6. Pray and think positive thoughts.
7. Know you are doing the right thing.
8. Avoid screaming by gagging yourself.
                                    —Daily TV Message

XXI
The River

Olson held tightly to the line as the speedboat raced him through the harbor, spray from the old aut hood he stood on cascading in frothy sheets all around, almost as if he were standing inside a bubble of water.

"Whoooee!" Jerry Joe called from the back of the boat, hooting through cupped hands. "You're a natch'l, boy. A natch'l!"

The harbor was jammed tight with commerce, boats on boats, but they didn't care. Huge rusted metal hulls loomed large in Olson's vision, only to skitter past inches from his face. Ragged men on skiffs shouted and shook their fists as his wake rocked them giddily and splashed their decks.

The noise they made was loud and biting, the only gas motor on the whole river, and it all blurred past Olson, who was having the time of his life.

"Turn around!" Jerry Joe screamed, and made circular motions in the air with his hands.

Olson smiled wide and waved at him. Putting his right hand where his left hand had been, he tried to spin around and put his left where his right had been. It was a wonderful idea in theory, but the execution went awry and he found himself flying through the air and cannonballing into the water at a high rate of speed.

It was then he remembered he didn't know how to swim.

The world turned dark and murky and he tried to grab a breath at the wrong place and the wrong time. The next thing he knew he was being pulled, gagging and sputtering, back into the boat.

They laid him on his back on the deck, dizzy eyes watching Jerry Joe and Junex Dinker, the driver, leering down at him.

"You shoulda seen yourself," Jerry Joe laughed. "You looked like a damned pig sloppin' in a mud puddle. Whoo!"

"You're supposed to swim in it," Dinker said. "Not try to drink it."

149

"Hell," Olson said, sitting up and shaking his head. "Figured I could just walk on it."

Jerry Joe slapped him on the back. "Whooee!"

Standing on shaky legs, Olson dried and started slipping back into his leathers. Jerry Joe and Herman both wore half exos, a light, summer style.

Going back to the helm, Dinker whined the motor and they were off again, "running" the harbor—patrolling it. Jerry Joe sat on a bench seat in the stern, patting the seat next to him.

"Take a sit," he told Olson.

Olson sat, using both hands to slide his wet hair back on his head. Jerry Joe smiled his dough-faced smile at him, his nearly shaved-to-the-bone head glistening sweat. He wasn't overly bright, but was nice enough. And he looked out for his people. Olson liked that.

"You ain't never run the harbor with me before," the man said. "How you like it?"

"Beats working," Olson replied.

"That it does," the man said, and looked away for a minute. He looked uneasy, and Olson figured he wanted to tell him something; so he just waited, giving the man his own time.

"That damned Hey-rab comes in today," he said at last, but Olson knew that wasn't what he really wanted to talk about. "Guess we'll have to get all done up and have a party with him or something."

"Guess so," Olson answered. They looked at each other for a moment, and when Olson couldn't stand it anymore, he said: "Did you want to ask me something?"

The man rubbed his hands on his face as if he were reshaping it. When he took them away, he was frowning. "What's with you and Rennie?" he asked.

"I don't get you."

Jerry Joe looked surprised. "Don't hold back on me, boy."

Olson shrugged. "It's no secret that we don't get along that well," he answered.

Jerry Joe pursed his lips and tried again. "Look. The man's a senior VeePee, which means he's got a shitload of folks working under him, people who'd just love to do something for him."

"Yeah. So what?"

"You're bein' followed."

"Where?"

The man rolled his eyes. "Everywhere, you dumb fuck. We got a couple on our tail right now."

Olson started swinging his head around.

"Don't look!" the man yelled. "Don't give it away."

"Why would he follow me?" Olson asked.

"That's what I want you to tell me."

"Look!" Dinker yelled from the controls, and pointed ahead.

Jerry Joe stood, craning his neck. "You're kiddin'. I thought we weeded them suckers out."

"Not unless we're both seeing things."

Olson stood too, trying not to show how wobbly his sea legs were. "What?"

The man showed him a creaky old boat with two masts. The ship flew a white flag emblazoned with a six-pointed star in blue.

"Yid liner," he said. "We kicked them all out of the harbor a few days ago."

"Not all of them," Dinker called over his shoulder.

"You just drive us the fuck over there."

Picking up his sidearm from the bench, Jerry Joe strapped it on. Olson did the same. "They been asking about you, too," he said, looking up from his buckling.

"Asking?"

"Questions," the man responded. "Like how's your work. What are you like. Shit like that."

Olson sat back down before he fell down. "What do you tell them?"

Pulling a cigar out of an inside pocket of his exo, Jerry Joe stuffed it in his mouth. "I tell 'em that you work for me, not them, and if they want to screw with you, to do it on your time, not mine."

"Thanks."

The man shrugged it off. "Just good business. You don't blow off your people 'less you got a good reason." He gave Olson a long stare. "Have I got a good reason, Cat?"

Olson returned the man's stare, and though he hated it that way, he knew there was nothing he could tell him. "It's just a personal thing, that's all. You worry too much."

Jerry Joe walked over to Olson's side of the boat to get a better look at the Yid liner. "I don't worry too much," he said. "Something's goin' on. And when somthing's goin' on with one of my people, it's goin' on with me."

Pulling the .45 out of its holster, he checked the clip, then shoved it back into the gun's butt. "Why'd somebody like Rennie go after a small fry like you? What's he got to gain?"

"Nothing," Olson said. "He's just a Jit-brain."

"Shit if he is."

They were pulling up alongside the old wooden tub. It had been some kind of a large fishing boat at one time, but was now a floating general store. Large lines were strung topside, dripping utensils, pots and pans, fish hooks, things that weren't produced locally and that LOW didn't supply. There were tables jammed high with clothes and hats, jars set with preserves. Every possible inch was jammed full with merchandise. Even the patchwork quilt of a sail they used was stuck with large hooks, displaying shoes.

Dinker cut the motor and they bumped up next to the thing. Several bearded men and curly-haired women were moving over to look at them.

"Throw a line out here!" Jerry Joe yelled. "Come on, hook us up."

A couple lines were thrown over. Olson grabbed one, used it to pull them up tight. "They're wearing beards," he said.

"They do what they want," Jerry Joe returned, as he watched Dinker pull up the other line. "The Hey-rabs gonna kill 'em whether they got hair on their face or not."

"How come?"

The man cocked his head like a dog. "How come Hey-rabs hate Yids? They just do, that's all. How come anybody hates anything?"

Olson tied his line down, and followed Jerry Joe as he climbed up a thick net full of sponges and onto the deck on the liner. When he reached the deck, Jerry Joe was already arguing with one of the Yids, a small old man with a gray beard and sharp eyes. He wore a good-looking brown suit and a small black skullcap. Gold chains hung around his neck and a large diamond ring weighed down his right hand. He wore a big sidearm, and Olson was amazed to see it was a laser.

"What for you wanna come around here and ruin my business?" the man said. "The customers take one look at harbor rats and go to somebody else."

"There ain't nobody else but you, Murray," Jerry Joe said. " 'Cause I run everybody else off. Just like I'm gonna run you off."

"What the hell you do that for?" the man returned angrily, waving his arms. "We do you a good job. Is this how you repay all we've done for you? Huh? Who got you that medicine that time when you put your plumbing in the wrong hole and had to grab the wall to piss, huh?"

"Just calm down, would you?"

The man raised his arms high in the air and turned around behind him. "Did you hear that, Myrtle?" he bellowed. "Mr. Fancy Schmanzy wants me to calm down."

An old woman in a flower-printed dress and earrings the size of grapefruits came stumbling up, hands on her hips. "Der all the same," she said in an irritating nasal voice. "Take what they can get from you, then leave you to rot. I warned you about this one, Murray. Didn't I? Didn't I?"

Murray put his hands on either side of his head and rocked it back and forth. "I shoulda listened to you. I shoulda let his plumbing rot off."

The rest of the people on deck had walked up to the conversation, glaring, shaking their heads. Olson smiled at them.

"So, what are we supposed to do, Mr. Big Shot?" Myrtle said. "Lose the last good weather and go starve?"

"You let me handle this," Murray told her.

"Yeah, sure," she answered. "You're doin' a fine job. Bunch of big shots, all of ya."

"Listen," Jerry Joe said. "You gotta go, 'cause one of them important Hey-rabs is comin' here today and we gotta make a big showin'."

Murray's hands went to his chest. "So, they're more important than us, or what? Who looks out for you when you're sick? Who gets you liquor when you want to get boozed up?"

"But—"

"No buts. You owe us, Mr. Harbor Rat. It's settled, then. We stay."

With that Murray turned and walked away, going down the gangway to the cabin section of the ship. Jerry Joe went after him, Olson tagging along behind.

They got down the gangway, into the narrow rocking hallway. The ship creaked loudly down there and it was dark. Olson could smell food cooking. Jerry Joe walked to a door marked PRIVATE and pounded on it.

"This ain't gonna hack it, Murray."

"Just a minute," came a muffled voice from the other side of the door.

"They find you in the harbor and they'll blow you out of the fuckin' water."

"Watch your language, there's ladies on board. Just a minute."

They waited. Jerry Joe turned to Olson. "Nice folks," he said. "Just a little emotional."

"I can see."

Jerry Joe smiled shyly. "About you and Rennie," he said. "I'll tell you the truth, I'm scared of the man. But, you're one of my people and I look out for my people." He searched Olson's blank face with his eyes, came away disappointed. "I don't want to die for you," he said quietly.

"Don't make such a big thing out of it."

Jerry Joe pounded on the door.

"Just a minute!"

"He's probably gonna bug you," he told Olson.

"Bug?"

Jerry Joe narrowed his eyes, wondering. Then he obviously gave up and his face relaxed. "Yeah. You know. Wire you with a listening device. Look around your apartment."

"And get rid of it?"

The man jiggled his head around. "No, no. Have I got to do everything for you? You just find it, then you bug him back and feed him info. It's the way the game's played. Everybody bugs everybody. What did you people do for fun in Dallas?"

Olson shrugged. "We didn't have much fun in Dallas."

The door opened and Murray stuck his head out. "What, you're still here?"

"You're gonna have to go, Murray. If you don't do it on your own, I'll have to get a tug and drag you out."

"So, that's the way of it, eh?"

"Yep."

Murray frowned and opened the door wide. They walked in. There was a small table set in the crammed-full cabin. There were new clothes stuffed everywhere, and hundreds of kerosene lanterns with shiny brass bases swung from the beams in the ceiling. The table was set with three places. The plates were piled high with steaming food.

"Sit," Murray said. "Eat."

Jerry Joe raised his eyebrows to Olson and they sat down.

"Fried matzo," the Yid said. "Try it."

Olson began eating right away. Applesauce sat on the plate with the matzo, and he found that the two things tasted delicious together.

"We really gotta go?" Murray asked.

"This is a big one," Jerry Joe said. "It could mean all our asses."

The man nodded thoughtfully. "When?" he asked.

Jerry Joe took a mouthful and talked around it. "Just as soon as we get off the boat."

The man sighed deeply and stroked his beard. "So be it."

"Sorry," Jerry Joe said.

"Not your fault," Murray said. "You're a good boy."

They ate in silence for a moment, then Jerry Joe perked up. "Say. How you fixed for bugs?"

Murray's eyes lit up and he winked. Getting up from his chair, he pulled a box out from under a bunk and started rooting through it. "We always got bugs," he said. "We do a good business with you boys."

Jerry Joe patted Olson on the arm. "My friend here is having a little problem."

The man stood up and dropped a gaggle of alien-looking electronic equipment on the table. "Well, these won't let you down, my young friend. My personal guarantee. And Murray Pizant's word is as good as blood."

Olson picked up the strange metal gear, turning it around in his hands. As good as blood, the man had said.

Marty Jerny and Billy Fain sat in the small paddle boat and peeked around the rusted hull of the old freighter. As soon as they saw Jerry Joe and Olson climb back into their boat and buzz off into the chaos of the harbor, they worked their feet on the gears and paddled themselves to the Yid liner.

The people on board were busy bundling up their goods, taking shoes down from the sails.

"Ho!" Jerny called up to the deck.

A young woman stuck her head over the railing and looked down at them.

"Where's your captain?" Jerny called.

"He's busy," the woman returned.

"Get him."

The woman looked at him for a moment, then moved away from the rail. A moment later she came back with an old man.

"We're packing up," the man said. "Nothing for sale now."

"That's what I want to talk to you about."

"So talk. I got ears."

Jerny stood up, almost losing his balance in the rocking boat. "Plans have been changed," he said. "You don't have to leave after all."

"Whazit?"

"The visit's just been postponed," Jerny said, smiling. "You can stay if you want."

The old man threw up his hands. "What's wrong with you people?" he yelled. "Can't you even make up your minds? What are we, your little rag dolls, pull us this way, pull us that way?"

"Stay or go," Jerny told him. "Makes no difference to me."

"You say that now," the man returned. "Just wait until you need something from us."

"I will," Jerny said, and looked at Billy. "Real soon."

* * *

> *The art of living is the art of knowing how to believe lies.*
>
> —Standard Operating
> Procedure Manual, LOW
> Corporate

> *Whoso commits aggression against you,*
> *do you commit aggression against him*
> *like he has committed against you;*
> *and fear you God, and know that God is*
> * with the godfearing.*
>
> —The Koran
> II. The Cow

XXII
LOW Building, Orleans

Olson and Gret crawled around the apartment on their hands and knees, talking inanities, looking. He doubted if Jerry Joe was right about the bug plants, but at this point it would be foolish to take the chance. Wexler sat crosslegged on the bed, unaware of what was going on, a giddy smile on his lopsided face as he watched them moving around.

"When is this high muck-muck guy supposed to show up?" Olson asked, as he felt under his nightstand and came away with a handful of cobwebs.

Gret had slithered under the bed on her back and was checking its underside, even though she was sure that creaking bedsprings was all a mike could pick up under there—especially given Olson's proclivities in that area. "He's not a muck-muck. He's Abdullah ibn Faisel Al Sa'ud and we're the dirt under his fingernails. We go up to meet him at two o'clock and wait until he shows up."

Olson rose to his knees, looking for another likely spot. Noticing Wexler on the bed and Gret beneath, he got the little man's attention, then made bouncing motions with his hands and body. Giggling, the Engy started bouncing on the bed.

"Hey!" Gret screamed. "What the . . . Would you . . . *Stop!*"

Both Olson and Wexler smothered their laughs with their hands as Gret came slithering out like a snake with its tail on fire. She sat up, fuming.

"I ought to knock both your silly heads together."

"Aw, we were only playing, weren't we, Wex?"

"A great deal depends upon one's definition of play—" Wexler began.

"Can it!" Gret said, and looked at Olson; but his eyes were not on her. They had moved up the length of one of the bed canopy posts and were staring at the frilly lace fringe around it.

Holding up a hand to quiet Gret, he stood slowly. The fringe was lumped out right next to the post at the foot of the bed. "Well, with all the work we have to do in the harbor, I think it's stupid to have us wait up on that damned roof for shit knows how long while Fingernails takes his good old time getting here."

"Look at it as a paid holiday," Gret returned.

He moved to the post and slid his hand up its sculptured length. Reaching the fringe, he slowly pulled it up, exposing the framework. Sure enough, a device similar to the one he had gotten from Murray was attached to the frame.

"When do you think it will rain again?" he said, pointing to the bug until Gret nodded her head.

"When it will hurt us the most," she returned with conviction.

He released the fringe and stepped back. "That's what I like about you, honey," he said. "Your undying optimism."

Gret threw her arms wide in question and Olson shrugged in return; then he looked at Wexler, still lolling his head around and grinning. He turned back to Gret, held a finger up.

"Wexler, my boy," he said. "Come right over here a minute."

He pointed to the bug post and Wexler slid across the bed to it, straddling the post with his legs and holding on to it with his little Engy hands.

Olson tousled his lifeless hair. "I've been wondering about the Jitterbug lately," he told the little man. "I want to know something of its history."

Wexler, true to form, started right in. "The Jitterbug was first introduced in the late twentieth century by one Is'al Dim ibn Fahad, ruler of Saudi Arabia. Its characteristic gold dome, put up supposedly as a mere symbol by every oil company in every city of the world that dealt with Arabian oil, in reality held the Herpes virus we know as Jitterbug. When the world was covered, the demands began."

Taking Gret by the hand, Olson led her to the couch that separated the bedroom from the living area. They sat down while Wexler droned on.

"No one took the demands seriously, of course, until Is'al Dim used the virus to destroy the Continent of Australia..."

"I don't think they'll be able to hear us over Wex," Olson said.

"What are we going to do?" Gret asked.

"We'll leave the bug in place for now," he returned. "At least until we talk to Mr. Elwood about it."

"What's Rennie up to?"

Olson shook his head. "Not sure. This has got to be more than just the mind match, though. I'll have to believe that he suspects something until I'm proven wrong."

"How could he?"

"You tell me. Probably my contact with Mr. Elwood." A copy of the Koran stood on the coffee table in front of the sofa. It was held in place by miniature gallows bookends. Reaching out, Olson flicked one of the tiny ropes, watched the hangman's knot swing back and forth. "His kind has a good instinct for this stuff."

They heard a scream from far away outside. It got loud quickly, then a shadow flashed past Olson's curtained window. He shook his head.

"Another one from the computer room," he said. "Guess they haven't found the problem yet."

"Hmmm."

Wexler was still talking. "Fully forty-five percent of the surface of the planet is uninhabited right now, thanks in total measure to the Jitterbug . . ."

"When are you going to plant your bug?" Gret asked him.

"Haven't figured that part out yet."

"Maybe I could help you."

"How?"

"How do you think?"

He stood up, turning his back to her. Walking to the window, he sided the curtain and looked down. A body lay on the pavement far below; no one was taking any notice of it.

"Look," he said to the window. "This is going to get pretty rough. I want you out of it. I don't want you involved at all."

She stood and walked over to him. He wouldn't turn to her. "Why?" she asked. "'Cause you don't want me fucking Rennie?"

He felt his jaw muscles tighten. "Not just that," he said, though he admitted to himself that it was a big reason.

"Then what?" she persisted.

He turned to her then, tried to take her in his arms, but she backed away.

"I'm just worried about you. I don't want anything to happen to you, okay?" He threw her own words back at her, but it didn't do any good.

"You just don't get it," she said. "No. It's not okay. You can't care about me. You're not allowed to."

"What's that supposed to mean?"

"What it means, is that I'm not a real person. I'm a walking love-juice machine, a giant two-legged masturbating hand."

She turned from him and went back to the couch, throwing herself on it. "On the day I was born they fixed it so I could never have any children. I've been made and trained for one purpose, and I'll never be anything else."

He started toward her. "But, Gret . . ."

She sat up quickly. "Stop it!" she said too loudly. "Get it through your head. I can never be what you want me to be. Fuck me, beat me, trade me, paint me green. For heaven's sake, kill me, send me away . . . but don't care about me."

"I can't help it."

He sat with her on the couch, and she quickly pulled herself into a ball and scooted away from him.

"Dogs are dogs. Peasants are peasants. I'm a Houris. It's not much, but it's what I am. You want a woman to care about? There's plenty out there. All from good families, good alliances. Care about one of them. Marry one—just stop making me wish for things I can't have."

She started crying softly then, burying her face in her bent-up knees. He reached out to touch her and she cringed from it.

She raised her head, eyes red, cheeks wet. Her face was pleading. "Don't cut me out of your power play. If it works, and I'm a part of it, I may be able to squeeze some benefits out of it, maybe even a pension. Do you know what happens to a Houris when she gets older?"

Olson shook his head, his mouth dry.

"It is estimated," Wexler droned, "that at any given second, there are three million living Jits on Earth, and that nearly a billion have already died from the disease."

"When you get old, they toss you out and replace you with a newer one, a tighter one. You're on the streets with nothing. Nobody wants to be around you because they hate you for what you are. The Execs don't want you, the peasants don't trust you. You don't have any skills, plus you've got this problem inside, this . . ." She twirled her hand in the air. " . . . craving."

Her hands were shaking, and Olson grabbed them to steady them. "You end up fucking on the street corner for a meal, and maybe they'll feed you and maybe they won't, because you're gonna fuck them anyway because you can't help it and what man in the world gives a damn after he's dumped his load.''

"You're bitter," he said, and his voice was raspy.

"Grow up, honey," she said coldly. "I'm scared shitless."

He stood up. It was getting to be time to change for the Arab's arrival. His insides were grinding like the gears on the dock cranes. "I won't cut you out," he said. "Is that what you wanted to hear?"

He began slipping out of his leathers.

"Yes," she returned, but her voice had softened somewhat. "But stay away from Rennie, just the same."

"Sure," she replied, but had already made up her mind otherwise.

"It's madness," Majid said softly, for the Elite commander stood near enough to them that normal conversation would be overheard.

Abdullah looked out the open gondola window at the lush, wet green of the Louisiana forest below. It spread out a patchwork of green and brown and gold, and their shadow blotted the colors, dulled them out with a curtain of night, Faisel's brand of night.

They traveled a thousand strong. Balloons flying in formation, nearly touching. The gondolas on either side were so close that the people in them called to one another, laughing and joking. Abdullah even saw a soldier smoking tobacco, another Western vice inflicted upon his people.

They filled the sky, a giant storm cloud moving swiftly, covering several square miles. And it was madness, Abdullah knew that. When he and his brother were children they would sometimes have brought to them the cobra and the mongoose, and would watch the mongoose slowly circle the snake, always intent, as the cobra tried to mesmerize it with the natural eyes on the back of its hood. Faisel would always laugh and say the animals represented the two of them, with Abdullah playing the part of the ferret. Then he would distract the mongoose with a stick and watch the cobra lunge, sinking its teeth in and holding on, gnawing, gnawing.

He looked at the Elite, then at Majid, and knew that the key around his neck was not so unlike a mongoose stick.

Below, thirty thousand Jits sat quietly, watching the man-made cloud drift overhead. Those overtaken with the seizures were covered with blankets and controlled. Milander lay prone on his litter watching the searchers trying to find him, feeling the cold, dark cloud seep across his body.

"Straighten me," he told his bearers.

Four burly men in brown robes and masked faces raised his litter up high above their heads and tilted it forward to face the throng that knelt quietly before them.

Milander spread his arms out wide. "O Lord," he called. "Please hear the cries of these, the least of your brethern. We are bringers of the word of love to the world, the harbingers of Life in a world of Death. Protect your people, Lord. If it is your Will, let this cloud pass away so that we may continue your good works."

He looked up then, looked at the bubble-bottomed quilt that covered the entire sky and knew that they would be safe.

He smiled at his people. "All is well!" he called. "We need not fear the infidel!"

They cheered, loud and wildly.

"If anyone wishes to marry," he called, "I will perform wedding ceremonies now. Line up!"

Abdullah heard a distant sound, like a monstrous chain being dragged across stone. "Did you hear that?" he asked Majid.

The man nodded grimly, and tried to stick his head out of a window so he could get a look at the sky between the balloons. "Hope it wasn't thunder," he said. "That's about the last thing we need."

*   *   *

> *Our fathers and ourselves sowed dragon's*
> *teeth.*
> *Our children know and suffer the armed men.*
> —Bedouin Lament

> *"Teach me work, such that when I perform it,*
> *God and men will love me." Lord Mohammed said,*
> *"Desire not the world, and God will love you;*
> *and desire not what men have, and they will*
> *love you."*
> —The Prophet Mohammed

XXIII
The Roof

In days crammed full with amazement, the most amazing thing of all was what Olson saw on the roof of the LOW Building, ninety stories from solid ground, nine seconds from instantaneous death, ninety feet from the clouds, and nine-tenths absolutely crazy.

They swayed up that high, swayed in the wind like some kind of sensual dance, and the low-hanging clouds drifted wispily past, sometimes dipping down to drown them in humid fog.

They were all up there, all the Execs in Orleans, walking around on the thick smoky glass that was Mr. Elwood's ceiling. They were done up in their three-piece suits of velvet burgundy and black shiny satin. They wore their ghutras in red and white check, the double wrapping cord nothing but symbolic in a society with no camels to rein in. And though they wouldn't allow Gret up there—after all, she was only a Houris—the married Execs all had their dutiful wives dressed in traditional robes and veils. And Olson hated them for what they made Gret, for what they made her think she was.

When Olson passed the weapons checkpoint and walked onto the wide roof, the first thing that caught his eye was the dome. It was large and imposing and sat atop a superstructure of crisscross beams. It was round, totally round, and apparently seamless. It gleamed, even in the dull light of a cloudy day, its gold sheen glowing like some kind of unattainable treasure high above their heads.

He stared at the dome for a moment, as people moved around him, and tried to figure out how such a thing could reshape a world. Walking up to it, he rested a hand on the superstructure, feeling a cold vibration humming through it. When he looked around, he noticed people staring at him. Smiling, he moved back into the crowd.

There were a lot of them, they filled the roof. There were

tables full of food, hot dogs and corn on the cob; and large
eunuch Engies dressed in ballooning trousers and green T-shirts
that bore the legend THERE IS NO GOD BUT GOD on the front and
MOHAMMED· IS HIS PROPHET on the back, carried trays full of
martinis that would no doubt disappear when the big shots
showed up.

The heads of the computer department were strung up like
fish on hooks and overhung the edge of the building. Olson
wandered over to get a look at them. A small scaffolding had
been erected of coarse wood. A long pole jutted out from it, over
the edge of the building. There were pulley wheels attached to
the pole that ran a length of rope through them. The rope
attached in heavy knots to the scaffolding, the other end dangled
the computer boys.

Walking to the edge, Olson looked over. He saw the men,
all trussed up and tied back to back, the pulley rope going down
into the middle of the pile. Their faces were drained of color and
emotion; they had resigned themselves to their fates, essentially
dead already. They looked up at him with eyes that held neither
joy nor pain. Beyond them, Olson was filled with the immensity
of the city that stretched out all around him. It was vast and
decaying, a compost heap Arab-style. The streets were still filled
with people and sounds and smells, but they were up too high to
know that; they were above it all, where it looked like a painting
of grays and rotted browns all closed in by the huge sides of the
wall, certainly Orleans's most impressive feature.

"I take no pleasure from that," came a voice behind him.

He turned to Mr. Elwood, resplendent in white tuxedo and
pure white aghal, then looked again at the prisoners. "Then why
do you do it?"

"Business," the man answered, and that was all there was
to it.

"Should we be seen like this?" Olson asked.

"I don't think it matters now," the man returned.

"Oh?"

"I got a memo this morning," Mr. Elwood said, and he
leaned his elbows on the chest-high wall that defined the edge of
the roof and watched the prisoners swaying in the breeze. Then
he yelled to one of them. "Hey, Mike! You sure you guys
couldn't find anything?"

All three men just stared at him as they slowly twisted in
the wind.

Mr. Elwood turned away from them and leaned his back on the wall. "Damn waste of manpower," he mumbled, and pulled a single cigarette out of his jacket pocket. Sticking it in his mouth, he lit it on a match he struck on the wall. Taking a deep drag, he coughed immediately, a painful hack. Determined, he tried again. This time he didn't cough.

"One of my boys in Agri says that Rennie has set his sights for you in a big way."

"He's bugged my room," Olson said.

The man raised his eyebrows. "You do anything with it?"

"Not yet. I've got one for him, though. I just wanted to talk to you first."

Mr. Elwood grimaced. "This doesn't scare you?"

"I'm too dumb to be scared." Olson smiled.

The man slapped him on the back. "You're okay, son." He hit the cigarette for a minute, the smoke blowing away quickly in the breeze. "I'd leave his and plant your own. He'll probably figure it after a while, but right now what you need is time."

"How do I plant it?"

Mr. Elwood shrugged. "Be creative. Use your Houris if you have to."

"I won't put her through that."

The man looked at him so hard that Olson wanted to run and hide from those eyes. "You got a problem there, Cat," he said at last. "Use the woman. That's what she's there for. This stupid attraction you have for her is just going to get you in trouble."

"Drop it," Olson said, and spit on the ground just to get away from Mr. Elwood's eyes. There was an uneasy silence then, and Olson studied the crowd, watched Rennie watching him. "What are we going to do about Rennie?"

Mr. Elwood tried to speak, coughed some more. He brought a handkerchief up to his mouth and it was stained crimson when he took it away. He threw his cigarette over the side of the building.

"A lot depends on how far he intends to go," the man said weakly. "In a couple of days, we'll have a meeting with my biggest support groups and I'll sell you to them, sell your protection to them." He cocked his head. "Rennie's a mover; he's got his own alliances. When he finds that you're under my protection, he can either back off or take it to the streets."

"And if he takes it to the streets?"

"Messy. He'll not only be challenging you then, but me too. It happens sometimes. There'll be assassinations and bloody interdepartmental mergers and repeated attempts on both our lives. That on top of the Arabs and the Jits..." Mr. Elwood shook his head.

"We can't do anything about the Arabs and the Jits right now," Olson said, and his eyes were still fixed on the party, "but if Rennie wants to screw with me, I can give him all he can handle."

One of the eunuchs walked up to them balancing a silver tray loaded down with martinis. He didn't have a name as such things went, but when he was among his own kind he liked to be called Raoul. He was totally hairless, part of the hormone engineering that gave him birth without a sex drive. When he thought, it was about food or sleep or about avoiding beatings. When he ate, it was as much as he could get. When he slept, he dreamed about the same things he thought about when he was awake. When he avoided beatings he was happy. When he couldn't avoid them, he cried.

"Drink?" he asked.

Both Olson and Mr. Elwood shook their heads no. Olson didn't want to get drunk like he did at the other party. Mr. Elwood had a deeper reason. The night before, he'd had the worst attack he'd ever had. He thought he was going to buy it that time. He had covered his silk sheets with blood and scared his Houris into crying in the closet. He had determined during those hours to avoid anything that might set him off until he could get Olson set solid in the system.

The Engy who called himself Raoul wandered off, wishing Mr. Elwood had taken a drink to lighten his tray. He moved to a tight-knit group nearby.

"Drink?" he asked.

A man in red was staring angrily at him, moving his head from side to side, and he realized too late that the man was trying to see around him.

"Would you get out of the...fucking way?" the man yelled, and shoved him.

Losing his balance, he went back, all the glasses sliding off the tray to crash loudly all over the smoky ground and splash on the pretty yellow robes of a large, fat woman.

And he was down there, cowering, trying to pick up the broken glass as everyone made angry faces at him and yelled terrible things, and he wasn't surprised when the Engy Master in his leather straps and weighted whips ran over and started to flail him.

He cried.

Rennie moved away from the commotion, watching Cat talking with Mr. Elwood and getting madder with each passing second. He had an entourage with him—Jerny, Billy Fain, and several others from his hierarchy in Agri. They were there as company, but also as a show of strength.

"He doesn't look good," Jerny said, nodding toward Mr. Elwood.

"He's on his feet," Rennie returned, "and that's too good. Allah, I wish I knew what they were talking about."

"They're talking about us," Billy said, and his voice was already slurring alcohol.

"For once, you're probably right," he said, looking at Billy in disgust. "You people haven't exactly been subtle."

He saw Olson looking at him, stared fire at him in return. "He's got something on Elwood," he said. "He's got to."

"What?" Jerny asked.

"If I knew that, I wouldn't be standing here with my thumb up my butt, now, would I?"

Jerry Joe in a blue denim suit and a stomach full of gin staggered over toward him, bumping into Junex Jordan's petite brown-haired wife in the process. He moved right up to Rennie and stared at him through red, blurry eyes.

"I want a word with you, you son of a bitch," he said.

"You're drunk," Rennie said, looking past him at Olson. "Sit down. Eat something. Respect yourself."

Reaching out, Jerry Joe took Rennie by the lapels of his red suit. "You're after one of my people," he said. "My people are like my family. I want you to stop it."

"Let go of the suit," Rennie said.

"You send your goons down on the river again to fuck with my people, and I'm personally coming after you."

Rennie had been carrying a drink around for effect. Without thought, he jammed it up onto Jerry Joe's face. It broke on contact, tearing the man's cheek and temple. His face exploded blood and when he grabbed at the place, Rennie grabbed him around the waist and shoved him toward the retaining wall.

They hit it hard, doubling Jerry Joe backwards. Rennie

hefted him up on the wall bodily, shoving him halfway over the edge.

"What are you going to do, cowboy?" he yelled. "What are you going to do to me?"

Jerry Joe had fallen part way over the wall. His hands scrabbled for a hold as he bled on the cement, one eye blinded by blood.

"Oh, please," he sputtered through torn lips. "Please."

"Beg me," Rennie spat. "Go ahead. Beg me!"

The man reached for help, but all that was around were Rennie's people, and they just stood there.

Olson saw it though and moved that way.

"No," Mr. Elwood called behind him. "Leave them be."

Olson paid no attention. He angrily shoved his way through the thick crowd that had gathered around the spectacle, physically throwing them out of his way until he reached Rennie.

Rennie flared around to him, could feel the anger bolting through his own body. It was exciting and frightening.

Jerry Joe managed to crook an arm over the wall and painfully drag himself up. Rolling off the wall onto the smoky floor, he lay there quietly, waiting either for death or the energy to move. Rennie prodded him with his toe.

And then Mr. Elwood was there, standing between them. "What in the name of Wahhab do you people think you're doing?"

"Nothing that would concern you," Rennie said.

Mr. Elwood jumped, startled. "In case you've forgotten, I run this place."

"Do you?" Rennie said. "I think you're too sick to run the place. I think you need a long vacation."

"I'm well enough to tumble your ass."

Rennie smiled then, moved up close to the Director. "Are you now?" he said softly, and saw the edge of sickness around the man's eyes. "I wonder . . ."

Olson grabbed Du'camp's arm and spun him around. "This is between you and me," he said through clenched teeth. "And I'm feeling real good today."

Rennie's people had formed a circle around them and were closing in.

"Move on!" Mr. Elwood said. "All of you."

There was the sound of shuffling feet.

"Stay!" Rennie said loudly. "Stay right there."

"There!" someone yelled. "Look!"

They all turned and watched the sky. At first it looked like some vast low-hanging clouds were moving in on them; then the image took on definition. Dirigibles, flying densely packed, were moving on the city. They formed a city of their own, covering all of Orleans like a helium umbrella. March musak blared from their speakers to trill loudly over the walls.

Olson watched in amazement as the monstrous shadow slowly spread over everything. Mr. Elwood was helping Jerry Joe to his feet, giving him over to the Engy Masters to get off the roof.

The dirigibles began dropping flowers onto Orleans. Millions of white petals floating down like fragrant snow, leaving an odor that would linger on the streets for days. And to Olson, the Arabs were trying to bury their handiwork under a blanket made by Nature.

And the cloud got right overhead and the flowers were falling on them, making the men laugh and the women squeal. Mr. Elwood passed a look with Rennie and the man moved off, satisfied with a standoff for the time being.

Mr. Elwood heard the music, watched the petals falling, and worried. He worried over the first serious assault on his authority in twenty years. He worried that all the flowers would clog up the already overworked drains of Orleans and contribute to the flooding.

The sound of cheering reached them from street level. The flowers excited them, the show of force frightened them, and the cheering was a nervous result. But it was large, large as the balloons, and thundered through the city, shaking the tower of LOW.

Rennie felt it all run through him like chain lightning. The glory and the majesty. He wanted it more than anything. And today, for the very first time, he felt seriously that he could have it. Elwood would be no problem, and Cat, the hothead, would be even easier.

The balloons overhead started moving around, changing formation. They jumbled for a time, but there was method. After several minutes, the crowd on the roof and the streets below all blew carbon dioxide into the air at the same time. The balloons, a thousand strong, had formed the image of a giant scimitar—the might of Allah—hung menacingly over the city of Nasrani.

"Is all this really necessary?" Abdullah asked Majid from the command balloon.

"We maintain order through fear," Majid returned, and he was gazing through the open window, binoculars fixed at his eyes. "It is the only way a relatively small force can control so many people. If we can do it with spectacle, rather than Jitterbugs, why not?"

Majid was watching the top of the LOW building, checking for anything out of the ordinary, finding nothing. He lowered the fieldglasses and smiled at his cousin.

"Are you ready for this?" he asked.

Abdullah returned the smile. "Do they smell?" he asked. "I heard that the Nasrani smell bad."

"Breathe through your mouth," Majid said, and ordered the command balloon down.

Olson watched the ornate balloon slowly descend, zeroing in on their position. The street crowds were still cheering even though the last of the flowers had settled like down and blanketed everything with a carpet of white.

When the gondola got close to the side of the building, ropes were thrown from it, and Mr. Elwood hurried to supervise the tying down of the thing with the beautiful scrollwork on the sides.

When it was secured, a door was flung wide, followed by a gangplank that cleared the retaining wall and rested on the roof itself. The crowd all pressed up for a closer look. First out of the gondola were a number of men dressed all in black robes, their faces covered except for eyes. Waves of whispers greeted them, for Nasrani had never seen Elite before.

The Elite moved into the crowd, moving them back away from the gangplank.

Mr. Elwood tried to remain close, but the Elite shoved him aside too, like so much refuse to be swept away. It angered him, but he kept it to himself, for there was no other logical place to take it. He saw commander Majid come down the plank and called to him, waving.

The man saw him and waved back, a gold glittering smile lighting up his dark face. He waved him forward, and Mr. Elwood scooted past the Elite before they could stop him.

"My friend," Majid said, and the two embraced warmly.

"You've been too long from my hospitality," Mr. Elwood said when they broke the embrace.

The man rolled his eyes. "A blessing, I think, eh?"

Mr. Elwood reached out and took his face in his hands.

"Maybe just a little." He honestly liked Majid. It was a shame that circumstances kept them from really being friends.

A man appeared in the doorway, a large Arab with a frowning face and a simple look about himself. Majid cleared his throat and addressed the crowd.

"His Imperial Majesty, First Vice-President and Secretary of the Board of the Light of the World Corporation, Minister of the Interior of Arabia, Progenitor of the Koran, Retired General of the Army of Allah, Protector of the Bedouin and Breeder of Prized Camels, Abdullah ibn Faisel Al Sa'ud!"

The musak blared loudly and all the Execs cheered shamelessly. Abdullah, looking a trifle embarrassed, walked down the gangplank and onto the roof, waving to his subjects the whole time.

Mr. Elwood went to him with outstretched hands. "Your Majesty," he said, bowing.

Abdullah took his hand, shook it. "I don't answer to Majesty," he said. "Abdullah will be fine."

Mr. Elwood nodded, but his eyes were attracted by the cord that hung around the man's neck. "This way, please," he told Abdullah. "I have a little speech to make."

They moved into the crowd, the Elite doing their best to keep people back despite Abdullah's protestations. Mr. Elwood leaned up close to Majid. "What of the Houston Jits?" he asked.

Majid frowned deeply, kept walking. "My forces engaged a sizable number of them on the edge of the Louisana forests and destroyed them. Thinking they had found the entire army, they returned home."

"You don't agree?"

Majid shook his head. "Their army was too large, their leader too smart to get caught that way. I think the bulk of their force is still somewhere in the forests."

They arrived at the scaffolding. "You think they'll come here?"

They shared eyes. "What better place?" he asked. "Evidence pointed to them turning and heading North, but I don't believe it."

"You think I should leave my people within the city, then?"

"That is your decision, not mine," Majid answered.

Mr. Elwood drew his lips tight and looked around. Rennie Du'camp had managed to avoid the Elite and was shaking hands with Abdullah, talking to him.

Quickly scaling halfway up the derricklike scaffold, he twined an arm through the wooden crossbars and took one look at his computer people before speaking.

"The City of Orleans and the employees of the Light of the World wish to extend our highest regards and warmest welcome to Abdullah ibn Faisel Al Sa'ud."

He stopped at the sound of applause and didn't continue again until it had died down. "This is a momentous occasion, the first visit of LOW hierarchy to the Western Sector, and we grieve that it is not under . . . more favorable circumstances. But we are confident that this visit will bear fruit that will be sweet to the taste of LOW Orleans and LOW Arabia. We extend every helping hand, every hospitality to our visitor from the East and wish him a happy stay in our humble city. As a sign of our good faith, we make you an offering of the department heads who were unable to find the problems that forced you to make such a long journey. They will cause you no further problems."

With that, Mr. Elwood reached down and flicked the release on the scaffold. The three men dropped without a sound and turned the white roses on the pavement below a dark, beautiful red.

*   *   *

To believe in one's dreams is to spend all of one's life asleep.
                                        —Eastern Proverb

He knows peace who has forgotten desire.
                                        —Bhagavadgita

XXIV
The Caravan

Faisel quietly lit the tall brown candle that sat on his side of the tent, and brought to flickering light the middle-of-the-night blackness within. Shadows stretched high on the canvas walls, then grayed and disappeared, only to thrust black again in the fluttering dance of darkness.

Moving close to the light, he checked his watch. He grunted, and began dressing, his eyes constantly roving to Nura's sleeping form on the other side of the tent.

He had lain naked in her company for two nights now, and still she would not acknowledge him or respond to his love and his misery. She wouldn't even talk to him except to answer questions or ask about her husband.

The gentle light played upon her, caressing her body, bringing out its richness even under the heavy sleeping robes she wore. Her back was to him, her dark hair wound around her head like a sleek satin pillow. And he wanted her. More than anything else in the world, he wanted her. More than his riches and more than his lands and almost more than his power, he wanted her. But he wouldn't take her by force.

There would be no victory in that, only a cause for revenge. It would be drinking from a poisoned well.

As much as he hated Abdullah, he loved Nura. The lust in him was great, nearly overpowering, but still he held her at a distance of respect. It was a war he fought continuously within himself. He needed to respect her, to have her respect in return. That was greater than sex, greater than control.

What he needed was more time for her to come around, more time for her to understand just what he could and would do for her. Then she would come to him, of that he was certain. A woman who had never had anything couldn't understand what that meant. She would have to be exposed to it.

"Faisel."

He heard the whispered voice outside the tent, saw Nura stir slightly, then settle again. Hurrying to the entry, he sided the flap.

Colonel Musa'id, eyes gleaming white in the blackness of the night, stood looking grimly at him. With him were the prophet and Naif, the old physician.

He motioned them in with a silent hand, the four men standing uneasily in the entry watching the woman sleep.

"You have it?" he rasped to the physician.

Naif frowned deeply, his wrinkled face puckering like a withered date. He held up the needle, a tiny clear drop of fluid glistening candlelight on its tip.

Taking the man by the arm, Faisel led him to Nura. He

stared at her for a second, his heart pounding, then knelt beside her, putting a large hand over her mouth.

Her eyes opened wide in terror and she began struggling immediately.

"Do it!" he said loudly, as he tried to hold her bucking body to the ground.

"But, she's . . . moving too much," the old man said.

"Colonel," he snapped. "Help me."

The man hurried over and grabbed her by the legs, while Misha'al stood watching everything with all-knowing eyes.

"Do it!" Faisel said again, above Nura's muffled screams.

The man hesitated slightly, then bent to her arm and pushed up a sleeve. He quickly jammed the needle in, its entry marked by her sharp intake of breath.

"It's done," he said after a second, and stood up, dropping the hypo to the ground.

"Shhh," Faisel said softly to her. "I won't hurt you. You have been kind enough to offer me your hospitality, and now I will return the kindness."

Her struggling became weaker.

"You'll see," he cooed. "I'll take good care of you."

Her eyes began fluttering and her head lolled backward. Within seconds, she was unconscious.

"I will take her," he said, and Musa'id moved quickly away from her legs.

Faisel bent and picked her up gently, cradling her in his arms. She was light, so light, and he held her close as he moved toward the entry.

"We leave now," he said, and they walked quickly outside into the night.

Without a word, they hurried across the dunes toward the convoy, the stark white of the sand glowing a pathway for them.

At Nura's tent, the old man, Thamir, lay faceup in the dune, the blood from the slit in his throat staining the ground, his eyes staring vacantly up into the black, black sky.

*   *   *

Verily, greed is poverty, and having no hope is richness; a man, when he has nothing to hope for, is independent.
                                        —The Prophet Mohammed

XXV
LOW Building, Second Floor Hall of Justice

The room was stark white and smelled of alcohol antiseptic. It had a double high ceiling that rolled conversation back in to echo on itself and a marble floor that threw footsteps up to the high ceiling in loud clicks. Mr. Elwood sat behind the big oak desk wearing his black judge's robes. On the wall behind him was a painting of blind Justice carrying the Koran in one hand and a sword in the other. He was flanked by a dictation Houris at a small desk to his right, and by the hooded Arm of Allah at his marble altar to the left. Doctor Don, dressed in white, stood beside the slab, and two accountants, each with a small CRT screen and typer, occupied desks beside Doctor Don. The halls outside were filled with supplicants.

They were getting a late start because of Abdullah's arrival, and would never be able to get to everyone, but Mr. Elwood knew from experience that if he didn't sit down and make some headway on his docket, he'd be backed up for a month.

"Send in the first one," he told the fuzztop who stood by the tall double doors. Picking up paper and pencil, he idly doodled while he waited, trying to figure out just how the hell to keep Rennie under wraps while he got Cat trained. Now that the man had attained VeePee status, it would be difficult to do anything to him without due process. Rennie knew that, of course, which was why he had pushed his luck on the roof. He was testing the water, sticking his foot in to see if he wanted to take the big plunge. He also knew that Mr. Elwood had enough on his mind already without having to worry about dealing with him.

Two fuzztops brought in a man dressed in overalls with no shirt or shoes. His hair was long and tangled and he was covered with caked-on mud.

Mr. Elwood leaned back in his swivel chair, twitching the pencil in his hand. "What's the charge?" he said wearily.

One of the fuzztops stepped forward. He was fat, fatter than his uniform. His face was all red and bloated, as if the uniform were pushing all his extra bulk up through his neck.

"Caught him stealing," he said, and held up a crusty loaf of round bread.

Mr. Elwood pointed with the pencil. "That's the . . . ah . . ."

"Yes sir," the man said, trying unsuccessfully to nod his boil-like head. "That's the evidence. I caught him taking it from a street vendor."

Mr. Elwood looked at the man, who stared nervously back at him. "What do you have to say in your own defense?"

The man's lips twitched for a moment. "We were hungry," he said. "We lost all our stuff coming through the gates, and the kids were cryin' and—"

"You realize that the law is very specific about stealing."

"Sir?"

"Papers," Mr. Elwood said, and the other fuzztop, a skinny one, handed him a small stack of official papers. There were originals and copies and copies of copies. He took out his rubber stamp and began inking each copy. "You admit to taking the bread," he said, not looking up at the man. "I have no choice but to find you guilty as charged under the wisdom of Islamic law and sentence you to the prescribed penalty. God help you."

Reaching out, he handed the Houris his stack of papers and rubbed hands across his weary face.

The fuzztops took the man over to the marble slab. Doc Don was ready with a needle for his arm. They gave him the shot and put his hands in the stocks set in the slab.

Mr. Elwood called out, "Next!" and stared down at the doodle on his paper. It was a crude drawing of a bug. He X'd it out, drew a box around it, then drew a circle around the box.

The Arm of Allah had slid the altar open on its middle hinge, exposing the steaming oil beneath. The hooded man then pulled a large cleaver out from under the slab and quickly chopped off the man's hands. His screams reverberated through the halls as they dipped his stumps in the hot oil to cauterize the wounds. Then they dragged him away as one of the accountants put the severed hands in an evidence bag along with the loaf of bread and sealed it up.

The fuzztops came in with a middle-aged woman in brown

burlap dress and a man in walking shorts and no shirt. Red knee socks protruded out of the top of his tattered boots.

Right behind them, though, Abdullah came storming in, flanked by two Elite. They swept past the supplicants and up to Mr. Elwood's desk.

"May we have a word?" Abdullah asked.

"Of course," Mr. Elwood said, and stood up to dismiss the fuzztops.

"No, no," Abdullah said, holding up his hand. "I don't wish to interrupt your schedule. Perhaps we could just . . . sit while you work."

Mr. Elwood looked at the Houris. "Adele," he said, motioning her away from her chair. "Take a break."

The woman stood, bowing, and walked off without a word. Coming around behind the desk with Mr. Elwood, Abdullah took the Houris's chair and slid it over by the Director's.

"Are you getting everything you need?" Mr. Elwood asked.

The Arab smiled. "Everyone has been most helpful. My people are down in the computer rooms now getting acquainted."

"And how about you? How are you doing?"

Abdullah shook his head. "There are many things I don't understand."

"Such as?"

"The calls to prayer."

"What?"

"Where is the Allahu Akbar?"

Mr. Elwood took a deep breath and said his own brand of prayers. "We have no calls to prayer in Orleans."

A look of confusion crossed the man's face. "No prayers. But that's sacrilege."

Mr. Elwood shrugged. "We've never had the calls to prayer."

Abdullah slammed a hand down on the desktop. "We will now. I can rig something up with one of those balloon things."

Mr. Elwood struggled to raise his weary eyebrows. "But all these people . . . won't know what to do."

Abdullah raised his head high. "We will show them. I will take the responsibility."

The Director sighed deeply. "Why not," he said at last. "What the hell."

Abdullah motioned for Mr. Elwood to go on with his business.

"What are the charges?" he asked a fuzztop.

"Murder," the man said.

"Murder," Abdullah whispered, and shook his head.

"What happened?" Mr. Elwood asked.

The woman stepped forward and pointed to the man in the shorts.

"He killed my husband."

"Not on purpose!" the man said loudly.

"How did it happen?" Mr. Elwood asked.

The woman frowned deeply. "That man was hanging out of a third-story window yelling at someone in the street, when he fell out, landing on my husband. He broke his neck, sir. Killed him and left us alone."

The man showed empty palms. "I didn't want to fall out the window. I hurt myself pretty good, too."

Mr. Elwood heard Abdullah clucking his tongue. He looked at the woman.

"What would you have me do?"

She fixed him with angry eyes. "I claim my right of retribution under the laws of Islam."

Mr. Elwood put the pencil to his mouth, resting it against his lower lip. "It is true that you have that right under Islamic law," he said, and thought for a moment. "I declare the defendant guilty, and for his sentence I will have you, madam, fall out of a third-story window on top of him so that you may have your just retribution. Next!"

They took away the protesting woman while the next case was being brought in.

"You have women working with the men," Abdullah said, as if he had been saving that.

"Yes," Mr. Elwood answered. "Sometimes."

"This is not Islamic. This is not Arabian."

"The women work cheaper."

"Then we will leave this system intact."

"What else?"

"While I am here, I want to see your operation. I thought we might arrange some tours of your various departments with the department heads present so that I may ask them questions."

Mr. Elwood thought about that for a second. Jerry Joe would be laid up in the hospital for quite some time. This would be an excellent opportunity to showcase Cat for everyone. He would have Cat lead the river tour in Jerry Joe's place. The seniority shifting would be minor, but not lost on anyone.

"We'll start with the river tomorrow morning," Mr. Elwood said with satisfaction.

"That will be wonderful," the Arab returned.

The next case stood before Mr. Elwood. It was a small man with a bald head. He stood alone, without fuzztops.

"What can I do for you?" Mr. Elwood asked.

"Sir," the man said. "I just wish to report finding a large sack of coffee beans down by the river. I didn't know who they belonged to, so I just came to tell you about them."

Mr. Elwood leaned way over the desk. "How did you know they were coffee beans?" he asked the man.

The man shrugged. "I prodded the sack with my big toe," he returned, holding out his foot.

The Director sat back. "The sack was not yours," he said. "You should have left it alone." He turned to the Arm of Allah. "Cut off his big toe," he said.

* * *

One is better off seated than standing, lying than seated, asleep than awake, and dead than alive.

—Arabic Proberb

XXVI
The Infirmary

Jerry Joe got a bed because he was an Exec. With everybody else it was simply a matter of surviving as best they could.

The infirmary was extremely large, taking up the ground floors of a whole block of crumbling buildings, but with the inherent medical problems rampant in Orleans at the time, there wasn't enough space to accommodate even a third of those who needed treatment.

Olson and Gret walked into a nightmare. The beds and all

the floor space were filled up with sick, dirty people. Those who couldn't find a place to lie down, stood. Those who couldn't stand, lay on the broken sidewalks outside the buildings.

The ceilings were low, the coal-oil lighting dim and filthy, leaving dark black patches in patterns on the already dirty walls. They could always tell when someone had died just by checking the layer of coal soot on his body. If you could write your name in it with your finger, you carted it out. The noise in there was constant, like the drone of a mammoth waterfall, pervading everything. And the smells were overpowering, rancid and nauseating.

"They brought Jerry Joe here?" Olson loudly asked to get above the noise.

"There's no place else to bring him," Gret returned. "This is it."

Olson contemplated the long rows of beds and bodies, then caught sight of a man in a bloody white smock moving from bed to bed nearby.

"Let's ask him," he said, and they walked in that direction, carefully picking their way over the moaning people underfoot.

Olson was getting to recognize the putrid odor of dysentery and the burning shakes of Yellow Fever, and saw a lot of it in there. There must have been several thousand just in this building, and he began to understand Mr. Elwood's concern over the strain of all those extra people inside the walls. The problems were epidemic already, and wouldn't be getting any better.

They caught up with the doctor as he bent over a man lying on the black-and-white-checked linoleum floor. He had the man's wrist between thumb and index finger.

"Excuse me," Olson said.

The man looked up, dropping the wrist in disgust. He had a handsome middle-aged face disfigured by smallpox scars. He seemed to have very bad eyesight, and squinting seemed to be his normal way of looking at the world.

"Just a minute," he said, and stood up. He turned away, twisting from the waist because there was no place to move his feet, and yelled, "Hey, Calli! Get Rosey, would you? You guys haven't been doing your damn job. This one's been stiff for several days."

A large Engy shrugged from across the room.

"What, do you wait until you can smell them all the way over there?"

The mutant shrugged again.

The man twisted back around. "That's his answer for everything," he said. Wiping off a dirty hand, he offered it to Olson, who shook it reluctantly. "My name's Jordan," he said. "You look healthy enough."

"I'm looking for someone," Olson said.

"Good luck," Jordan returned.

"His name's Jerry Joe," Gret said. "He got his face cut up in a fight."

The man pouted out his lower lip. "The Junex. I remember now." He started twisting around again, searching. "Aha!" he said. "This way."

Picking their way through the mess, they moved down the rows of beds. "Don't know why they even come in here," Jordan said over his shoulder. "Not a thing we can do for them—a place to lie down, an occasional bowl of soup. The dysentery's the worst. It thrives in a place like this."

"How's my friend?" Olson asked.

"He'll live," the man returned. "He lost an eye, part of a lip. His face is pretty hacked up, but I think they're making a leather half-mask to cover it up." Jordan chuckled back at them. "If he doesn't catch dysentery in here, he'll walk out on two legs."

They stopped once in front of a woman on the floor. Shaking his head, Jordan bent down and examined her swollen, pus-draining leg. He clucked down in his throat, and pulled a red tag on a string out of his smock pocket. He tied it around her hand and stood up.

"Hey, Calli!" he called to the Engy, who was still standing in the same place he had been before. "Clean off a table in the OR and take her in." He was pointing downward. "Sharpen up the saw; we've got to take a leg off. I've red-tagged her!"

Calli just shrugged.

They moved on. Olson saw Jerry Joe before Jordan did, and ran over to him. The man was asleep, a swarm of flies buzzing around the blood-soaked bandages on the left side of his face. The sheets and pillow were also bloody, as was Jerry Joe's hair. It had thickened and matted in there.

Shooing away the flies, Olson shook the man. The good eye, the one not covered by the bandages, fluttered open. He smiled with the exposed half of his mouth.

"This is what you call keeping your mouth shut the hard way," he mumbled out of the right side of his mouth.

"You just take it easy," Olson said.

Jerry Joe nodded. "I'll take it easy, and *then* I'll kill the son of a bitch."

Olson laughed deep. Gret and Jordan had gathered around the foot of the bed. "That's the spirit. The doc says you're going to be all right."

"No more beauty contests, though," Jerry Joe added.

Olson nodded. "I want to thank you for standing up for me back there."

"Had to," Jerry Joe said, and closed his eye. It might have been a wink, but there was no way of knowing. "I let 'em screw with my people, next thing I know, they're screwing with me. No. You're the one who stuck his neck out. You interfered with a Corporate dispute at a higher echelon, and Rennie can use that against you."

"But I saved your life," Olson said.

"And I'm grateful," Jerry Joe mumbled. "But Rennie could bring you up on charges of insubordination and probably make it stick."

Olson turned and looked at Gret. She nodded slowly.

"Hell with Rennie," he said.

Jerry Joe raised his good eyebrow. "Sometimes you don't even talk like an Exec," the man said.

All at once, there was a commotion at the door. Mr. Elwood was entering, along with an entourage of fuzztops to clear a path. They caused quite an amount of turmoil, shoving people out of the way so the Director could walk past them. He had a large green handkerchief tied around his nose and mouth to block out the stench. When he saw Olson and Gret, he waved and moved in that direction.

Many of the sick ones were on their feet now, tripping over those still on the ground. There were loud shrieks of pain then to go along with the constant moans. Mr. Elwood reached them quickly, pulling his mask down around his neck.

"How's it going, hot shot?" he asked Jerry Joe.

"Never better," the man lied, moved that the Director would personally come to see him.

"You're supposed to *drink* out of glasses, not smash them on your face," Mr. Elwood said.

"I'll keep that in mind," Jerry Joe returned, eye lit up.

Mr. Elwood turned to the doctor. "How's it holding up?"

The man frowned. "We get several hundred a day with dysentery," he said. "Something less than that in Yellow Fever.

We passed our bottom-line capacity a few days ago, and things are getting worse by the minute.''

Mr. Elwood looked at him sadly. "Do the best you can," he said, then looked around. "Look, I own a 'safe' building just down the block. I'll see if I can get it opened up for your overflow." He shook his head. "Probably won't do too much good, but it's all I've got to offer."

The man almost smiled. "I appreciate it; I really do."

Mr. Elwood reached out and patted him on the shoulder. "You're doing a good job here. I'm the one who appreciates it."

They shook hands and Jordan wandered off.

" 'Safe' building?" Olson said.

Mr. Elwood licked dry lips. "Upper-management Execs will buy buildings in town where they can keep their people in case of mergers. You'll own some, too."

Olson started to ask him something about it, but Mr. Elwood was already busy gathering everyone up near the headboard of the bed.

"I've got something I want to do," he said, looking around to make sure no one overheard them, "but I have to ask your permission, Jerry Joe."

The man narrowed his good eye. "Something, like what?" he asked.

The man rubbed his always tired face. "The Arab wants a tour of the river tomorrow," he said. "Since you're laid up, I want Cat here to lead the tour."

The eye wandered from one of them to the other. "Something's goin' on," he said slowly, choosing his words carefully so as not to offend his boss. "Cat's way down on seniority."

Mr. Elwood bent down close. "I've taken a . . . personal interest in his career," he near-whispered.

"I don't understand."

Brown eyes rolled around. "I want him to move up quickly."

"To where? My job?"

"I'd never take your job away from you," Olson said.

"Calli!" Jordan called from across the room. "Here's another one!"

"I want a guarantee," Jerry Joe said.

Mr. Elwood and Olson looked at one another, and Olson shrugged with his eyes the way Calli did with his shoulders. Finally, the Director spoke to Jerry Joe.

"We're involved with some . . . interdepartmental politics

right now," he said. "If you help us out and things work, you have my personal guarantee that you will get a department-head job on the river."

"What if things don't work out?"

"You'll probably be killed."

"Does this have anything to do with Rennie?" the man asked.

"Everything," Olson told him.

Jerry Joe growled deep in his throat. "I'll do whatever you want," he said.

"I want you to play dead," Mr. Elwood replied.

Rennie stood with VeePee Fagin on top of the wall, overlooking the city gates. The sky, as usual, was overcast, and a light drizzle was falling; but it fell in disconnected sheets around the edges of the massive balloon umbrellas that covered the entire city. Fagin had fieldglasses riveted to his eyes, and the megaphone attached to his mouth made even private conversation boom out in loud crescendo to whomever wanted to listen in. He had a patch on one eye and a monocle on the other. Instead of an exo like Rennie wore, he had a long lead-lined raincoat that made him walk with a stoop because it was so heavy.

"I know that I owe you," the man whispered, and it was like a shout. "I just think this is a bad time to think about collecting."

"I didn't choose the timing," Rennie said, looking around to make sure nobody was listening. "It's all ready to fall apart now, and I want to know whose side you're on."

"Aha," Fagin said, pointing around the binoculars. "We've got company."

Rennie followed his finger, and saw the distant figures of several people running toward the gates.

"Riflemen!" Fagin called, and the megaphone rolled the word out like thunder.

"It's going to happen whether we want it to or not," Rennie said. "Elwood's old and sick. He's done for."

Fagin looked up and down the length of the huge wall. His riflemen were waving from their posts.

"Wait till they're close!" his voice boomed. "Use no more than one shot if possible. Aim for their legs. All you need to do is slow them up!"

"When the leadership changes," Rennie said, "it's going to be me who comes out on top."

Fagin turned and stared at him, his eyes just barely able to see over the rim of the instrument on his mouth. "What's in it for me if I help you?"

"You owe me, remember?"

"Yeah, I remember," he whisper/shouted. "If you hadn't set up Hewett that time, I'd have never made VeePee. But a little extra incentive would certainly juice my spirits."

"How large is the Gate Guild?"

"I got about five hundred working under me."

Rennie stared back over the wall. The small group of people was drawing closer, excited and laughing to have made safe harbor.

"You know," Rennie said, "when I take power, all of Elwood's support will need to be divided among those loyal to me. I don't think it would be out of the question to say that you could probably . . . double the size of your department by combining it with Maintenance and Motor Pool, with a corresponding raise, of course, to go with your new responsibilities."

"Of course," Fagin said, and Rennie could see him smiling through the mouthpiece of the gadget.

The man stuck out his hand. "Honorable men," he said. "Honorable cause."

"For the good of the Company." Rennie smiled back.

Fagin looked over the wall. The people were within fifty yards. "On my signal!" he yelled to the riflemen.

He let them get almost up to the gate before letting the riflemen open fire. They were quick and efficient, and abruptly ended any possible Jit contamination from the outside. They used their ammo sparingly, saving it for later use.

"Cease fire!" Fagin called up and down the line. Then he leaned over the wall, looking down. "Firemen!" he yelled.

Below, the gates were quickly opened, and three men with flamethrowers strapped to their backs ran onto the soggy ground outside the walls. Torching their hoses, they set the corpses on fire, burning them relentlessly, leaving little piles of carbon ash that would either blow away or be merged with the ground by the all-pervasive rain.

*   *   *

If a piece of worthless stone can bruise a cup of gold, its worth is not increased, nor that of the gold diminished.

—Sa'di

O Lord! Keep me alive a poor man, and let me die poor; and raise me amongst the poor.
—The Prophet Mohammed

XXVII
LOW Building, Room 615

Gret stood outside Rennie's door for several minutes before knocking. Her hair was set in long ringlets and her dress was yellow and filmy, like spun sugar. She was nervous, shaking slightly, and the small package she carried within herself made walking uncomfortable; but she was going to go through with it—of that she was certain.

She had managed to get hold of the microphone when Olson was out of the room, and she was going to plant it for him, help him whether he was smart enough to accept the help or not. She had a talent. It would not go to waste.

Taking a breath to calm herself, she knocked.

"Who is it?" came Rennie's muffled voice.

"My name's Gret'amaine," she said, trying to make her voice husky. "I'm Junex Catanine's Houris."

The door flung open immediately, and Rennie poked his head out, looking up and down the corridor. When he saw it was clear, he turned his gaze slowly to her, a strange smile seeping onto his face.

"And what brings you to the viper's den, little sister?" he asked, voice low and menacing.

186

She pursed her lips. "Cat thought you might be . . . lonely," she said, "wanting some company."

He stared blankly for several seconds, then opened the door all the way to admit her. She stepped in. Rennie's apartment was twice as big as Olson's, and was done up all in heavy woods and black leather. The carpets were red. Rennie, stripped to the waist, wore a pair of tight red shorts and carried a sword in his hand.

"Don't think you'll need that one," she said, looking at the sword.

He smiled and leaned the weapon against the wall. Another Houris came walking out of the bedchamber dressed in a flimsy robe. She flashed fire at Gret.

"Kind of late for company," she said.

"Take a walk, Myrt," Rennie said casually to her. "Get some exercise."

"Do what?" the woman replied.

"Get out," Rennie said.

The woman's face was set in rage. "And do what?"

"Think about what it would be like to live outside," Rennie returned.

Myrt's fragile crystal face blanched white and she walked across the room, head high, and out the open door, still dressed in the robe.

"Shut the damned door!" Rennie called after her.

She returned and quietly closed the door. After it clicked shut, Rennie turned his attention to Gret.

"Cat sent you?" he asked.

"Sure," she responded. "Why not?"

"Gesture of friendship?"

She shrugged. "I'm just a Houris."

He walked right up to her. "So you are," he said. "I'm going to have to search you."

She held out her arms. He began rubbing his hands on her body, squeezing, caressing, pushing all the right buttons, and almost immediately she felt her mind start slipping its gears. She was already fighting to remember why she came and what she had to do first.

"You're unarmed," he said, and pushed himself against her, his erection insistent between her legs.

"You're not," she sighed, and lolled her head back, a hiss escaping her lips.

The liquid fire was spreading through her, rolling away her physical presence, rapidly turning her into a sentient machine. Putting a finger to her lip, she bit down hard.

"Owww!"

He was staring at the blood running down her finger. "What the . . ."

"I got carried away," she said, pulling back from him, breathing heavy. "Have you got something I can put on this?"

"In the bathroom," he said, pointing back through the bedchambers.

She leaned up and kissed the end of his nose. "Don't go away. I'll be right back."

"Don't worry," he said.

She moved off, every nerve in her body alive and tingling. It was all she could do to keep from running back and throwing herself at him.

Damn me. Damn me.

His apartment was dark like a cave, the walls seemed wet and damp. Her senses were keen, sharp-edged, as the after-shocks of sensations kept kicking her relays in and out.

She got into the bathroom and closed the door, leaning against it for support. Her whole body was vibrating there in the dark. She flicked on the light, and the room exploded in harsh, sterile white—porcelain and ceramic on bright white wood. Going to the sink, she turned on the water and washed her finger. There was pain there, she was sure of that, but the other sensations were in control and blotted out something as inconsequential as physical pain.

She washed the blood away, then cleansed it with a small bottle of camel urine she found in the medicine cabinet.

Her breathing was labored, but she was getting it under control. Sitting on the edge of the tub, she spread her legs and fished the tiny microphone out of her vagina.

She held it in her hand, looking around. It would have to be in here; she wouldn't chance trying to place the thing anywhere else. She kept trying to gear her mind, kept trying to push the incessant desire off to the side. Finally she hooked the mike under the lip of the sink and left the bathroom.

The bathroom exited into the bedroom. Rennie had lit several tall candles in there, bringing to flickering light the contrived blackness of the place. Everything was done in blacks and dark walnut, even down to the sheets on the big four-poster.

Rennie was lying on the bed, naked, the orange light playing across his muscular body and rejuicing the synapses of her brain.

"Come here," he said, and held out his arms.

She moved to him—willingly and without will. Walking out of her sandals, she knelt on the bed and pulled the dress up over her head and threw it on the floor.

He pulled her down on top of him and kissed her, igniting her lips with his tongue. His large hands moved across her body and she could feel herself being sucked into the vortex.

Rolling her onto her back, he climbed on top of her, his penis jamming tight against the entrance of her cunt, and she could hear herself sobbing down in her throat, and when she opened her eyes she could only see Olson's face where Rennie's dark, coiled leer should be.

"Do you like it?" he whispered.

"Yessss."

"Do you like it a lot?"

"Put it in. Please."

His mouth darted to her nipples, sucking and biting. Hard, too hard, but she was beyond the pain now, and his hands held her arms outstretched, wide open.

And somewhere back in the vibrating mist of her brain, she felt something, something wrong. Hands. Too many hands. She opened her eyes, tried to focus them.

Someone else was in there doing something to her hands. She tried to sit up, couldn't. Her hands were tied to the bedposts.

"What . . . what . . ."

"This is my friend Marty," Rennie rasped. "He's going to help us out with our little experiment."

She fought the pleasure, the overbearing pleasure. She fought for possession of her senses, and she kept losing the fight.

Rennie had climbed off her, and he and Marty Jerny were securing her ankles, spread wide, to the foot of the bed. She was panting, her pelvis jerking up and down on the mattress.

"Oh, please," she muttered. "Please."

"What do you think, Marty?" she heard Rennie say.

"Looks like love to me," the man returned, and they both laughed.

"Please do it," she pleaded. "You can't . . . leave me . . . like this."

Rennie was down beside her, his lips at her ear. "Oh, I'll do it," he said sweetly. "We just have to have a little talk first."

"No. No talk."

"Now, now." He stroked her hair, gently, soothingly. "This is going to be real easy. Just relax."

He nodded to Jerny and the man, fully dressed, sat on the bed on the opposite side from Rennie. Reaching out his hands, he began to slowly run them up and down her body. His touch was electric, her skin springing up at him where he gently kneaded it. Then Rennie's hands joined Jerny's, and Gret was a mainspring winding tighter and tighter.

She was gasping for air, head flung back, her body arching without control against the bonds that kept her from floating away. And the ergs built up in her relays to the point of shorting out her whole system.

"Stop," Rennie said calmly, and all the hands were gone from her.

Her body was shaking as if chilled and she was crying, and if she could only touch herself, she'd end the insanity—the torture.

"Fuck me," she spat, and couldn't look at them. "Would you . . . please fuck me!"

She screamed it, then she just screamed.

"Lot of spirit," Jerny said.

"Tell me about Cat," Rennie whispered in her ear.

"Wh-what?"

He reached out and lightly flicked the lips of her cunt, sending lightning spasms charging through her.

"Does Cat plan to take Mr. Elwood's job?"

"Fuck me, please fuck me!"

"Just help me out and I'll help you out," he whispered. "Really."

Jerny had climbed between her legs and was kissing the inside of her thighs, and the agony tore through her as the unreleased tension in her brain began seeping into her whole body, making her physically sick but not lessening the desire.

"Does Cat plan to take Mr. Elwood's job?" he asked again.

"Yes!" she screamed, revulsion mixing with the out-of-control desire, and she wanted to die almost as badly as she wanted release.

Jerny had moved up farther with his mouth, the pressure building within her to where she feared coming apart physically.

"When is he going to make his first move?" Rennie asked.

"P-please," she cried. "Don't do this."

Jerny was right there, and she tried to buck herself against his face, but he pulled away, leaving her muscles spasming out of control. She was having a full-blown seizure.

"Answer the question," Rennie cooed.

"Nooo."

"It'll all be over if you answer the question."

Jerny's lips were on her again, pulling away again.

"Tomorrow!" she screamed. "On the river!"

"How?"

"Please!"

"How?"

"He's taking Jerry Joe's place on the tour."

"Jumping seniority?"

"Yes!"

Jerny lifted his head to look at Rennie. "The river," he said.

Rennie bent over and kissed Gret, long and passionate.

"Perfect, my love," he said softly.

She was filled with hatred, her desire a disease to her. And still she cried for release—from desire, from humiliation, from her betrayal, from life. The tears were from the pain and from the hurt that goes deeper than pain. And if her hands had been untied at that second, she would have taken her own life; she would have strangled herself to death.

"You know what to do," Rennie told Jerny, and the man reluctantly got off the bed.

"Enjoy yourself," the red-haired man said.

Rennie shrugged. "I'm just doing her a favor," he returned, and climbed between her legs.

Her body was flopping like a grounded fish. He lay heavily on top of her to smother the quaking. Without preamble, he entered her.

"You're going to have to stay here for a while," he said, but she was beyond that.

She strained against him toward climax, hating the act, hating herself, and when the release came, it was more painful than the waiting.

When he was finished, he got up, blew out the candles, and

left her alone in the dark. She lay there, still tied, feeling his seed oozing back out of her, leaving the sheets wet and clammy beneath her.

She lay that way for hours, crying softly in the dark, feeling the room pushing in on her, in and in, suffocating her, driving the life from her.

Olson and Mr. Elwood stood huddled in the dark, slick alley, the Director shifting from foot to foot as Olson smeared streaks of mud on his face and messed up his hair.

"This is stupid," Mr. Elwood said.

"Everything's stupid," Olson replied, using the Director's own brand of discourse against him. "Hold still."

"What if somebody sees us?"

Olson stood back and examined his handiwork, adjusting the man's olive-drab parka so that it hung all the way to the ground, totally covering his exo.

"Plenty of people are going to see us," Olson replied. "That's why we're going in disguise."

"You know what I mean."

Olson reached into the ankle-deep water and came up with his own handful of mud. Working quickly, he smeared it on his face and into his disheveled hair. "Look," he said. "We're going to do this. If you really didn't want to, you would have stopped me when I first suggested it."

Mr. Elwood rolled his eyes. "I didn't think you'd really go through with it."

Olson showed him even rows of teeth. "You're stuck now."

"I've just figured that out."

"Come on."

Before the man could change his mind, Olson turned and splashed toward the mouth of the alley and the army of citizens who marched aimlessly up and down the main thoroughfares. Without a backward glance, he moved into the flow and started walking. It was with relief that he saw the Director walk up beside him. People were crowded all around, pushing and yelling.

"I must be as crazy as you!" Mr. Elwood yelled to get above the racket.

"Crazier!" Olson returned, and it felt good to be out on the streets with people he understood. Out here, when people shoved you, you shoved back and if they didn't, you knew they meant no harm.

They walked for several minutes, and every time Olson looked at Mr. Elwood, the man had a smile on his face. Finally, Olson saw what he was looking for, the place they had scouted out earlier. Grabbing the Director's arm through his parka, he pulled the man out of the street and up to the entryway of a crumbling building.

"Where are we?" Mr. Elwood whispered, his face nearly invisible in the darkness. Olson put a finger to his lips and walked up to a barricaded place where a door had once stood. He banged on the barricade of piled-up crates.

A box came sliding out of the middle of the pile of boxes and a dirty, scarred face replaced it.

"Yeah?" the face said.

Olson turned and winked at the Director. "Hair of the dog," he returned.

The man frowned, his face creasing deeply. "Who sent you?"

"Nobody," Olson answered.

"Hit the road," the face said, and started to replace the box.

"You might want to look at this first," Olson said, and in his hand were two small plastic disks.

The eyes widened. "Where'd you get plastic?"

Olson closed his hand over the disks. "Where'd you get such a big mouth?"

The face looked inquisitive for a moment, indecisive. Then a bushy eyebrow arched and boxes were pushed aside. "Come on in, brothers," the man said when a large enough hole had been opened.

They entered, Olson slipping the doorman the plastic, knowing that he'd pocket one of the disks for himself.

"Up the stairs to your left," the man said as he bit down on the plastic to test its thickness.

"I hope you know what you're doing," Mr. Elwood said as they started up the long flight of dark, rickety stairs.

Olson turned, walking slowly to keep his exo from clattering under the parka. "I'm going to have some fun." He smiled. "And so are you."

The aroma of roast dog reached them halfway up the stairs, and it stirred embers in the Director that he thought long dead.

And then he knew why Olson was bringing him to this place in the midst of the Chaos of Orleans. It was the connection between the two, the tether that held them together. At that moment he decided that the Freebooter was right. It was time to strengthen the bond, time to look to the future without torturing themselves with the past.

They opened a door at the top of the stairs and the noise hit them like a Gulf hurricane followed immediately by a shifting wall of smoke. They went in.

It was a large room filled with citizens, lucky ones who had enough barter in their pockets to buy their way in. Men mostly, with notable exceptions, and all of them grimy and loud. They laughed and yelled through clouds of carbonized dog flesh that hazed the room to acrid fog. They swilled something vile in crocks and forgot that the world was coming to an end outside. The Director experienced several seconds of fear and unease before realizing that down underneath the gold exo and the scrubbed-clean skin he was just like they were. Olson smiled over at him.

"Let's get drunk and eat some dog," he said.

"Fuck right," Mr. Elwood answered.

They made their way through the crowd, finding a table made from an old computer console. They pulled up a couple of crates like the ones blocking the door and sat down. A burning tin of butter sat in the center of the table.

"How'd you find this place?" Mr. Elwood asked.

Olson put an index finger up beside his nose. "Never lets me down," he said, then jerked his head toward a long counter at the other end of the hazy room. "Drinks!" he yelled loudly.

A woman with stringy gray hair and wearing an old red flannel overcoat shambled over to the table, setting two crocks down before the men. "Welcome to Smoky Joe's," she said in a monotone, sniffling and wiping her nose on the coat arm. "No fightin', no killin', and no complainin' about the service."

"We're hungry," the Director said.

"No complainin'." The woman glared and moved off.

Mr. Elwood tipped his crock up and took a deep drink. He hadn't had tater juice for over thirty years and it was as rank as he remembered, which made it just fine with him. He swallowed hard and waited for his stomach to come apart.

It didn't, and he was surprised.

"What's a safe building?" Olson asked, his voice nearly lost in the din of the room.

The Director leaned his elbows on the table and drank again, nearly emptying the crock. "When push comes to shove," he said, "and you have to fight mergers, you're not going to want your people living at LOW. We all have buildings like this scattered around the city where we can split up our people and hide them. I'll deed mine over to you when I step down."

"When will that be?"

Mr. Elwood answered with another question. "Have you learned the pecking order?"

Olson showed empty palms. "I know the departments and who runs them. I know basically whose loyalty we can depend on when we make our move..."

The woman walked up and set a plate of steaming meat pieces on the table. She refilled their crocks from a large pitcher and walked off before anyone could complain.

Both men drank again. The Director was beginning to feel it.

"I never had a father before," Olson said, and his voice was slurring a touch.

The Director drained his cup. "You're not going to go and get morose on me, are you?"

"Drink!" Olson yelled, and the woman hurried over with the pitcher.

"Slow down," she said, sloshing juice in the crocks and all over the tabletop. "I'm an old woman."

"You look young enough to me," Mr. Elwood said, patting her on the rump.

"Better watch it, Black Pete," she said loudly, and laughter rippled through the room like wind through a sail. "I could haul your ashes all the way out and back again."

"Annie used to be a Houris!" somebody yelled.

"Annie's still a Houris," the old woman returned sadly, and hobbled off.

Mr. Elwood watched her walk off, then picked up a piece of white meat and stuck it in his mouth. He smiled. It had been a long time. "I've never had a son before, either," he said.

Olson stuck some meat in his mouth and took a big drink. "How come you never married?" he asked. "You could've had your pick of the litter."

Mr. Elwood sat up straight. "I could say I liked the Houris

too much, but that would be a lie.'' His face tensed, eyes dancing the reflection of the yellow butter flame. "Maybe it was my rebellion against the aristocracy, my way of not giving in completely to the system. Though in retrospect, I sure wish I'd had children. I sure wish that.''

"You got me,'' Olson smiled, and the old man returned it.

The door burst open across the room and a man dressed in patchwork overalls and no shirt walked in, dripping wet. He carried a long pole with several fat, sleek rat carcasses dangling from stout lines. He walked to the bar and laid the pole across it.

"What's it like out there, Herm?'' someone called.

"Rain's getting worse,'' the man said, as the bartender filled a crock for him. "Say, anybody want to trade one of these things for a good piece of shaving glass?''

A tall, gaunt man in tattered, stringy pants moved to the bar. He had a piece of window glass in his hand. "Half,'' he said.

The hunter nodded. "Fair enough,'' he replied, and watched as the man scored the glass with a knife and broke it across the end of the bar.

The hunter took a long drink as the other man picked out a large rat and unstrung its body from the pole.

"You'd think the assholes who ran this place would have enough sense to have more people down at the river sandbagging,'' the hunter said. "This whole city's gonna be underwater in a couple days.''

"Then we'll at least have fish to eat!'' somebody called, and the room pumped full of laughter.

"I think the whole city's done for anyway,'' the tall man at the bar said, sticking his rat in his pocket and sliding the glass across to the hunter. "Elwood's too old; he can't run a city this size anymore.''

The Director rolled his eyes at Olson.

"I got a friend in Agri,'' a woman who was sitting with a large group of men said. "He said he overheard some of the bigwigs talkin' the other day and they said that Du'camp's going to be taking over.''

"Over Elwood's dead body!'' the Director said loudly.

"Is there any other way?'' the hunter said, and everyone laughed. "Honest to Allah, I'll be just as happy to see him go. Maybe some new blood is what we need around here.''

"You people have short memories,'' Mr. Elwood said.

"Who saw to it that you all had houses to live in? Who made the rules about getting people fed during bad harvests?"

The rat man put his hands on his hips. "You Black Petes all stick together," he said. "Hell, that was ancient history. All we get anymore is a gutful of trouble from our supervisors to make quotas we couldn't reach in a lifetime. No, a change couldn't do any harm at all."

"But Du'camp's a maniac," the woman said.

"They're all maniacs," the hunter replied. "Du'camp will take it because he's strong and Elwood is old and weak. I'll bet he takes him soon, during the Jit crisis."

"There's street odds on that," the rat man said.

The hunter continued. "And I'll bet he takes him in one of Elwood's strongholds."

"Mining," Mr. Elwood said.

"You're a fool," the hunter returned. "He'll take him in Manufacturing, right under everybody's nose."

"He wouldn't dare," the Director said.

The hunter drained his crock and slammed it on the bar. He began to sing in a loud, crystal-clear tenor:

> *We drink because we're happy*
> *And we drink because we're sad.*
> *We drink because the river's up*
> *And we know we've all been had.*
> *We know that we're the deepest slime*
> *In the bottom of the wellllll!*
> *So we keep on drinking anyway*
> *To cover up the smell!*
> *Ohhhh . . .*

Everyone stood up, including a laughing Olson and Mr. Elwood, to join the chorus.

> *We drink to the life we lead*
> *Because it's all we get.*
> *We drink to remember*
> *That it's better to forget.*
> *We drink to the Junexes*
> *Who work us till we're dryyyyyy!*
> *We drink to wet our whistles,*
> *Hope to spit it in their eye!*

The woman with the friend in Agri climbed up on the bar
and shouted it out:

> *We know the river's risin'*
> *'Cause our feet are getting wet.*
> *Execs are runnin' ragged*
> *Over Jits they haven't met.*
> *And if that isn't bad enough*
> *Young Rennie gets this verse!*
> *He's going to start a merger war*
> *And make a bad thing worse.*
> *Ohhh ...*

They sang the chorus, everyone laughing and stomping feet.
Old Annie waved for a verse. She picked up the hem of her skirt
and danced while she said:

> *I used to be a Houris*
> *When my hair was sleek and long.*
> *The VeePees used to love me*
> *But I'm sure you've heard the song.*
> *They beat me, bruised me, fucked me, used me*
> *Never told me whyyyyyyy!*
> *Then they waltzed me out the big front door*
> *And said, "Good luck, good-bye."*
> *Ohhh ...*

The chorus started in again, both Olson and Mr. Elwood
screaming along with it. While he was singing, Mr. Elwood
made himself a mental promise to beef up the security at
Manufacturing, but he forgot the promise right away.

*   *   *

> *Dictators ride to and fro upon tigers from*
> *which they dare not dismount.*
> —Hindustani Proverb

Wearing coarse, hard cloth, and eating coarse
food is not abstinence from this world;
abstinence from this world is only shortness
of desire.

—The Prophet Mohammed

XXVIII
Rub Al Khali

They had to dig Thamir's grave deep in the shifting sands
lest the wind bring his murder back into the light of day. They
gathered in a dune bowl, the entire clan, and to Bandar the
monstrous walls of sand that surrounded them all around were
like a mass grave for all his people.

So, they put the old man to rest there in the bowl, deep
down, but not deep enough to forget. There would be no marker
for the grave since the blowing sand covered all, but that didn't
matter. Thamir was part of the sand now. Bandar wanted to
believe that the rest of them could be part of the wind.

And they put him to rest in a deep place where his toothless
mouth could never laugh at the sky again. They were on the
run, hiding from the eyes of Faisel. They prostrated and recited
the Koran and the old women mourned and his possessions were
divided among his sons and his widows were married to his
brothers and heirs and life went on—but they watched over their
shoulders the whole time.

Bandar lay back on the sloping sand next to Ahmad and
watched the mourning rituals. High above him, at the top of the
slope, the line of camels carrying their possessions stretched into
the distance in stark silhouette.

He turned his head and stared at Ahmad, watched the age
lines sunk more deeply around his eyes than he remembered.
"And what happens with us now?" he asked.

Ahmad picked up a handful of sand, let it sift through his
fingers. "We travel," the man returned, "as far and as fast as
we can. And perhaps we can outrun our dishonor."

"The desert is not that wide."

"What would you have us do?"

"Seek vengeance," Bandar replied immediately, for his

mind had already set on this thing. "Get back that which was taken."

Ahmad lay back and stared straight up at the blue sky. "Faisel has armies," he sighed. "We are barely sixty men. What would be served by dying uselessly?"

"I'm not concerned with Faisel's army. I'm only concerned with Faisel. And for him, there are more than enough of us."

Ahmad turned and stared into Bandar's smoky eyes. "You speak as if you have something in mind."

Reaching into his thobe, Bandar pulled out a folded piece of paper and handed it to Ahmad, who opened and handed it back.

"You know I can't read," he said.

Clearing his throat, Bandar spoke slowly, haltingly. "The woman will be safe for now," he read in a monotone. "If you wish to seek her release, come with the new month to the covered bridge at the mosque at Riyadh."

Ahmad sat up, face set in a hard frown. "Where did you get that?"

"I found it on the carpet in Abdullah's tent."

"Who left it there?"

Bandar shook his head. "Someone who either wants to help us or finish us off for good."

"And if they want to finish us?"

Bandar stood up, brushing sand from his mishla. "Then we will die for an honorable cause," he said, and walked off.

Nura, five inches tall, walked around the bedroom of the luxurious suite that Faisel had given to her. He watched her on the television box that he had set next to all the Orleans boxes in the room of televisions.

Faisel was tired and nervous. He had dreamed about her again, *that* dream, waking up when the fire crackled all around him. He had the dream almost every time he slept, and every time he had it he became more agitated.

He had watched her sleep through the television box—sleep and eat and undress and bathe—until he knew how she lived. He knew her movements, and perhaps her thoughts. He knew everything there was to know about her except why she wouldn't come to him. Abdullah still lived. There was still plenty of time.

Turning his gaze to the screen to his left, he watched the computer room in the Orleans LOW building. It was nighttime there. The room was dark except for a single flickering CRT screen that bathed a single figure in ghostly blue light. The man sat before the screen, hunched over the typer, intent. Faisel leaned down closer and studied the man for a moment before tiring of it and returning to Nura. The man was fourteen thousand miles away, as far away as one could get on this round planet, and his image jettisoned twenty miles into space to get flung through a communications satellite before ricocheting to the Rub al Khali and Faisel's narrow gaze.

His name was Paul-Paul Baggins and he watched his screen intently, senses alert, on edge. Things were getting tighter now, nearly too tight to bear. He typed:

CANNOT CONTINUE OPERATION . . . DANGER TOO GREAT.

The screen answered after a few seconds:

YOU WILL CONTINUE AS PLANNED.

He stared at it, wanting the letters to arrange themselves differently. He typed again:

FEAR DISCOVERY . . . MUST DISCONTINUE.

He waited—and waited. After several minutes, his own face appeared on the screen, along with the readout of his executive clearance and statistics. He looked at it, heart pounding.

ENDORSEMENT CANCELED began flashing on the screen.

ENDORSEMENT CANCELED . . . ENDORSEMENT CANCELED . . . ENDORSEMENT CANCELED . . . ENDORSEMENT CANCELED.

Closing his eyes, he banged the response key and typed in the letters:

OK.

And he jumped at the sound of thunder outside, rumbling low and long like a metal trash can down a windy alley, and then it . . .

Cracked like a whip, Mr. Elwood's eyes snapping open, his body wet with cold sweat. The chills were on him, the shakes, and the fire in the pit of his stomach did nothing to warm him. The evening caught up with him after all.

A Houris whose name he didn't even know lay beside him in bed, sleeping, breathing deeply in drug-induced stupor. Mr. Elwood slipped quietly out of the cold, wet bed, lightning flashes skittering daylight brightness in and out of his house of glass, only to plunge it back to middle-of-the-night blackness—starless, moonless.

And the rain came. Hard finally, it pounded in heavy sheets, his windows a blurry curtain to the reality without.

A spearhead of pain shot up his neck, doubling him over. His breath came ragged, in small gulps.

"Oh Godddd," he rasped, and fell to his knees. Crawling to the nightstand, he reached up, fumbling in the drawer for the syringe that was waiting for him, ready to go. Grabbing the small rubber hose, he managed to wrap it around his upper arm and knot it tight with his teeth. Flexing up a vein, he jabbed the needle in and slowly pushed the central-nervous-system depressant into his bloodstream so he could fool himself for just a little longer; so he could pretend to be alive just a little longer.

The pain subsided in moments, and when he was able to stand, he walked, naked, to the blurring windows. The balloons were gone, and he hadn't even noticed it until this minute. The streets were already filling with water and, as he feared, the flowers were clogging the drains and would soon plunge the city into a new kind of fear.

And as he watched from the ninetieth floor, someone else watched from the seventeenth. Olson stood at the window, lights out, Wexler dutifully at his side. The little man sat happily beside him, hugging his leather-clad leg.

He looked for Gret, and didn't know where else to look, so he watched out the window, as if she'd magically appear there. She'd never left him alone like this before, and he was worried about her. He depended on her for everything, but that wasn't the nature of his fear. He had never been able to reach out to anyone before, to make someone's life as important as his own; and yet he couldn't protect her as he did himself and it drove him crazy. Was this love? If so, it hurt deeper than any pain he had ever known.

He looked down at the water-flowing street again.

Down.

Down.

"It is a large country," Abdullah said groggily, as he and Majid leaned on the open window places and stared down at the eternal forest beneath them. "One could hide several armies in there."

Majid nodded. "We must find them," was all he said, but he wanted to say much more.

The lights were turned out in the gondola, most of the Elite already sleeping, curled up on the floor. They had decided at the last minute to take the balloons back to New Mecca. Abdullah wanted to see if he could use the Elite radio to call his brother.

Majid was overcome with the realization that he had to find the Jit army before they made their move, and he wanted to be back at his headquarters to quadrant off a map and begin a serious search. They were down there; he was convinced of it. Just as he was convinced that his failure to stop them could result in the end of this land he had learned to call home.

"Byat," he whispered. "Home."

"They're going home," Ted Milander said, looking up into the rain, watching the carpet of balloons passing overhead.

"Will they be back?" Danny Ford asked, his words slurring and garbled, his hemorrhaged brain running out, slowing down like an old motor, ready to burn out completely.

Milander lay flat on his pallet, his left side completely paralyzed, his aide's features barely visible in the dark, rain-dripping forest. Reaching out with his right arm, he pulled the man close, hugged him with all his strength, and kissed him on the lips.

"Yes, Danny, they'll be back," he said, and rocked gently back and forth, holding the man in his arms.

"Will they . . . hurt us?"

"They can't hurt us," he returned. "Not really. You see, they're not real. They're just an illusion."

"They look . . . r-real."

Milander began crying softly, rocking, holding the man to him. "We are life," he sobbed. "The new life, the New Age. They are Death, and dead themselves. They must kill themselves to make way for us. They can never hurt us because they're dead, and the dead aren't real. They're only memories. Do you think that memories can hurt you, Danny?"

"I d-don't know, Mr. Milander," Danny said. "I don't really . . . h-have any more m-memories."

"That's because memories are dead, Danny, not real." He kissed him again. "We are real. Our message of love is real. That's all that's important. That's all that matters. That's all there is."

* * *

Surely God wrongs not men anything, but themselves men wrong.

—The Koran
X. Jonah

> *Mankind has grown strong in eternal struggles
> and it will only perish through eternal peace.*
> —Adolf Hitler, *Mein Kampf*
> —Old World Wisdom

XXIX
The River

Olson, stuffed into his exo, walked to work that morning. It was early, sunrise, and he hadn't slept all night. Gret never showed up, either at his place or her place in the Houris's dorms, and he was worried about her.

A moderate rain was falling as he sloshed through ankle-deep water that was rising higher thanks to the petals of millions of white roses. Citizens milled through the streets, unable to stop lest they be sitting in water. Their fires were out, and a great many of them had managed to get on top of buildings and were living up there, at least until their combined weight collapsed the roofs. Engies got it the worst, of course. Looked down upon by all humans, they were always expected to give up their spots if a "real" person demanded it, so the streets were alive with giants and dwarves and tall thin fruit pickers and scaly, gilled fishermen and squat bug eaters and planter Engies with the L-shaped backbone and four-armed two-headed factory Engies who could sleep and work at the same time.

A balloon floated low overhead, an electronic bell chiming with monotonous regularity blaring from it. A platform was attached to the underside of the gondola and an Arab soldier stood on it, petrified.

"*Call to prayer...Call to prayer,*" boomed a heavily accented voice.

Everyone looked up, pointing and laughing.

"*You will face Mecca,*" the voice rang along with the bell, and the soldier on the platform was pointing to the East.

"*You will face Mecca!*" the voice demanded again.

The soldier on the platform made a very deliberate show of removing his sandals and holding them up for the crowd. Then he got down on his knees and bowed to the East.

"Remove your footwear," the voice demanded. *"Prostrate yourselves."*

The street crowds were applauding wildly as the soldier continued his prostrations. When the balloon voice began reciting from the Koran, Olson quit watching and moved on.

Abdullah watched his balloon drift down to the docking platform on top of the LOW building. They connected up with a jerk, and several Elite jumped out with the tie-down ropes, securing them to the building.

The man rubbed his face wearily. He had been up all night and felt it. First, he spent fruitless hours trying to force the Elite captain to let him use the radio, a request that was ultimately rejected by Faisel himself. Then he spent the next several hours making the trip back to Orleans.

The gangplank was lowered by the Elite and Abdullah walked out onto the deserted roof. About a half inch of rain stood on the roof, the continuing rainfall increasing that depth in constant ever-expanding ripples.

The Elite captain was right behind him as he splashed off the gangplank.

"I've never seen rain like this before," Abdullah said.

"It is God trying to drown the Nasrani," the Elite returned.

They walked toward the exit blockhouse. "You don't need to constantly follow me around," he told the man. "I'm not going anywhere."

"We are here to protect you," the man said. "Wherever you go."

"Protect or watch?"

"You play with words, Abdullah. What difference the reason? It is the will of Faisel that you not be left alone, and we are the instruments of his will."

Reaching the door, Abdullah turned the knob and entered, going down the short staircase to the ninetieth floor.

"You didn't inform us of your intention of making these inspection tours," the Elite said as they walked to the elevator. "We would have rejected such an idea. You will not make any more plans unless you have cleared them through me."

Abdullah chuckled, but it turned to anger. When they reached the elevator, he turned to the man. "I have gone easy on you while you have constantly degraded and humiliated me. I will not stand for it any longer, do you understand?"

He angrily mashed the down arrow and spit on the ground. "I go where I want, when I want, with whomever I choose. I clear nothing through you, I suggest nothing to you. I do what I want, and if you don't like it—quit. Better still, I fire you. Go on. Get out. You're fired."

"I work for Faisel ibn Faisel Al Sa'ud," the Elite said calmly. "Only he can terminate my . . . employment."

"Well, as far as I'm concerned, you don't work for Light of the World Corporation any longer. I will take no more abuse from you. You are what the scholars call persona non grata as far as I'm concerned."

The elevator doors opened and Abdullah stepped in and pushed the close-door button. The Elite slipped in before the door closed. Abdullah pushed the lobby button and they started down.

"We will wait for the others downstairs before going to the river."

Abdullah ignored him. They rode in silence. Twenty floors down, the elevator stopped and the door slid open, but nobody was there waiting for it, so they continued on their way.

"Your brother had some information to pass along to you," the Elite said after a time.

Abdullah looked at him, but didn't speak.

"He wanted you to know that he has a houseguest for a time . . . an indefinite period of time."

"What are you getting at?" Abdullah said.

"Your wife, Nura, is living at the LOW Headquarters." Abdullah could see the man's eyes dancing above his veil. "Isn't it wonderful that Faisel is caring for her in your absence."

Abdullah's stomach muscles knotted up tight, and he could feel his hands ball into fists of their own accord. His brother had Nura.

The bell rang and they jiggled to a stop on the first floor. When the door slid open, they climbed out.

"We'll wait for the next car," the Elite said.

Abdullah looked at the lobby tv. Faisel's grim face occupied the screen as he read his taped message from the Koran, and Abdullah tried to remove all thoughts from his mind about how Nura came to be where she was.

They waited for the arrival of the next car before going to the river.

*   *   *

The LOW barge sat waiting for Olson at the end of the main dock. It was quite large and painted Arab green. Steam-powered, it had a big paddle wheel on the back and two tall black smokestacks jutting out of the sides of the double stories of rooms and luxurious suites. It was boxy except for the bowed prow. The gun sat on the prow. It was a large gun, and powerful. It was painted black and polished to the point of being shiny blue. It was a gun from a time when guns really meant something. It was the biggest gun the Arabs allowed anyone to have. It had a big round sight on the top, and cranks on the side so that the gunner, who sat on a hard metal chair, could adjust quickly through the sights. There was a dwarf Engy who lived with the gun, who rarely left it. His job was to keep it cleaned and polished. They called him "Pop" after the sound of the gun.

The ship was LOW's royalty barge. It was always freshly painted and kept in perfect repair. Mr. Elwood used it to tour the Mississippi and let everyone know just what the concept of order out of chaos really meant.

The city was coming alive, the rain sky lightening with the backlight of Sun. The river was up high, swollen and pregnant, and for the last several days Mr. Elwood had authorized food payments to citizens in exchange for labor filling sandbags. Already, two warehouses on the wharf were filled with sandbags, with more coming.

It was going to be another muggy one, Olson already starting to sweat under his exo. He climbed onto the pier and walked toward the barge, passing a couple of Rennie's people going the other way. A trouble bell rang in his mind, but he never heard it. His thoughts were too occupied by fear for Gret.

A small set of stairs led up to the first deck. He climbed aboard and started exploring. He was in charge of the tour, but had never been on the boat before.

As he looked around, the rest of the river Execs showed up one at a time. All would take the ride with Abdullah.

Jerry Joe actually ran the river. He was the supervisor. Above him were a VeePee and a senior VeePee, both of whom made decisions but stayed off the river, preferring to deal with the books and the kickbacks. Below Jerry Joe were five other senior Junexes before reaching Olson's slot. Olson was low man on the totem pole, and everyone treated him that way. LOW Orleans ran on seniority. It was the way of things.

Olson leaned over the top rail on the second landing and

watched a big silver aut pull up to the end of the pier. Mr.
Elwood climbed out and moved toward them. Everyone else was
congregating on the main deck. Going down the wooden stairs
amidships, he joined them just as the Director climbed on deck,
looking dazzling in his own gold exo.

"Good morning, gentlemen," Mr. Elwood said in his
practiced manner. "I want to have a little talk before we get this
under way. Let's move up front where we have some room."

He moved past them and walked toward the bow. Going
directly to the gun, heat on its metal chair and swiveled it around
to where they were gathering. Olson picked out a large coil of
thick, prickly rope and sat on top of it. Pop stood at attention
beside his gun when he saw everyone congregate.

"First of all," Mr. Elwood said, "I want to thank you for
getting down here on such short notice. This tour wasn't even
decided on until yesterday afternoon, and you've done a lot with
a little time. I'm sure that Mr. Abdullah ibn Faisel will be proud
of all of you."

They all looked around then, smiling inanely at one another.

"Next, I want to talk about the tour itself. I will not be able
to join you for it. Unfortunately, I have to rush to the other
departments and make sure they're ready. But I know that our
esteemed visitor will be in good hands."

The Director leaned back, studying each one of the men in
front of him. Olson tensed himself, knowing the bombshell was
coming next.

"As you are no doubt aware," Mr. Elwood said, "senior
Junex Jerry Joe had an accident yesterday that resulted in some
serious injury. As a result, he will be unavailable today for the
tour. He and I have discussed the situation at some length, and
his recommendation is that today's tour be conducted by Junex
Catanine."

"Who?" someone said, and everyone started looking around
silently, the only sound their clicking exos.

Junex Wilkes, next in line behind Jerry Joe, spoke up. "No
disrespect intended, Mr. Elwood," he said, "but shouldn't this
simply be a matter of seniority? That's how we've always run
everything before."

Mr. Elwood slipped off his seat and walked to the rail,
looking into the dark, churning waters, the light rain slicking
down his exo. "The seniority system has always been a conve-

nient way of running things. It's not a hard-and-fast law. This time Jerry Joe and I have decided not to use it.''

"It's not fair," Wilkes said, and turned to the rest of them. "It's not fair to any of us. If you can break the chain for this, you can break it for anything.''

Mr. Elwood nodded sleepily. "That's true. Yes.''

"Well, I don't accept that.''

Olson walked to the front of the group and stared fire at them. If he was going to run the show, he'd have to start acting like it.

"If you don't like it, Wilkes," he said, "you can come and talk to me anytime.''

Wilkes met his gaze, inner tension evident on his face. The man had a fake nose. It was made from a piece of metal, with skin taken from his shin stretched across. Cutting off the nose was the penalty for adultery. Olson had seen many like Wilkes.

"What right have you got to walk in here and jumble our seniority?" the man said harshly, but Olson could already tell he was going to back down.

Olson took a step toward him, and he cringed slightly. "What right do you have to go against the wishes of your immediate superior, and the Director?''

The two VeePees were keeping their mouths shut. Mr. Elwood must have talked to them already.

"Well, it's just that . . .''

"And now you're going to try to give me an excuse for your disloyalty.''

The man's face blanched. "I'm not disloyal!''

"Then stop acting like it!" Olson yelled at him. "Instead of prissing around and worrying about your precious seniority, you should be down on your hands and knees every day—''

"Five times a day," Mr. Elwood mumbled.

"—thanking Allah that you have such a wonderful job. So what if I've been picked to do this one job? So what? What possible difference could it make in the scheme of things?''

The man was slowly blending into the crowd, making himself invisible by degrees. "Since you put it that way . . .''

"Yeah," Olson said. "Since I put it that way.''

He was having a good time with this. It was a lot easier to tell people what to do than he'd ever thought. Turning his back to them, he winked quickly at Mr. Elwood, who widened his eyes and shook his head. Then he turned back around.

"What we're going to do," he said, "is to take the Arab down the river and show him a good time. We're all going to work together, and we're going to be enthusiastic and smile a lot."

He stretched his lips out wide with his fingers in an exaggerated grin. They all laughed, even Mr. Elwood.

"And who knows, maybe the man will like us so much, he'll promote all of us. What do you say?"

There was some spontaneous applause and they all grunted positively, including Wilkes. Mr. Elwood began moving away from the scene.

"Thank you, gentlemen," he said, waving. "I'm leaving everything in Mr. Catanine's capable hands."

And the word "Mister" was lost on no one.

Olson walked him to the gangway.

"You're going to be okay," Mr. Elwood said.

"Do me a favor," Olson said, and the Director narrowed his eyes. "Find Gret. She was gone all night."

Mr. Elwood smiled slightly. "That's a Houris for you."

"Would you do what I ask?"

Mr. Elwood backed up a pace. "You're really worried, aren't you?"

Olson nodded.

The Director patted him on the arm, his razored gloves scraping on Cat's exo. "I'll see what I can do," he said, and went down the stairs and walked off.

Halfway down the pier, he met Abdullah ibn Faisel coming the other way. Olson watched them exchange greetings before they each went on their way, Abdullah moving toward the boat with several of his Elite.

Olson greeted him at the top of the gangway.

"Permission to come aboard?" Abdullah asked before stepping onto the ship.

"Permission to come aboard your own boat?" Olson returned, shaking hands with the man. "I hardly think you need it."

Abdullah smiled easily. "My boats have four legs and they walk on top of the waves. This is all a mystery to me. You will have to explain things very carefully."

Olson returned the smile, found himself liking the man. "To tell you the truth, Mr. Abdullah . . ."

"Just Abdullah."

"To tell you the truth, Abdullah, I don't know anything

about boats either. This one's floating. I think that's a good sign."

Abdullah grabbed him and hugged him close. "At last, an honest man. I am glad to make your acquaintance..."

"Cat."

"Cat?"

Olson shrugged. "It wasn't my idea."

"Well, Cat. We will discover the joys of this marvel together." He turned to the Elite, who hadn't been able to get past him to come aboard. "You may wait here for me. We will return in..." He looked to Olson, who held up one finger. "One hour."

The Elite captain stared hard at him. "One of us shall go with you," he said, and Olson was surprised at the man's boldness.

"Him," Abdullah said, and grabbed one of the Elite by the arm, bringing him up the rest of the gangway and on board.

"So be it," the Elite captain said, and backed down onto the wharf.

Abdullah stared hard into the face of the man dressed in black. "Stay out of my way," he hissed, and pushed him aside. The man tensed, crouching, but didn't say or do anything.

"Are you ready?" Olson asked.

Abdullah raised his eyebrows. "Is the day ready for the passage to night? We go, ready or not."

So Olson gave the orders and they got under way, thick black smoke hooting through the big stacks and the paddle wheel swishing the river, churning the murky waters and frothing them white and alive.

Being careful with his people, Olson introduced them, by seniority, to Abdullah and was never at a loss to say something complimentary about each one. Wilkes was still obviously upset about the turn of events, but he kept it pretty well to himself.

They toured the engine room, where short squat Engies with powerful arms fed coal to the steam furnace, and the wheelhouse and the dining room, finally ending up on the prow with the magnificent gun.

"How's it going, Pop?" Olson asked the little Engy, who reminded him of Wexler.

"It's going great guns." Pop smiled and patted the weapon. Then he took out a rag and polished where he patted. "Betsy's clean and happy and keeping peace on the river."

Abdullah looked down at Pop. "You've done well," he said, and patted the man on the head.

"It's my job," the Engy said proudly.

Abdullah looked around, and Olson knew he was trying to see past the foul smells and the filth and the poverty to get to the beauty of the river beneath.

"You'll get used to it," Olson told him. "Faster than you'd want to believe possible."

"What is the bondage that makes people stay here?" the Arab asked after a moment.

"Fear," Olson answered without hesitation. Elwood had taught him well. "Fear of the unknown, the most powerful bond of all."

Abdullah searched Olson's eyes. "It saddens me," he said.

"Yeah," Olson answered. "Me, too." And out of the corner of his eye he caught a glimpse of the Elite who dutifully followed them around at a short distance, and he wondered just what kind of bondage Abdullah lived with.

"How does the commerce work here?" the Arab asked.

Olson perched himself on the white wooden rail with the ornate hand-carved balusters. "We do three basic types of business on the river," he said. "First we have our own fleet of ships." He pointed back the way they had come. "You can see their masts sticking up back there. They carry tribute payments to the House of Sa'ud, and bring back plastic and oil on the return. They also do our necessary business with other branches by carrying goods for trade that supply our basic needs. We barter on the river with independents who come in and deal their wares directly to the people on the docks. We also load and unload the ships that come from the other branches with our trade consignments."

"Sounds like you keep busy."

"Depends on the time of year."

"Cat!" someone called from the second landing.

Olson turned to see Wilkes standing up top, pointing out the wheelhouse window. He turned and followed the man's finger. There, dead ahead, and not more than one hundred fifty yards distant, was the Yid liner, the one they had tossed out the day before. It sat there big as you please, its starred flag unfurled and rippling proudly in the river wind.

"Yid liner!" Wilkes shouted up and down the boat, and he

was going to make an issue out of it whether Olson wanted to or not.

"You allow them in this harbor?" Abdullah asked, his voice husky.

"We threw them out yesterday," Olson returned, and knew immediately that words weren't going to solve anything.

The other Execs were already gathering on the prow, and Pop was nearly jumping up and down with glee. Something would have to be done.

"Get the gun ready," Olson said, and Pop started whistling. Climbing up on the gun, the Engy straddled the long barrel and shinnied up it to unplug the thing.

"What are you going to do?" Abdullah asked.

"We're gonna blow them out of the water," Wilkes walked up and said. "They shouldn't have been here at all."

"We thought they were leaving yesterday," Junex Harry said from the midst of the crowd.

"'The company does business with Yids?" Abdullah asked.

"Not as a general rule," Olson replied, flinching. What were they doing here? He was sure they were leaving.

The Elite had run to the rail, climbing up on it. "Devils!" he screamed, shaking his fists. "Infidels!"

Confusion reigned on deck. Everybody was talking at once and moving around. Olson kept looking from the Yid liner to the cannon and back again. Pop was unlatching the safety catches.

"Load it up!" VeePee Norman with the long nose and thick lips said. "Let's go!"

And the back of the thing was unscrewed and Wilkes was there shoving one of the big, heavy shells into it, and Olson still couldn't figure out why the Yids were still around.

"Let's go!" VeePee Norman said again.

"She's ready!" Pop called.

Olson had no idea how to fire the gun. He also had no desire to shoot at the Yids. He quickly saw a solution that would help on all accounts.

"Wilkes!" he said. "Take the gun!"

The Junex looked at him in something akin to amazement, unable to figure out why such an obvious Mover would step away from such obvious glory.

"Yes sir!" he said, and climbed up into the metal seat. Olson and Abdullah stepped aside so he could have a wide berth.

Wilkes began cranking, the gun swinging to the right, the

barrel tracking downward. "Come on," Wilkes purred, "come on."

His hand poised over the firing mechanism. "There, there . . . gotcha!" he yelled, and banged the fire control.

In that instant, Olson knew there was a reason why the Yids had stayed on the river, and he knew there was a reason why he saw Rennie's people on the dock, and he knew there was a reason he hadn't seen Gret all night, and he knew that all the reasons were the same reason.

Even before he saw the spark in the mechanism, he was moving. Abdullah was closest to him. Throwing himself at the man, they both broke through the rail and fell, and the whole deck went up in a huge explosion before they even hit the water.

And Olson's mind flashed as the barge went up in a huge fireball of wood and metal splinters and pieces of bodies. He heard two splashes as gray smoke blew over like hot fog, and then the world closed in around him, enveloping him in a warm and protective cocoon.

* * *

Why is betrayal the only truth that sticks?
—Old World Lament

Said Lord Mohammed, "Now the adultery of the eye is to look with an eye of desire on the wife of another; and the adultery of the tongue is to utter what is forbidden."
—The Prophet Mohammed

XXX

The Streets

Olson dreamed of quiet, murky peace, and when the voices invaded the dream, he didn't want to leave it. He remembered fire; he remembered water; he understood betrayal. Gret was the only one who'd know he would be leading the tour, the only one who could have betrayed him to Rennie.

They were pulling on him, but he couldn't—or wouldn't—help them. Voices jumbling in, yelling that other fella's name, and he tried to tell him to bury him in his own name, but the words just wouldn't come out.

He was lying flat on a board, being carried above everyone's head. He tried to open his eyes but could only focus on the broken shards of the mirror of his existence. People everywhere, staring, yelling, raining words and water and millions and millions of white, white roses.

They came for Gret sometime in midmorning. She knew it was daytime because a tiny crack of gray light had edged its way around the tightly pulled bedroom blind several hours earlier and hazed the room to recognizable form.

She hurt all over from the position she had been forced to assume all night. With no way to help it, she had loosed her bladder and bowels onto the bed and then been forced to lie in it. She felt violated in every possible way, less than human in any possible way.

Marty Jerny and Billy Fain were leering at her from the bedroom door.

"Smells kinda bad, don't it?" Billy said, holding his nose, and Jerny laughed along with him.

"Looks like this one hasn't been housebroke yet," Jerny replied.

She looked at them with dead eyes, as they moved toward her, Billy shaking his head. "Sure is a looker, though," he said, and began running hands along her body, pulling roughly on her breasts.

She suffered the hands on her, abstracted them to the dusty trash bin where the bad memories go; but when she felt herself starting to respond, she screamed at the top of her voice out of sheer saturnalian repulsion.

The scream was deep and guttural, so animalistic that it made the men jump back in amazement.

"God," Billy rasped, voice shaken.

"Let's just get her out of here," Jerny said, and they quickly began to untie her. She lay there impassive, not caring whether she was untied or not. What difference would it make? What possible difference?

"C'mon, sweet thing," Jerny said, and they grabbed her under the shoulders and hoisted her up. "Time to go home. The party's over."

She was on her feet, moving them, surprised that she even could. Still holding her arms, they guided her through the living room where Myrt, the Houris from the night before, sat curled up on the sofa, smiling wide and nodding her head in satisfaction.

Moving her to the front door, they opened it and shoved her out into the hallway, where she stumbled, fell hard against the wall. Billy tossed her wisp of clothing out after her.

"Y'all come back now," he said, and slammed the door.

She lay there for a moment, huddled against the wall until she found the will to get into her clothes and wander away.

Not knowing where she wanted to go, she made it to the elevator and pushed the button, hoping that it would simply take her where she needed to be. The doors opened after a time and she stepped in.

Two Execs who she didn't know were already in there. They crinkled their noses in distaste when they saw her. Keeping her head lowered, she stared at the floor and stood against the wall, her arms crossed protectively across her chest.

"What do you think happened?" the taller of the two Execs said to the other.

"A vendetta," the other said. "That's the only thing I could figure. Pop kept that gun in perfect order."

Gret could hear their words, and somewhere in there, they began to make sense to her.

"How did they get around Pop to get to the gun?"

"He spent about an hour in the galley getting breakfast," the smaller man said. "That's all the time they would have needed. It's funny, too. That new Exec, Cat, and the Arab went overboard. Everybody else got blown to pieces except for Pop. Everything came apart around him and missed him completely."

"What's funny about that?"

"When he saw what happened to his gun, he killed himself." Both men laughed loudly.

"What about Cat?" Gret asked in a tiny voice.

"What?" The men glared at her.

"What happened to Cat?"

The smaller man grimaced and shook his head. "Don't know," he said. "They took him to the dispensary, but I don't know what kind of shape he was in."

When the elevator reached the lobby, Gret at least knew where she was going.

"Here he comes. Here he comes. Come ahead on, boy. Come ahead."

Olson's eyes fluttered to see Jerry Joe, the whole left side of his face encased in slick brown leather, looking down at him.

"Welcome back." He grinned with the right side of his mouth. "Ya got my old bed."

Olson tried to sit up, but a bolt of burning pain that ran straight up his spine and exploded in his brain drove him back to the mattress.

"What kind of shape am I in?" he asked. His mind had turned to Gret, but he forced it away.

Mr. Elwood and Abdullah ibn Faisel joined Jerry Joe, looking down.

"Ya just got hit up the side of the head with Wilkes's head," Jerry Joe said. "A little shrapnel, a little concussion. You'll be up kickin' ass before you know it."

Abdullah had laid a hand on his shoulder. "You will live," he said with authority. "I will see to it. You saved my life. My gratitude is without boundaries."

"You're okay?" Olson asked, and almost slipped back into unconsciousness.

"You're a hero." Mr. Elwood smiled. "A bona fide hero."

"What about everybody else?"

"Dead," Mr. Elwood said immediately. "The whole stinking boatload. What happened?"

"Rennie," Olson replied. "I think he was trying to get me. I saw a couple of his people on the dock when I went aboard."

"But how—"

"Not now," Olson snapped, and Gret's face kept popping into his brain. He clenched his fist, saw the stitches on his arm. "Everybody's dead?" he asked.

Jerry Joe nodded. "Couldn't find enough of most of them to bury."

Olson forced his brain to gear. If the whole department was wiped out, there was nothing to stop him from moving up. He looked at Jerry Joe, the only man senior to him on the river.

"How'd you like to die?" he asked him.

*   *   *

Gret sloshed quickly through the rain and the water, her flimsy
gown stuck tight to her, and it was probably only the horrible cast to
her face that kept the street people from approaching her.

She reached the hospital block, and the crowds got much
thicker. They were everywhere, far worse than the day before.
They tumbled out of the front of the building like a human
cornucopia, spilling out onto the rain-filled streets. The stench of
disease and death hung physically over everything like the rain
clouds hung over the city. Crying and moaning echoed up and
down the block. The dead and dying lay in the water, some
floating in the deeper sections.

Picking up the hem of her dress, she covered nose and
mouth with it and moved into the logjam, picking her way
carefully to the hospital door. Hands reached for her, filthy
hands, hands begging someone who was at least clean to do
something for him.

She reached the door. It was open, a stand of sandbags
blocking the water out. Climbing over the barricade, she was
stopped by a fuzztop with a rag tied around his face.

"Full up," he said, holding out a hand. "No more room."

"I've come to see someone," she said.

"No more room," the fuzztop answered.

"Please," she said. "An Exec."

"Who?"

"Junex Catanine," she returned.

The man chewed his lower lip for several seconds before
pointing out Cat's bed to her. It was the same one Jerry Joe had
been in yesterday.

She saw him through a curtain of people, moving and
shuffling, trying to keep from falling over one another. Her heart
jerked. He was still alive!

She flooded with feeling when she saw him, realized how
much his life had entangled with hers. She moved to him
automatically, without thought, picking her way over the bodies
that separated them. She had nearly caused his death; she had to
see how nearly.

Olson caught sight of her halfway across the large room,
and if he could have willed her away, he would have done it.

"Leave me for a few minutes," he said to the others, and
there was a catch in his voice.

Mr. Elwood turned to follow the line of Olson's sight.

When he saw Gret, he flashed back around, not understanding why his face had turned the color of the bandages on his head.

Without words, they all stepped away from the bed, Abdullah watching the woman's progress with keen interest.

She moved to him, past Mr. Elwood and Jerry Joe without a word. Her head was set, intent, her face was a mixture of pain and relief. She reached him, reached out to touch him.

"Oh, Cat, I . . ."

"What do you want?" he said, jerking his arm away from her.

She stepped back a pace, lips quivering. "I . . . I just wanted to see that you were all right. I . . ."

"Well, you can tell your friend Rennie that it didn't work out the way it was supposed to."

She was shaking her head, her eyes spilling over with tears. "No," she whimpered. "That's not the way it was."

His eyes were diamond bright and just as hard. "Then suppose you tell me how it was. Tell me that you didn't betray me."

"Cat . . ."

"Tell me!"

Her eyes were wide and vacant as she backed away from him in horror. Olson was the power and he could hurt her. Stumbling over a body on the floor, she went down hard, Mr. Elwood hurrying to help her up.

She looked at the Director, eyes darting, then pulled away and hurried into the crowd, leaving Mr. Elwood standing there staring after her with his hands on his hips.

Abdullah moved quickly to Olson's bedside. "You sent the woman away," he said. "She had love in her eyes for you."

Olson laughed dryly and turned his face to the wall. "She's just a Houris," he whispered.

PART THREE

And of His signs
is that thou seest the earth humble;
then, when We send down water upon it,
it quivers, and swells.
Surely He who quickens it is He who
quickens the dead; surely He is powerful
over everything.
                                        —The Koran

Who breathes must suffer, and who thinks must
*   mourn;*
And he alone is blessed who ne'er was born.
                                —Old World Wisdom

    The dogs bark, but the caravan
    Moves on.
                        —Bedouin Proverb

XXXI
The Streets

Gret ran through the crowded streets, the grimy clawers
somewhere behind her, laughing, trying to catch her. She was
nearly naked, her Houris clothes hanging in muddy tatters,
flapping behind her as she ran.

And there were people all around, a nightmare world of
people, jamming, grabbing, shouting. It all passed before her in
flashes as she tried to keep her feet, to keep moving through the
sea of reaching hands. She was drowning in an ocean of people,
alone, terrified.

A hand reached her in the middle of a crowd, grabbing her
by her flowing hair, jerking her back. She fell in the mud, feet
shuffling past, threatening to trample her. Almost giving in, she
somehow found the strength to crawl through the moving legs
and the nightmare images.

Something ahead, an opening, a clearing. She struggled to
knee level, crouching, staying below the shouts of her pursuers.
Men, all men, her enemy. She struggled through bludgeoning

knees and curses and reached daylight—an alleyway, jammed
full with broken crates and old televisions, a television graveyard.

She jumped up and charged into the alley, diving up and
over a large pile of trash, coming down hard on her shoulder and
rolling to a stop in the middle of a pile of televisions.

They were still shouting for her, still looking, but the
sounds were getting farther away. The ocean current had carried
them farther down the street. She was safe for the moment.

She lay there panting, getting her breath, moving gingerly,
hoping that nothing was broken.

"They're gone," a voice said, and she jerked around
behind her to see a giant Engy staring down at her. She jumped
up, tried to run, but he grabbed her shoulder, pulled her back
while she struggled against him to no avail. She had seen giant
sport Engies fuck before; they could literally tear a woman apart.

"It's all right," another voice said, a female voice. "We
won't hurt you."

She writhed in the giant's grip, twisted her head to the
woman. She was a citizen. Two small children stood beside her.
She let herself go and listened to the giant's vibrations, feeling
nothing but goodwill oozing from him.

Breathing deeply, Gret calmed her mind, tried to slow down
the skip-jumps to something more natural. The Engy released
her.

"We'd better get you out of sight," the woman said. "Your
kind are not very welcome on the streets right now."

Gret opened her mouth to speak. "Th-thank . . . you," she
managed to rasp through a throat strained from screaming, for
her nightmare on the streets had been a long one.

"Save your strength," the woman said. "Follow me."

She turned and walked farther back into the alley. Gret
made to follow, but once the terror had drained out of her, the
energy went with it. She slumped back against the Engy, weak.

"Carry her, Jorge," the woman said, and her tone was
kindly.

The Engy grunted and picked Gret up easily, as if her
weight had also drained away with her energy. She remembered
looking into his face, at the genuine smile there. And then the
whole world spun around. . . .

When she awoke, she was in a house, a house made of
televisions. The walls were piled up tv's, their dead eyes staring
listlessly inward, reflecting on every screen the small campfire

that burned in the center of the room. The chairs were small tv's, the tables large ones.

A group of people ringed the house. They all stared at Gret. There may have been ten of them. Day had turned to night, and the rain still fell, part of it dripping inside through the cracks in the pyramidlike television roof of the house. A hole was left open at the top to allow smoke to exit.

Someone had thrown an overcoat over her and it felt good, secure. She snuggled up tighter under it.

"Welcome back," said the woman who had first talked to Gret. She moved over to her, stroking Gret's hair. "Are you feeling any better?"

"How long have I been . . . been . . ."

"A long time," the woman said.

She tried to sit up, but was still awfully weak. Getting up as far as her elbows, she gazed around the campfire. There were several children and several citizens, men and women. Besides the giant, there were two other Engies—one a male Breeder with the gene-mix computer grafted onto his torso, the other a female Picker/Harvester with an L-shaped spine that made her permanently bent over. Pickers were usually paired with squat stocky Miners who could carry them around on their shoulders when away from the fields, but if this Picker had a symby-partner, he was nowhere to be found.

This was the first time Gret had ever seen humans mixing with Engies, and she realized that she had a measure of acceptance here because of that fact.

"My name's JoBeth," the woman said. Her hair was dark and long and she had managed to keep it reasonably clean. She was a young woman made old by hard years. She wore a dress made from resewn jeans.

Gret managed a smile. "Gret," she returned. "I want to thank you for what you did back there. As soon as I can get myself together, I'll be on my way."

"Nonsense," the woman said. "How long since you've eaten?"

Gret shook her head; she was unable to separate the nightmare into time frames. "I . . . I don't know," she said. "Days, I guess."

"That's what I thought," JoBeth replied. "Harley. Get this lady something to warm her insides."

A man in a tattered jumper grunted himself to his feet and

moved to the fire. A kettle made from a cathode tube bubbled over the flames.

"Another mouth to feed," the man grumbled.

"Oh, shut up," JoBeth said, turning to him. "You always manage to get your belly full."

"I really don't need to . . ." Gret began.

"Shh," JoBeth said, putting a finger to Gret's lips. "Harley's a good man; he's just got a big mouth. Who's Olson?"

Gret sat up straight. "What do you mean?"

JoBeth narrowed her eyes. "You kept calling for him when you were out before."

Gret sagged. "Just someone I used to know."

"Then you're alone?" the giant Engy asked from across the room.

Gret nodded. "Alone," she said.

Harley walked up and handed her a tin filled with a murky gray liquid. "We'll have to get her some clothes," he said to JoBeth.

"We'll work it out." The woman smiled. "There's always room for one more."

Gret brought the tin to her lips. It had a gamy odor. She drank gratefully, realizing how hungry she was for the first time.

"Rat soup," JoBeth said, "with a little barley mixed in. Best we could do."

"It's wonderful," Gret said, and meant it.

"Why'd they kick you out on the streets?" Harley asked.

JoBeth stood up and slapped him on the shoulder. "Would you be good!" she said. "Gret's personal life is no concern of yours."

"I made someone mad," Gret said between sips, "someone powerful. I left before they could kick me out."

"Made 'em mad, huh?" Harley said, smiling. "Then left on your own. Well, anybody that can walk on an Exec is okay with me." He wiped a dirty hand on his dirty pants and held it out to her. "Welcome."

Gret shook his hand.

JoBeth slid over a television and sat beside Gret while she ate. "Guess we're all kind of misfits here," she said. She shook her head. "The crowd on the streets is like some kind of . . . animal or something."

"The group mind," Gret said.

"Not too much like people," JoBeth continued. "We all

came in here to get away from it, to try to keep something together. Guess we're all family now.''

"Family," Gret repeated, and the notion appealed to her.

"Do you have any fresh news about the Houston Jits?" one of the other women asked.

Gret shook her head. "I'm sorry," she said.

"Well, I'd just as soon get back to the fields and take my chances," Harley said.

"If you got out, you'd never get back in," Gret replied.

"Sometimes I think maybe that wouldn't be so bad," the man said.

And for the very first time in her life Gret found the concept of living outside the walls something other than a fate worse than death. She was beginning to find the limits within herself, and it made her feel good—strong, like rat soup on an empty stomach.

* * *

> *And if they desire treachery against thee,
> they have tricked God before; but He has
> given thee power over them; and God is
> All-knowing, All-wise.*
> —The Koran
> VIII. The Spoils

XXXII
Convent, Louisiana
Western Sector—America

They propped Milander up against a tree where he could watch the swollen Mississippi rumble past on its headlong charge towards Orleans and the sea. All around him, the old city crumbled to ruin as nature reclaimed what was once hers completely. Ivy climbed cement and brick walls; thick, choking weeds pushed up through buckling asphalt streets; the hulks of old auts twinkled rust red in the always humid air and provided homes for a number of different types of bugs and small animals.

Despite the wetness, his people worked, the sounds of saws and hammers setting up a clack-clack cadence to go along with the steady shush of the rain. They were building rafts out of pieces of the old buildings, rafts that would be taking some of them to Orleans.

The river was busy, too. For the two days they had been camped at Convent, a steady stream of Jits came to meet them. Somehow the others knew, others from everywhere. They were flocking to Milander, joining his army of love.

They knew.

They just knew.

And they all came down the river, each boatload a joyous event and a cause for celebration. Milander's army was growing, swelling like the river. Orleans was barely three days away. It would have to topple; it could not withstand his assault on its emotions. After Orleans, it would all fall, every bit of it.

So he lay there, propped up on his stretcher, and watched the boats come down the river to him. The Mississippi wasn't just a river; it was an artery, an artery that he was getting ready to tap and drain.

"M-Mr. Milander?"

Milander turned his head away from the rushing waters and looked at Danny Ford. "Yes?" he returned quietly, and smiled with the side of his face that wasn't paralyzed.

Danny worked his mouth silently for a minute before speaking. "The g-generals are . . . here to s-see you."

"Good," Milander said. "Bring them over."

Danny limped away, returning a minute later with the generals. There were four of them, all of them stubble-bearded, all of them naked. Milander didn't believe in uniforms, but knew the troops were going to have to recognize the generals at a glance. Taking their clothes was the perfect solution—distinction without ego gratification.

He then gave them names to fit their duties. Admiral Nelson would be taking the rafts down the river. General Eisenhower would be the main assault leader. Hannibal coordinated the mass troop movements, and Napoleon commanded the artillery.

They stood at attention before him.

"The beards are growing out very nicely," he told them. "At ease."

They slouched, Napoleon, the smallest of them, rubbing his

beard. "It itches," he said, and shoved his cowboy hat a little farther back on his head.

"That will pass," Milander said, and remembered reading that somewhere once. "Would someone get me a stick?"

Hannibal retrieved a broken branch from the ground and cracked it over his knee, handing the smallest part to Milander.

"Thanks," the man returned, and began drawing in the dirt. "How are the preparations coming?"

"The rafts will be ready by tomorrow," Admiral Nelson spoke up. "It's going quicker than we had expected because of the influx of new people who already have rafts or boats."

"Excellent."

With that, the admiral fell, twitching, to the ground, caught heavily by a grand-mal seizure. The others ignored it and went on.

"The river will be dangerous for us," Milander said. "They will have it carefully defended, and I don't feel our greatest success will be in that area."

"Then why do it?" Eisenhower asked.

Milander stopped drawing in the dirt for a minute and pointed the stick at the general. "Because it will force them to divide their troops to defend the river and the walls. We'll only put our sickest people on the river."

Nelson began gagging loudly. Napoleon knelt quickly beside him and jammed a small twig in his mouth to keep him from swallowing his tongue.

"As soon as the rafts are finished, we'll move on," Milander said. "We still have the element of surprise on our side, but it's only a matter of time before they discover us. I want to be as close as possible to the city before that happens. Somewhere we can dig in."

"We are nearly sixty thousand now," Eisenhower said.

Milander nodded, his attention centered on his scrawl in the ground. "Is there enough to eat?"

"More than enough," Hannibal said.

"How's morale?"

"Spirits are high," Napoleon said. "Our purpose is solid and clear . . . even with the new people. We will spread the word to Orleans."

Milander smiled. "It is a battle we cannot lose. We have sixty thousand separate chances at achieving victory. Look here."

He was pointing the stick down at his sand picture. "I want you to build me one of these," he said.

They all squatted down around the picture, studying it.
"What is it?" Hannibal asked.

"It's called a catapult," Milander said.

"What's it for?"

"You'll see."

Admiral Nelson was beginning to come around. Moaning
slightly, he gagged back to wakefulness, his eyes focused on the
sky. "Balloon," he said weakly.

Milander looked down at him. "What?"

The man rubbed his face. "Balloon," he said again.

They looked up to see a Light of the World balloon floating
gently overhead.

"They've found us," Eisenhower said.

Milander grunted. "Bring me the laser," he said.

Hannibal and Napoleon hurried off, returning quickly with
the ornate little cannon.

"Do their balloon," Milander told Napoleon, "but don't
drain the charge. I want to save some of the juice for later."

"Yes, sir," Napoleon said, saluting.

They set up the weapon on a large tree stump. Sighting was
easy with such a large, slow-moving object. When he had it
dead, he squeezed the juicer, and slid a tiny pink hot line of light
across the wide expanse of the balloon's surface.

"Enough," Milander said, and Napoleon shut down the
laser.

The balloon hung for a time, then began losing altitude,
falling in extra slow motion to the ground.

"Be careful with them," Milander said. "And bring the
survivors to me. I want to kiss them."

*   *   *

*So God makes clear His signs for you; haply
you will understand.*

—The Koran
II. The Cow

XXXIII

LOW Headquarters
Rub Al Khali

The studio lights glared hot as the desert Sun as Faisel ibn Faisel Al Sa'ud sat with Misha'al in the small studio. He sat at a desk, his hands folded upon it, and the prophet sat on a folding chair just outside camera range. Behind Faisel hung the flag of Sa'ud, a background of pale green with a scimitar seemingly cutting a swath right through the back of his head.

There were three cameras that operated automatically, and the man who ran it all sat chained in the glassed-in booth, lest he be free to take advantage of Faisel's vulnerability.

"I have the dream every night," Faisel said. "It becomes more alive, more vivid with each passing day."

"Perhaps it is something you ate," Misha'al returned, his black robes wrapping him bodily in the shadows.

"This is serious!" Faisel snapped. "I fear something is happening."

"Mike test," came the amplified voice from the booth.

"Testing," Faisel said as the boom mike dropped closer and closer to his face. "Testing...sifre...wahhed...etnayn. Testing."

"Okay."

"You brought the woman here," Misha'al said. "You killed to bring her here."

"I brought her here on your recommendation."

The prophet laughed. "Since when does the lowly servant of the King of the World command the master?"

"What will I do?"

Misha'al shrugged and pulled his feet up on the chair with him. "You could always let her go."

"No!" Faisel said loudly. "I love her...I must have her."

"But not while Abdullah lives."

"You know the law."

"Yes."

231

Faisel laid his head on his arms on the desktop. "I feel I am caught up in something I have no control over," he said wearily. "I cannot let the woman go, yet I fear every minute she is here—unreasoning fear. I want her for my wife, yet I cannot have her. I stand on the edge of madness with this, yet am unable to jump either way."

Misha'al smiled slightly. "You must obey God's Will."

"Which the oracle translated as taking the woman."

"According to the law."

Faisel slammed both fists on the table. "You talk in circles!"

"Watch those decibels," came the higher authority in the booth.

"You've done all you can," Misha'al said. "You must have patience."

"We are receiving transmission from New Mecca," came the voice.

Faisel sat up quickly, straightening the blue ghutra on his head. "Put it through here," he said, pointing to the small monitor screen inset in the desk.

A minute later, a head shot of the captain of the Elite staticked on the screen. "Greetings from the Western Sector," the man said.

"What has happened?" Faisel said. "I felt a tremor in my heart."

"There has been a tragedy," the man said, "an explosion on the LOW barge. One of our number has been killed."

Faisel felt his pulse thumping. "And my brother?"

The Elite blinked. "He was thrown clear of the blast and was unhurt."

Faisel clenched his fists. "Who caused this terrible explosion that nearly undid my brother?"

"I do not know," the man replied.

"You really don't know?" Faisel returned.

The Elite shook his head.

"Just stay close to him. You never know when he may need your . . . help."

The man's eyes widened somewhat above his veil. "He resists our attempts at control very strenuously. He even attempted to fire me."

"You work for me," Faisel said. "Always." He tapped his

chest with an index finger. "Just remember that no one can offer you what I offer you."

"That would be difficult to forget."

"Stay in constant touch."

"As you command."

The monitor face vanished in a haze of snow, and Faisel studied it for a moment. When he turned to Misha'al, his dark eyes were shining. "Let us set a limit to my pain," he said.

Misha'al narrowed his eyes. "You have something in mind," he said.

Faisel spoke to the control booth. "Tape this for showing in the Western Sector," he said.

"Right," returned the voice. "Fifteen seconds."

He took several deep breaths, and settled his face into an angry scowl.

"Five seconds . . . rolling!"

Faisel looked deeply at the camera with the red light glowing like a demon eye. "People of the West," he said, voice low and melodious. "A disturbing report has just reached me concerning your behavior toward my brother, Abdullah. I sent him to the City of Orleans as an ambassador of peace and goodwill. You repaid me by making a traitorous attempt on his life."

The red light switched to the close-up camera, and Faisel turned to face that. "The justice of Allah is swift and severe, and your treachery will be repaid in kind. You have seven days to successfully complete my brother's mission for him. At the end of that time period, if total reparation has not been made, my brother has the authorization to use the Jitterbug key on your gold dome."

Pulling the ring of keys out from around his neck, Faisel held them up for the close-up camera that automatically dollied up for a good look. "Remember," he said. "Seven days."

Then, just for good measure, he jangled the keys around.

"Cut!" came the booth voice. "Excellent."

Faisel nodded. "Run that message forty times today," he said.

* * *

There is a polish for everything that taketh away rust; and the polish for the heart is the remembrance of God.

—The Prophet Mohammed

Dispatch is the soul of business, and nothing contributes more to Dispatch than Method.

—LOW Corporate Motto

XXXIV
Orleans—The Streets

The old church building was of a style that had been out of use when the building was made. It was a remnant of a time gone by, a time that existed somewhere in the winding corridors of memory, a time that was real once, but held no reality for the people who built the church. It was from a fantasy time, a time of angels and devils and good and evil—a time of Hope.

The church had long stone steps leading up to concentric archway entrances. Stone on stone, the building then spired majestically toward the rainy heavens, thrusting gray-brown towers into the low-hanging clouds. The church was made for rain, looked comfortable in it. Perhaps it shared the rain with the fantasy time, a link with a reality that once was. Perhaps the building was simply as dreary as the rain. The church was locked up now, used as a storehouse.

Gret huddled in the alcove at the top of the stone stairs. The burlap robe she wore was rough on skin used to the feel of more delicate fabrics. Her long, glowing hair was smeared with mud to cut the highlights, and she had it tied back behind her head in a severe bun. Her face was dirt-dusted to hide the spray of freckles, and dark glasses put out the fire that was her eyes. She was surviving, helping the family survive.

"Did you bring it?" she asked the large man who stood before her.

The man's flat face was twisted out of shape by the weight of misery to where he looked like a human mask of tragedy. He wore a tattered black coat that hung all the way to the ground. From within the coat he produced a small loaf of bread, holding it out to her.

She reached and he snatched it back.

"After," he said.

She nodded. "Fair enough."

The streets ran equally with rain and people. They milled aimlessly, directionless. Faisel's message of impending doom lay heavily on everyone, and the city with its locked gates was beginning to look like a prison to them all. Gret could physically feel the tension that permeated everything, and knew that when human beings were pushed to the wall they would fight more viciously than the most vicious animal.

"Let's go," the man said.

Gret reached out her hands. "I'm going to touch your face," she said, and he flinched slightly before allowing her cool fingers to rest on the raw nerves that made up his psyche.

Closing her eyes, Gret let herself escape the doom which her unwitting betrayal had brought to her, and sank into the dusty pit that her client called home.

"You work with your hands," she said, "in the factory."

"Yeah," he crooned. "That's right."

"Your father beat you . . . and your mother."

"Yeah."

"They both died when you were young."

"They got ground up in a machine."

Gret had left before she could be arrested. Apparently she had enough survival instinct for that.

"You've fathered five children by two wives," she said, and the sheer weight of sorrow of the man's life was a huge boulder pushing down on her. "Both of your wives died in childbirth. Two of your children survive, but you don't know where they are."

The man's eyes welled tears and he wiped his nose on the sleeve of his filthy coat. "That's right."

Gret was crying, too. "You have pain," she stammered, "deep inside of you."

She put her hands on his chest, tapping the pain, wishing she could drain it.

"Will . . . will I survive?" he asked.

"None of us survive," she returned.

"Will I survive the Jitterbug?"

She looked deeply into his troubled eyes and saw all the way through him. Death rolled off him like gas off the marshes. He was immersed in death, swooning in it, drowning in it.

"Yes," she managed after a moment. "You will survive."

"Damn him!" Mr. Elwood spat, as he watched another replay of Faisel ibn Faisel's message on the television in the antechamber. "What's he trying to do to us?"

Olson turned to him from the rain-splattered fiftieth-floor window. "A lot going on down there," he said, tapping the window obliquely with his knuckles. "The street crowds seem to be all worked up."

"It will get worse," Mr. Elwood returned, and his throat seemed constricted. "It will get a lot worse."

Jerry Joe got up from behind Mr. Elwood's desk and walked over to join Olson at the window. "There's gonna be blood in the streets before this is all over," he said, and Olson turned to watch the reflection of the window light on the slick surface of the man's leather half-face.

"What are we going to do?" he asked.

"Not a damned thing," Mr. Elwood replied. "What can we do? We're locked in here because of Jits on the outside, and now the whole city's afraid of Jits on the inside."

"The river," Olson said. "We'd better protect the river."

Jerry Joe stared at him with his good eye. "You got a point," he said.

Mr. Elwood moved to the telephone that sat on his desk and picked it up. "Hello . . . hello," he said. "Can I get . . . would you please get off the line? Operator? Operator?"

There was a knock on the door.

"Disappear," Olson told Jerry Joe.

The man nodded silently and moved to a closet on the other side of the room.

"This is a priority call," Mr. Elwood yelled, a finger in his free ear. "Operator . . . would you please clear the lines . . . I need the office of Port Authority . . . no, not Mort. Port. Port! Would you clear the fucking lines?"

Olson moved to the door and opened it a crack. A graying fuzztop peered through the crack. "They're all here," he said, inclining his head over his shoulder.

"Thanks," Olson returned, and shut the door.

"Operator!" Mr. Elwood yelled. "Clear the line, this is a priority call! Hello . . . hello?"

He slammed the phone down and sat at the desk, writing furiously on bright white rice paper.

Jerry Joe stuck his head out of the closet. "All clear?"

"Come on out," Olson said, "but make sure that door always stays locked."

"Sure," the man answered, and moved out of the closet. He went over to the small tableful of food that was set out for him and began to nibble. "Guess if you gotta stay somewhere, this is as good a spot as any." And he plunked himself down in a deep cushioned chair with a sigh of contentment. Olson wondered how long he would stay contented.

"There," Mr. Elwood said, heating the sealing wax on a candle and fixing the seal with his big gold ring. He folded the letter in thirds and began rooting through a drawer for an envelope. "I've authorized the fuzztops to go in and close down the harbor. We'll block the streets leading to it and not let anybody in at all."

"We're going to need to clear the river itself of traffic, too," Olson said, and put a hand to the back of his head, feeling the small bandage that was the only remnant of his brush with death at the river.

"You can take care of that later," Mr. Elwood said, stuffing the letter into the envelope that he dug out of the bottom drawer. "Why don't we get Gret to deliver this."

"She's not here," Olson said, moving to look out the window again. One of the balloons was floating by, trying unsuccessfully to call the citizens to prayer.

"Where is she?"

"Gone."

"Why?"

Olson turned to look at him. "She's just gone, that's all."

The old man shrugged. "You depended too much on her anyway," he said, and put it out of his mind.

"The department heads are out there," Olson said, angry at himself for missing Gret.

Mr. Elwood looked at his watch. "Good. We've got a little time until the full board meeting begins. Let's go."

They moved to the door, Jerry Joe getting up to follow them that far. "Don't forget I'm here," the man said.

Olson smiled at him. "Lock up behind us," he said.

They moved into the boardroom, Faisel's bigger-than-life image on the wall taking on new meanings for all of them. Out of the twenty departments that ran Orleans, nine of them were represented at this preliminary meeting. Seven department heads sat at the large oblong table. Olson represented the river, Mr. Elwood administration, making nine. They were all dressed in their best three-piece suits, and their red-and-white-checked ghutras were cleaned and pressed, the tails hanging in neat creases around their heads.

Olson took a place at the table, and Mr. Elwood groaned into his big chair on the dais. The room got silent immediately.

"We're here for a reason," he said, and paused a moment to look at them all. When he spoke again, it was slowly, with marked intensity.

"There will be an attempt to unseat me at this meeting today," he said without inflection. "It will come upon my recommendation conferring senior-VeePee status on Junex Catanine."

There was a buzz around the table, and Olson noticed everyone stealing glances at him.

"Probably most of you have never seen Mr. Catanine before . . ."

Olson watched the eyebrows go up.

"But I'm sure you've all heard of his heroic deed at the river yesterday that saved the life of Abdullah ibn Faisel."

They all applauded politely.

"You are all here because of either your loyalty to me or your hatred of VeePee Rennie Du'camp, who is even now marshaling his support against me. I'll not mince words here. I have chosen Mr. Catanine to succeed me as Regional Director."

Mr. Elwood waited until the furor died down before continuing. "I'm not a well man. I do not have long to live. I know that all of you have more seniority than Mr. Catanine, but do you have the power to hold my office if Du'camp tries to take it from you?"

Getting up, the Director walked to the jump window and

pushed it open. "Evaluate carefully your ability to stand up to Du'camp, and remember what happens if you fail."

He returned to his seat. "Mr. Catanine's strong and fair. I'm sure he will reward your loyalty to him a hundredfold. He's a hero, so maybe the citizens will even get behind him. These are troubled times; they demand strong leadership.

"I'm sure many of you are totally unconvinced. Fine. Think about it, but vote with me today. I'm going to stick my neck out on this thing a mile. If I lose this vote, Rennie will take it as a no-confidence mandate and call for another vote right away. You people better remember which side your bread is buttered on. You have anything to say, Cat?"

Olson stood up and walked to the front of the room, his white silk suit moving fluidly with each step. He turned and stared at them. "I know how most of you probably feel," he said. "I'm the new kid in town and don't deserve anything. I understand that feeling; I sympathize with it. But that's as far as it goes. You're businessmen and this is a business deal. Put aside your feelings and vote your pocketbook. I guarantee I'll help out each and every one of you when I take over. I also guarantee I'll bury those of you who don't help out."

He pointed to Mr. Elwood. "This man runs the Company in Orleans, and you are all Company men. I expect you to do the right thing."

Short and sweet. He strode resolutely back to his seat, his face set, his jaw tight. When they looked at him now, the glances were furtive, fearful. He wanted them to realize just what was on the line here; he thought they did now.

"Questions?" Mr. Elwood asked.

VeePee Glower from Manufacturing Branch cleared his throat. "You're talking about a complete change of leadership here," he said. "When is all this supposed to take place?"

"As soon as we can work it out," Mr Elwood said.

"What happens if you get your vote today?"

Mr. Elwood drew a ragged breath. "VeePee Du'camp has already challenged my leadership. He won't back down from that."

"That means interdepartmental war," Glower said. "In the middle of all this."

Mr. Elwood shrugged. "It wasn't my idea."

The door at the end of the room opened, and two of

Abdullah's Elite slid silently in, heads darting. Abdullah himself strode in behind them.

"I hope you don't mind," he said.

"Not at all." Mr. Elwood smiled, standing. "Come. Take this chair."

"No thank you," Abdullah said, and walked to the jump window. "I'll stay here by the fresh air."

With that, he pushed open the oft-used window and sat on its ledge, looking down. Taking a deep breath, he looked over at Olson. "It makes me happy to see you in such excellent shape."

"Me too," Olson returned.

At that moment, Rennie walked in, lean and hard in his red suit. The Elite rushed over to check him at the door.

"That won't be necessary," Mr. Elwood said with annoyance. "Weapons are not allowed in here."

"Thank you . . . Mr. Director," Rennie said, moving to his seat.

The other board members followed quickly behind Rennie, leading Olson to suspect that the man had conducted his own private meeting beforehand.

When everyone was seated, Mr. Elwood opened the meeting with a recitation from the Koran:

> It is not for any Prophet to have prisoners
> until he make wide slaughter in the land.
> You desire the chance goods of the present world,
> and God desires the world to come; and God is
>   All-mighty, All-wise.
> Had it not been for a prior prescription from
> God, there had afflicted you, for what you took,
>   a mighty chastisement.
> Eat of what you have taken as booty, such as
> is lawful and good; and fear you God; surely
> God is All-forgiving, All-compassionate.

When he was finished, he sat quietly for a moment before speaking. "I thank you all for coming on such short notice. I know things are kind of rough right now, what with the weather and our enlarged population, but it is precisely for these reasons that I felt it necessary to call this special board meeting.

"First of all, I have an unhappy announcement to make. We

must add another name to the tragic toll lost in yesterday's river accident. Junex Jerry Joe died this morning from wounds received in a fair and lawful fight with VeePee Du'camp. We grieve his passing.''

"He wasn't hurt that bad," Rennie said.

"You're obviously mistaken," the Director returned, and spoke again immediately to change the subject. "Secondly, we are here to pay homage to Junex Catanine and his heroic efforts during the river crisis in helping save the life of Abdullah ibn Faisel Al Sa'ud.''

The applause was there again, led by Abdullah himself, who shook his fists high in the air and bellowed loudly.

"And now we have arrived at the problem," Mr. Elwood continued when the noise died down. "As you know, keeping the river clear and protected during these difficult times is of the utmost importance. We have no time for the usual politicking that goes along with succession to office. It has always been my decision in the past to stay out of the process of Exec selection, preferring a more Darwinian approach to leadership. On this occasion, however, I step out of character. With yesterday's tragedy, all senior Execs from the Port Authority were wiped out with a single stroke, leaving Mr. Catanine the sole remaining river Exec. Considering his intelligence and poise under pressure and his obvious track record of late, I find that we would be horribly remiss in not immediately nominating and electing Mr. Catanine to the position of senior VeePee of Port Authority. Do I hear such a nomination?''

"Right here," said Glower, raising his hand.

"I second," Olson said.

"Protest," Rennie said, raising his own hand.

"We recognize VeePee Du'camp," Mr. Elwood said.

"First, I protest Junex Catanine's presence at these proceedings. Second, I certainly protest his seconding of his own nomination.''

Mr. Elwood pursed his lips. "The chair overrules the first protest. Our bylaws are very clear in stating that the highest senior Exec votes at board meetings until such time as someone more senior assumes the position of leadership. Your other protest will stand as a matter of good taste.''

Mr. Elwood glared at Olson, who shrugged in return. "Withdraw that second," he said meekly.

"I second the nomination," said VeePee Pembeck from Raw Materials, one of Mr. Elwood's people.

"The nomination has been made and seconded," Mr. Elwood said. "We will now bring it to a vote."

"Protest," Rennie said matter-of-factly. "The floor should be opened to debate before the vote is cast."

Mr. Elwood nodded tiredly. "Is there any debate on this nomination?"

Rennie raised his hand.

"The chair recognizes VeePee Du'camp."

Rennie stood up and walked to the front of the room, looking and acting invincible. "I'm really surprised," he said, "that a man of Mr. Elwood's character would stoop to trying to shove his nomination down our collective throats."

The room suddenly became quiet as a grave. To attack the Director in public was an unheard-of assault on his position. Rennie smiled like a perpetually grinning skull.

"Before we vote on this," he continued, "I think it behooves us at this time to examine the possible motivations for such a ludicrous nomination. I agree with Mr. Elwood that the river is too important to leave hanging. I also think it's too important to leave in the hands of someone with less than a week's worth of seniority in Orleans. Why not appoint a temporary department head, say a junior VeePee from Shipping and Receiving with close ties to the river. Then, after we've made a decent search for a replacement, we can vote on it."

There were murmurs of affirmation around the table, and Olson watched Mr. Elwood's jaw muscles clenching and unclenching.

"Why is Mr. Elwood in such a hurry for us to confirm his protégé?" Rennie said. "A man whom we know nothing about except that he was lucky enough to fall overboard and take a high official with him. Why is it so important? Why this man?"

Rennie turned and looked accusingly at Mr. Elwood. "Why?" he said loudly, pointing a finger.

"It is not my place to explain anything to you," Mr. Elwood said. "I have made my recommendation."

"See that?" Rennie said theatrically. "He's got no reason. Well, that's all right, because I'll tell you the reason. Mr. Elwood is a sick old man, a man incapable of making reasonable decisions anymore. His obvious incompetence in this matter is the proof. You all know he's incompetent. Vote your knowledge.

We need leadership right now, strong leadership, not old men with flagging brains and two-day wonders from Dallas. Vote this ridiculous nomination down and let's get on to something more constructive.''

With that, Rennie walked back to his seat to a smattering of applause. When it had ceased, Mr. Elwood spoke.

''Apparently this vote is to be a judgment of my competence. So be it. I need explain nothing, except to say that Mr. Catanine is, in my judgment, the most competent person available for the job to be done.

''I have run this city for a long time, and despite our present ills, it runs smoothly, more smoothly than any branch of the tree of LOW. VeePee Du'camp should be so incompetent.''

There was laughter around the room, Abdullah joining in loudly.

''Perhaps it is VeePee Du'camp's motivations we should question,'' he continued. ''What does he stand to gain if the vote goes against me? Are you prepared to back him in a power struggle? That is what he's asking of you.''

The Director smiled and shook his head. ''No. I don't think that's what you want. Now, why don't we stop this foolishness and put Mr. Catanine into office where he belongs?''

''I move we close debate,'' Olson said.

''Second.''

''In favor?'' Mr. Elwood said.

The ayes carried it.

Mr. Elwood licked dry lips. For the first time in many years he was worried, really worried, about his ability to carry this off. His words were fine, but Rennie's had the ring of truth to them.

''All those in favor of conferring the status of senior VeePee on Junex Catanine, signify by raising your hands.''

The hands went up. All of Mr. Elwood's people stayed loyal, but only one from the other group voted with them.

''I count ten,'' Mr. Elwood said weakly.

''Yes, ten,'' someone said.

''All those opposed please raise your hands.''

Mr. Elwood had hoped for an abstention, but it wasn't meant to be.

''Ten,'' Rennie said. ''A dead tie.''

He stood up, a huge grin consuming his face. ''Without a clear majority, the motion fails.''

Olson felt his insides come apart. It was all over, all wiped out in a show of hands.

"Hold it just a minute," Abdullah said, and got off his window ledge. "You gentlemen have forgotten something. As a senior board member of the LOW Corporation, I have voting rights at all board meetings, including yours. My vote will break the tie."

He walked around the table until he stood behind Olson. "And I vote for my friend Catanine!"

With that, he bent down, taking Olson in a bear hug and lifting him bodily out of his chair, both men laughing and wrestling around.

There were cheers from Mr. Elwood's people, and the Director himself leaned heavily back against his chair in relief.

"This settles nothing!" Rennie yelled, standing up. His face was flushed, the anger blowing over him like a nasty wind. "You'll never be able to hold this together," he warned. "Never."

The man drew a breath, calmed down. "The vote has been taken, but it's not the last vote." He glared around the room. "The words have been said . . . but not the last word. I reserve that for myself."

With that, he deliberately moved toward the door. "I go to do my job and defend the city. I will no longer be a party to these corporate politics when so many matters of real importance are going on."

He left, the nine who voted with him right behind.

Mr. Elwood watched them go with some sadness. Rennie's next step was ordained. It would be war, hard and bloody.

*   *   *

> *The most excellent Jihad is that for the conquest of self.*
> —The Prophet Mohammed

XXXV
New Mecca

The Sun was setting in blinding reds and yellows when Abdullah stepped off the gondola that had returned him from

Orleans. As he walked across the field toward the garrison, several Elite and a computer man in tow, it amazed him that it could be so clear here and so rainy in Orleans.

"So, when can I expect results?" he said to Kanaly, the computer expert. The man was small and dumpy, with a wide round face that made him look like the man in the Moon.

"It's a slow process," Kanaly answered lethargically, his eyes moving, refusing to meet Abdullah's. "We're having to go through each disbursement program and check them against the master lists. Since we don't know what we're looking for, we have to look for everything."

Abdullah fixed him with dark, staring eyes. "When?" he said again.

Kanaly turned away, stared at the ground as they walked. "There's no way of telling," he said quietly.

Abdullah stopped walking, grabbed the man by the lapels of his jumper. "The way of telling, is that in six days everybody dies."

"I have no control over this," Kanaly returned, his voice quaking. "Don't you see? This computer nets with every computer in the whole world. The whole fucking world! I'm looking for a grain of black sand in the desert."

Abdullah released him to fall backwards on the hard-packed earth. Turning, he stared at the Elite and their blank, veiled faces. "What matters to you?" he asked them, but they had nothing to say in return.

He walked quickly to the gates. They opened as he got to them. "Majid," he said to the gate guards who stood huddled under a fan palm, smoking tobacco. "Where is he?"

They showed him empty palms.

"Bah!"

He pulled the cigarettes out of their mouths and strode on. "Majid!" he yelled from the middle of the courtyard. "Majid! Where are you?"

A window facing the courtyard opened, and Majid poked his unsmiling face out. "Up the stairs," he called, pointing below him.

Abdullah broke into a trot. Running under the ornate archway, he took the stone steps two at a time. When he entered the upstairs hall, Majid was standing by an open doorway. Smiling automatically, he gestured Abdullah into the room.

Entering, he went directly to the window that overlooked

the courtyard. The Elite who had followed him in were standing in the yard with their hands on their hips, looking around. Abdullah drew the curtains and sat heavily on a wooden chair.

"My brother has given us six more days," he said.

The man nodded. "I know."

"The computer people tell me they cannot predict a conclusion to this thing."

"I knew that all along," Majid answered, and walked to a huge map on the wall. "We have other problems to add to these. Look."

He pointed to the map. It filled the whole wall of the small, plain room, and showed the Western Sector, gridded off into sections.

"I sent the balloons out today," he said. "I was looking for the Jit army. Each balloon had the job of patrolling its coordinates."

He stopped and looked at Abdullah, and there was fear in his eyes. "No one reported any Jits," he said quietly.

"That's good, isn't it?"

"One of my balloons failed to report in," he said, and pointed to a section just East of Orleans. "Right here. When they failed to respond to our transmissions, we sent the next closest balloon to go look for them. They also failed to report. Neither balloon returned to base."

"Orleans," Abdullah said.

"Just as I feared. They move on Orleans."

"When?"

"A matter of days."

Abdullah leaned forward, burying his face in his hands. "What happens?"

Majid just stared at him. "We've had other reports," he said after a moment. "Jit movements from other sectors." He pointed to a wide range of Western Sector coordinates. "They travel in packs. For some reason, all the packs are traveling in the same direction—toward Orleans."

"What do you propose to do?"

"Stop them however I might," Majid said. "It bothers me that they have knocked two of my balloons out of the sky. It means they have artillery and know how to use it."

"It means something else, too," Abdullah said, standing up and peeking out the curtain at the courtyard. The Elite were nowhere in sight. "It means that they probably have at least two of your laser cannon."

Majid's eyes widened at the prospect. "Scuttling the cannon is always the standing order in these types of emergencies," he replied. Then he laughed and added, "But that doesn't mean it was done. I think you have just ruined my sleep tonight."

"Will you attack them tomorrow?"

"Tomorrow is Eed el Adha, my cousin. A holiday for New Mecca."

"A wasted day."

There was a knock on the door. Both men looked at one another. Majid nodded, frowning, and Abdullah moved against the wall.

Going to the door, Majid opened it to several Elite.

"We seek Abdullah," one of them said.

"He's not here," Majid said.

The Elite tried to push past him. "We will check for ourselves."

"Not in my camp," Majid said, blocking the way. "Not if you place any value on your miserable lives."

The men stared silently at one another for a brief eternity, then they were gone. When Majid turned back, he was smiling a real smile.

"I have an idea," he said, raising a finger. "We will call a hunt for tomorrow, for sport. We will make sport with the Orleans Execs."

"What will that do?" Abdullah asked.

"Wait and see," Majid returned. "Tomorrow. Are you hungry?"

Abdullah moved out into the center of the room. "I got something on the ride back. Sleep is what I really need, though I guess my black-robed friends will be waiting patiently for me by my bed."

Majid, laughing, embraced Abdullah, then put an arm around his shoulder. "I think I have the solution to both of our problems. Come on."

Moving to the door, Majid opened it a crack and peeked out. When he didn't see anyone there, he opened it and looked up and down the hall. Turning to Abdullah, he motioned with his hand. "Hurry," he whispered.

Puzzled, Abdullah followed him into the hall. It was dark there, the evening Sun long gone behind the walls. He moved them toward the blank far wall of the building.

"Sometimes I need to get quietly away," he whispered;

then, winking, he took out a big ring of keys, using one to open
a door at the end of the hallway. They entered through the door,
to find themselves in an empty room. A tapestry depicting
Mohammed's victory at Vadr filled one of the blank walls. Majid
walked right to the tapestry, then lifted it to reveal a door behind.

"Watch your step," he said. "It will be totally dark in
here." With that, he disappeared through the doorway. Abdullah
followed quickly and found himself on a long, dark flight of
stone steps.

"I'd been here three years before I found this," he said.

"Where does it go?"

"You'll see."

The steps evened out somewhere below ground level. Majid
lit a kerosene lamp he had down there and in the dim light
Abdullah could see they were in a long, rambling hallway.

They walked for a long time before coming to the ladder
that led back up. Climbing, Majid pushed on a trapdoor to let in
the last rays of the dying day. He climbed out, followed by
Abdullah.

The trapdoor had a fake rock anchored on top to hide it.
They came out on the far end of the landing field, right next to
the last balloon on the field.

"Get in," Majid said, indicating the balloon.

Walking to the door, Abdullah opened it and entered. The
entire inside of the gondola was a huge bed, fat pillows all
around; and upon the bed, a naked Nasrani woman—a blonde.

Abdullah started to turn around, to leave, but he felt the
balloon rising. Looking out the still-open door, he saw Majid
letting out the tether and waving.

"I'll bring you down in the morning," he called, and
waved again.

Closing the door, Abdullah looked at the woman.

"Hello," she said.

"Are you cold?" he asked.

She shook her head, a sly smile on her face. Her breasts
were large, the nipples pink and distended. He felt himself
beginning to respond. She spread her legs.

"I guess we're going to be in here all night," he said.

"Uh-huh."

He walked across the bed to her and she sat up, stroking
him through his robes.

"Like what you see, huh?"

"Always."

She pulled him down on top of her. "We'll see."

And for all too short a time, he forgot about everything else and tried unsuccessfully to recapture a real feeling.

*   *   *

> *Im-mo-late.*
> *Im-mo-late.*
> *If it's your Fate,*
> *Then it can't wait.*
> *Don't be late.*
> *Take the bait, and*
> *Im-mo-late.*
> *Im-mo-late.*
> —Jump-rope Rhyme

> *The Prophet said, "The best of you is he who is the best at repaying."*
> —The Prophet Mohammed

XXXVI
The River

The torchlights sputtered and flickered in the hard rain, their dancing flames barely lighting the long lines of people who were futilely stacking sandbags against the relentless surge of the Mississippi.

"The guy in the bar was right the other night," Olson said as he and Mr. Elwood swept along the hastily constructed sea wall, rain sheeting down their exos in blurring patterns. "It's too little too late."

Mr. Elwood stopped walking, turned to stare out across the churning waters. They were on the wrong side of the sandbags, the rising river licking their boots like the tongue of some incredible beast. Behind them the lines fanned out in two directions—giant Engies along the wall stacking the bags, and long snaking lines of citizens fingering out from the wall to the wharf warehouses where the bags were stored, handing the bags one to the other down the line.

"You've got to be strong," the Director said, "like the river." He turned to stare at Olson through the eye slits of his gold helmet. "When you screw up, you just live with it, knowing that even though you make mistakes, you can still cut the mustard better than anybody else."

Olson stifled a smile. "That sounds like excuses to me," he returned. "What if you're wrong?"

"There's no such thing as right and wrong," Mr. Elwood said flatly. "There's only ego, self-image."

"I don't get it," Olson said, and the river surged suddenly, swelling up almost to his knees before subsiding.

"Doesn't matter," the Director responded, and started walking again. "What you do need to know is the way to deal with the other Execs. They appreciate strength and audacity. They're basically weak men who are not especially skilled at creative thought. If you give them a reason to accept you as their leader, they'll do it. It's really what they want."

"Strength," Olson repeated.

"Have you heard about the hunt?" Mr. Elwood asked, as a sandbag slipped off the top of the three-foot wall and fell at his feet. He bent down to pick it up.

"Hunt?" Olson said, watching the Director heft up the sack with a grunt and place it back on the wall. They continued walking. "You mean like for squirrels or something like that?"

"Jit," Mr. Elwood returned. "We're going to hunt Jit."

"When?"

"Tomorrow morning. Majid called it."

Olson stopped walking, sat on the wall and took off his helmet. "What exactly do you mean by hunt?"

Mr. Elwood moved up next to Olson and sat on the wall beside him. "I mean it just the way it sounds, boy. We're going to try to flush some out and kill them."

Olson stared out across the dark waters, at the boats still remaining in the harbor, their tiny deck lights shining out across the river in long, choppy streamers. "They're holy people," he said. "I can't kill them."

"Yes you can," Mr. Elwood said flatly.

Olson didn't even look at him. "Don't tell me what I can and can't do. They see the visions, they see . . . God."

A giant Engy moved up behind them, sandbags loaded up in his arms. "Need space," he said.

Mr. Elwood stood, pulling Olson up by his arm. They began walking again, farther into the curtain of the night. "I know how you feel," the Director said. "I felt the same way when I got here."

"If you knew how I felt, you wouldn't ask me to do this."

"I said I knew," Mr. Elwood said angrily, "not that I sympathized." He put a foot up and over the wall. Olson climbed after him. "Let's get some caffeine."

They walked toward the food lines that filled one of the warehouses.

"I'm not going to change my mind," Olson said as they sloshed through calf-deep water.

"Yes you are," Mr. Elwood returned.

They reached the building and moved through its open door. There was light in there, electric light, and it bathed the entire room in a yellow warm glow. The place was packed full of people waiting for something to eat and drink. The deal was, food for work, a fair trade-off for sandbag labor.

"I'm not going to debate their holiness with you," the Director said as they shoved their way through the lines to get to the food tables. "I'm going to talk to you about commitment. You realize that the Jits want to destroy all human life?"

"What makes you say that?"

"Why do you think they're coming here?"

"Never thought about it."

They made their way to the head of the line and spoke to the fuzztops who were serving. "Two caffeines, please," the Director said, and the man reached under the table, coming out with two black, gummy-looking cakes and two crocks of water to wash the mess down.

"Thanks," Olson said when he got his, and immediately took a bite of the bitter cake.

There was a commotion farther down the line. A giant Engy was complaining that his food ration wasn't nearly large enough for the work he was doing. The fuzztop wasn't buying any of it and kept ordering him away, threatening.

"Why not give it to him?" Olson asked.

"We're on strict rations," the Director returned. "We're trying to make our food supplies last through a long siege."

"But he's so much bigger than a normal man."

Mr. Elwood made a face as he bit into his cake. He took a large drink immediately. "First off, rations are rations. Secondly, Engies are not men."

"Yes they are."

"What would you have me do?"

Olson smiled. "Let everybody eat as much as they want," he said. "Your rations will never make it to those hungry enough as long as they're under Exec control. Also, with a full belly, your people out on the docks will sure work a lot harder for you."

Mr. Elwood shook his head. "Tell 'em," he sighed.

Olson patted him on the shoulder. "That's the spirit."

He leaned way over the table so the fuzztop could see him. "You there!" he said. "Give that man what he wants."

The fuzztop looked puzzled, but began filling the man's tin with oatmeal. Olson wheeled around and spoke to the throng. "Everybody!" he yelled. "Listen! Keep your place in line. Don't shove. There's plenty for everybody, and everybody gets as much as they want!"

A loud cheer resounded through the room and Olson waved to the folks.

"Does it feel good?" Mr. Elwood asked.

"Yeah. Real good."

"These are your people," Mr. Elwood said. "Your adopted people. If you care so much about them, why are you willing to let the Jits come in and kill them all?"

"I never said I wanted that," Olson replied.

"If you refuse to fight for them, it's the same thing."

"No it's not."

They moved back through the still-jostling crowd in the warehouse, got out by the door to finish their caffeine and water.

"Whether they're holy or crazy doesn't matter," Mr. Elwood said. "Fact is: I don't see that there's any difference. The Jits come here en masse every time there's a kill somewhere. They're drawn here and to the other branches. They think they're the next evolutionary step or something."

Olson choked down the last of his cake. "You trying to tell me they want to replace us?"

"That's right, boy. They're inhuman; they're monsters. And they want us to die so they can start all over."

Olson looked around. "Maybe that's not such a bad idea."

Mr. Elwood slapped him hard across the face. Olson glared, but held back his own anger.

"You'd better listen to me," the Director said, low and menacing. "You pick your side, either us or them. There's no in between because it's war to extinction. You want to be a Jit? Fine. I'll walk you to the gates myself. But, by God, if you throw in with us, you'd better damn well be ready to fight for us. You'd better be ready to kill in cold blood for us, and without provocation."

The man was more worked up than Olson had ever seen him. It was almost frightening. "I love you like my own," Mr. Elwood said, and his eyes were glazed. "But, so help me, if you don't stand up with us, I'll kill you myself."

Olson pushed through the door and into the rain-night, dropping his crock on the ground to pop loudly. Mr. Elwood followed him out.

"I don't want to kill anybody," Olson said.

"Who does?" Mr. Elwood returned. "We're talking about survival here."

"I've got to think."

The Director walked up to him, took his face in his hands, and kissed him on the lips. "You're sincere," he said, "and I respect that. But if you've got to think, do it fast. Tomorrow will be too late."

"Tonight's too late," came a voice from out of the night.

Both men wheeled to the sound. A Junex in exo walked out of the darkness, followed by another. Olson heard Mr. Elwood slap his wrist against his thigh to engage his wrist laser. Lowering his hand slowly, he did the same.

"Something to tell me, brother?" Mr. Elwood asked.

The two men stepped forward.

"That's far enough," the Director said, his voice firm and commanding.

Olson's helmet was still locked firmly under his arm. He wished that he'd left it on.

"You're too old," the Junex in the light blue exo said, and his voice quavered somewhat. "You're no more good for the city or for LOW."

"And you're going to do something about it?" Olson said.

"Our fight isn't with you," said the man in a dark green exo. "You can just walk away right now."

"I like it here," Olson said.

"Then you'll share his fate."

Olson smiled and very slowly, very deliberately put his helmet back on, surprised that they let him. "Better his fate than yours," he said quietly.

"Did Rennie send you?" Mr. Elwood asked.

"We're here to save the city," the man in green said.

That's when Olson heard the other footsteps. He turned his head slowly. They had a small army of citizens with them, all armed with knives and aluminum bats.

"Nothing like a fair fight," Olson said.

"Assassination," the man in blue corrected, and raised his lasered wrist.

At the same instant, both Olson and Mr. Elwood dived to the ground, rolling into the surrounding men. Then all became confusion.

Pink-hot lines lit the night, lasers cutting into the gyrating crowd of men. Olson was struggling up, swinging out with razored gloves, as blows rained down on him and the idiots with the lasers chopped down their own people in their haste to do the job.

All at once, Mr. Elwood was beside him. Back to back, they fought the paid killers, while the Junexes used up the charge in their wrists.

And after a minute there was nothing but moaning and the sound of running feet as the citizens scurried back to their hiding places. Fifteen people lay on the ground; two Junexes stood looking at them, the charges used up on their weapons.

Mr. Elwood shared a look with Olson. "What should we do with them?"

Olson shook his head. "It's your party," he said.

The men drew swords, but stood, waiting, knowing that neither Olson nor the Director had used his laser.

"Did Rennie send you?" Mr. Elwood asked again.

No response.

"You are Junexes," Mr. Elwood said. "Guardians of a proud tradition. I owe you at least the death of a man." He looked at Olson. "Life is harsh," he said. "I didn't make it that way, but I'm not going to run away from it, either."

With that he killed his two assailants, as Olson knew he would.

"Think about it," the Director said. "I'll call you later."

He walked off, clacking and splashing into the night. Olson went back into the warehouse and arranged for some help in disposing of the bodies.

*   *   *

Love is like war: you begin when you like and
leave off when you can.

—Corporate Wisdom

XXXVII
Olson's Apartment

Olson lay on the big four-poster and looked at the microphone that was barely peeking out beneath the fringe of the canopy. He'd spent the whole day since the board meeting getting a serious dose of corporate politics, LOW style. He'd learned about tribute; he'd learned about mergers; he'd greased so many axles he figured he'd slip out of bed if he didn't take a shower.

Wexler sat on the living-room couch, crying softly.

"Stop it," Olson said.

"C-can't," the little man with the lopsided head sobbed.

"Stop it," Olson said again, and he was staring hard at the mike, remembering.

"Miss Gret," Wexler said quietly.

"Gret's gone," Olson returned, and the words caught in his throat. It made him angry that she could affect him still, after all she'd done.

"Why?"

"Gret was bad," Olson spat, sitting up, his eyes still fixed on the canopy. "She went away."

The little man trundled up to Olson, climbed, with assistance, onto the bed with him. "No," he said. "Gret wasn't bad. She loved me. She was my m-mother."

He flung himself into Olson's arms, crying in earnest, his

little frame quaking violently. Olson held him tightly, smoothing his hair. He wanted to speak, but was afraid he couldn't get the words out, and that would make him even madder at himself and at her.

There was a loud ringing sound. Olson jerked his head around, looking.

"What?" he said.

"Telephone," the little man said into his chest.

"What do I do?"

Wexler looked up at him, his big brown eyes a tear factory. He sniffled. "You have many choices in life," he said.

"About that?" Olson said.

"You pick it up."

Olson slid off the bed and padded across the carpet to the instrument on the coffee table in the living area. He picked it up, holding it near his head in an approximation of the way he had seen Mr. Elwood do that afternoon.

"Hello?" came a distant voice full of static.

"Hell no?" Olson responded.

"Cat? Cat? Is that you?"

He recognized Mr. Elwood's voice, and pulled the receiver away from his face, holding it at arm's length. "What do I do?" he asked.

"Do?" Wexler returned, and his wide eyes got wider. Olson could see the wheels turning in the little man's head as a whole world of possible solutions churned through him.

"With the telephone," Olson said. "I don't want to talk."

"Say you don't want to talk."

"I can't do that, it's Mr. Elwood."

"Cat . . . Cat . . ."

He could hear the tiny voice drifting over to him from the phone. Wexler had his hands on his head, rocking back and forth.

"You either talk or not," he said. "Talk or not. What other choices are there? What kind of question is that?"

"Cat . . ."

Olson knew that Mr. Elwood wanted to put him on the spot about their earlier conversation, and he just wasn't ready for that.

"Cat?" Olson said.

"Is that you?"

"Who?" Olson returned.

"Cat!"

"Let me talk to him."

"Who is this?"

"Wexler," Olson said. "This is Wexler."

"Cat isn't here," the voice said.

"Then why did you say he was?"

"Can you take a message?"

"Message. Yes."

"Tell him to be in the lobby at seven sharp tomorrow morning. The Saudis have called a hunt for tomorrow. He needs to attend."

"Why?"

"Just give him the message."

The line clicked off abruptly, and Olson turned back to the bed. So much had been happening that he had forgotten the transmitter the Yids had given him. Maybe it was time to get it out.

Walking to the closet across from the foot of the bed, he opened it and rooted around on the shelf above the hangers. He found the box and slid it out.

Moving to the bed, he dumped the contents of the box out on the rumpled satin spread. The receiver was there, and headphones, and extra dry cells to run it, but the transmitter was missing.

"Have you been playing with the stuff in this box?" he asked Wexler.

The little man shook his head. "Gret did," he said.

"Gret," Olson repeated, and picked up the receiver, turning it around in his hands. He reached out and flicked the knob, and voices jumped out at him. He shut it off quickly, and began to feel a strange sensation inside of him.

Getting up, he moved to the bathroom, closing the door behind him when he entered. With shaking hands, he turned on the receiver again. Two men were talking above a static sound that he realized was running water. It was Rennie and, perhaps, Jerny. One of them was taking a bath, so he surmised that the transmitter was somewhere in Rennie's bathroom.

"You get anything off it yet?" Rennie's voice asked the other.

"Not much," the other voice replied, and Olson was convinced that it was Jerny. "Somebody called him, but he didn't want to talk, and him and that little Engy of his have been talking about the Houris.''

''What about her?''

''She disappeared. I think they know that she had something to do with that river business, and she took off before they could get her.''

''Too bad,'' Rennie said. ''We might have used that again.''

Jerny laughed. ''Look what happened last time.''

The running water stopped, and was replaced with the sound of splashing. He heard Rennie sigh as he sank down into the tub. ''The idea was sound,'' he said. ''The circumstances just backfired a bit.''

''You think you put your foot in it today at the board meeting?''

''Nope.''

''It looks like Abdullah is siding with fucking Cat.''

''Doesn't matter,'' Rennie said. ''I've never seen anybody try to get rid of anybody more than our esteemed ruler is trying to get rid of his brother. When we come down on Cat and Elwood, we'll just take care of the Arab, too.''

''That's quite a chance to take.''

There was more splashing. ''I don't think so,'' Rennie said. ''I think Faisel would just love for us to get rid of Abdullah for him. Besides, he's got the goddamned key. We're going to have to take him out anyway.''

Olson sat listening for several more minutes. They were talking strategy and he should have been interested, but all he really wanted was more information about Gret.

Shutting off the machine, he walked back into the bedroom and retrieved the headphones. He found the jack and plugged them in, turning the machine back on.

''So, you don't think you know where Gret's gone,'' he said to Wexler, and heard shushing noises over his headphones. Good, they were listening to him again.

The little man cocked his head, the sad look returning to his face. ''There are many, many places she could have gone. Her first decision would be to decide whether or not to stay in the city. After that—''

''I understand,'' Olson said, cutting him off. ''But you think we can trust her?''

''Trust?'' the little man replied. ''I don't really understand ideas of that nature.''

''She's not a bad woman?''

"No," Wexler said emphatically. Olson was beginning to agree with him.

"Well, maybe we can find her and bring her back," Olson said. "I miss her too."

He walked toward the door and called from across the room, "I'll be back later." Then he opened the door and closed it without leaving.

Wexler started to say something, but Olson silenced him with a finger to his lips. The Engy got a look on his face that a cat gets when encountering a new kind of bug and sat down on the floor. Olson listened.

"Maybe I was wrong," Jerny said. "Maybe they don't suspect her."

"And I'll bet she's too scared and too smart to ever tell anyone what happened," Rennie returned.

"And she's awful close to the new VeePee." Jerny laughed.

"We may not be through with the woman yet," Rennie said softly.

"Next time we tie her up, I get to go first," Jerny said. "I can get shit out of her same as you."

"Like the rope, huh?"

"You might say that."

"Marty, my friend," Rennie said. "She's all yours."

Olson grabbed off the headphones and threw them to the ground. They had tied her up, probably tortured her sexually. The anger came first, flushing through him like piss through an alky, but it was replaced immediately by the pain. Gret's pain and his rejection of her. She must have gone to Rennie's to plant the bug for him, and they took her.

He rushed to the window, staring down into the rain-soaked night. The streets were alive with torchlight, processions that stretched out in all directions like an army of fireflies. The citizens were frightened and angered over Faisel's message; they were filling the streets the way pus fills a boil, and soon enough they would burst.

And Gret was down there somewhere.

Wexler walked up to put his hand in Olson's. Reaching down, Olson picked up the little man and hugged him close, both of them looking at the street crowds.

"Will we find her?" Wexler whispered.

Olson just looked at him, and he could feel the tears wetting his own cheeks.

"Wait here," he whispered, setting Wexler on the floor.

He went to the door, then ran. He ran down the stairs to the streets, then ran through the rain-running alleys and gutters of Orleans. He ran like a crazy man, letting off the pressure that had built up in him like a steam engine. He ran screaming her name over and over until the rain-black night turned into rain-gray day and the brocaded suit he wore swelled up like a sponge and weighed a good fifty pounds. Near the alcove of an old church, he ran past a woman who said she could tell the future, but who couldn't tell her own very well because she shrank back in the shadows in fear when she saw him and let him pass without a word.

*   *   *

> *You were longing for death before you met it;*
> *now you have seen it, while you were*
> *beholding.*
>
> —The Koran
> III. The House of Imran

> *Visit the graves, for verily these will make*
> *you indifferent to the world and remind you of*
> *the hereafter.*
>
> —The Prophet Mohammed

XXXVIII
The Hunt

The fuzztop with the bullhorn stood on the shoulders of a giant Engy and tried to keep order among the crowds who pressed ever larger against the gate.

"PLEASE FORM DOUBLE LINES. NO PUSHING OR SHOVING WILL BE ALLOWED. THE GATES WILL BE OPEN LONG ENOUGH TO ACCOMMODATE ALL OF YOU. PLEASE KEEP ORDER."

The sky, as usual, hung heavy gray, a light drizzle falling steadily as it seemed it was going to do forever. It was early morning, still early enough for the wall lights to cast shimmering reds and greens up and down its length. Several inches of water stood on the choked streets, and the area around the gate was even thicker in mud.

During the night, the crowds pressed the gates, demanding release. They feared the inside more than the outside. Mr. Elwood had been forced to make a decision. It had always been his policy during Jit scares that the gates, once closed, were never to be reopened until the threat had passed. That was obviously impossible this time; he was faced with the possibility of forced exit that could damage the gates themselves and render everyone in trouble. Instead, he made a historic decision: the gates would be opened for a period of one hour per day for the next five days. Once out, however, there was no return. Hence the green cards.

Olson sat in the backseat of his hunt aut along with Mr. Elwood and waited to get his green card. Abdullah, strangely exuberant, sat in front next to the driver, an Arab sergeant with a heavy mustache and a permanent scowl settled onto his dark face.

The other auts lined out behind them, next to the throngs of dirty citizens who smelled of mildew and sweat and fear. The hunt auts were different from any others Olson had ever seen. They were older, it seemed, of a different design. They had no tops, no defensive gear, and plush sofas where aut seats usually were.

"You look like you haven't slept," Mr. Elwood said, and Olson thought the Director looked more than a little cramped in his gold exo.

Olson shrugged, shifting the M-16 around on his lap. "I'm fine," he said, but he really wasn't. He took a breath, watching the people crammed all around the aut, their mud-streaked faces peering down at him.

Faisel ibn Faisel's face was screaming out at them from the rows of televisions set into the wall.

". . . hour of your retribution draws closer. Six days you have to satisfy my brother. Six more days before the justice of Allah is meted out in deserving measure. Think about it. Six days!"

Lightning flared brightly, whitening the gray sky for just a second, thunder blaring a long rumble to mix with the never-ending rumble of people thunder.

"These hunts are for sport," Mr. Elwood was saying, "so they're set up a little bit differently than we usually do things. No lasers. No radar or any other electronic detection gear. No automatic-weapons fire." He pointed to Olson's rifle. "In fact, you'd better set that thing for semiautomatic fire."

"What's the point of all this?" Olson asked.

"Sport!" Mr. Elwood replied loudly, and slapped him on the leg. "C'mon, wake up. We're going to have some fun."

"What's the real reason?" Olson asked.

Abdullah turned to them, a large smile on his face, partly from his evening, mostly from the fact that the Elite were in another aut. "The real reason is that today is Eed, a holiday for my people. Majid called the hunt so that he could try to locate the Jit army."

A loud engine noise made Olson turn. It was Majid, throttling through the crowds on a motorcycle, mud splattering out indiscriminately from the back tires, covering Majid and everyone near him in a dark, speckled coat.

He skidded to a halt next to Abdullah's aut, and pulled his goggles up to rest on his aghal. His face was mud-caked, except for the light mask area made by the goggles. He smiled, glinting gold, and held up a handful of green cards.

"Take the one with your name on it and display it on your clothing!" Majid yelled above the crowd and his engine. He handed several of the cards to Abdullah. "Remember: don't lose them. These are the only things that will get you back in the gates!"

The fuzztop with the bullhorn was talking again, as Abdullah handed Olson and Mr. Elwood their cards.

"REMEMBER. ONCE YOU LEAVE YOU CANNOT RE-ENTER THE WALLS."

Olson turned the green card around in his hand. It was plastic, quite valuable and impossible to duplicate, and it had his name and status printed on it.

"YOU WILL NO LONGER BE UNDER THE PROTECTION OF THE LOW CORPORATION, OR THE CITY OF ORLEANS."

Olson used the pin on the back of the card to fix it to the heavy leather of his right glove. He was feeling a strange unease at having to leave the walls.

"I have to give out the other cards!" Majid yelled. "I will ride with you when we go."

There were gunshots behind Olson. He turned to see one of the VeePees in a following aut standing on his seat and firing point-blank into the crowd with his rifle.

"I told you to get back!" he screamed.

"Save it for the Jits!" Mr. Elwood called back to him.

"ONCE OUTSIDE THE GATES YOU BECOME A POSSIBLE JIT AND HARMFUL TO THE REST OF US. YOUR STATUS WILL BE THE SAME AS A JIT, AS WILL BE YOUR FORTUNE—DEATH ON SIGHT."

With that, the big gate was creaked open by a contingent of gate guilders pushing for all they were worth against the dragging mud. A wild cheer went up from the crowd and they jammed up immediately, trying to get out. There were several thousand of them, a drop in the bucket compared to those who stayed, but this was just the first day. Olson hesitated to think of what it would get like closer to the deadline.

The crowds jostled by, as Mr. Elwood yelled for the fuzztop to toss him the bullhorn. It came tumbling into Olson's lap, and the Director grabbed it, standing up in the seat and turning back to the other auts.

"GOOD MORNING, GENTLEMEN. I KNOW IT'S EARLY, BUT I THINK WE HAVE SOMETHING IN STORE THAT WILL GET YOUR BLOOD CIRCULATING."

All the hunters yelled and shook their fists in the air. The hunting party was made up exclusively of department heads, all of them lining out in their auts precisely the way they did at the board meeting. Rennie occupied the last aut in the line, which he was assigned to by Mr. Elwood and which was just fine with Olson.

"DOES EVERYONE HAVE HIS GREEN CARD?"

More yelling and affirmation.

"GOOD. DOES EVERYONE KNOW THE RULES?"

Everyone, apparently, knew the rules.

"ALL RIGHT. JUST TO SWEETEN THE POT, WE'RE GOING TO ADD A LITTLE EXTRA TO THE HUNT BY MAKING IT A COMPETITION. THE EXEC WITH THE GREATEST NUMBER OF CONFIRMED KILLS WILL RECEIVE A ONE-YEAR OIL RATION FREE OF CHARGE!"

The Execs were yelling, but it was mostly lost in the din caused by the exiting throng. Olson kept watching the crowd, hoping to catch sight of Gret. He hated the idea of the open gates. He could lose her forever that way.

"IF WE'RE ALL READY ... LET'S GO HUNT SOME JITS!''

The aut engines roared to life, the Execs yelling and firing their weapons in the air. Olson's aut took off with a jerk, Mr. Elwood tossing away the bullhorn as they left.

They drove right into the crowd, depending on the people on foot to get out of the way. The feeling was that these were nonpeople anyway, good as Jits, so good as dead.

So, the citizens scattered as fifteen old-style auts without tops coughed and sputtered through the mud into the wet morning, and thirty exo-clad Execs and assorted dignitaries prepared for a morning of invigorating fun and adventure.

The firing started just as soon as they cleared the walls, rifles popping from auts bringing up the rear, firing upon the citizens who were just leaving. Olson could tell from the frown on Mr. Elwood's face that these kills wouldn't be counted as part of the contest.

Majid came ripping down the line on his motorcycle to ride beside the lead aut, his face settled into something of a grimace due to the push of the wind against it.

Mr. Elwood pulled a silver flask out of a pocket set in the back of the driver's seat. Unscrewing the cap, he took a long pull and handed it to Olson.

"Martini," he said.

Olson took it from him and took a long, hot drink, hoping to dispel some of the dampness that had settled onto him during his long night on the streets. He started to hand it back to Mr. Elwood, but the Director pointed to Majid.

He reached his arm over the side of the thing and the Arab steered closer, taking the flask with a nod of his head. He drank, trying not to tilt his head too far back lest he lose the road. Olson noted that Abdullah was scowling at Majid the whole time.

The Arab handed the flask back, nearly running into the aut when he did. Then he shouted across to the driver.

"Follow me!"

With that, he pulled out in front of the aut, and drove off the roadway, going overland. The driver turned with him, and they were bouncing crazily on nonexistent shocks across muddy pitted ground.

"Drink?" Olson asked, shoving the flask toward Abdullah.

"A good Moslem doesn't indulge in alcohol," Abdullah responded, frowning once again in Majid's direction.

"Don't be too hard on him," Mr. Elwood said, patting Abdullah's arm. "You can't live with another culture and hope to understand them without adopting some of their ways. Majid is a good man . . . and a good Moslem."

"The Koran is our life," Abdullah said. "To ignore the Koran is to ignore God . . . to ignore our reason for being alive."

"Allah works in mysterious ways," Mr. Elwood countered. "Even among the infidels."

Abdullah grunted. "I will think about that."

They bumped and sloshed like that for several hours, Olson's lower back feeling like he had been dropped fifty feet. The only relief came when they would get stuck in a mud hole and have to get out and push, and Olson, sweating in his exo and feeling like his spine had been replaced with a bough from a hickory-nut tree, found himself wishing more and more for mud holes.

It was while stuck in an overflowed creek at the bottom of a ravine that they had their first real contact. They had been coming off a flat stretch of bayou dripping Spanish moss from dead skeletal trees. The first three auts plowed into the creek, two of them getting stuck. The others had pulled up behind, everyone getting out to help.

Olson and a couple of the other VeePees were pushing from the back of the rusted machine, while Mr. Elwood and Abdullah stood with their hands on their hips, watching officiously. There was a great deal of drinking and laughing going on, and Olson realized that it was mostly relief at being away from the all-pervading atmosphere of Orleans. Du'camp seemed to stay away from the general action, talking from time to time privately with his people. Olson noted that this, also, was not lost to Mr. Elwood.

"There," Majid whispered harshly, pointing farther down the creek. "Quiet."

A hush fell over the group and they turned to Majid. The man had binoculars to his eyes, his finger still pointing.

Olson looked down the creek, around the trees that ran up to it on both sides. It snaked a path within sight for over a hundred yards, then turned abruptly to the right, getting lost around the groundswell that led up the hill. He could barely make out several figures near the bend on their hands and knees getting water.

"How do you know they are Jits?" Abdullah asked.

Majid kept the binoculars to his eyes. "I know them when I see them," he answered with confidence.

The Execs moved quietly to their auts and got hold of their weapons. Their faces had suddenly turned somber.

"Let Mr. Elwood have the first shot," someone said, and it was picked up as a general cry.

The Director smiled wide and shook his head. "I accept your contract for first shot," he said, "but subcontract the job to our newest VeePee, Catanine."

"Don't do this," Olson whispered, walking up to him.

The Director looked hard at him. "Why not?"

"I've never fired one of these before," he said, holding up the gun.

Mr. Elwood shrugged. "You just look down the barrel and squeeze the trigger. I'll help you."

"Yeah."

The Director tightened his lips. "It's now or never, Cat. You got to crap or get off the pot."

Olson looked at him hard. He wanted to give him an answer, he really did; but he knew that until he was actually looking down the shiny barrel of that M-16, he wouldn't know if he could do it or not.

"Don't worry about it," he said, because it was all he could think of to say.

Mr. Elwood grabbed the gun away from him, turning it over in his hands. "It's all up for grabs right now," he said. "Everything we've been working for." He checked the mechanism, pulling the clip out and staring at it before shoving it back into place. "And all you've got to say to me is, 'Don't worry about it'?"

Olson tried a half smile. "Best I could come up with."

The Director shoved the gun back into his hands. "Do the right thing," he said, and his eyes were cold and hard.

The others had joined them at the aut, guns at the ready. "Okay," Mr. Elwood said. "We'll see how close we can get. Mr. Catanine gets the first shot. After that, it's open season."

They moved off through the trees, their feet sinking deeply into Louisiana spongeland. Using the trees for cover, they were able to get within thirty yards before having to deal with the clearing that the Jits occupied.

There were about fifteen of them, all in different stages of the disease. Men, women, and children, they sat by the creek.

They appeared to be resting. Some were bathing in the water, others just lying beside it. They seemed at peace somehow, a thought that Olson had to forcibly shake from his mind.

Mr. Elwood waved his arms in both directions, telling the hunters to take up positions in the trees. They made some noise doing it, but it didn't attract any attention from the Jits, who seemed totally unconcerned, as if they were off on a picnic somewhere on a warm, lazy day.

Olson got behind a China elm tree, leaning his rifle against it for support. His hands were shaking noticeably and his insides from the combination of the bad ride and the bad feelings were jangling like wind chimes in a hurricane. Mr. Elwood crawled up next to him.

"Take the safety off," he whispered, and Olson did it. "All right, now, sight down the barrel."

"Mr. Elwood, I . . ."

"Listen to me," the old man said. "They're not people, they're killers worse than the worst killers you can imagine."

"They're women and kids."

"They're murderers. They want to murder us and ours, and they'll do it if we let them. They have to be destroyed. Sight down the barrel."

"All right."

"Pick a target."

Olson picked a large, ugly man, who was standing up, scratching his back on a tree.

"Pick a child," Mr. Elwood said.

Olson glared at him.

"They're monsters," the Director said. "Killers. There."

He was pointing to a petite blond woman who held a spasming baby in her arms. She was cooing to the baby as if its gurgles were something other than an epileptic seizure.

Olson sighted on the baby, and he knew he had to make a decision.

"Ready," Mr. Elwood whispered up and down the line of riflemen, and they all raised their rifles.

Olson took a long, calming breath and blinked some sweat out of his eyes.

"Do it," the Director rasped to him.

He sighted again, the crosshairs set directly on the child's head.

"Do it."

And Olson faced the natural consequences of all his actions. He was no longer a sitter by the side of the road. He had taken sides, made decisions, cast his lot. This was the outgrowth of all that had gone before. He took another breath and knew what his decision had to be.

He squeezed the trigger, and the gun jumped in his hands. The baby's head exploded red, along with the mother's left breast. A second later, the whole world came apart.

Their blind was full of smoke as the weapons discharged rapidly. The clearing kicked mud and Jits, as they fell, twisting, writhing the death agony, and Olson was firing right along with the others, fulfilling the duty that he had taken upon himself, dying a little with every shot.

"Some are getting away!" Majid yelled, and began running. Abdullah and Olson and Mr. Elwood were running with him.

They thrashed through the underbrush, all of it passing Olson in a blur. It was as if he were watching it all on one of the television boxes, watching it happen to someone else, someone who didn't care if they were holy people or just crazy, someone who didn't care whether he blew up little babies or not.

Three of them had gotten away. They were charging up the hill. Olson splashed through the creek, then up the rock-strewn incline. He was a person removed from his body, a floating mind. His insides churned with a fire that wasn't physical and it amazed him in an abstract way that he had the energy to climb the hill after his long night.

The hill rose steep and long, nearly straight up. They gained quickly on the slower-moving, limping Jits, but not before they crested the hill and disappeared on the other side.

He could hear Abdullah panting beside him. Majid was slightly ahead, Mr. Elwood slowing behind. Turning on the speed, Majid reached the top of the hill, only to stop dead in his tracks, the .45 he held in his hand dropping to his side like a dead limb falling from a tree.

Abdullah grunted, but Olson didn't say anything. He was still intent on the escaped Jits. He and Abdullah reached Majid's side at the same time, and the sight he saw would never be equaled in this or any other lifetime.

The hill was just as steep on the other side, falling away to a long flat plain through which the Mississippi wound. The plain was full of Jits, stretching back into the distance as far as he could see.

They moved like some monstrous circus parade, dressed in rags, dressed in finery, and naked. They jumped, they sang songs like a choir. Many were sick and crawling, many were jerking crazily, lost in the Jitterbug frenzy. They filled the plain, and filled the river—on skiffs and steamboats and flat-bottomed rafts of lashed-together logs.

They were an army, as large and formidable as anything Olson could imagine.

He heard Abdullah retching beside him, but couldn't pull his eyes away from the spectacle below long enough to look.

Mr. Elwood came wheezing up beside them. "Say, why aren't you . . ."

He stopped dead, staring.

"Oh my God," he whispered. "How many?"

"A hundred thousand at least," Majid said.

"A pestilence," Abdullah said.

"They're heading the way we just came from," Olson said.

"How long before they reach Orleans?" Abdullah asked, his voice strained.

"Two days," Majid said. "Three at the outside. Look down there, at the front of the procession."

Olson looked. A man on a litter was being carried by many hands at the head of the line.

"That's their boss," Mr. Elwood said, "their company president."

"And behind him . . ." Olson said.

Majid made a sound in his throat that Olson had never heard before. "Our lasers," he choked out. "Three of them."

Abdullah turned to Mr. Elwood. "Do you still have that flask?" he asked.

Mr. Elwood nodded, pulling it out of the utility pouch that hung from his exo. Without a word, Abdullah took it from him and, tilting it to his lips, drank the whole flask in one long gulp.

They stood there watching for a long time, and then, when they couldn't think of anything else to do, they went back down the hill and helped the others burn the bodies.

*　　*　　*

Dreaming men are haunted men.
                    —Bedouin Proverb

*Assist your brother Moslem, whether he be an
oppressor or an oppressed. "But how shall we
do it when he is an oppressor?" Lord Mohammed
said, "Assisting an oppressor is by forbidding
and withholding him from oppression."*
                    —The Prophet Mohammed

XXXIX

Riyadh, the City of Bridges
Saudi Arabia

The Islamic year totals three hundred fifty-four days, each
month beginning when, and only when, the proper authorities
have seen and corroborated the appearance of the new moon. It
was under this cloak of darkness that Bandar ibn Mira and
Ahmad ibn Rizul rode into the ancient city of Riyadh.

Once the seat of power of the Kingdom, Riyadh had been
the headquarters of Arabia's first great modern leader, Abdul
Aziz, the first to be called Al Sa'ud, and a direct ancestor of
Faisel ibn Faisel.

The camels clopped easily, their hooves sounding hollowly
on the brick streets. Bandar rode sedately, his mind immersed in
their purpose, while Ahmad, edgy and suspicious, kept turning
in his saddle, watching the empty streets behind.

They had been riding for two full days, the water in their
goatskins nearly gone. For food, they had existed on the butter
carried in lizardskins on their bandoliers and the dates strung on
the pommels of their saddles. Their rifles were close at hand.

"If it is a trap," Bandar said, "there is very little we could do about it."

"I understand that," Ahmad returned. "But I also believe that worrying about things is what keeps them from happening."

"You mean that if you didn't worry, that's when we'd have to worry."

"Precisely."

Bandar shook his head, patting his camel's coarse-haired neck. "Sometimes I wonder how you survived to adulthood."

Ahmad pointed a finger at him. "I survived because I worried about it."

Both men laughed and continued down the narrow, building-lined streets, the solitary footfalls of their camels the only sound echoing through the sleepy streets of the once-great city.

When Abdul Aziz rode triumphantly into Riyadh in 1902, he married a woman named Tarfah, the daughter of Sheikh Abdullah ibn Abdul Lateef, qadi of the town and chief ulema. He built her a beautiful mud palace next to the mosque, then connected them with a covered bridge above the streets so that he could journey from his majlis to the mosque in privacy. It was at this place that Bandar and Ahmad were to meet with their secret benefactor—if, in fact, that was what he was.

Hobbling their camels beneath the crude curving bridge with the small square air vents inset, they entered through the mosque and up the narrow, winding stairs to the bridge.

It was dark in there, and sweltering. Both men took heavy breaths, disliking the feeling of confinement. The vents let in the barest starlight, but it wasn't enough to cover the terrible smothering effects of the bridge.

"My hatred abounds for this place," Ahmad whispered.

"We have no need to cower," Bandar said loudly. Then, to the darkness: "Is anyone here?"

A lighter flared a high flame at the palace end of the corridor. Bandar walked toward it immediately, Ahmad following a little too slowly behind.

As soon as Bandar reached the flame, it went out, plunging them back into darkness again.

"You will relight the flame," he said.

"This is sufficient," a voice rasped out of the darkness.

"No," Bandar said. "I will see face to face who I am dealing with or I will not deal at all."

"My identity must remain a secret."

"We can speak as men only when we both share knowledge of one another. Your letter speaks of villainy and heroism. I make no such plans with a spirit."

There was no response from the darkness. Bandar tightened his lips and nodded. Turning abruptly, he strode away, nearly running into Ahmad.

"Wait," came the voice.

Bandar turned, staring cold fire.

The lighter flared again, and Bandar returned to its source. He stood, staring straight into the flickering orange face of Misha'al ibn Abdul, confidant of Faisel himself. The man's eyes burned black like a tar pit, his tight curly beard like dark wires. He smiled with thick lips.

"You are a forthright man," he said.

"Why did you hide yourself from me?" Bandar asked, trying to read the mask of Misha'al's face.

"Quite simply," the man returned, "I was trying at all costs to protect myself. You wouldn't allow me to do that, and that is to your credit. For now we have something on one another, is that not correct?"

"You left the note in Abdullah's tent?"

The prophet's dark eyes danced. "Yes," he replied.

"Why?"

"I hoped that perhaps we might be able to help one another."

"How?"

"You certainly get right to the heart of it."

Bandar felt the sweat creeping down his face. He couldn't stand to be in that place much longer, and that, probably, was the reason that Misha'al had picked it.

"I am a direct man," he said. "I know no other way."

Misha'al let the flame go out. "It was getting hot," he said. Then, "I will tell you how we may be able to help each other. You want the woman called Nura. I want solace in the desert."

"Why?"

The lighter went on again. "I have been . . . liberating large amounts of cash and commodities from Faisel's storehouses," he said. "I have amassed a very sizable personal fortune that I sincerely wish to live to spend. I have the ability to help with the woman's escape, if you will let me stay with you for a time, until it is safe for me to journey to my stronghold. Do you understand?"

Bandar shook his head, and the light went out again. "No," he said. "I don't understand the reasons, but I do understand the deal."

"Do you accept it?"

"I would not have come here otherwise."

"Good."

Bandar heard a rustling sound, Misha'al bending over, then straightening. When the lighter flared again, he held a small black box in his hand.

"Take this," he said. "It is a radio receiver. I will send you messages on it. You cannot get in touch with me through the box, only I you. We will never meet like this again until everything is taken care of; it is extremely dangerous for us to meet."

"I understand. What is your plan?"

"I will radio the details of it to you," the prophet answered, and he was beginning to get nervous. "Just remember, I face the same dangers that you do in this enterprise. Trust me."

"I do not trust you," Bandar replied. "But I have intended from the first to do as you say."

The light went out.

"Then go. You will hear from me."

Bandar turned and walked with Ahmad out of the bridge. It wasn't until they had taken the camels and were riding through town again that Ahmad spoke.

"Why didn't you talk with him of vengeance?" he asked. "Why didn't you tell him what you intended for Faisel?"

"We don't know all of his plans," Bandar replied, his mind lost in thought. "There is no reason for him to know all of ours. Time will answer everyone's questions."

And they made the journey back to the caravan in silence, each perceiving events according to his own will.

The shell was hard and tight all around him, too tight. Walking around in it was difficult, and he was always just ready to fall down. The air was hot, stifling, as Faisel stumbled through the red, red haze. The room was large and lost in the red haze shadows, and the wall was wet, running a steady thick trickle of water all along it.

He stumbled into thick red smoke, and the smoke was cold smoke, freezing smoke.

The air was thick and dead and didn't want to come into his

mouth as he labored through the heat and the ever-tightening shell.

And there was the woman, in the cell where he had left her at the far end of the room, past the hissing cold smoke, past the thick wet air. She paced the cell, naked, every now and then staring without emotion into the fuzzy red darkness.

He lumbered toward her, falling before reaching her side, falling again. He was there, but she could look right through him as if he weren't. He called her name over and over until the rumbling started and everything shook.

She burst into flame then, red on red, and she looked right through it like she looked through him.

The flame leapt higher, leapt all around him, and it got hotter and hotter. . . .

He sat up screaming, his body dripping stale, cold sweat, the sleeping covers drenched. The room pulsed pale bluish colors from the wall-sized television box that pictured a mammoth version of him reading the Koran. The woman who had been beside him in bed was curled up in horror on the floor against the far wall.

His heart was pounding, and if the dream had been any more real, it would have burned him.

There was a pounding on the door, and the muffled sound of someone calling his name. He took deep breaths to calm himself.

"Yes," he called at the door, but the pounding continued. "Yes! *Yes!*"

The pounding stopped. "The woman's gone," a distant voice said.

Faisel jumped out of bed and ran, naked, to the door. He flung it open to see a large Elite staring at him. "How long ago?"

"Don't know," the Elite said. "She was checked two hours ago."

Faisel turned and walked back into the room, flipping on the light as he passed the switch. The Elite followed him, staring as the concubine jumped up and ran out into the hallway.

"She can't have gone far," he said, slipping a thobe over his head. "Have them put extra people on the security monitors. She'll turn up."

He hurried to the large marble bathroom and grabbed a towel to wipe his sweaty face and hair. "I'll have someone's head for this," he said, frowning as the Elite came into the room. "What are you waiting for?"

The man's eyes widened above his veil. "May I . . . use . . ." He was pointing into the room.

Faisel realized that the man wanted to use his intercom, and waved his hand. "Yes, anything. Hurry."

The Elite ran for the control console that sat behind the heavy drapes of the majlis. Faisel moved to the doorway, watching him across the length of the bedroom. His heart was still pounding from the memory of the dream, and for one instant he almost wished that Nura would get away.

"Get Misha'al when you're finished with that," he said. "I want to see him."

Faisel turned back into the bathroom, pulling the thobe back over his head. He toweled his whole body in a vain attempt at toweling away the dream. Then he dressed totally, his blue ghutra no stranger to sweat. The Elite was already calling him as he finished. He hurried to the sitting room.

"They've found her," the Elite said as he searched for the toggle that would activate one of the small screens that was inset in the console. "She's hiding in life support."

"Let me see," Faisel said, shoving the man out of the way and flipping the proper switch.

The screen came up staticked snow. "Security," Faisel said into the flex-pole mike in front of him.

"Roger."

"Give me that image up here."

"Right away."

The screen crackled to life. It was a wide shot of the life-support subbasement, the heavy drone of the huge silver electric turbines drowning out all sound. The woman was plainly visible as she crouched behind the first storage tank in a long line of storage tanks that stretched back out of the range of the camera and beyond.

"Security," he said into the mike. "I'll go get her myself, just so she does not get away again. Have a squad waiting at the door. You can do that, can't you?"

He clicked off before the man could respond.

"I'm going for her," he told the Elite, and swept out of the room. He took the cart to the subbasement entry, then the long flight of stone stairs down to the thick concrete bunker. The green-suited security force was waiting next to the heavy iron door marked DANGER.

"Is she still in there?" he asked.

"As far as we know," the pale-skinned sergeant replied.

He frowned at the man and swung open the big door. "Stay out here," he said.

"She may be armed," the sergeant said.

Faisel stared at him, memorizing his name badge. "She is my guest," he hissed, and entered the room.

Closing the door behind him, he slid across the big bolt and wondered why the room was designed to be locked from the inside.

The room was large, and all of it was filled with sound. It rumbled inside of Faisel, vibrated him. The large generators hummed and the turbines whirred and all of them were roundish like mosques with no square corners. This was the heart of LOW, the total self-contained energy that ran the underground fortress.

"Come out!" he yelled to get above the noise.

She didn't answer. Circulating air blew against his face from an unseen vent, but it didn't dispel the petroleum smell of the place.

"I have watched you on the television box! I know you are in here! Come out or I bring in my people to flush you out!"

She came out then, slowly, with great dignity. She was still wearing the nightclothes she had worn when he had taken her, clothes she had refused to trade for the ones Faisel had provided.

The dream was still in his mind, and when he saw her, he flushed with anger. Closing the distance between them, he grabbed her by the wrist, tugging on her.

"Is this how you repay my hospitality?" he said, dragging her toward the metal door that sat opposite the one he had come in.

She refused to walk, fell to the floor. Reaching out with both hands, he took her wrists and dragged her bodily. "What kind of a demon are you?" he spat. "What kind of a spell have you cast on me?"

"The demons are in your brain!" she yelled at him through clenched teeth. "Why don't you just kill me now? Do it!"

He got on his knees before her face. "I love you," he said. "I wouldn't hurt you. I have never felt this way before."

Jumping up, he began to drag her again. "If you will not

accept the hospitality of Faisel ibn Faisel,'' he said, ''I will show you how inhospitable I can be.''

Reaching the door, he let go of her hands and fished out a ring of keys. Taking off a long, thin one, he used it to unlock the door.

Nura got to her knees, and Faisel grabbed her under the arms and stood her up. ''Welcome to your new home,'' he said, and shoved her into the room.

It was big and open, an extra boiler room in case the building were ever expanded. There was a cellblock at the far end of the room. Faisel roughly took Nura under the arm and propelled her toward it.

''I want you with a fire that consumes me,'' he said, moving swiftly.

''You don't want me,'' she returned. ''You want Abdullah's happiness.''

''I dream of you every time I sleep.''

''Happiness comes from within, not without.''

''You have put me in some kind of trance.''

''Your evil is what consumes you!''

Why didn't she understand? Why couldn't she see that she was forcing him to desperate measures? She could change it with a word, a look—a crumb of bread for a starving man. She was making him act crazy, insane. He didn't know what he was doing anymore.

''Why are you doing this to me?'' he pleaded. ''I don't want to hurt you.''

''Do your worst,'' she said. ''It is no business of mine.''

He screamed loudly, an animal sound. If she wouldn't love him, she could hate him, at least feel something for him, know in some measure the pain that he lived with.

He reached the cellblock and used the same key to unlock one of the cells that he had used to open the door. ''I put my wives here when they misbehave. Since you are going to be my wife, you may want to get used to it.''

She turned and stared at him, rubbing the place on her arm where he had held her. ''You may take me, but you'll never own me.''

Lips twitching, he reached out rough hands and ripped the nightgown from her body, leaving her naked. She stood looking at him, head held high.

''Is this what you want?'' she said, spreading her arms

wide. "It's skin, and blood. And it's no different from all the other skin and blood you have known in your life."

He stared at her, mouth dry. "Now you won't do any more running in the halls," he said, and his breath was coming ragged.

"Is this it," she asked, "or is there more to your humiliation?"

And the anger made him jump, and he wanted to shove her words back into her smirking mouth. He grabbed her and threw her to the dark-stained mattress that served the bare cell as a bed.

She didn't struggle; she didn't scream. She just lay there with staring eyes. He pushed himself hard against her, hating her the whole time for making him do it. Then he saw her eyes and stopped, pulling away.

"No," he said, standing. "You'll come to me. You will come to me. And when Abdullah dies, I will do the right thing and marry his widow as prescribed by Law."

She sat up on the mattress, looking at him, looking through him. "You're afraid to take me," she said. "Somewhere inside, you know that the dream isn't real, and that frightens you to death."

"Dream," he whispered, and what really frightened him was that he feared the dream was real. He backed out of the cell, clanging the door to lock, the bars between them.

"You will stay here until you come to me and ask me to take you out."

"Then I will stay here a very long time," she said, and gathered up the remnants of her torn clothing.

He reached through the bars and snatched the clothes away from her. Without a word, he turned and strode from the room, trying to get control of the jangling in his stomach.

The Elite he had left in his bedroom was waiting at the outside door with the security team.

"I have tried to contact Misha'al," he said. "I cannot find him anywhere in the building."

"Not in the building?" Faisel said. He had never known Misha'al to leave LOW without a reason. "Put out a message for him over the television boxes of the world. I want him back here with me."

He climbed the stairs then, trying to figure out what kind of life Misha'al had besides with him.

*   *   *

Death is a camel that lies down by every door.
                                    —Persian Proverb

XL
Mr. Elwood's Apartment

The pain had been intense that night, more intense than he had thought possible. The Jits were on the move; the city streets were full of torches and rioters, and he had foolishly gone charging up a hill like a fifteen-year-old.

Sitting alone in the dark by the windows and watching the torches and the occasional flashes of lightning in the ever-grumbling clouds, it struck him for the first time that maybe there were worse things than being dead. The pain was an ever-constant companion, a friend of long and terminal duration. He took some pills, a lot of them because the pain was so bad, and then he shot himself up with massive doses of central-nervous-system depressants and lay down to get some sleep. Somewhere between three and four in the morning he woke up, his belly heaving, his brain off in a fog somewhere. He had to throw up.

Getting up, he stumbled toward the john. He was more asleep than awake, more dead than alive, more unconscious than not.

He somehow made it to the bathroom and fell to his knees before the porcelain bowl. He knelt there, teetering on the brink for several seconds, then fell back to sleep, pitching forward.

He drowned, very quickly and unceremoniously, in the toilet, touching off a controversy that would rip the city to pieces.

PART FOUR

Perchance the unbelievers will wish that
*   they had surrendered:*
leave them to eat, and to take their joy,
and to be bemused by hope; certainly
*   they will soon know!*
Never a city have We destroyed, but it
*   had a known decree,*
and no nation outstrips its term, nor
*   do they put it back.*

—The Koran
XV. El-Hijr

Riches are not from abundance of worldly goods, but from a contented mind.
                    —The Prophet Mohammed

XLI
Louisiana Skies

Majid kept the binoculars glued to his face so long that he etched circular crease marks around his eyes and could barely manage to focus when he pulled them away. His entire balloon force was in the air, but the weather conditions were making it extremely difficult to navigate properly. The clouds roiled low, and the wind had picked up. The really heavy showers were finally making themselves felt.

He sat by the big laser, watching the dark ground below. His binoculars were in one hand, a microphone in the other.

"Damn you," he whispered to Ted Milander somewhere on the ground, and even if he'd shouted it, Milander wouldn't have been able to hear him.

After the run-in of the day before, Milander had scattered his people into deep forests, spread them out to get to Orleans on their own. It made them impossible to track, especially in the bad weather. Several times Majid had seen small groups scurrying to hiding when he passed over, but they were a drop in the bucket, not worth the battery drain on the laser. He'd never felt so helpless in his life.

He frowned. "I'm going to get you, son of a bitch," he whispered again.

A gust of wind blew past, shaking the balloon, wagging its gondola. Majid felt like he had left his stomach at New Mecca.

"Can't you keep it any steadier than that?" he yelled into the mike.

The pilot's voice crackled back in his headphones. "We shouldn't even be up here in this weather."

"You let me be the judge of that!" Majid said angrily. "Take us to the river."

They began a long, slow turn, but more wind came up and bounced them lightly against the balloon on their left.

The crash was loud, as people and equipment went flying. Majid was thrown to the ground, his radio coming down on top of him. Luckily he caught it and set it back up on the stand.

"What in God's name are you doing?" he yelled into the mike, as green suits picked themselves and their equipment up off the rocking floor. "Damage estimates!"

"I think we're all right," the voice returned. "We'll check it out in detail."

Line two was buzzing lightly. He flicked it on.

"Station three, station three," came a barely audible, crackling voice.

"Yes," Majid said.

"Midair collision," the strained voice said. "Three balloons down."

Majid slapped the table. "Any contacts?"

"No. We're fighting for our lives up here, we're—"

"Pick up the survivors," Majid interrupted. "Have your squad return to base."

He clicked off and looked out the window. They were coming up on the swollen Mississippi, its serpentine path knotting into the horizon.

The river was full of traffic, coming and going. There was no way to distinguish the Jits from everybody else. He briefly considered destroying everything on the river, then thought better of it. Hopefully VeePee Cat and his river people could strain out the Jit boats at the river checkpoints before they could get into the harbor. That was the supposition anyway.

He began to reconcile himself to a siege of Orleans. When they all got to one place and stayed, that's when he'd have to get them. He spat loudly on the floor. And get them he would.

They stayed up awhile longer, but when he watched out his window as two of his balloons collided, one dropping a gondola full of screaming men, he knew it was time to go.

Turning the balloons around, Majid headed them back to New Mecca, where they arrived just in time for afternoon prayers.

* * *

We were with the Rasul on a journey, and some
men stood up repeating aloud, "God is most
great"; and the Rasul said, "O men, be easy on
yourselves and do not distress yourselves by
raising your voices; verily you do not call to
one deaf or absent, but verily to one who
heareth and seeth; and He is with you; and He
to whom you pray is nearer to you than the
neck of your camel."

—The Prophet Mohammed

It is better to go to the house of mourning,
than to go to the house of feasting: for that
is the end of all men; and the living will lay
it to his heart.

—Eastern Wisdom

XLII
The River

The oil tanker moved into the harbor like a huge cockroach, bloated and ugly, and totally unwanted. It was an Arab delivery, and the Arabs respected neither the authority of the river check-points nor the inherent danger of the situation. They just floated their monstrous boat in, displacing more water in an already overflowing river, and demanded that they be serviced immediately. Olson decided to ignore them.

He stood in the passenger side of the speedboat, the bull-horn in his hand. Junex Jansen was driving the boat. He was one of the new Execs who had transferred from other departments friendly to Mr. Elwood to help Olson on the river.

The rain was coming hard, dripping Olson's hair down his bare head, slicking in sheets down his exo. They pulled up beside a small pontoon boat full of beef jerky stuck in long strips on cords strung around the deck. Barrels of hardtack filled the horizontal spaces.

"YOU WILL HAVE TO LEAVE THE HARBOR IMMEDIATELY," Olson called as they lapped gently against the side of the thing.

Two dirty-looking men were busy rolling the barrels closer to the center of the deck.

"We're gettin' packed up as quick as we can!" one of them yelled.

"LEAVE NOW," Olson said. "RAISE ANCHOR OR YOUR BOAT WILL BE CONFISCATED. DON'T COMMUNICATE WITH OTHER BOATS ON THE RIVER. THEY MAY BE JITS."

The men walked toward them to try to explain why their situation was special.

"Let's go, Jan," Olson told the driver.

The stocky man ran a hand across his shaved slick bald head and throttled the engine. "You know," he yelled, his quick takeoff throwing spray into the faces of the men on the pontoon, "even animals have enough sense to get in out of the rain!"

"We're men," Olson called back. "We've evolved past things like that!"

The harbor was emptying slowly, and would never empty totally due to a large number of boats that belonged there for one reason or another. It was a slow business trying to root out the leeches, but Olson could hardly blame them—he wouldn't want to have to get back on the river knowing there were Jits out there with him.

"What about the Arabs?" Jansen asked, nodding toward the tanker.

"They just want to dump our monthly ration and get a little R&R," Olson returned. "They'll just have to wait their turn."

"Their turn is usually first," Jan said.

Olson tightened his lips. "We've got other priorities at the moment."

A loud horn blared out from the wharf offices, crying across the sounding board of the water, continuing to echo long after the horn stopped.

"What is it?" Jansen asked.

"Something's wrong," Olson said. "Take us back to the dock."

Jan turned a wide arc, sending a curtain of frothy spray in a graceful curve beside them. Opening up the engine full, they ripped through the gentle waves, bouncing along their tops as the piers rushed past them.

Pulling up to the wharf, they slipped into their reserved space and tied it down. Then they quickly climbed the only two above-water rungs of what used to be a long wooden ladder up to the metal dock.

There were people moving around on the wide pier, fuzztops mostly and employees with authorization. The two-story wooden houselike office structure was set on the land side of the pier. Up and down the river, they were still fighting a losing battle with the sandbags.

Junex Valuska, tall and passive, was waiting grimly for him at the door.

"What's wrong?" Olson said, moving past him into the room. The office was old creaky wood. It smelled of rot and fish and was filled with several gunmetal-gray desks. A large map of the harbor hung on the wall.

"We just got the news," Junex York said from his desk. He was older, too old to be a Junex. He was a scrapper who was better at opening his mouth than shutting it. Covered with scars and with a missing thumb and forefinger on his right hand, York had been busted back so many times that he had begun to think of success in very nonlinear terms.

"News about what?" Olson asked.

"Mr. Elwood," Valuska said, walking back in the office and shutting the door.

Olson sighed, sitting on the edge of his desktop. "What's he want now?"

Valuska studied him with dark eyes. "He's dead, Cat."

Olson was on his feet without realizing it. "You're sure? How? When?"

"They found him a little while ago when they went to clean the room," York said, his gravelly voice low and concerned. "It looks like he drowned in his fucking toilet."

"What?" Jan said.

York raised a hand. "Honest to Allah," he said. "Drowned," he said. "In his fucking toilet," he said.

Olson felt dead himself, all hollowed out inside. His life was in a shambles again, just like on the outside; except on the outside you were careful not to care about people. He wanted to blame somebody, to hate somebody for it.

"Did somebody kill him?" Olson asked.

Both Valuska and York shrugged.

"What's this going to do to us?" Jan asked.

Olson turned to him, eyes narrowing. "What do you mean by that?"

Valuska stepped closer, clearing his throat. "What he means is that we've stuck our necks out by siding with you and Mr. Elwood. Rennie might have the strength to take over now. What does that mean for us?"

Olson looked at each of them in turn. "Why do you ask me about this?" he said, thinking about the Jit baby. "You each made your decision on your own. You came to me because you saw an opportunity to move up in a hurry. You knew the risks at the time. What do you want me to give you, a written slip telling Rennie you won't be bad boys again?"

York stood up. "We don't deserve that from you," he said. "We know what we let ourselves in for, and we're willing to accept that. We just want some idea of what happens now."

"Okay," Olson said, walking to the map and staring at it, his back to them. After a moment, he turned back around. "If you're still willing to stick with me, what we do now is whip Rennie's ass and take over the Company. When we're through, I can guarantee each of you, and the others who came to me on the river, a department-head job when this is all through."

"That's good enough for me," York said. "Hell, at my age, this is the only shot I've got at the big time. Count me in."

"Me too," said Jan. "I always was a dumb fuck."

Valuska smiled. "I'm in too," he said, "but for reasons completely opposite Jan's. I think you can pull it off."

Olson moved for the door. "Things are going to get sticky now," he said. "I want you all armed all the time, and I want you to stick close to me. Let's get over to LOW."

He walked out into the rain, the others right behind. Moving through the sparse crowd, they made their way to the barricades.

"Parker made Jit contact out on the first checkpoint today," Valuska told him as they walked.

"Any trouble?" Olson asked.

"The flamethrowers did the trick," the man responded.

They moved up to the barricades, the crowds thick on the city side. Several fuzztops cleared a path into the crowd for them.

"Did they burn the boat, too?" Olson asked, people pushing all around him.

"Yeah," Val returned. "They burned everything."

"Remind me to put out a memo on the taking of souvenirs," Olson said. "We've got to make sure everything gets burned."

The mob was thick by the barricades, but thinned pretty well a block or so later. Their main problems were with water. Several of the more low-lying streets were completely flooded, making them continuously find alternate routes. They walked through the tenement section that was once called the French Quarter, then into the more elevated areas.

Just outside of the Quarter, they were attacked by a small band of citizens armed with knives and aluminum bats. They beat them back easily, leaving several dead and scattering the others. York, especially, showed great style in combat, attacking with a viciousness rarely seen in someone his age. It only lasted a few minutes, and when it was over, Olson would swear that he caught a glimpse of an exo slipping around a corner. He was convinced then that Rennie hired the locals to do a little of his dirty work. If that were the case, he was going to have to do much better than that.

When they arrived at the LOW building, it was a whirlwind of confusion. There were large, milling crowds outside the building generating the natural fear that comes upon the death of a father figure. Inside was much worse.

Execs shuffled around aimlessly, talking in small groups, then moving on to other groups. The topic was serious politics, the kind practiced with the cutting edge of the sword. A momentary hush fell over the assembled when Olson and his entourage walked in. He glared around the room, playing the game, and everything returned to normal. The first thing he noticed was that the weapons racks were all empty. The second thing he noticed was that Rennie's people seemed a lot more organized, a lot more positive, than his. He called them his, though he had no idea if they thought of themselves that way.

They walked into the middle of the room, Olson looking around, hands on hips.

"Looks like some of these folks would just as soon murder you as look at you," Jansen said.

"You're here to keep them from doing just that," Olson returned. "Stay alert."

VeePee Glower and VeePee Hennessy spotted Olson from across the room and moved toward him. Glower ran Manufacturing and Hennessy was Administrative VeePee, the next step below Mr. Elwood's. With Mr. Elwood's death, he would succeed him in seniority. Glower was a step behind Hennessy.

"This is a terrible day for the Company," Hennessy said, shaking Olson's hand. "What a tragedy." He was an older man, early sixties, with runny blue eyes and a tired face. He looked weary and frightened.

"Was it murder?" Olson asked for the second time that day.

"Difficult to say," Glower said, studying Olson with dark, apelike features. He was probably the biggest Elwood loyalist in the city. Olson didn't worry about him. "He drowned, that's all we know."

"What are we going to do?" Hennessy asked.

"The same thing we were going to do before," Olson returned, playing it by ear.

"And what was that?" Glower asked, eyes hard.

Olson turned and met those eyes, overpowered them. "We're going to turn the Company over to me," he said flatly. "Unless, of course, you have a better idea."

"I have a better idea," Glower said. "We follow the line of advancement and run the Company ourselves."

"Do you think you can stand against Rennie and me?"

Glower's eyebrows began bobbing madly. "You?"

"This Company is my legacy," Olson said, "and I mean to have it. So help me, I'll get you, no matter what it takes, if you cheat me out of what's mine."

"For God's sake," Hennessy said. "If he wants the damned thing, let's give it to him. Rennie would eat me alive . . . it's really not something I'm looking forward to."

Glower rubbed his face gently, stroking, thinking. "Besides," he said to Olson, "if we turn things over to you, Rennie will no doubt try to take it from you. Perhaps you two young bucks can fight it out and destroy each other, leaving the way open ultimately for a wise old Company man."

Olson smiled at Glower's threatening "honesty." "A little competition never bothered me," he said.

Glower's gaze didn't vary. "How would we do it?"

"Not here," Olson said, glancing around the room. "I want to see the body."

"Up in the apartment," Hennessy said.

Olson nodded. "We'll talk in the elevator."

They took the elevator up, Olson and his people, plus the other two VeePees. Once they started up, Olson spoke: "If nobody changes sides on us, we'll still have a majority on the board."

"If you count Abdullah in there," Hennessy said.

"You leave that to me," Olson replied. "We'll have to call a meeting, probably tomorrow, to officially confirm you as acting Branch President and Regional Director. When that happens, you will nominate me in your place, since, as I understand it, Branch President is not necessarily a seniority job."

"It's an interim job by seniority," Glower said, his look still uneasy. "Usually, though, once somebody's in, it's tough to get him out."

Olson took a breath, listening to the creaking of the pulleys. "So, we'll nominate and second. When we vote, it should break down exactly as it did the last meeting, and I'll be in, and all of you get to keep your jobs and your heads."

"Sounds too easy," Glower said.

The doors slid open, and the small hallway that led to Mr. Elwood's door was jammed with people. Many wore exos, and a great many more carried weapons in a section of the building that had never allowed weapons before.

They shoved their way through the crowd, the voices loud around them. Fuzztops guarded the door, but allowed them access immediately when they saw that Hennessy—Mr. Hennessy— was part of the group.

As they went in, Mr. Elwood's current Houris was being led out, crying loudly. When she saw Mr. Hennessy, she stopped, throwing her arms around him, crying into his shoulder.

"Oh, sir," she wailed. "It's so sad. He was so young, so far from retirement."

"There, there," the man said, and gently pulled her away, putting her back in the hands of the Junexes who were helping her.

"Nice girl," he whispered.

By all accounts, she really was something special. Mr. Hennessy would inherit her by Law, and probably keep her.

The apartment was fairly empty. A few VeePees milled about; a handful of fuzztops looked around for clues in their comical way.

"Rennie won't take your idea lying down," Glower said, then pointed down the hall. "The body's in the bedroom."

"We'll need to have a council of war right away," Olson said, "to set up some sort of mutual defense pact."

"Isn't there some easier way of doing this?" Hennessy asked.

They moved down the narrow hallway, Junex York taking point, Jan and Valuska bringing up the rear. "Well, we could just turn LOW Orleans over to Rennie Du'camp," Olson said, "but I don't think you'd like the results of that, either."

Hennessy rubbed a soft hand across his soft face. "I'm too old for this shit," he said.

Olson put a rough hand on his shoulder. "Then you'd better find a fountain of youth somewhere in a hurry."

York took up a position beside the bedroom door. Olson walked in just in time to see Rennie Du'camp bent over the body on Mr. Elwood's bed. Loudly clearing his throat, Rennie spit on the dead man's face.

Olson was in motion without thought. "Bastard!" he screamed, and threw himself across the bed, banging into Du'camp.

The man growled, grabbing him around the throat. They rolled, thrashing on the bed, knocking Mr. Elwood's naked body to the floor.

Olson had the man in a bear hug, squeezing, but Rennie was also wearing an exo and wasn't feeling much. They rolled over, falling off the bed onto Mr. Elwood, and many hands were pulling them apart.

The atmosphere of the room was supercharged as the two camps pulled back their champions, straining still to get at one another.

"I'm going to kill you!" Rennie screamed.

"Try it! Try it!"

Rennie broke free temporarily, and they were at each other again, then pulled apart again. Rennie's people dragged him toward the door.

"Enjoy your last days!" Du'camp screamed as they got him out of there. "Fun's almost over!"

Olson stood, breathing heavily, his chest rising and falling. He looked and noticed the hands still on his arms.

"I'm all right," he said quietly, and they released him.

Hennessy and Glower were picking Mr. Elwood up by the shoulders and legs. They laid him on the bed, folding his already stiffening arms across his chest.

"Would you leave me alone with him for a minute?" Olson

asked, and everyone filed out quietly. York hung by the door for a moment, looking as if he were getting ready to say something. Then he thought better of it and went out, closing the door behind him.

Going up to the bed, Olson sat next to Mr. Elwood. He stared at him. The eyes were closed, the muscles slack; but Olson found it interesting that Mr. Elwood looked years younger. He finally realized that it was because the man's face wasn't creased in pain anymore.

"I've had two friends in my whole life," he whispered to the corpse. "Now one of them's dead and the other is gone." His voice was beginning to choke up. "You told me about all this, but you didn't tell me how bad it was going to hurt when you went away."

And his thoughts turned to Gret, and he thought that maybe, just maybe, when he took over it would be easier for him to find her.

"You weren't much of a father to me," he said, "but you sure as hell were better than nothing."

With that, he laid his head down on Mr. Elwood's chest and cried for a long time.

*   *   *

No absolute is going to make the lion lie down with the lamb: unless the lamb is inside.
—Arabic Saying

It is your own conduct which will lead you to reward or punishment, as if you had been destined therefor.
—The Prophet Mohammed

XLIII

1438 Bourbon Street, Orleans
LOW Manufacturing

VeePee Glower sat and drank scotch at his big desk overlooking the interior of one of the large warehouses, and tried to put it all together. This Cat person was so forceful, so sure of himself, that he wasn't quite sure what to think of it all. There were rules, regulations, codes of conduct—all important stuff. It all seemed meaningless to Cat, as if accomplishing his goal was all that mattered and to hell with the regulations. Glower couldn't figure that in a man. They had a saying in the factories: Hire in masses, train 'em in classes, then fire their asses. Cat seemed beyond that system, as if he were starting his own.

He glanced out the overlook window to the huge, open warehouse below. Men, his men, moved crates around with fork lifts and two-wheelers, sweating and cursing, and knowing what their job was. Glower had always thought that he knew what his job was, too. Now it was different. He'd have to decide for himself. Follow Cat or not? The alternative was Rennie, not any better. Maybe a lot worse.

He heard a commotion outside. Rising heavily from his spring-creaking chair, he moved suddenly to the window. It was late, too late, and the bottle of Yid scotch on the desktop was a lot emptier than it should have been, but what the hell, it was the end of an era.

Siding the curtain that looked out on street level, he gazed out into the dark, rain-filled night. Auts, a lot of auts, were pulling up to the curbs and blocking the streets. Heavily armed men in exos were hurrying out of the machines, while many citizens with bats and knives waited to be told what to do.

He dropped the curtain. Damn. And he wasn't even wearing an exo. Running to the office door, he hit the emergency siren and it immediately blurted loudly into the building. Going back to the desk, he lifted the telephone receiver with one hand while rummaging through his desk for a laser with the other.

The phone lines were dead.

"Fuckers!" he screamed, and shoved the phone off the desk to clatter loudly on the cement floor. He grabbed the shiny silver laser and checked the charge before shoving it into the belt of his three-piece suit.

There was an explosion at the sliding front doors, and the mammoth slabs of metal blew inward, bringing with them white-gray smoke and Rennie's people.

They charged in like a plague of locusts, screaming and firing all manner of weapons. The warehouse night shift was off guard and without security. They didn't have a chance.

The fighting swept in, explosions filling the building with

smoke, as laser lines zipped hot pink in and out of the frothy confusion.

Glower pulled his own weapon and took off the safety. His office was connected to the warehouse floor by a steep metal staircase. A dark green exo came through the smoke fog with an automatic weapon in his hands, and started up the stairs. Glower let him get about halfway up before firing himself, the laser line making a neat black pinhole in the safety glass of the window.

The man stood for a moment, the tiny hole in his head smoking gray, then he tumbled backwards, somersaulting down the steps to lie in a jumble at the bottom.

Then other figures emerged from the smoke, other exos with no-peek faces. They took cover behind wooden crates and lay down a barrage of fire at the office.

Glower ducked back, as glass and chips of wood flew through the room in an obscene dance of death, and he knew that when the firing stopped they would rush him.

Putting his back against a filing cabinet, he slid to a sitting position and prepared for the inevitable. Rennie would do right by his wife and children, he didn't fear that anyway, and all he really could figure was that at age fifty-four, it had all seemed to go by awfully fast. At least he was spared the agony of having to make a decision about Cat.

Mr. Elwood's Houris's name was Regina, and she was everything that Hennessy had been led to believe. She sat astride the old man on the big bed, pounded him mercilessly while screaming like a fat soprano at the Orleans opera house.

Up and down she rode him, pulling all the way off his dick, only to slam down again as if she were trying to stuff his whole body up into her cunt. He knew he'd be black and blue in the morning, but for now the pain felt good. It was like a taste of something he could almost remember, but not quite. Sitting up slightly, he took a long fingerlike nipple between his wrinkled lips and tried to suck some of her life into himself.

And that's when the door burst open and the Junexes with the machine guns strode in.

"Already?" was all he could think of to say, and they hurried and pushed themselves to orgasm just as the first bullets slammed into their bodies.

*   *   *

Olson lay awake in bed, even though it was his sleep time. The M-16 lay beside him, ready. In the living area, York snored loudly, while Jan and Valuska played cards in the dim light. Wexler slept the sleep of innocence in the bathtub.

No one spoke, that wasn't the deal. Olson had made it perfectly clear near the microphone that he wanted to be alone that night—to think. He wanted to see if Rennie would hear him and take the bait.

He would send Jan in the morning to watch the gates for Gret while they were open. If he could just hold things together long enough to take power, he could use all of LOW's resources to find her and get her back. He needed her now, more than ever. He needed her to help him understand his empire; but that was the furthest thing from his mind. What he really needed was her laughing eyes, and godalmighty tilted nose, and the fact that sadness and happiness were absolutes to her as they are to a child.

He sat up in bed. It was too quiet in the hall.

Grabbing the gun, he hurried over to the sofa, nudging York to wake him up. The man sat up quietly, shaking his head to clear it.

Jan and Valuska dropped their cards and took up positions behind furniture, while York doused the small table lamp and plunged the room into total darkness.

A small sliver of light from the hall was filtering in under the door. They watched as several shadows moved to the door and obliterated the brightness.

"Aim for their faces," Olson whispered harshly. "Wait for me to shoot first."

There was a small scraping at the lock, and he knew they were using the passkey. The door swung open easily on well-oiled hinges that hadn't been oiled earlier that day. Several backlighted silhouettes filled the door space, then quietly slid into the room. There seemed to be more in the halls.

Olson let them get in a few steps before opening up. He pulled the trigger at head level and held it down. The small room was filled with sound as it strobed in and out of blackness with the flare of many rifles. In flashes he could hear the screams and see people falling by degrees, frame after frame, and the gunpowder smell was pungent in the small room.

It was over almost before it had begun. Olson heard feet retreating down the hallway toward the elevators. He jumped up from behind the chair and ran to the door over a carpet of bodies. They had already made the elevator and the door was closing. Shouldering the rifle, he emptied the clip into the machine, and saw several of them go down before the doors closed completely.

He turned back into the room. The lights were on, and his people were pulling exo masks off the bodies of six Junexes.

"Lookee what we got here," Jan said, grinning, his bald head shining in the light. He pulled a head up by the hair. It was Billy Fain, Rennie's boy. He let go and the head fell to the floor with a thud.

"Drag this crap out into the hall," Olson said, then looked up to see Wexler peering sleepily around the bathroom door-frame. He turned back to Jan. "We're going to need a new place to stay."

* * *

> Do not appear rejoicing at the misfortune of
> thy brother, for God may be merciful to him
> and put thee into trouble.
> —The Prophet Mohammed

XLIV
The Joust

Olson marched thirty strong up to the warehouse that used to house VeePee Glower's offices. There was a merger party going on in there now, attended by Rennie Du'camp and several hundred of his very closest friends.

Rennie now had control of Manufacturing, which switched the balance of power over to him. That fact, coupled with the assassination of VeePee Hennessy, heir apparent to Mr. Elwood, spelled desperate trouble for Olson and his coalition. Olson had underestimated Rennie for the last time. Now he was hoping that the underestimation would be on the other foot.

The rain fell in torrents as Olson and the Junexes he could gather quickly sloshed through the low-lying sections of Bourbon

Street toward the several-square-block section of warehouses. The streets were drowning in silence and darkness, and the light and noise at the end of the block drew them magnetically.

"They could easily kill us all," Jerry Joe said, and his blue exo covered up his face and features pretty well.

"Going to anyway," Olson returned. "If we don't show some sort of unified front, we won't be able to muster any support at all."

"What are we going to do?" York asked.

Olson turned and stared at him through sheets of water. "I'm open," he said. "Got anything in mind?"

York smiled wide. "Kick some ass," he suggested.

Turning all the way around, Olson looked back down the line behind him, at his men and the burden they carried above their heads. He hadn't lost anybody yet, which was a surprise in itself. All the other VeePees were alerted and prepared now. He didn't suspect that any more ground would be lost tonight, but it was time to show his leadership, or the momentum of Rennie's initial thrust would end the war right here. Olson had lost two key people through violence; he wasn't about to lose any through simple osmosis.

They drew closer to the warehouse and the loud bass rhythms of the musak reaching their hearing. Then they heard the mourning wails of those who had lost people in the attack, mixing with drunken shouts of the revelers within.

They began passing people carrying bodies, families with nowhere within the walls to bury their dead. The habit of late was to pillage the oldest standing graves in the cemeteries and add a new body to the bones in the old coffin.

Olson held up a hand to stop the flow. "Jerry Joe," he said, "Jan, York, Valuska . . . all of you come with me. The rest of you, hide yourselves out here. If trouble starts, I want your asses inside."

He looked at the warehouse half a block down the street. Glower's bullet-riddled body was hanging from a telephone pole just outside, his wife on her hands and knees crying, the water almost covering her.

"Somebody cut him down," he said, and his throat was dry. "And give us that bundle you've got."

York waded over to the Junexes and took their burden, slinging it over his shoulder.

Olson moved to the warehouse, past the pile of unclaimed

bodies half-floating in the flooded street. The big sliding doors were missing, blown away, and sandbags covered the entrance to keep out the water.

There were two guards by the door place, but they were sitting on the sandbags, facing into the party, watching. Olson was surprised at the lax security, at Rennie's overconfidence. He watched as his advance people sneaked up to the guards and pulled them out into the water, drowning them quietly.

Stopping just before reaching the sandbags, he looked at the others. "I don't know what I'm going to do in there," he said. "Just try to follow my lead. And for God's sake, keep my back protected."

With that, he stepped over the sandbags and through the big doors into the bright yellow light and the merriment.

All the warehouse crates had been moved against the far walls, leaving a large section in the middle of the place wide open. It was filled with people, men and women, some in exos, most not. There was a long table full of food, hot dogs and bread and cheese and fruit, and everyone was eating freely, obscenely. Naked Houris ran around, giving and taking to anyone who was sober enough to reach out an arm and grab. Martinis were being served from huge barrels by giant Engies. A cigarette- and dope-smoke haze hovered by the lights like a manmade rain cloud, and the sound was loud, overpowering, as everyone yelled to get above the already earsplitting musak. The large mind-match screen from the stadium had been moved into the place and people were lined up for matching, winner take all as long as someone could hold out against all comers. The screen image was of two gamecocks, pecking at each other's eyes and clawing with razored talons.

Rennie was near the table, drinking heavily. Olson had never seen the man drink before, and it made him angry to think Du'camp had lowered his guard because Olson was no match for him.

As he moved closer to the center of the room, he could hear it get quiet by degrees, as more and more people noticed his arrival. His own people formed a loose semicircle around him, weapons ready, eyes wary.

Olson fixed on Rennie, walked deliberately toward him. By the time Du'camp saw him, everything but the musak had stopped dead.

Putting aside his drink, Rennie shoved his way through the

people near him and strode toward Olson, hatred flashing through his dark eyes. The two men stopped no more than a foot from one another.

"Welcome to my victory party," Rennie said loudly to get above the musak. "Have you come to concede?"

"You left some trash at my house," Olson returned, and their eyes were locked tight. "I just wanted to return it. York!"

The man stepped forward and dumped his package at Rennie's feet. It was Billy Fain, tongue hanging out, his dead eyes opened wide in fear and pain.

The crowd surged forward, and Olson's men brought up their weapons. Everything stopped. Stalemate. Marty Jerny, red face redder with alcohol, came running out of the crowd to kneel down before the dead man, a puzzled expression on his face.

Rennie looked down at Fain, then up at Olson, locking eyes with him again. "Would somebody shut that fucking thing off!" he screamed, and seconds later the musak died away and they stood there in the overpowering quiet.

"What do you want here?" Rennie asked quietly.

When Olson spoke, it was loud and confident. "I want to tell you you're a shit," he said so that everyone could hear. "I want to tell you that you'll never control this city, that you don't have the guts to take it or the balls to hold it."

"I could fry you right here," Rennie said.

Olson jammed the barrel of his M-16 up into Rennie's neck. "What have I got to lose?" he said. "Hell, we'll both go and leave the city to the Jits."

Jerny stood up, face contorted. "He killed Billy," he said. "You've got to do something."

"Shut up," Rennie said, not taking his eyes off Olson.

"Billy was a bad boy," Olson said; then his eyes caught sight of the now blank matching screen. "Tell you what: I'll give you the chance to get even."

Jerny stretched his frame higher. "You name it," he spat.

"No!" Rennie said.

"He killed Billy," Jerny said. "We gotta do something."

"Unless, of course, you'd like to do it yourself," Olson said to Rennie, and he could watch the possibilities flash through the man's eyes.

The crowd was up for it now, crying drunkenly for blood. A Houris was grunting somewhere in the background as someone did her behind a crate. Rennie was drunk and knew it; he also wasn't stupid enough to risk everything he had gained in one foolish moment. He closed his eyes and slumped his shoulders.

"It's your funeral," he said to Jerny.

The man smiled broadly. "What's it gonna be?" he asked.

"Mind match," Olson said.

The man's features darkened for a second, then sprang back stupidly. "You're on."

The crowd cheered and cleared a path for them to the screen. Olson's Junexes kept tight around him, always ready. Olson and Jerny sat at the table, the screen to their sides. Locking eyes, they fixed the alpha rings around their foreheads.

"We need a starter," Olson said.

Someone wandered out of the crowd with a round piece of plastic in his hand. "Call it," he said to Jerny, and flipped the thing with his thumb.

"Blue," Jerny said.

The plastic hit the floor, and the man bent down to read it. "Blue it is," he said. "Junex Jerny's advantage."

"Do it," Olson said, and closed his eyes. . . .

He was hurtling down the highway at a high rate of speed, the aut he sat in precisely like the one he'd ridden in on his first day. He looked down at the instruments; they were as alien to him as the ones he had seen. He wasn't wearing an exo, but a knife sat beside him on the passenger seat. The landscape was moving past him in an incredible blur, and if he'd had enough sense to know any better, he would have been scared to death.

A blip was flashing on the radar screen, and he knew that it was Jerny bearing down on him. All the equipment lay before him—machine guns and rocket launchers and lasers—but he didn't know how to use any of it.

An explosion sounded beside him, rocking the aut, and he had to grab the control pistols to keep the thing on the road. He got Jerny on visual, barreling toward him, machine guns blazing.

The roadway kicked up all around him and bullets raked the hood and windshield, and Olson was swerving, nearly losing control.

He somehow kept the road, getting control just as Jerny flashed past him, mere inches from him, the man's leering face close enough to reach out and touch.

Olson was moving down open highway. His impulse was to keep moving, to take the imaginary aut straight down the imaginary road and see where it led, but he knew he couldn't do that.

He did know how to work the brakes and gas. Slamming on the brakes, he shifted the pistol grips and skidded the aut into a semispin, coming to rest facing the way he had just come. Gunning it, he headed back down the road, frantically trying to figure out how to work the fire controls.

His radar was bleeping again, Jerny closing in. His eyes dashed over the toggles and buttons, but none of it made any sense.

The highway exploded in front of him, orange fire flowers blossoming loudly. The aut was bouncing wildly, black smoke bleeding from under the hood, turning the windshield dark and slick with oil. Olson fought the grips, and Jerny was right there, charging through the smoke to sideswipe him as they passed, bright white sparks showering out of their contact.

And Olson pulled the aut out of it one more time, skidding around for another pass. This would be the last one. The smoke had dissipated somewhat, probably because he was running out of oil. Picking up the knife that lay beside him, he stuffed it in the belt of his suit and put his foot on the gas.

He picked up speed, but the aut was dogging it, crying down deep inside of itself. The radar was bleeping again, and he slammed on the brakes, then pushed on the gas. Missiles exploded far down the road, anticipating him prematurely. He gunned for the missile fire on the roadway, braking as he reached the black and gray smoke. Turning sideways, he blocked the road.

He jammed the door release, and jumped out of the aut, pulling the knife as he did so. He dived for the shoulder just as Jerny's aut screeched loudly and slid into his with a terrible tearing of metal on metal as both cars caught fire.

Olson ran around the choking smoke in time to see Jerny, shaken up, climbing out of the cab, his own knife out and ready. The man stumbled away from the holocaust and it exploded, sending a huge ball of orange/black fire high into the blue, nonraining sky.

Jerny looked over and saw Olson, his eyes widening.

"Sorry, Marty," Olson said, thinking of Gret. "It's not going to be that easy."

He walked toward the man, the hatred welling up within him, overpowering him. All the frustration, all the angers, were giving themselves vent. He wouldn't lose now, and somehow Jerny sensed this. The hesitation was obvious on his face.

"You're going to die, Marty," Olson said.

"Don't count on it," the man returned, but his voice was quaking.

Olson moved to within striking distance there on the hard-packed flatland, the dead auts still spewing fire on the highway.

He feinted a slash, and Jerny thrust. Olson ducked and made a wide arc with the blade, gashing Jerny across the exposed forearm.

The knife fell from the man's hand and Olson charged, driving him away from it. Jerny grabbed his arm, blood flowing freely onto the dirt.

Olson charged again, and Jerny backpedaled, stumbling over a rock. He fell to the ground, hard, and Olson was right on top of him. He stabbed deeply into the man's other arm at the shoulder, ripping the blade lengthwise as he did.

Jerny lay whimpering on the ground, crying for mercy.

"Is that how Gret cried?" Olson asked, and the man's eyes darted back and forth. "Is it?"

"No...please," Jerny rasped. "You don't understand, I..."

Olson punched him in the face to shut him up. Then he used the knife to cut off the man's pants. He castrated him then, leaving him to scream for several minutes before slitting his throat and finishing the job....

The image faded, and Olson shook his head, back in the warehouse. He pulled the alpha ring off and threw it down. Jerny lay dead on the floor, curled up in the fetal position, the band still around his head.

The room was absolutely quiet, everyone staring at him with mouths open.

"It's you next time," he told Rennie.

"This *is* the next time," Rennie said, then turned to the crowd. "Take him! Don't just let him walk out of here!"

"Not so fast," Jerry Joe said, and he was pointing at the door.

The rest of Olson's people had come in. Thirty guns were trained at the crowd. No one moved.

Olson and Rennie exchanged glances, and as he turned to walk out of the warehouse, Olson knew that neither would underestimate the other again.

* * *

God's it is to show the way;
and some do swerve from it.
If He willed, He would have
guided you all together.
　　　　　　—The Koran
　　　　　　XVI. The Bee

Do your duty, and leave the rest to God.
　　　　　　—Corporate Wisdom

To win without risk is to triumph without
glory.

　　　　　　—Bedouin Proverb

XLV
Computer Central, Orleans

"It may not be anything," Kanaly said. "It doesn't make any sense."

The computer man and Abdullah walked quickly, shoving their way through the jam of Arab regulars and lower-management personnel in the basement hallway.

"What in the name of Wahhab is going on down here?" Abdullah asked, trying not to lose the little man in the crowd.

"Power settling," Kanaly told him. "The whole city is in turmoil since Mr. Elwood died. If someone doesn't take control soon, this whole place is going to come apart."

"Are we going to be able to keep this building open?"

The man turned to answer and ran into a green uniform. He jumped, startled, then continued. "Majid assured me that keeping the computer rooms clear was the priority."

Abdullah frowned. Their time was running out. He couldn't afford to lose any more of it. They walked past a wall screen showing Faisel's message for the day. It was a long, graphic video of someone dying from the Jitterbug, and Faisel's face inset saying they only had four days left. Abdullah noticed that people were beginning to look at him with something less than love in their hearts.

They reached the computer-room door. Kanaly nodded to the two regular army guards and motioned Abdullah inside. They left the confusion of the lower levels and entered a quiet, orderly workshop. The lights were on, the machines whirring away, but the place was empty except for Jackson, the other computer man, who sat staring at an open terminal, a cup of coffee in his hand.

Abdullah walked quickly to his side. "What have you found?" he asked.

The man looked up at him for several seconds, then removed his black frame glasses before speaking. "I honestly don't know what it is," he said, then looked back to the screen. "Look at this." He tapped the CRT with his glasses.

Abdullah walked around to face the screen. It was scrolling a list of disbursements to the Wichita branch, regular trade-off items, though quite a lot of them.

"So what?" he asked.

Jackson looked at him again. "There is no Wichita branch."

"What?"

The man frowned, put his glasses back on. "When we started this," he said, "we didn't know what we were looking for, so we started in the obvious place. We checked every tribute payment to Corporate to make sure it wasn't being siphoned. Everything was in order. So we began to methodically run through every asset and every disbursement to see how the two things offset one another. It was coming out fine, too, but we kept running into trade-offs to the Wichita branch."

The man leaned his chair back on two legs and took off his glasses again to rub his eyes. "Well, I've been working with LOW computers for the last twenty years, and I just didn't remember ever doing any business with a branch office in Wichita."

Kanaly walked around beside Jackson. "We checked Accounts Receivable and couldn't find anything coming in from Wichita, so we checked back through the files at the home office and discovered there was no such branch."

Abdullah looked at the still-scrolling list. "You mean that someone has been shipping goods and materials to a nonexistent city?"

"It's stranger than that," Jackson said, righting his chair. "This isn't the only city doing it. We got on the net and had a look at everybody's disbursements. Fifteen other cities all over the world are doing the same thing."

There was a commotion at the door. Abdullah looked up to see Cat forcing himself past the door guards. They had hold of him, as he tried to break free.

"Abdullah!" he called across the room. "Get these goons off me."

"It's all right," Abdullah told them. "Let him in."

Cat jerked away from them and moved toward the computers.

"If the branch doesn't exist," Abdullah asked, "then where do the shipments go?"

"We think it's possible," Kanaly returned, "that someone is creating a real city with these materials. A real city with real people and real commerce."

"Who?"

Both men shrugged. Cat walked up to join them.

"You've got to do something," he told Abdullah.

"About what?" Abdullah returned.

"Declare martial law or something," Cat said. "Get some order."

Abdullah looked back at the screen, resentful of the intrusion. "I am not here to interfere with intrabranch politics," he said, then looked at Kanaly. "Is there someone here doing it?"

"Undoubtedly," the man answered, "but I don't think the trouble originates here."

"That's no answer," Cat said. "It's anarchy out there."

"Would you wait just a minute," Abdullah told him. Then, to Kanaly: "Why do you say that?"

"Someone has to coordinate. Someone has to give out the passwords."

Abdullah arched his eyebrows. "You mean someone from the home office?"

The man held up his hands. "Don't quote me on that."

"Jits are pounding on our river defenses," Cat said, "and we're so busy fighting one another that we're not dealing with it."

"It's not my problem!" Abdullah spat. "Now, would you kindly wait until I'm finished with this?"

"Go to hell," Cat said, and marched away.

Abdullah took a breath and shook his head. "Guards!" he called when Cat opened the door. "Detain that man!"

There was a brief scuffle, after which Cat was subdued and brought back into the room, kicking and screaming.

"If you cannot contain yourself," Abdullah told him, "I can have you bound and gagged!"

Cat quieted down.

"Do you have any suggestions?" Abdullah asked.

"Give it to the home office," Jackson said.

Abdullah shook his head. "That I cannot do. First, there may be complicity with LOW Arabia. We don't know who or why. They could destroy records, purge the files to protect themselves. Second, even if we could pass this information on, we don't have anyone to blame here, no culprit."

"Then I suggest we catch them in the act," Kanaly said, his pink moon face smiling wide. "Then we can make them talk."

"Yes," Abdullah said. "We'll have to reallow access to the computer room and hide someone to watch. When the thief shows up, we'll grab him."

"If we haven't already chased him away," Jackson added.

"So be it," Abdullah said, and laid his hand on Jackson's shoulder. "You two have done a good job."

The computer men looked at one another, then at Abdullah. "Could we ask you a favor?" Kanaly said.

Abdullah narrowed his gaze. "What is it?"

"Since we're finished here, can we spend the rest of the time at New Mecca?"

Abdullah looked at the man's frightened eyes and couldn't blame him for wanting to be away. "Yes," he said, turning away from them.

Cat still sat at the far end of the room under guard. Abdullah moved to join him. "Go back to your posts," he told the guards. Olson sat on a terminal chair, the dark screen beside him. Abdullah pulled up a chair to face him. "I have much on my mind," he said.

"So do I," Cat returned.

"Perhaps we can begin again," Abdullah said, then smiled slightly. "It is good to see you."

Cat brightened and rolled his eyes. "Good to see you, too. Got a few minutes to talk?"

"Of course."

"You know what's going on?"

Abdullah grimaced and looked at the blank screen. Trouble at the source, in Arabia. "Mr. Elwood has died. Those left behind fight for control of what was once his."

"More specifically, Rennie and I are fighting," Cat said.

"Just so."

"I want you to help me," Cat said.

"It's against Company policy," Abdullah returned.

"I don't care about that."

Abdullah stood up, turning away from him. When he turned back around, he had made a decision. "Do you know that my wife is being held hostage until I complete my task here, and that my task may include the destruction of Orleans?"

Cat's features slackened. "I didn't know about your wife."

"If you ran this city," Abdullah asked, "what would you do if you knew I was on my way up to the dome to release the Jitterbug?"

"I'd have to stop you."

Abdullah sat back down and leaned up close. "I like you," he said. "I honestly do, but I can't involve myself in these local politics."

"I'd be a lot easier to work with than Rennie," Cat returned.

"Probably."

"You owe me your life," Cat said.

Abdullah stood up abruptly, his chair scraping loudly behind him. "I will think about it," he said, and strode away.

*　　*　　*

> *He who humbles himself for God, him will God exalt; he is small in his own mind, and great in the eyes of the people. And he who is proud and haughty, God will render him contemptible, and he is small in the eyes of the people and great in his own mind, so that he becomes more contemptible to them than a dog or a swine.*
>
> —The Prophet Mohammed

XLVI

LOW Headquarters
Rub Al Khali

Misha'al sat with his computer, the Wichita readout scrolling quickly, faster than the eye could read, double columns of numbers growing larger. He watched with no small amount of satisfaction. His job was nearly done; his city nearly ready.

Already populated with those who had helped him before, Wichita thrived and prospered. Well prepared to be self-sufficient and well stocked with those things it could not be self-sufficient in, the city was his reality and his dream, the crowning jewel in the LOW crown—and Faisel didn't even know of its existence.

If things went correctly, Faisel would never know. Misha'al could bargain Nura to the Bedouin in exchange for a hiding place and passage to Jeddah, where the steamer captain he had promised a shipyard to would ferry him up the Red Sea to the Mediterranean, then the Atlantic, and finally to the Western Sector and freedom.

Quitting the program, he returned his computer to full-time Koran readings, and walked to his tiny bed, getting down on hands and knees to look beneath it. He reached under and slid out the pile of old clothes. Tossing the clothes aside, he came away with the small stainless-steel box that he had made himself in LOW engineering during the sleep periods. He studied it carefully, moving it around in his hands so that it caught the dull light of his room and slid it lengthwise in tiny streamers along the top of the thing. This was his ticket to freedom, the simple hinge upon which all his plans would turn.

And the door burst open, Faisel ibn Faisel Al Sa'ud, hands on hips, filling up the open space.

"I have been in need of you, and you have not been here," the King of the World said.

"I have been in need of privacy," the prophet said, and set the box casually on the bed, "and you, obviously, have not given it to me."

Faisel walked in and slammed the door. He would not be put off so easily this time. "Where have you been?" he demanded.

Misha'al walked to the table at the farthest point from the box and sat down. "I made a pilgrimage to Riyadh," he said. "There is no law against it."

"Why?" Faisel demanded, hands still planted firmly on his hips.

"I hoped there would be answers there," he said.

Faisel walked across the room, noticing all the clothes on the floor that Misha'al had strewn around when getting the box. "You are a messy person."

"I have an organized mind," Misha'al returned.

Faisel sat opposite him at the table. "Answers to what?" he said, his eyes like flamethrowers.

Misha'al took a breath, tried to calm himself. "I went to the mosque of Abdul Aziz in Riyadh," he said. "I prayed there that I might be able to help you understand the dreams that plague you."

Faisel brightened. "Yes? You found answers?"

"Perhaps."

"Bah!" Faisel stood up, pacing the room like a caged animal. Misha'al had never seen him so distraught. "I seek solutions and you give me more questions. I rapidly lose patience with you, ulema."

"And I with you," Misha'al returned, but his usual fire was gone. For the first time, he was beginning to be afraid of Faisel, afraid of the forces that were now controlling the man. He couldn't explain away the dreams, couldn't even imagine what they were.

Faisel walked back to the table and stared hard at Misha'al. "What did you find out in Riyadh?"

"The mosque is old, long abandoned," he said. "The floor was covered with a thick layer of dust, and in the dust was scrawled these words:

Whosoever thinks God will not help him
in the present world and the world to come,
let him stretch up a rope to heaven,
then let him sever it, and behold
whether his guile does away with what enrages him."

Faisel narrowed his brows, a tongue snaking out to lick thick lips. "You think the dreams are some kind of test?"

"Perhaps a test of the Law versus your feelings. Perhaps the vividness of the dreams is the severity of the test. You want the woman, yet you wait to have her lawfully."

Faisel struck a heroic pose. "If that is the case, then I pass the test well."

"I think that you have," Misha'al returned, knowing that this ploy would work with Faisel only until the King had another dream and had to survive the terrible fear again.

Faisel walked to the bed and sat down heavily. He picked up the box and began idly to toy with it. "Perhaps you did go to Riyadh on my behalf," he said. "I certainly hope that is the case."

"You do me an injustice," Misha'al returned.

"I have always given you much freedom here," Faisel continued, "because you've never abused it. But I do not like secrets at my expense." He stood up, dropping the box on the bed, where it bounced once then fell onto the floor.

He moved to the door. "Even when the secrets are on my behalf. Don't leave the compound again without my permission and an armed escort. Even in your capacity, you know too much to be running around loose. It's all for your own good."

"Of course," Misha'al said. "I will be more careful in future."

Faisel opened the door. "Yes," he said. "You will."

And the King was gone.

Misha'al took a ragged breath, noticed that his hands were shaking slightly. Getting up, he moved quickly to the door and peeked out. The hallway was clear. It was beginning to unravel quickly; he couldn't hold things together much longer.

Closing the door, he turned and hurried to the box on the floor. He picked it up and removed the cover. The intricate clockworks on the inside seemed undamaged. Secreting the box within the confines of his mishla, he left immediately and hurried to the subbasement where they had moved Abdullah's wife. Using keys he'd had for many years, he entered the extra boiler room and crossed to the cells.

Nura sat, naked, in the corner on the floor. Her knees were pulled up in front of her and her arms were wrapped around them. Her eyes were wary but alert.

"Have you been getting enough to eat?" he asked her.

"Who are you?"

"A friend."

"I have only enemies here."

"You are wrong," Misha'al said. "I bring you greetings from Bandar."

She stood up, unashamed, and ran to the bars, wrapping slender fingers around them. "What news?"

Misha'al looked at her eyes. To look anywhere else was folly. "We have very little time," he said. "Just listen. Even at this moment, Faisel could be watching us. Your husband still lives."

He watched her sag against the bars, her face awash with relief, and for the first time he realized the mental anguish that was her constant companion.

"Bandar and the rest of the clan are on the move. I have spoken with them."

"Y-you have?"

"We have arranged an escape."

She pulled herself up to her full height, her head set, face determined. "I will do whatever is necessary to help."

He nodded and pushed the steel box through the bars to her.

Bandar waited until the sky was soft with night and the evening prayers were finished before bringing out the huge carpet and stretching it out on the sand. When all the men had been assembled, he had them stand around the edges of the carpet, which was fully twenty feet square.

"To be Moslem," he said, "is to be rigid and unbending. We have taken upon ourselves an oath of vengeance upon the most powerful man in the world. We do not have the power to be rigid in this case."

With that he tossed an apple into the center of the carpet, quite far from anyone's reach.

"The carpet," said Bandar, "is the Kingdom of Faisel. The apple is Faisel himself. The problem is to reach the apple without treading on the carpet, for in truth we cannot stand against the might of the Kingdom."

A small child came running from the tent area. It was one of Bandar's sons, and he was soon tugging on his father's robes.

The man looked down at him. "You disturb me," he said.

"The box talks," the boy said.

"Dwell on this," Bandar told the clan. "I will return quickly."

Following the child across the still-hot sand, Bandar entered his tent and squatted down in front of the receiver. Misha'al was speaking.

"...I will repeat this one more time. Go to Holmes Air Base with the morning light. Tell them you seek audience with Faisel. They will tell you that it will be a long time before you could have such an audience. You will tell them that you can wait, and then demand hospitality. They will not reject this demand. You will then go to the place assigned and wait. You will hear from me very soon."

That was that. Static replaced the voice. Bandar stood up, smiling down at the box. Everyone had a surprise in store.

He rejoined his brothers at the carpet. They were all still staring at the apple. Bandar fell to his knees.

"We need not walk on the Kingdom to reach the King," he said, and began rolling up the carpet. "All things can be accomplished if they are handled properly. That is what Abdullah taught me."

He rolled the large rug, walking with it on his knees. When he got close enough, he reached out and snatched the apple.

"Faisel will be ours," he said, and took a large bite from the bright red fruit.

* * *

> *Death is a favor to a Moslem. Remember and speak well of your dead, and refrain from speaking ill of them.*
> —The Prophet Mohammed

> *Solitary trees, if they grow at all, grow strong.*
> —Old World Wisdom

> *This world is a prison for the faithful, but a paradise for unbelievers.*
> —The Prophet Mohammed

XLVII
The Funeral

In the middle of the night, Rennie tried to take the harbor. He was turned back by Olson, but not before both sides had sustained heavy losses.

Three hours later, two of Rennie's VeePee allies were assassinated by machine-gun fire as they ate a cold breakfast in the LOW cafeteria. The man who did it was said to have had a leather mask that covered half his face.

Shortly thereafter, an aut bomb was detonated just outside the LOW Light and Power Headquarters on Farrow Street. The facade of the building was damaged extensively, but no upper-management people were hurt. There were forty-eight casualties on the streets, however, including seven Arab regulars who were there to give public instructions on the call to prayer.

One hour later, Abdullah ibn Faisel Al Sa'ud called the cease-fire.

Abdullah and Majid floated high above the city in the command balloon, watching the huge funeral procession snake through the flooded streets toward the cemetery in the center of town.

"This is no place for the balloons," Majid said again, and Abdullah was getting extremely tired of hearing it.

"We have declared peace," he replied. "Now we have to enforce it."

Majid swallowed back what he wanted to say and looked out around him. The sky above the city was filled with the might of the House of Sa'ud, while the Jitterbug army marched unobstructed on the city gates.

"They will be here soon," he said.

"Yes," Abdullah answered, but his mind was several thousand miles away.

314

"We will have to relieve these men sometime," Majid said. "They cannot go on without rest, or food, or fuel."

Abdullah moved away from the window and stared at his garrison commander. The man's smiles had not come so readily of late. "Just what would you have me do?" he asked. "There is a civil war going on down there. Not much use in stopping the Jits if we have nothing to stop them from."

Majid moved up close so they were nose to nose. "If you don't stop the Jits, the stupid feuding will not mean anything. Give me my balloons back! Let me have the weapons I need to stop this plague!"

"I have called the cease-fire. That is my word. The balloons stay!" Abdullah looked down and saw that his fists were clenched. He turned away from Majid, taking deep breaths. "I did not ask for this," he said quietly, then turned back around. "In the name of Allah, I'm a camel herder. All this . . ."—he gestured with a broad hand—"is . . . craziness. I cannot weigh lives against lives. I do not know what is right or wrong anymore. What's any of it worth?"

The two men stared at one another for a moment. Then the radio buzzed loudly. Without taking his eyes from Abdullah's, Majid reached out and flicked it to life.

"Yes," he said obliquely.

"We are above the river," the voice staticked. "Boats full of Jits are pounding the defenses here. They won't hold much longer."

Majid raised his eyebrows, his mouth a slash.

Abdullah sighed deeply. "Yes," he said, and shook his head. "Take me down first. Then do what you need to do at the river."

"I'm on my way," Majid said to the radio, then toggled it off.

He closed the distance between himself and Abdullah, taking his cousin in his arms. The two men held on fiercely to one another, each drawing strength from the other.

They picked the biggest sarcophagus they could find in the city for Mr. Elwood's body, then proceeded to slosh the two miles from the LOW building to the graveyard to plant it.

Olson led the processional, followed by his allies. Rennie and his people brought up the rear because Rennie wasn't about to give Olson a free shot at a public display. Behind the VeePees,

Junexes marched hundreds strong, followed by the citizens, thousands strong.

The tension was thick, like the water in the streets. All the Execs wore full-dress exos and were armed to the stubble of their hairless chins.

And the sky was full of rain and balloons.

When Olson reached the big wrought-iron gates, two giant Engy gravekeepers swung them open for him. Standing aside, he directed the pallbearers through the opening. The pallbearers were: York, Valuska, Jan, and Jerry Joe, not necessarily in that order.

The cemetery was large, the aboveground graves a field of gray stone sentinels. Olson's mood was dark, his passion the black passion of hatred and sadness. All the colors of the world were wet and runny, dripping like sweat. There was no light, only overcast, and had he only looked, he would have been able to see Gret standing in the drizzly shadows outside the gates saying her own good-bye to someone who had been kind to her.

The Engies were pointing to a small cement pathway that wound to the right.

"Let's get it over with," Olson said, and moved along the narrow road, the spongelike ground drooling water onto the path.

Only the VeePees were allowed inside the gates, on Olson's orders. After they passed within, the Engies shut and padlocked the things.

Olson could barely stand to be in the same world as Rennie. To be in the same proximity was maddening. And the damned cease-fire. He had asked Abdullah to help him, not throw dirt into the works.

The gravesite sat at the fork of the path. It was a marble mausoleum the size of a large room. Its long-locked door had been torn aside by Engy hands.

Olson walked up to, then into the crypt, small marble cherubs with cracked bodies smiling angelically down at him, their little wings chipped and broken, their little white faces creased with dirt and mold.

Inside, the crypt was plain and unornamented. A large candle provided as much light as they needed. There was a stone slab in the middle of the room with an ornate coffin resting atop it. Olson unslung his M-16 and stood it up against the wall. Then he moved to the slab.

Grunting, he shoved the coffin off the slab to crash loudly

onto the ground. A small pile of bones rattled out onto the floor. One of the Engies came in and kicked it all aside.

Olson's people squeezed through then, the simple box Mr. Elwood rested in hoisted up on their shoulders.

"Right here," Oson said, pointing to the slab.

They hefted the body onto the stone, and Valuska set up the photographs on the white pine box. One pictured Mr. Elwood on a trip to Arabia, receiving his twenty-five-year-service pin, while wearing a pith helmet, from a smiling Faisel ibn Faisel. The other was a certificate that showed that Mr. Elwood participated in the LOW profit-sharing programs through payroll deduction. Olson clucked down in his throat. He hadn't known about that.

Putting his hands flat on the coffin top, Olson stared down at it.

"Do you want us to . . . to . . ." Jan began.

"Yes," Olson said. "Leave me for a while."

They left, and Olson was alone with his mentor. He felt alien, totally cut off from feeling and understanding. What a strange road it had been to get all the way from nowhere to somewhere that turned out to be nowhere after all.

"Why don't you climb in with him?" a voice said. He looked up to see Rennie standing in the doorway. "Do everybody a favor."

Olson's jaw muscles tightened. "'Cause I'm not through whipping you yet."

Du'camp walked into the crypt, followed by the other VeePees.

"You can have your chance anytime you want."

Olson looked down at the coffin, then up at Rennie. "There are better times to talk about this."

"I don't think so," Rennie returned. "I've been wanting to get you in a graveyard for a long time."

"Don't you people even respect the dead?" came a voice from the doorway. Olson turned to see Abdullah standing there, his mishla wet and hanging, dripping mud from the bottom. "Get on with your service."

Everyone stared at him, an interloper where he wasn't wanted.

"Reverend," Olson called, and a skinny man dressed in a black exo slipped in under Abdullah's arm, which at the time was holding the doorframe in place.

The man, nose too big and darting eyes, walked to the

coffin, the LOW Bible, Standard Operating Procedure, in one hand, the Koran in the other. He spread his hands above the coffin.

"Oh, Allah," he said loudly. "You have seen fit in your infinite wisdom and understanding to take our brother, Northrope Elwood—"

"Northrope?" several people repeated loudly.

"—to your bosom. We are glad that you found him so pleasing and worthy to take away from us. He was a good Company man. He was a great Company man. He always filled out his time cards punctually, and never let his vacation days accrue unnecessarily. He was a believer in black ink, and consistently showed a profit year after year, to your great honor and glory. He paid his tribute well, and never, until the present crisis, gave any trouble to your arm of vengeance, Faisel ibn Faisel Al Sa'ud, Chairman of the Board, King of the World."

"Hear, hear," the assembled mumbled.

"When are we going to straighten this out?" Rennie said to Abdullah. "This city is mine; I want it."

"I want to call a meeting for later today," Abdullah responded. "You people have either got to find a quick way to settle this or find some way to work together until the Jits are taken care of."

"I know how to settle it," Olson said, raising a fist.

The reverend was still talking. "Cost reduction was his biggest virtue. He was a man among men, a man who wasn't afraid to spend less plastic than was fashionable. He discouraged waste, and promoted waste-reduction campaigns to the fullest...."

"You have a city to run," Abdullah said. "There are people to feed, pay envelopes to give out. Someone has to be in charge!"

"Nobody but these two want it," Fagin from Wall Maintenance said.

"Yellow Fever has reached an epidemic stage," VeePee Greely, head of Human Services, said. "We've run out of places to put the victims."

"His books, until now, were always in order," the reverend said. "And he was happy to time-share his computers with anyone if it promoted the greater glory of the Company. He never hired anyone who couldn't do the job and never fired anyone unless he felt they deserved firing...."

"I've got the seniority," Rennie said.

"I've got the support," Olson said, "and the blessing of that man right there." He pointed to the coffin. "He told me himself that you'd run the Company into the ground."

Rennie started around the coffin for Olson, his own men trying to pull him back. Olson came around unobstructed, and for one brief instant Abdullah considered letting them have it out right there.

"Stop it!" he yelled. "At least finish the ceremony."

But it wasn't to be.

There was a terrible rattling of machine-gun fire outside, followed by screaming. They ran out into the rain and saw Arabs bailing out of balloons, drifting to the ground in large green parachutes, firing away at the melee that had broken out among warring factions on the ground. Some gas bombs were tossed, and before anyone really knew what was going on, the entire funeral procession rapidly dispersed without even thinking to close the door to the crypt.

There was a burning logjam blocking the river. It was all the Jit boats that Olson's people had set on fire. They blocked everything, confused everything, curling thick black smoke through the entire landscape.

Majid watched it all from above, through fieldglasses. His troops fired continually into the smoke and the churning gray of the waters, lest so much as one Jit try to swim beneath the conflagration and drift into the city like a cloud drifting across the icy blue heavens.

The first checkpoint consisted of a concrete bunker on each side of the river connected by a small metal bridge that spanned the waters. There were two other checkpoints like this one before the walls and the harbor. And that was fortunate, because this outpost was in the process of being abandoned.

The fire was everywhere, hot, orange fire, and Majid decided that Milander had purposely sent ships along that would burn this way.

He used the glasses to look farther upriver. There were boats as far as he could see, all coming this way. He wanted to travel that direction and take as many as he could, but everyone was needed here. There were so many of them, so many.

He looked back down, watched the Junexes and their soldiers running away from the outposts as fire danced along the white concrete of the bunkers. They seemed so small from up here, so quiet amidst the continual death rattle.

Then he watched as his gunners shot down the Junexes and their soldiers just in case one of them had gotten contaminated. They would fall back to the next outpost now. That's all they could do, fall back.

*   *   *

> *Fuel is not sold in a forest, nor fish on a lake.*
>
> —Eastern Proverb

> *When the whole world turns clown, and paints itself red with its own heart's blood instead of vermilion, it is something else than comic.*
> —LOW Computer Analog,
> discovered in memory
> banks and expurgated

XLVIII
The Stadium

"Point of order!" Rennie said, and the microphone picked up his voice and echoed it back to him around the speaker system of All-Sports Stadium.

"The chair recognizes VeePee Du'camp," Abdullah said from his table in the center of the field, his own voice booming, a word explosion.

The crowd of forty-thousand-plus was loud and rowdy. They got in free to the debates, and had turned them into some kind of mammoth celebration of anarchy. They were dogs off the leash who responded by running madly around in circles and yipping at the wind. Every fuzztop in the city had been routed to the stadium, and for the first time in Orleans history, they were allowed to carry weapons. This was perhaps a better concept in theory than in practice, since the fuzz felt it their duty, since they had the guns, to use them at the least provocation—which caused a great many more problems than it actually solved.

Rennie stood at the long table set on the sidelines, Olson at a similar table on the opposite sidelines. Both had a long row of advisers seated next to them. He picked up the microphone.

"Mr. Chairman," he echoed. "After thoroughly checking my SOP, I have to conclude that this entire proceeding is out of order and not in accord with Company policy. I hereby move that we adjourn this meeting immediately and allow the leadership in the city to settle at its own level."

"Second," someone at his table said.

Abdullah turned and consulted with the black-hooded parliamentarian seated next to him, a hand over the microphone mouthpiece. Rennie had no doubt but that the chair would rule against him, but at this point he felt he had to try it. With Abdullah so friendly to Cat, he didn't feel he had much of a chance unless he would pull something strange out of the bag.

Abdullah turned and leaned down to the mike. "The chair regretfully denies your motion, VeePee Du'camp. Under chapter fifteen of the Uniform Conduct Code in the appendix to the Standard Operating Procedure Manual, any ranking Corporate board member may declare martial law and suspend charter rules in times of extreme crisis when the regular chain of command breaks down. In other words, Mr. Du'camp, I can and will do whatever I feel is best."

There was loud cheering and foot stomping, accompanied by gunshots as the fuzztops tried their best to reduce the population of the city a citizen at a time.

"Point of order, Mr. Chairman," Rennie said again.

Abdullah frowned. "Yes, VeePee."

"I take exception to your totally arbitrary decision in declaring this a state of 'extreme crisis.' "

The crowd loved that one, laughing and shouting for a good five minutes before order could be restored.

"Sit down, VeePee," Abdullah said.

"Yes sir," Rennie said, and sat. He had figured to lose that one, but he still had other shots. If he couldn't make them work, however, he was going to have to do some fast thinking. He was sure of two things. One was that Abdullah was Cat's friend and benefactor. The other was that most of the city would back the man backed by Corporate. It was only natural. He would have to find a way to kill Abdullah. He had already made several minor attempts in that direction, but the Elite who followed him everywhere were impossible to get beyond.

"The chair must remind everyone," Abdullah said, "that we are speaking here this evening of most grave matters that concern every citizen here present. The city is at a total standstill. Disease and sickness are rampant. Essential services have been shut down. We must solve this problem of leadership tonight or your city will not survive."

There was more yelling and cheering, and Abdullah couldn't decide whether they were cheering his words or the death of the city. His Moslem heritage was one of fatalism, but he had never seen anything like this. He moved around uneasily in his seat, the exo Majid had forced him to wear uncomfortable under his robes.

"Mr. Chairman," Cat said, raising a hand, his words booming, then howling as the speakers caught a wisp of feedback and turned it into a hurricane.

"The chair recognizes VeePee Catanine."

The man rose and walked around the table to move to the center of the field, stretching his mike cable as far as it would reach. He was cheered and booed in equal measure.

"My advisers and I think we have worked out a compromise that may work until such time as we can have a proper reunification of city government."

"Excellent," Abdullah said. "The chair will be happy to hear your proposal now."

"Thank you," Olson said, and he hoped he could railroad this through with or without Rennie's approval. "In the current crisis, I suggest we handle things as follows: we divide the city government into two sections, administrative and manual. The administrative branch will handle the actual running of the Company and the city, setting policy and making the decisions. The manual branch would have the charge of running the systems that implement administrative decisions. I further suggest that I be put in charge of administrative, since that was what I was being trained for by our late Director, and that VeePee Du'camp be put in charge of manual. This to last until the end of the crisis, or six months, whichever comes first."

Oh that's great, asshole!" Rennie shouted. "You make the rules, huh?"

Abdullah was pounding the butt of a rifle on the table as the crowd went wild. "You have not been recognized!" he yelled at Rennie.

Du'camp moved into the field, too. "Why don't you just propose that I be thrown off the tower?" he said. "It'll be a lot quicker!"

"That can be arranged!" Olson returned, and the men were several feet apart, both held in check by their mike cables. And the crowd went crazy.

"I will have order!" Abdullah shouted, looking uneasily around the stands at the powder keg whose fuse was not being dampened by the steady rain. "If you gentlemen cannot work this out, you will be forced to live with a proposal of my choosing."

Rennie and Olson looked at one another, rumbling volcanoes ready to erupt. The hatred passed between them in undulating waves, overpowering, fueled by other people's hatreds that were all focusing on this single matrix.

"I can solve the problem," Rennie said quietly, and the entire stadium quieted with him.

Abdullah looked around, his eyes finally drifting into the early-evening sky and the reassurance of the balloons that gave them a helium ceiling.

"The chair recognizes VeePee Du'camp," he said.

Rennie paused, his red exo slick with water, running the stadium lights in elongated bars. "There is a simple way to settle a dispute such as this," he said. "Trial by combat."

There were no boos this time, no confusion of purpose. The crowd generated a solid stream of positive noise.

"One on one," Rennie said above the cheers. "Winner take all!"

Olson felt the smile curl the corners of his lips. This was real; this made sense. In the midst of all the nonsense, this was rock solid.

"I accept the challenge!" he yelled.

Abdullah was banging the rifle butt again. "Order!" he shouted. "Order!"

When the noise finally died down, he said, "Will someone put that in the form of a motion?"

"I move," Rennie said, "that the matter of who will succeed to the position of Branch Manager be decided by trial by combat between myself and VeePee Catanine."

"Second!" Olson said.

"The motion has been made and seconded," Abdullah said. "All in favor..."

The ayes nearly lifted the stadium off the soggy ground.

Abdullah stood. "The motion carries!" he said amidst the tumult. "A mind match for the city!"

While the crowd screamed out its approval, the large screen was dragged out, gouging deep crevices into the muddy field with its legs. The table was brought out to the center of the field, Rennie and Olson hooking themselves up immediately.

The two combatants stared across the table at one another, psyching themselves up for the contest. So intent was Olson upon this task that he nearly missed the toss of the plastic. Rennie won.

"Are you ready, gentlemen?" Abdullah asked.

"Ready," Olson said.

"And me," Rennie said.

"The nature of this contest must necessarily be to the death," Abdullah said. "Good luck, and may Allah give one of you a relatively painless end."

One minute the crowd was cheering, filling Olson's senses. The next instant he was hot and dry, staring at eye level into the face of a snake.

He was an animal, a small furry rodentlike animal, an animal like he had never seen before. The snake was large and hooded, and it turned its back to him, two eyes on the back of its hood. No, wait. Those weren't eyes, they were spots. He watched the spots hypnotically, let himself drift with them. He moved around the snake on four small legs, the creature being careful to keep its spots within Olson's line of vision.

Olson circled, an ever-decreasing spiral. He watched the spots... the spots...

The snake turned and lunged, but Olson skipped out of the way just in time. Drawing itself up full, the snake towered over him. It lunged again, and he felt its teeth on his neck just before he slipped away. He knew instinctively that the snake would have to get a good bite to hurt him. It injected its venom slowly, painfully....

His brain popped like one of Abdullah's balloons. It was abrupt, a shock to his system. He shook his head to clear it and saw that Rennie was doing the same, and the boos of the crowd were overpowering. He and his adversary shared a puzzled glance before Abdullah's voice broke through the last bits of mist in his brain.

"I'm sorry to stop the competition," he said, but the crowd was drowning him out. "Please! Please! Listen to me."

The crowd quieted somewhat so the man could continue.

"I've just been handed a note," he said, holding up the paper. "It says that the Jits have reached the city gates in force!"

People were up and scrambling before he even got the words out. He had to shout the rest of it.

"Everyone of Exec rank please report to the main gate immediately!"

Olson stood. He took a step toward Rennie, but the mob was on the field now, choking up the distance between them along with everything else. Abandoning himself to the crowd, he let them push him on the flow, out of the stadium, and into the canals that used to be streets.

People were wading in knee-deep water. Auts could not run the city streets anymore. Boats, or what passed for boats, were the order of the day—doors, telephone poles, anything that floated, became the mode of transportation for the city of Orleans.

Olson had grabbed his rifle on the sidelines, and now was holding it above his head as he waded, his brain still foggy from the ill-conceived match.

"Cat!" somebody called, and he turned to see Jerry Joe standing up in the harbor-patrol speedboat, waving his arms. "Get your ass over here, boy!"

Olson sloshed to the boat and climbed in, rolling heavily onto the deck. Getting up, he moved fore, taking the passenger seat next to Jerry Joe. "What's it look like?" he asked, checking his wrist lasers to make sure they hadn't gotten wet.

Jerry Joe slid down to his seat and gunned the engine before starting them off slowly down the middle of the street.

"All the damned Jits in the world are out there," he said. "Man the spot, will you?"

Olson turned on the hand spotlight beside the windshield and rotated it to light the way directly in front of them. A great deal of debris floated by, some of it supporting rats that would soon enough be somebody's dinner. People filled the streets, most of them on foot, but they stayed out of the way of the large craft.

"How about the river?" Olson called.

The man shook his head, then blared the horn to get several children on a log out of the way. "They're hammering the second outpost pretty well," he said. "We may not make it through this one, partner."

Buildings rose on both sides of them, people hanging out the windows, many of them throwing debris down on Olson and Jerry Joe. The Junex wasted several laser tags on them before he decided to conserve his charge for the real problem.

They moved slowly, but steadily, the inboard chugging away at the faintest throttle. They passed a flooded aut with a Junex standing on the hood calling for help. They didn't stop though. It was one of Rennie's people.

It took nearly an hour to reach the wall, and on the way they passed many large fires built up on anything above the waterline. Judging from the smell of the smoke, Olson surmised that the cemeteries had run out of room for the dead.

The walls were crawling with exos when Olson jumped out of the boat and climbed the stairs to the pillboxes, Jerry Joe on his heels. They reached the top, the sound of the guns deafening. Olson pulled his helmet off his belt and put it on just to soften the sound a little.

Near the main gates the walls were totally filled with riflemen. Olson ran farther down the rows of snipers and settled into a niche far less populated. There was no one to give orders, but for once, it wasn't necessary. Everybody knew exactly what to do. Kill Jits.

It was just getting dark, gray day turning to black night. A half mile in the distance he could see the bulk of the Jitterbug army, spread out wide, moving casually forward. The force was immense, larger, if possible, than the last time Olson had seen them. It was as if they filled the entire world except for the city.

Jerry Joe pulled up next to Olson, laying his rifle in the cutout section made for the weapons. He pointed downward. There were several thousand people shouting at the gates, being mowed down in even rows.

"They look all right to me," Jerry Joe said. "Don't see a jerker in the bunch."

Olson grimaced. "Those are some of the ones we let out over the last few days," he said, "trying to get back in."

"Son of a bitch."

"That's the reason the Jits are hanging back. They're letting us waste our ammo on our own people."

Barrels of precious gasoline were brought up onto the wall and dumped on the people below. They used Molotov cocktails to start it up.

Olson didn't watch as the citizens burned; he kept his eyes and his mind fixed on the Jitterbug army. The balloons were moving from their positions above the city, drifting over the Jits, and soon he could see distant laser lines raking through their columns, lighting up the night. And the crackle of machine guns sounded like faraway castanets.

When the fire burned down, the Jits moved in. The wall had gotten quiet as everyone prepared for the onslaught. Giant Engies moved up and down the wall carrying boxes of extra ammo to each station.

The Jits were pushing several large wooden contraptions along with them that rose a good forty feet into the air.

"What are those?" Jerry Joe asked. "Some kind of ladders?"

Olson shook his head and watched the Jits move into range. "Look!"

A balloon was moving erratically, losing altitude. The Jits had gotten it with one of their lasers and it was trying to make it back over the wall. Forty feet from Olson's station, it smacked the wall hard, the gondola breaking loose and spilling Arabs out onto the charred ground. Those who could run made for the gates, but there was no one to open up for them.

When the Jits got in range, the wall people opened up on them, knocking them over in large numbers; but there were larger numbers waiting to take their place, and for the first time Olson wondered if there was enough ammo in the whole world to kill all of them.

One of the wooden machines sprung itself, its large arm flinging something toward them. It went over the gate to splash into the street. It was a body.

"Oh my God," Olson whispered, slumping against the wall. "They're throwing their dead in here."

"Firemen!" people were screaming, and soon lines of liquid fire were eating away at the dead Jit as all the arms went into motion, slinging bodies as quickly as they could string them up.

And twilight became black night, while the spent cartridges piled up around Olson's legs like a metal snow.

*   *   *

*"O Prophet of God!" said one of his disciples,
"I have heard so many things from thee, and I
fear that I may forget their end and aim, so
tell me a word that may contain everything."
The Prophet said, "Fear God according to what
thou dost know, and act accordingly."*

—The Prophet Mohammed

XLIX
Somewhere Over Arizona

The balloons limped back to the garrison sometime in the middle of the night, their lasers spent, their numbers greatly decreased. Abdullah sat on the floor of the command gondola, his back against the uncompromising wood, Elite stretched out all around him sleeping. Majid sat at the radio table under a dim yellow bulb, taking the reports and writing down the bad news as he had been doing for several hours.

Finally, he leaned back, rubbing his eyes with the heels of his hands. He pulled the headphones off his ears and dropped them on the table. The noise made Abdullah start, bringing him out of a half-sleep reverie.

"Are we almost there?" he said.

Majid stood up, stretching out the pain in his lower back. "Yes," he said simply.

"How does it look?" Abdullah asked, though he really didn't want to know.

Majid sat down again, hand massaging his back. He stared at Abdullah for several seconds. "I'm going to have a cigarette," he said.

Abdullah nodded, waving a hand in his general direction.

The commander took a machine-rolled cigarette off the top of the radio, lighting it on his hand laser when he couldn't find a match. He dragged slowly, let it out slowly, spoke slowly.

"We've lost well over two hundred balloons," he said, weary, "nearly twenty-five percent of the entire force."

He laughed, a coarse, dry cackle. Smoke came out with the laugh. "They could have had all of us, but they wanted to conserve their laser charges." He shook his head, holding his hands in the air. "We sit up in the sky like bubbles under a waterfall. They can't miss us."

"And now they've got more lasers," Abdullah said.

"A few more," Majid said. "After the other balloons were lost, I did some scuttling drills. From everything I've seen, I think we've kept most of our ordnance out of their hands."

"Well, that's something," Abdullah said, closing his eyes and letting his head fall back to lean on the wall.

Majid drew on the cigarette again. "It's something, but not much. The second river checkpoint will fall before morning, too."

"What do we do now?"

"A couple of things. I've begun to have an amount of respect for Mr. Milander, the leader of the Jits." Majid took a deep drag on the cigarette, then flicked it out a window space. Abdullah wondered whether the rain would put it out before it hit the ground. "He's unearthed an old aut graveyard just outside of town and has...infested it. He seems to be playing a waiting game. We will try to do the same. I won't send all the balloons at once anymore. We'll do it in shifts so that there will always be fresh balloons. We'll try to use the wall for protection from their lasers, and maybe use height, too, though that will cut our own efficiency. The one advantage that we have is that we can recharge our lasers and they cannot. Perhaps we can make that work for us. I've also got some napalm."

Abdullah stood up. He felt creaky, old. "What are our chances?"

"What chances?"

"That is really not what I want to hear."

"All right," Majid returned, and he reached out and flicked off the tiny light, plunging the gondola into darkness. "Perhaps if we can find some way to get rid of Milander himself, we can beat them. He is their cohesive force, the reason they are so organized. He's a natural-born leader. If the gates of Orleans are to be opened, he is the key. Lose the key, and the gates could stay locked."

"Any ideas?"

"No."

"Think about it."

"I will," Majid answered. "I certainly will."

* * *

The line stretched out down the old stone steps, down through the calf-deep water of Lafayette Street and way around the block. It was four in the morning and Gret had all the business she could handle.

She was piling up food, had already accumulated enough to help feed JoBeth and the others at the television house for quite a long time—longer, she feared, than any of them would be around to enjoy it. It made her feel good to be making a contribution to the family, made her feel useful.

Down on her knees, she held the small, frail boy's face in her hands and looked into his eyes. She sensed gentleness and nonaggression. She sensed a love of people and of life, and a dogged will to preserve that life. She saw none of the darkness of death or hatred. Releasing his face, she took him in her arms, holding him fiercely to her, as if she could take a little of his goodness into herself. And for the instant that she held him, it did work.

Standing, she smiled at the boy's mother, and felt some of his qualities shining from her. "There's nothing wrong with him that some fruit won't cure," she said. "He's going to be fine."

"If I had some fruit," the woman returned, hugging the boy to her hip.

Gret smiled. "I think I can help you out."

Disappearing into the shadows of her alcove, she got into her food stock. Business had been very good, especially since the appearance of the Jits. It wouldn't hurt her a bit to give back to the citizens something of what they gave to her.

Reaching behind a sack of flour, she pulled out a small net full of apples. She came out of the shadows and handed the apples to the woman. "Don't tell anyone where you got them," she said.

The woman's lower lip began to quiver, and she hugged Gret close. "Miss . . . I . . . I . . ."

Gret put a finger to the woman's lips. "Shhh. Just go on," she said. "Lots of people waiting."

The woman nodded, wiping at her tears with the tattered sleeve of her shift. Hiding the apples under her wet shawl, she trudged down the stairs with the boy, who kept turning back, watching Gret.

The parade moved forward a notch. Gret's next client was a thirty-year-old man who looked sixty. He had one arm, and a rat was peeking its head out of the pocket of his heavy wet overcoat.

Gret had just begun to take his pain upon herself when the commotion started.

A small cadre of Execs had come down the street in a rowboat, bumping up onto the steps. Jumping from the skiff, the men pulled it farther up on the stairs.

Gret's eyes went wide. One of the men was wearing a bright red exo that she would have recognized a mile away—Rennie.

She merged back in the shadows.

Rennie looked around. He felt tired and hollowed out. They had been killing Jits faster than the barrels of their guns could cool. Some of the fiftycals had even melted, and still they came, oblivious of their losses, singing and happy. Balloons were down everywhere, and they were rapidly depleting their gasoline resources just burning the Jits who were dying in front of the wall.

He stood wearily on the stairs. "Thumper," he said to a Junex all in black. "Watch the boat."

The man nodded as Rennie turned to Gret's line. "What the hell you people doing here?" he snapped. "Get on! Go ahead. Move!" He made a mock run at the line and it scattered to the winds.

VeePee Fagin laughed loudly. "Hoo! What a frightening figure you are!"

Rennie walked back, shaking his head. "Just like children," he said, then turned to Lars Harken from Public Health. "You say this is the place?"

The young man ran a hand through his blond hair to get the wet strands out of his face. He was an OB, a step below Exec material; but he had dreams; that could certainly be said for him.

"I was here inspecting for scrap melters a couple of weeks ago and stumbled across them. I've been trying to decide ever since whether or not to tell anyone."

Rennie put an arm around his shoulders and walked him up the stairs. "Lars, my boy. You did the right thing in coming to me, and if all this works out, there will be a good bonus in it for you."

"Just working with you would be bonus enough for me," the man returned, and Rennie felt another pair of teeth nipping at his ass that would one day have to be dealt with.

"I still don't know what this has to do with anything," Fagin said, wiping water off his eye patch. "So, what if they are there?"

"We'll see," Rennie returned.

They reached the top of the stairs, and Harken let them in with a key he kept on a large ring of keys that dangled on his pants loop under his bright yellow slicker.

They pulled open the big wooden door and entered the darkness of the old church. Kneeling, Harken picked up a fat candle that he had left there last time.

"Mostly old office records and broken-down equipment in here," he said, striking a match on the stone wall and lighting the candle, which he could barely wrap his hand around.

The candle threw off a hazy yellow glow, dispelling some of the dark. It was creaky in there, smelled of mildew and wood rot. Water dripping in from many places in the high, peaked ceiling puddled on the fake marble floor, making it slippery and clean in small sections. Dust and large cobwebs covered everything else. Crates and equipment jammed most of the floor space—filing cabinets, typewriters, PBX systems, dictating machines, water coolers—rusty, space-taking things that should have been melted down for bullets earlier.

"Back here," Harken said, and knocking down several cobwebs, he proceeded to take them through the storehouse.

"We need to start worrying about saving our asses," Rennie said to Fagin.

"What's that supposed to mean?"

"It means that we'd be fools to think that we'll end up with the city even if we kill all the Jits."

"Unless we can get to Cat and Abdullah."

"Right. Or unless we can work out something totally different."

They moved to the back of the sanctuary, where Harken held the candle over a crate that was half falling apart, the wood rotting from a continual half-century barrage of dripping water. Rennie bent down and easily ripped the lid off the box. Reaching in, he pulled out one of the stark white suits and held it up in front of him.

"Con-tam suits," Fagin whispered harshly. "The real thing."

Rennie whistled low. "The most illegal item in the empire," he said, smiling. "And it doesn't hurt a bit."

Outside, Gret peeked around the edge of her alcove at the boat guard. He was sitting on the steps beside the thing, watching debris float down the street. Hurrying from her hiding place, she moved across the stairs and through the partly open door.

She could hear Rennie's voice at the far end of the building, so she edged closer, walking cautiously, hiding behind whatever was handy. Finally she was able to get within ten feet of Rennie and hide behind a printing press.

"We can communicate with them now," Rennie was saying as he counted the suits in the crate.

"But why would we want to?" Fagin asked.

"To make a deal," Rennie returned.

"With the Jits?" Harken said.

"Sure," Rennie said. "They're people just like us. They probably want the same stuff."

"What would you offer them?"

"I'm thinking about half the city."

"What?" Fagin said.

"Fifteen," Rennie said, folding up his suit and putting it back with the others. He looked at Fagin, smiling. "Enough for my close friends."

"What about me?" Harken asked.

Rennie grimaced. "Yeah, you." He scratched his head. "My problem with you is that you already know too much."

He pointed a lasered finger at the man's face and burned him a third eye right between the other two. The man fell in a heap on the ground.

"He was a real go-getter," Rennie said, looking at the man. Jostling the body out of its slicker, he wrapped it around his own shoulders.

"You want to give the Jits half the city?" Fagin asked.

"Just for a while," Rennie said. "Look. There are some good natural divisions in the city. With a little well-placed dynamite, we can blow some bridges and a few strategic buildings and divide it off pretty well. Then, once the Jits come in the front gate . . ."

"That we leave open for them?"

"That we leave open for them. They'll take care of Cat and all of his nasty friends; then, some night soon, when they're all asleep, we can sneak over to their side and burn it down. Hell, we'll all be heroes."

"That's the craziest idea I've ever heard," Fagin said.

Rennie cocked an imaginary finger-gun at him. "Is that crazy-crazy or wild-crazy?"

"When do we do it?"

"First thing in the morning, when the attack starts again

in earnest." He winked at Fagin and holstered his imaginary gun. "Like the man says: more than one way to skin a Cat."

* * *

> *The higher an ape mounts, the more he shows his breech.*
> —Old World Wisdom

> *It is not the oath that makes us believe the man, but the man the oath.*
> —Ancient Proverb

> *The more violent the love, the more violent the anger.*
> —Burmese Saying

L
Orleans Public Library

Olson stood on the sixth-floor roof of the old building and looked at the night city through fieldglasses. A large cook fire rain-sizzled beside him, fed by piles of old books that they had found in the basement of the aged structure.

In the distance, occasional flashes could be seen where the continual catapulting of Jits inside the walls brought out the flamethrowers. Other than that, things were fairly quiet as everyone rested, preparing for the next day's onslaught.

He was using this safe building as his command center, better to be away from LOW. Several hundred of his people were housed within the structure, with hundreds more spread out in various buildings in the city. It was part of his inheritance from Mr. Elwood. The rain still came, with most of the city now under several feet of water.

He was tired, too tired to sleep. He was lonely and alone,

and wondered more and more often if he was getting to be too much like those he hated. People depended on him, and that made him feel good. At this point, it was probably the only thing that kept him hanging on.

"Cat," came York's voice behind him.

He turned. The older man looked awake and angry, and Olson wondered just how he kept himself pumped up so much.

"Something?"

The man jerked the stub of a thumb back over his shoulder. "A citizen wants to talk to you."

"What?"

"There's a citizen waiting back there, who says she has an urgent message for you."

Olson smiled and tried unsuccessfully to get a look back in the shadows. "A citizen with an urgent message," he repeated.

York shrugged. "What can I tell you? She's been convincing enough to get this far."

Olson laid the binoculars on the retaining wall and turned to stare at the fire. "Well, let's not disappoint the lady with the urgent message. Send her over."

Putting his hands behind his back, Olson let the fire have access to most of his body. He was out of his exo for now, and though sweat was replacing the rain that wet his face, the fire was doing much toward drying out his clothes.

He heard them walking up behind him, but didn't turn around.

"Here she is," York said.

Olson spun to let his back get the flames. "Now, what is this I've . . ."

He was staring into Gret's eyes.

The world stopped for him then, the Jits and the water and the sickness all fuzzing off into some vaguely remembered nightmare. They stared at one another for several eternities in a world only they inhabited. And with neither of them remembering closing the distance, they were in each other's arms.

"Gret . . . Gret." He was squeezing her tightly, trying to physically merge her into him so she wouldn't slip away again.

"God," she cried. "Kill me if you want to, I couldn't stay away."

"My love, my love." He held her, rocking back and forth. "I'm so sorry. I've searched for you every day." He pulled her away from him, staring at her. "Kill you? I love you, I could never . . ."

Her lips quivered. "But I thought . . . Oh, the hell with it. Hold me."

They embraced again, smiling uncontrollably, joyous.

"I take it you two are already acquainted?" York said.

They both laughed.

"Junex York," Olson said, "I'd like for you to meet my future wife, Gret'amaine."

"A citizen?" the man asked, incredulous.

"A Houris," Gret said.

York shook his head. "Times sure have changed," he said.

Olson stared at the woman, started to ask her about the way she looked, then realized that it had everything to do with survival. Instead he said, "You've brought the Sun back into my life."

She nodded up at him, the firelight highlighting her pale blue eyes. "You're not so bad yourself," she returned; then suddenly her face darkened. "God, I almost forgot why I came to begin with."

He searched her face. "What?"

"I saw Rennie," she said, "in the old church on Lafayette Street."

"What was he doing there?"

"Making trouble. He's got hold of some con-tam suits that will keep him isolated from the disease. He intends to slip over the wall in the morning and try to make some kind of deal with the Jits."

"Deal?" York said.

"With Jits?" Olson said. "What kind of deal can you make with Jits?"

"It doesn't make any sense to me," Gret returned. "I overheard him tell Fagin that he wants to open the gates to them if they promise to take only half the city and give him the other half."

"That's insane," York said. "Totally crazy."

"Not from Rennie's standpoint," Olson said. "He's got nothing to lose. He figures that I'll get the city because of my relationship with Abdullah . . ."

"Which isn't that good," York finished.

"But Rennie doesn't know that," Olson said. "He feels like he's looking down the end of the road and it's a blind alley.

He'll either get it from the Jits or from me. This other way, he'll have me taken care of and only have to worry about them.''

Gret cocked her head. "You've changed," she said.

Olson nodded. "For the better, I hope."

"When does this all happen?" York asked.

Gret tightened her lips. "I think he intends to take the suits from the church at first light. I don't know where he goes after that."

"Do we wait for him at the church?" York asked.

Olson shook his head. "We don't even know if he'll go there anymore himself. I want you to go down there now and wait. Follow whoever grabs the suits and report back to me as soon as they make a move."

York nodded grimly and moved off, passing Valuska halfway to the door down. The Junex hurried over to Olson.

"Thought you'd want to know," he said. "We've just gotten word that the second outpost has fallen."

"That leaves one," Olson said, and took a deep breath. "Get out there with a hundred replacements. Fortify that last checkpoint. We can't let them have the river."

"Got it," Valuska said, and hurried off.

"It's falling to pieces," Gret said.

Olson pulled her close again. "Not really," he said into her hair. "It fell to pieces several days ago. It's the pieces that are falling to pieces now." He began pulling out the pins that held her hair up, letting it spill over her shoulders like thick honey.

He stepped back a pace. Spitting onto his hand, he began wiping the dirt off her face. "There's my Gret," he said softly, and let his hand drift down to her breasts.

A look of pain shot across her face and she jerked away from him, moving to the retaining wall, looking out over pain multiplied by a million.

"What's wrong?" he said, walking up beside her.

She turned and looked up into his eyes. "I've changed too," she said.

"Changed how?" he asked.

She started to talk several times before getting any words out. "That night with Rennie . . . I . . ."

She broke down crying, her whole body convulsing. Olson held her again.

"Something happened that night," she sobbed into his shoulder. "Something . . . I don't know, snapped, inside of me.

I've felt vile and dirty ever since. I've never felt that way about myself before. I'm some kind of unnatural freak or something.''

"No!'' he said, angry. "You're sweet and wonderful. Whatever happened to you was because of Rennie. He used you like he uses everything. He used your own goodness against you. You can't blame yourself for his perversion.''

"I can control it now,'' she said firmly.

His eyes narrowed. "The sex . . .'' he began.

"I'm stronger now. My mind is stronger, my . . . determination.'' Her face was bunched up, muscles tight, and he couldn't help but believe her.

"I love you no matter what,'' he said.

"I'll never betray you again,'' she said.

He shook his head. "You don't have to—''

"Never.''

She moved slowly away from him, looked out over the city again. "I've spent a lot of time with the citizens,'' she said quietly, and he put an arm around her shoulder, which she didn't shrug off. "I really grew to love being with them. There's something . . .''

"Real,'' he said.

She smiled at him. "Yeah. Something real about life out there that they don't have in LOW.''

"I know,'' he said.

"I understand that now,'' she replied, then stared at him for a time.

"Say what you're thinking,'' he told her.

"This is going to sound strange coming from me,'' she said, "but would you mind if we didn't make love for a while? Maybe we can start over again, get to know one another.''

"We're both new people,'' he said. "It's only right that we get to know one another.''

"Thanks,'' she said, and cuddled up next to him, his arm protectively on her shoulders.

And for once in his life, Olson knew what it must feel like to be King of the World.

They came banging into Abdullah's room no sooner than he had gotten to sleep. The sound startled him, made him jump, bleary eyes blinking at the Elite who formed a semicircle around his bed.

"He wants to talk to you,'' one of them said.

"Who?" Abdullah said, rubbing his eyes.

"Faisel."

He jumped out of bed and slipped into his still-damp thobe. "Well, come on," he said, and hurried out the door. Moments later, he was in the Elite barracks wearing a headset, waiting for the static to clear on the small screen in front of him.

Faisel's face juiced to life, filling the screen. "So, my brother," he said. "We get to have a little talk."

"Where's my wife?" Abdullah said. "What have you done with her?"

Faisel metronomed an index finger slowly in front of his face. "My brother," he said. "You must relax. We have many things to talk about. I wish to bask in the light of our love for one another first."

Abdullah swallowed back what he wanted to say. Arguing with Faisel was useless, a waste of everyone's time. "What do you wish to speak with me about?"

"That's better," Faisel said. "How goes your mission?"

"We have made progress," Abdullah said.

"How so?"

"We have found the discrepancy. Now we await him who caused the problem."

"Who is this person?"

"I do not know."

"Why is he stealing from me?"

"That I also do not know."

Faisel grinned. "How is he stealing from me?"

"I do not wish to say at the moment."

Faisel laughed then, threw back his head and laughed. "You certainly have made progress," he said when he was able. "Why will you not tell me the nature of the problem?"

Abdullah closed his eyes. The thing he feared was that Faisel was doing it himself from LOW Corporate. "I don't want to make accusations until I am absolutely convinced of the culprit and his crime."

Faisel pursed his lips. "Speculate," he said, and it was not a request.

"Where is Nura?" Abdullah returned.

"You want your wife?" he said, sneering. "Does my brother pine for his bundle of sweet flesh and good teeth?"

"What have you done to her?"

"Well, see for yourself."

The camera pulled back to reveal Faisel's private rooms. Opulently done in stuffed purples and yellows, it was a room of priceless hangings and obscene elegance, a large room of fat pillows and squat, polished tables. A woman was there, standing to the left of and slightly behind Faisel. She wore a long flowing gown the color and shimmer of gold, but soft as a summer wisp of cloud. A veil of black film covered the lower half of her face, but it was Nura, there could be no doubt.

"My love," Abdullah choked, reaching out to the screen.

The woman took a step forward, but a look from Faisel stopped her in her tracks.

"You see?" Faisel said. "Nura is here with me and doing quite nicely."

"Let her go," Abdullah said.

Faisel showed empty palms. "I do not keep her here," he said. "She stays of her own free will, enjoying my hospitality. Isn't that right, Nura?"

"Yes," the woman said quietly, eyes on the floor.

"Nura?" Faisel said gently. "We didn't hear you."

She looked up at the screen, drew a breath. "I want to be here," she said. "Faisel has been very good to me."

"No," Abdullah said. "I do not believe you."

"What?" Faisel said. "Do not believe your own eyes, your own ears? You certainly are a strange fellow. Do you not know when you have been replaced?"

Abdullah felt the tide of anger swell within him, but he held it in check. "Let her go," he said. "I'll do anything you wish."

"You are already doing that," Faisel said.

"You bastard!"

"You know better than that," Faisel returned, shaking his head. "Since you are my brother, I wanted to spare you this embarrassment, but I suppose I have no choice. Tell him, Nura."

Abdullah stared black hatred at the screen as his wife walked closer to it, looking once to Faisel before speaking. "I...I don't love you anymore," she said. "I love Faisel and want to stay with him."

"Lies!" Abdullah screamed. "I know he's making you say those things."

Faisel walked up to the camera. "I am an honorable man," he said. "I would never respond to the advances of my brother's wife, no matter how beautiful she is. I will always do the right thing."

Abdullah sat before the screen, fists clenched, hands shaking. "Do you think for one second that I would believe your vile schemes?" he said. "I have known you for too long, and have known my wife just long enough. What did you threaten her with? Tell me!"

Faisel's eyes went wide. "Me? My brother, I was just trying to protect your feelings."

"You listen to me," Abdullah said, and his voice was cracking like his heart. "Before I left, you made me swear a bay'ah to you. Now I swear my own oath. You will die by these hands, serpent. By my blood and the blood of my children and my entire clan, I swear to you that I will be the instrument of your death."

Faisel's expression turned dark and angular as he stared back at Abdullah. "You have one day, jackal. One day left. Your hollow threats mean nothing. Your own death, I fear, is much more imminent than my own."

He brought the camera in close and smiled to fill its screen. "But do not worry, my brother. I am an honorable man and will do the right thing by your widow after you are gone."

At that point, Abdullah put his fist through the tv screen. He cut his hand deeply and had to be rushed to the infirmary, where he took fifty-four stitches without anesthetic and reswore his oath on the blood that lay in a puddle on the linoleum floor.

"We've lost transmission," the technician behind the lights said.

Faisel turned away from the camera to stare at Nura. "You were not very convincing," he said.

"I told you he wouldn't believe you," she returned, and it was all she could do to keep from going at his face with her nails. "But I kept my end of the bargain, and I expect you to keep yours."

Someone switched off the hot lights, darkening the room to a twilight haze. Faisel turned to the video people and the Elite who were guarding them. "Leave me, all of you." They began scurrying around, gathering up equipment. "Now!" Faisel yelled, and they all hurried off without their gear.

He turned back to Nura. "The bargain was that I would promise not to kill Abdullah if you could convince him that you were in love with me. You didn't convince him."

She stared hard at him. "How does a man like you live with

himself?'' she said. "Does nothing matter to you? You say you want me to love you, yet you show me the base selfishness of a little boy."

His eyes searched hers. "Nura, I . . ."

"You're not a man," she said. "You're no part of a man. Being around you chills my blood. And now, please take me back to my cell. I far prefer it to being around you." She began to take off the clothes he had made her wear.

"No," he said. "Please. Keep the clothes."

"I will only wear my own clothes," she replied. "I want nothing of yours."

"Please keep the clothes," he said. "I attach no meaning to the wearing. Please. I don't know where I put yours, but you need not go around naked anymore."

She slipped the gown over her head. She would have taken the clothes under ordinary circumstances, but now she couldn't, she couldn't because of the plan. "I will only wear my own clothes," she said, tossing him the gown.

And he turned his eyes from her nakedness, ashamed at last.

*   *   *

The Greeks have been vanquished
in the nearer part of the land;
and, after their vanquishing,
they shall be the victors
in a few years.
To God belongs the Command
before and after,
and on that day
the believers shall rejoice in
God's help; God
helps whomsoever He will; and
He is the All-mighty, the
All-compassionate.
                              —The Koran
                              XXX. The Greeks

LI
The Sewers

"Take a left at the next junction," Thumper said, and he pointed to the place on the map that he had taken from the old files in Public Works.

Rennie nodded, holding the flashlight on the map, then sweeping the beam back into the murky darkness after he had looked.

The tunnels were rusted and dank, thick black stringy goo dripping from every overhang, the sludge on the floor congealed like pudding as they trudged through it. The tunnels were alive with creatures that thrived on decay, creatures that hurried to get away from the flashlight beam because it threatened their world of darkness. And Rennie's white suit was turning darker and darker.

"Here it is," he said, and his voice came nasal-sounding through the mouthpiece of the self-contained con-tam suit.

The tunnel branched off, and Rennie didn't hesitate as he moved down the left fork, Thumper and VeePee Fagin following dutifully behind.

"We'll look for the sign on our right," Thumper said. "It shouldn't be too much farther on."

They moved forward, Rennie playing the beam against the round sidewall of the metal tunnel. His light found the sign quickly. It read:

CITY OF NEW ORLEANS
SEWAGE TREATMENT #3

There was a small metal ladder attached to the wall beside the sign. Hooking the flashlight on his belt loop, Rennie scaled the thing. A small trapdoor was inset at the top. He unlatched it, rusted flakes of iron drifting down with the activity, and pushed. The thing wouldn't budge.

"Give me some help up here," he said, pushing while he

343

talked. Fagin got up there with him, both sharing the ladder by using only one foot on the rung. The two of them grunted with the strain for several minutes before the door moved.

They pushed open to daylight, mud and small stones falling in on top of them. Rennie climbed out. He was standing in thick weeds on the site where a cement building had once stood, the vaguest outline of a foundation the only hint that anything manmade had ever occupied that place.

He turned back to look at the city. They were several hundred yards from the wall, the fighting already gearing up in the early-morning light.

"Come on, let's go," he called down the hole as Fagin climbed out. "Let's get this over with."

"It's not too late to change your mind," Fagin said as he, too, looked back at the wall. "We can turn around right now."

Thumper climbed out, pulling his flamethrower up after him and strapping it on his back again.

"Are you having problems with my plan?" Rennie asked Fagin.

"You know I'm with you," Fagin replied.

"Good." Rennie looked at the wall again, an imposing sight. They were North of the city, on the Lake Pontchartrain side, the bulk of the fighting taking place at the front gates to the West and South. "There should be an old aut graveyard nearly due West of here," he said, pointing. "That's where Milander is supposed to be bivouacked."

"So, are we just going to walk in there?" Fagin asked.

"That's about the size of it."

And that's what they did. Moving swiftly, the sound of gunfire nothing but a distant rumble, they hurried toward Milander's headquarters. At one point, an Arab balloon rapidly losing air drifted lazily overhead to crash a quarter of an hour later into the lake, its inhabitants apparently not willing to take their chances with either the Jits or the citizens.

They reached the graveyard within thirty minutes, entered the labyrinthian corridors of piled-up ancient carriages many hundreds of years old. The pathways were narrow, the walls of metal high. Thumper walked cautiously, his flamethrower ready, turning in circles to watch behind him. Fagin carried a sawed-off shotgun, while Rennie had his wrist lasers strapped on the outside of his con-tam suit. No balloons floated overhead; Milander used his lasers to restrict the air space over his headquarters.

"Milander!" Rennie called every few feet. "I want to parley!"

He carried a white handkerchief which he waved above his head.

"Milander!"

All at once, a man was blocking the path ahead of them. He was a young man who looked old, a man whose body had been twisted all out of proportion.

"Wh-what you waaant here?" the man slurred.

"We just want to talk," Rennie said. "Are you Milander?"

There was laughter then, from all around. Thumper looked up to see many of them high above his head, atop the piles of old auts.

"Do I . . . l-look like M-Milan . . . der?"

Laughter again.

"This shit makes my skin crawl," Fagin whispered.

"Shut up," Rennie rasped; then, louder: "We're here to make a deal with Milander."

Someone was coming up on them from behind. Thumper turned loose with the flamer for a second, just to drive them back.

"Easy with that," Rennie said, low. "We still need to get out of here."

"M-Mr. Milan . . . der don't make no . . . d-deals," the man said.

"Tell him I'll open up the gates," Rennie said.

The young man's good eye got wide. The other side of his face was totally paralyzed and didn't do anything. He hobbled off, and they were alone again.

Majid and Abdullah walked out into the balloon field with the morning light. The Arizona sun burned bright on a valley of high blue sky. It was hot and dry. Dry. Abdullah felt as if he would never grow used to the dichotomy of this land. Within a matter of hours he would be in another part of the country where it rained all the time.

"Are you sure you are well enough to go into Orleans?" Majid asked, gesturing toward Abdullah's bandaged hand.

"My brother has given me one more day," Abdullah replied. "What do you think?"

The man nodded. "I suppose you have seen the television box this morning?"

Abdullah couldn't help but laugh. He was wearing an exo under his mishla, crossed bandoliers of bullets and power packs; he carried a rifle in his left hand, and near to his right, a holstered laser. The television was juicing a continual picture of him, with Faisel's voice telling the Western Sector that this was the man who was going to turn the fury of hell loose on them.

"Yes," he said simply. "I have seen the television. What have you decided to do with the balloons?"

"We're going to run them in shifts," Majid said as they reached the command gondola, the Elite already untying the moorings. "A third of what we have left will go to the city with us this morning. Another third will relieve us in eight hours, the remaining third to relieve them in eight hours."

Majid cracked the gondola door, frowning at the Elite who stared blankly at him, as balloons rose majestically all around them. He started in, then stopped, taking a long look back to the garrison.

"What is it?" Abdullah asked.

The man shook his head, the tail of his ghutra sliding around his shoulders. "A feeling...I don't know. I sense a problem here at the garrison."

He shook his head again, climbed into the already stuffy gondola. Abdullah followed him in.

"Have you thought any more about Milander?" Abdullah asked.

Majid smiled at him. "I packed a surprise in the cargo hold this morning," he replied.

"What is it?"

For the first time in several days, Abdullah saw Majid's gold teeth flashing. "A secret," he said, and winked.

Rennie was taken around enough twists and turns before being led to Milander that he wasn't even sure what direction he was facing anymore. Finally, double doors were cracked open on a large yellow vehicle that had the words ST. CHARLES PARISH SCHOOL BUS painted in black on the side, and he was led in with Fagin, Thumper staying outside on guard.

It was hot in there, the humidity a physical presence, like an extra person. Rennie was getting very uncomfortable in his suit, and wished that he could rip the helmet with its steamy plastic visor off his head for just a moment to breathe some fresh air.

There was a man on a stretcher in the back of the big aut.

His stretcher was propped up against the back emergency door, facing forward. The young man they had spoken with earlier was sitting next to him, a hand on the man's arm.

"Are you Milander?" Rennie asked, walking toward the man.

"Yes, my son," Milander answered through the left side of his mouth, the unparalyzed side.

Rennie grimaced. The man apparently had use of one hand and part of his face—and his brain. *This* was the man who was holding the city of Orleans and the might of LOW at bay?

"I extend my heartfelt greetings to you," Rennie said.

Milander nodded, a cat smile on half his face. "And a fine day to you too, VeePee Du'camp."

Rennie sat down on one of the bench seats close to Milander, turning toward the aisle to face him. "I thought that if you had a minute, you and I might talk a little business."

"I have nothing but time."

"You want the city," Rennie said.

"I will have the city," Milander returned.

Rennie was dying for a cigarette, fought the thought from his mind. "Suppose I can make it easier for you."

The man closed his eyes for a second. "Danny has told me that you said you could open the gates."

"Yes," Rennie said. "I can. If we can come to some sort of . . . arrangement, you and I."

Milander drew a difficult breath. "You have something in mind, I presume."

Rennie looked at Fagin, then back to Milander. "I am prepared to open the gates for you, right now, today, if you will promise to make certain concessions to me in return."

"I'm listening."

Rennie took a deep breath, a cigarette breath, and let it out. "If I open the gates for you, you must promise in return to occupy only half the city. We can divide it right down the middle, each getting the goodies on his particular side. We can make mutual trade agreements, live in peace."

"Why do you make me this offer?"

Rennie chuckled. "Because I want part of the city, and this is the only way I can think to get it. A leader of men like yourself could certainly understand that."

"Certainly."

Rennie watched out the side windows as several men with

lasers strapped on their backs went walking by with a gunner behind.

"So what do you think?" Rennie asked.

"We would live in peace together," Milander said. "Each on his separate side."

"Absolutely," Rennie said. "Fifty-fifty, right down the middle."

"We would make trade agreements."

"One hand washing the other."

Milander stared down at his paralyzed hand. "Your offer is attractive, since I don't relish the idea of losing all my people just trying to get through the gates."

"Half a city is better than none," Rennie said firmly.

"Well put," Milander returned. "Couldn't have said it better myself."

Rennie stood up, turned, and smiled at Fagin, who never came in any farther than the double doors. He walked closer to Milander. "I knew you were a businessman," he said. "Gotta have good business sense to have made it as far as you have."

"Well, you sure were right."

"Have we got a deal, then?"

"Deal."

Rennie stuck his hand out, then jerked it back in. "I'll dynamite a dividing line in the city for us. We'll try to open the gates for you right at dark tonight. Remember. Half and half."

"Fifty-fifty," Milander said, nodding.

Rennie turned and walked back to the front of the aut. He turned just before going down the stairs. "After all this settles down, we'll have to take a lunch."

"And have a few drinks," Milander added.

Rennie winked. "Later," he said, and walked out.

Danny and Milander sat silently for several minutes after the citizens left.

"Wh-what did that . . . m-mean?" he asked.

"It means that perhaps they will open the gates and let our love flow in of its own accord," Milander said.

"Will you g-give h-him half the . . . city?"

"No."

"But you . . . p-promised."

"They are not real, Danny. You don't make real promises to illusions."

*   *   *

Majid's balloons floated to the East, just as the caravan approached New Mecca from the West. The caravan was long, but not as long as it once was. The continual deterioration of the Western sector had affected even the scavengers.

Iffa rode on his camel to the front gates. Behind, fifty creaking wooden wagons pulled by fifty camels kicked up a dust cloud that could be seen as far away as ten miles.

Iffa was what was called a slaver in the East and a pimp in the West. He took whores to the garrisons and outposts, and in return managed to make enough plastic to keep himself fat with food and vodka and sex. It wasn't much, but some people don't need much.

Putting up a hand, he halted the wagons. The green suits were gazing down at him from the top of the walls.

"I have returned!" he called up to them, and it was difficult to be cheerful, since he had awakened that morning with a stomach ache.

"We cannot allow you entry," a guard called down to him.

Iffa made an expansive gesture. "I have traveled for eight days to reach you here. You cannot turn me away."

"There are too many Jits around," the voice returned.

Putting a hand to his breast, Iffa looked shattered. "I have no Jits with me. What would that do for my business? We have been here many times, and there have never been any Jits."

"We are under orders."

"Orders," Iffa mumbled, fingers scratching his fat, sweaty face. "I have cigarettes!" he screamed.

Nothing.

"Whiskey!"

"Orders."

"I have deodorant . . . candy!"

"Do you have drugs?"

The man raised his arms high. "I have hemp, gentlemen. I have endorphins. I have lysergics reported to be gleaned from the long-lost chemicals of Owsley."

"Too risky."

Iffa hefted his huge bulk off the camel and readjusted his robes. This was not the first time of late that he had been denied entry to a garrison. It was a situation he was well prepared for.

Going to the back of the first wagon, he pulled aside the heavy canvas drape. Several young men sat looking back out at him. "David," he said. "Come out here."

The boy dutifully climbed out of the wagon. He was only fifteen, but possessed of an endowment that left those who saw it gaping in disbelief. Iffa didn't know where he'd be without David. The boy was also a natural blonde, quicksand for any Arab. David hadn't failed him yet.

They walked up to the gate.

"Does this look like a Jit?" he called up to them, then looked at David. "You know what to do," he whispered.

Without a word, the boy lifted his robes up over his head and stood before them naked. A born exhibitionist, he began stroking his organ until it grew to immense proportions, the ultimate symbol of cleanliness—the no-Jit dick. The catcalls from the wall gave way very quickly to silence. Then, ten minutes later, the big gates squeaked open and Iffa brought the wagons in.

In the last wagon was a twelve-year-old boy named Jeffery who was young and extraordinarily beautiful. Iffa had picked him up the day before at the Scottsdale outpost where he was trying to get in. He had passed Iffa's lie-detector test easily and when the man found out he was still a virgin, he took him under his wing immediately.

What neither of them knew was that he had contracted the Jitterbug mere hours before he had met Iffa, from a stranger he had shared a meal with on the road, a stranger who didn't even know that he had the Jitterbug because he had picked it up from someone who had been turned loose from College Station days before that.

Jeffery's wagon bounced to a halt in the garrison's stone courtyard. Seconds later, a dark, bearded face was peering in at him, whites of his eyes glowing in the darkness.

He was reclining on the wagon's back mattress. Smiling with a keen, innocent face and sharp eyes, he said, "Hi, my name's Jeffery, what's yours?"

Fifteen minutes later the boy experienced his first orgasm. A minute after that he became totally impotent for the rest of his young life. Twelve minutes later he experienced his first severe intestinal disorder. Barely fifteen minutes after that he was killed and burned when they realized what he was. But it was already too late.

Olson stood on the wall, binoculars fixed on his eyes, watching the place where Rennie had come up from underground. He could barely see the radio that he had placed by the trapdoor and left on. Beside him, Jan checked the countryside, while York, Jerry Joe, and Valuska shot Jits off the wall.

"There," Jan said, pointing to the West.

Olson blurred a line across the countryside with his fieldglasses, finally settling on the three white-clad figures that were crouching low, hurrying back to their rabbit hole.

He followed them with the glasses as they approached the hole, smiling when they got within range of the transmitter.

" . . . charges should be set by now," Rennie's voice crackled over the radio that Olson had set on the wall.

"I'll take care of the gate myself," Fagin's voice said, and they were very close now. "I have a private office in the base of the wall."

"What the hell!" Thumper yelled. They must have spotted the radio.

"Oops," York said loudly, and they all laughed.

Olson put the microphone to his mouth as he saw Rennie bend to examine the radio. "It's my victory party," he said, and watched Rennie stiffen. "Come to concede?"

Rennie started swinging around looking. "Where are you, you son of a bitch?"

"Up here," Olson said. "On the wall."

He waved his arm, and watched through the glasses as Fagin pointed to their position.

"Fuck you!" Rennie said.

"Since you like it on the outside so much," Olson said, "I thought I might fix it so you could stay out there all the time."

"What's he mean?" Fagin said. "What the hell is he talking about?"

Rennie made a gesture. "Fuck him," his voice crackled over the radio. "Let's go."

He bent to open the trapdoor.

"I wouldn't do that," Olson said.

Fagin's voice was near hysteria. "What's going on? What's he talking about?"

"Button it!" Rennie ordered, but he didn't pull open the door.

"I knew this was a bad idea. I knew it wouldn't—"

"Shut up!" Rennie yelled.

Fagin turned to the wall. "Please," he whined. "I didn't

want to have anything to do with this. I'll do anything you want, say anything—''

Rennie cut him off with his laser, burning a hole through the back of the man's head that bubbled out of his eye patch. He fell to his knees, stayed there.

"What did you do?" Rennie said congenially, pointing to the trapdoor.

"It's a surprise," Olson said. "Don't you like surprises?"

Rennie bent to the door again.

"Don't do it," Olson said.

Rennie stopped. Thumper walked up to him, moved him aside.

"I'll do it," he said, and jerked open the door that set the trip wire that detonated the charges that Olson had placed all through the tunnels.

The ground shook, rumbling like an out-of-tune motor. Then large sections of it collapsed, a geyser of dust spewing into Thumper's face through the open manhole.

"I told you not to open it," Olson said. "Now it looks like you're trapped out there."

Rennie looked up to the wall, smiling wide, arms outstretched. "Okay," he said. "You win. I give up. I freely admit that you're the better man, and I'm happy to step aside and let you have the city. Now, how about getting me back in?"

"Listen," Olson said. "We're all full up right now, but leave your name with my secretary, and we'll let you know as soon as we have an opening."

"Cat!" Rennie said. "Please."

"Sorry," Olson said, "but I've got an appointment."

With that, he flicked off the radio and walked down off the wall. He was needed at the river.

*   *   *

Have you considered the water you drink?
Did you send it down from the clouds, or
did We send it?
Did We will, We would make it bitter; so
why are you not thankful?
                                        —The Koran
                                        LVI. The Terror

Every day cannot be a feast of lanterns.
—Eastern Wisdom

The big drum only sounds well from afar.
—Persian Proverb

LII
The Clouds

They watched from the gondola of the command balloon as the Arabs in the oil tanker were plucked one by one, like dates, off the deck of the big ship and lifted by rope ladder into one of the balloons.

Wexler applauded from his position in Gret's arms as one of the men fell from the ladder, legs flailing wildly, into the churning waters of the Mississippi.

Gret giggled, hugging the little man close. He responded by throwing his arms around her neck and giving her a big, sloppy kiss on the cheek.

"Is this your first balloon ride?" she asked him.

"It depends," Wexler responded.

"Uh-oh," Olson said.

"I don't think that my physical body has ever ridden in a balloon before," he said, "but I have memory of such things, so perhaps my RNA donor had done such before, although it may be possible that he had just seen pictures of something like this on the television, or maybe I simply remember balloon rides because sometime in my past I saw television pictures and don't remember that I did . . ."

Olson crossed to the other side of the gondola, where Majid and Abdullah stared upriver toward the fires at the last checkpoint. There were still thousands of boats crammed end to end and side to side trying to force their way through the outpost which was an attachment to the city wall. A huge column of fire crackled upward, black oil smoke relighting and bursting orange fifty feet above the conflagration.

Abdullah shook his head. "I have never seen people welcome death the way they do."

The boats kept coming, plowing right into the flames, as riflemen on the walls fired into their midst, and the dense packed balloons overhead dropped napalm and laced the area with laser lines blurring out pink haze as the cannon panned.

"It is a war of extinction," Majid said quietly.

"What?" Olson said.

"Milander, their leader, is out to make the human race extinct." Majid looked at each of them in turn, and Olson noticed a cast to his eyes, a darkness, that hadn't been there before. He remembered that Mr. Elwood had said the same words. "This is not random. Jits are being drawn here by some . . . force of some kind. It is methodical. We don't just fight for the city here; we fight for the whole human race."

As Olson looked out the windows, he could see nothing that would make him think it was not the end of the world. Smoke rose from the walls as continual gunfire blurted into the small groups of Jits who stormed the towers with ropes and crude ladders, trying to get in, wanting nothing more than to get in. Balloons crisscrossed the fighting, trying to help out but avoid Milander's lasers at the same time. They would go down, some outside the walls, some in. Many buildings burned within the gates, the results of collisions with LOW dirigibles. Bodies flew from catapults, as boatloads of Junexes with flamers rowed to them, making a contest out of who could burn the most, and the dead filled the streets, floating dead from sickness and fire and violence of a more personal nature. The hospital was underwater, but it didn't matter; they couldn't handle the load anyway. Nature was flushing out the hospital, taking care of the bloated dead, bringing it all up as the water rose in the cemeteries, taking all the dead out together, and Olson thought of Mr. Elwood, floating, floating on the fat dark current, his beautiful dream drowning in a sea of water and blood. The citizens huddled in the dark towers, waiting for someone to come and take them—either Allah, or LOW, or Jits—and it didn't matter who anymore. Waking up from the nightmare was the only thing of any importance. And waking up was the only thing that none of them could do.

"Where are your replacements?" Abdullah asked.

Majid shook his head. "They should be here anytime."

"They should have already been here."

"I know."

The Elite who was running the radio looked up from his console. "VeePee Catanine," he said.

"Yeah," Olson said, and moved to the table.

The man handed him the headset and Olson held it up to his ear without putting it on. "Cat," he said.

"Valuska," a tiny voice crackled.

"Yeah, what you got?"

"At the rate we're using up ammo at the front gate, it won't last us through the morning!"

"Okay. Look, we've got more people than we need up on the walls there anyway. Move about half of them over to the river, and while you're at it, find a place to stash a bunch of that ordnance so we'll have it in reserve. Ration it out; we've got a long way to go."

"Gotcha."

Olson rubbed his dirty face with a dirty hand. "How are the negotiations going with Rennie's people?"

"They're still holed up in their buildings," staticked the response. "I think they realize he's gone now. They're taking some kind of vote."

"What's it feel like?"

"I think they'll come around soon."

"How's the food situation?"

"We're rationed . . . I don't know what the citizens are eating."

"Okay. Keep me posted."

"Roger. Out."

Olson handed the headset back to the Elite and rejoined the others. Abdullah was still staring intently out the window, and Olson realized that he really wasn't looking at anything.

"I saw you on tv," he said.

The man turned dark eyes on him. Said nothing.

"Will this day bring you the answers you seek?" Olson asked, persisting.

"Perhaps."

"What is the precentage of your perhaps?"

The dark eyes flashed. "What business is it of yours?"

"It's all my business."

Majid stepped between them. "Maybe this isn't the time," he said. "We have many other problems."

"Listen to me," Olson said. "I'm real sorry about your wife and all, but the problem is a lot larger than that. If we don't do something, we're going to lose this city and everybody in it. Now there must be some kind of extension you can get from your brother, something—''

"My brother sent me here to die!" Abdullah yelled. "He doesn't want me to find anything. Why do you think he's been showing my picture around like a prized stallion? There have already been four attempts on my life today.''

"But you have the key," Olson said. "The decisions are in your hands.''

"My wife's life is in my hands." He pointed a shaking finger at Gret and Wexler. "Would you kill them for the sake of the city? Would you?''

Olson looked over at them, faces wide and innocent. He let his eyes drift to the floor. "Thank God," he whispered, "I don't have that decision to make.''

Abdullah's voice calmed. "I pray that the decision will be taken away from me somehow before the time comes. I do not know what else to do.''

Olson let his eyes drift upward. "My prayers are the same as yours, my friend." He reached out and put a hand on Abdullah's shoulder. "Because I hate to think of what's going to happen if things don't work out.''

"VeePee," the Elite at the radio said, and he was holding the headset out for Olson again.

Olson moved to the radio and held the gadget up to his ear. "Go ahead," he said.

It was Valuska again. "It's over!" the man said happily. "Rennie's people have just voted to throw their support behind you. You're the man, Cat. You're the one!''

Olson was in shock. There was nothing surprising about the turn of events, except that it had happened. He held out the headset, and the Elite plucked it away from him.

"What is it?" Gret asked when she saw the look on his face.

He gazed up at her. "The city's mine," he said softly, and they shared a look that spoke volumes in seconds. She smiled a half-smile, nodded.

"Congratulations," Abdullah said dryly, and he made an expansive gesture. "It's all yours. What are you going to do with it?''

Olson walked to stare out the window, at the churning

organic machine of the city that was rotting before his eyes. "I'll be damned if I know," he said.

* * *

> *If you do not raise your eyes you will think*
> *that you are the highest point.*
> —Bedouin Saying

> *He who knoweth his own self, knoweth God.*
> —The Prophet Mohammed

> *All Moslems are as one person. If a man*
> *complaineth of a pain in his head, his whole*
> *body complaineth; and if his eye complaineth,*
> *his whole body complaineth.*
> —The Prophet Mohammed

LIII
Light of the World Headquarters

The screen was fifty feet high and one hundred feet across. It was filled with a mammoth parade, people marching and cheering, hundreds of thousands of them.

"London," Faisel said from his cushion in front of the screen. Nura sat on a cushion next to him, wrapped in the robe that she had agreed to wear while she viewed the pictures.

"They loved me in London."

Bobby fuzztops pushed the crowds back as the royal aut plowed slowly ahead, Faisel waving to his loyal and loving subjects through four inches of impact-proof glass.

The picture switched to another crowd, this one with a definite Oriental look. It was another parade, moving down a wide, tree-lined boulevard.

"Bangkok," Faisel said proudly. "Just last year. Three-quarters of a million people showed up. Unfortunately, I had to destroy them a few weeks after these pictures were taken.''

Nura was getting a stiff neck from looking up. For two hours Faisel had been showing her pictures of him triumphantly entering city after city. Her eyes were beginning to hurt also.

"Do we have to watch anymore?" she asked, rubbing the back of her neck with a balled fist.

He looked at her in puzzlement. "Is this not exciting to you?"

"Why should it be?"

"This, all this," he said, "will be yours to share with me."

"No," she said simply.

His eyes flashed and he picked up the small microphone that lay next to him. "Enough," he said, and seconds later the screen went blank and the house lights came up.

He looked hard at her. "I thought to make you understand," he said, and stood up. "This building, the ground it was dug in, the desert, all those cities and all the people in them, the ground all the way to the core, the sky as far as you can see, everything—it all belongs to me."

"I understand that," she said.

"And I control it all," he said, shaking a fist.

"I know."

"And I have picked you to share it all with."

She shrugged. "I am not interested. I've told you that many times."

He squatted to get eye to eye with her. "How can you not be interested?"

"You have offered me the whole world," she said. "There's only one catch: I'd have to take you with it." She shook her head. "It seems to me I'd be getting the worst of that bargain."

He reached out and grabbed her by the shoulders, shaking. "You mock me!" he screamed.

"Yes!" she screamed back.

He stood again, turning his back to her. "Why do you treat me this way?" he asked quietly.

"You can ask me that after all you've done?"

He turned around slowly. "I am truly sorry for everything," he said. "And this is the first time in my life I've ever apologized."

"Is that supposed to set everything right?"

"I only acted out of love for you."

"If you love me you will bring my husband home to me."

"What can he give you that I can't?" he asked. "You've seen the vastness of my empire, the glory of my reign . . ."

"I've seen the unhappiness that it has brought to you," she answered. "I wouldn't trade one minute of my time for your whole miserable life. Now, are you going to bring Abdullah back to me?"

He sat back down on the cushion. "My brother has sworn a blood oath against me. I cannot bring him back now under any circumstances."

"Please, Faisel," she said softly. "Everything still hangs by a thread. It is not too late to set it all right."

He stood up again, paced. He felt listless, tired all the time. But sleep brought the dreams. He nearly scaled an inner wall, but turned away from it at the last second. "He swore an oath. One of us must die. Abdullah will never return from the Western Sector. Can we just accept that as a given and begin from there?"

She stood up too, blocked his path as he paced. "If my husband dies, his oath will be mine also."

"You don't mean that," he said. "It is not for the women to take oaths."

"Let me put it this way," she replied. "You may take me, I cannot help that, but fear your life if you ever go to sleep around me."

"But I love you."

"Then sacrifice for me."

"I am the King of the World!"

"You are a pathetic, selfish, unhappy man."

He walked away from her then, walked away realizing that the one thing the King of the World never had to deal with was Truth.

"You forgot something," she called after him, and threw the robe he had given her on the ground.

Bandar and Ahmad ran around opening all the windows in the barracks that the green-suits had given them at Holmes Air Base. It had been difficult enough to pitch the tents in the sheet-metal structures, but when they lit the cook fires, it not only roasted them in there, but filled the entire room with thick gray smoke.

"How do the hadhar live in such places?" Ahmad coughed, using his ghutra to try to fan the smoke through the windows.

"Perhaps they do not cook their food," Bandar called to him from farther down the row of windows.

Most of the clan had rushed outside to escape the smoke and were now enthralled by watching a tank truck refueling one of the big jets.

"Can't we pitch our tents outside?"

Bandar shook his head. "We were told to wait here until . . ."

And the radio started talking before he could finish his sentence.

"You will listen to me," the voice said, Bandar and Ahmad hurrying over to squat before the small box on the ornate carpet they had provided.

"You should now be occupying building E-14, the supplicants' chambers." Bandar nodded at the correctness of the words. "At the end of the building are a group of lockers. Pick up the radio and move to the lockers now."

They stood, gathering up the box and walking to the lockers.

"One of the lockers in the line should have a combination lock on it."

Sure enough, the center one held a large, heavy-looking lock. "I will give you the combination twice," the voice said. "Open the lock."

Bandar had never opened a lock before; it was a new and exciting experience for him that carried with it a wonderful sense of accomplishment. He messed up the first time, but got it open on the second try.

"Now take off the lock and pull open the locker."

He did. It wasn't a locker at all. It was a door that led to a deep shaft with a metal ladder leading down.

"What you are looking at is the escape tunnel from the LOW building. Only Faisel and I know about it."

"And us!" Ahmad said.

"The ladder will lead you to a tunnel that will incline sharply downward. The tunnel is very long, and should take you several hours to walk. Try to be at the other end of it by evening prayers. Leave now. I will meet you there with Nura."

"And then we will have our day," Bandar said grimly.

The radio continued. "If you have all of that information, I want you to destroy the radio. It will send a signal to me."

Bandar didn't pretend to understand what any of that meant, but it had all worked properly so far; so he stood up with radio in hand, and proceeded to smash it on the floor. The machine cried a little death whine when it died.

Misha'al heard the feedback in his headphones and sighed deeply. Then he quickly smashed his own radio, threw the pieces in with other trash, and practically ran to the incinerator to get rid of it.

When he came back, the door to his room was open. His heart was pounding as he walked in to find Faisel conducting a search with several of his Elite. They were tearing up the room in a very methodical and direct manner.

"Hello, ulema," Faisel said, and Misha'al didn't like the tone of his voice. "We hate to inconvenience you this way, but it couldn't be helped. You see, we've been getting reports of unauthorized radio transmissions coming from somewhere within the building."

"And just who am I supposed to be calling on a radio?" Misha'al said.

"You're the prophet, you tell me."

The man went to his table, righting it and a knocked-over chair, and sat down. "I can tell you that I resent this intrusion," he said, his confidence back a bit.

Faisel walked over and righted another chair, sitting opposite Misha'al. "Take it easy. We're checking everyone."

"You just happened to start with me."

Faisel shrugged. "You have unlimited access and no controls," he said. "You are the obvious choice."

They pulled the mattress off his bed and slashed it open with the daggers they carried in their belts.

"There is no radio here," Misha'al said.

"I believe you," Faisel said. "Where is it?"

"I do not own a radio."

"Nobody owns anything but me," Faisel said. "Are you going to betray me?"

"I love you," Misha'al said, and Faisel was slapped in the face by his own words.

The Elite moved to the table. "We found nothing."

Faisel nodded. "You are off the tether for now, prophet. But we will speak further after I have checked on some things."

He stood up, inclining his head toward the door. The Elite walked out. Faisel wandered slowly to the door. "I'm thinking about releasing the woman," he said.

The man's eyes widened. "When?" he asked, and his voice cracked.

"She refuses to go out in anything but what she came in with," he said. "As soon as I find her clothes, she's gone."

Misha'al took a breath. "Why do you not sleep on that decision," he suggested.

Faisel just looked at him. "Do not leave your room," he said, "until we've straightened this thing out. And in case you must wander, I'll leave one of our friends outside to keep you company."

He left, slamming the door behind him, and Misha'al got up immediately and went to the small dresser that sat beside the bed.

Pulling the drawer open, he sifted quickly through the balled-up mess the Elite had left him and grabbed out Nura's clothes.

He took a deep breath, sighed it out. Fortunately, the Elite had only been looking for the radio. He had picked up the clothes knowing the woman would want to wear something out of the complex.

Folding the gown carefully, he placed it back in the drawer and tried to figure out how he was going to get rid of the guard on his door.

*   *   *

> *Whomsoever God guides,*
> *he is rightly guided;*
> *and whom He leads astray—*
> *thou wilt not find for them*
> *protectors, apart from Him.*
> *And We shall muster them*
> *on the Resurrection Day*
> *upon their faces,*
> *blind, dumb, deaf;*
> *their refuge shall be Gehenna,*
> *and whensoever it abates*
> *We shall increase for the*
> *the Blaze.*
> *—The Koran*
> *XVII. Night Journey*

LIV
Fire and Water

The mouth of the harbor was a solid sheet of flame stretching nearly a mile upriver. And still it wasn't enough. Jits were sneaking through on anything that could float, and where there was nothing to float, they tried to swim.

"TIGHTEN IT UP!" Olson said into the bullhorn, as Jerry Joe took the speedboat through Olson's ragged armada of rowboats and commandeered barges, the last vestige of hope between the Jits and his city.

"DON'T WASTE YOUR SHOTS. MAKE EVERYTHING COUNT."

Night had fallen and the rain continued, while the fires lit the Northern sky like an artificial sunrise. Several balloons still drifted overhead, but they were useless bags of air, their bombs and napalm depleted, their lasers in need of charge. They could have perhaps held the last checkpoint had it not been for the balloons. The reinforcements had never shown up.

He turned aft, watched Jan crouched over the radio, his hands clamping the headphones tight over his ears.

"Jan!" he called, but the man didn't hear him. "Jan!"

Putting the bullhorn to his mouth, he called, "JUNEX JANSEN!"

The man jumped, startled, then pulled off the headset.

"Any luck raising Majid?" Olson called.

Jan made an exaggerated show of shaking his head. "No one knows where Majid is!" he called over the battle noises. "They're trying to find Abdullah now!"

Olson gave him the thumbs-up sign and turned fore. "TIGHTEN IT UP!" he said again, as his loose semicircle of defense continued to draw up closer to the raging fires, trying to keep the Jits from slipping through the cracks.

"They're like cockroaches!" Jerry Joe said, and his half-face was glowing orange from the firelight, sweating like a baked apple. "You just can't kill them all."

363

"We'll never hold them this way!" Olson yelled. "We need more balloons, and fast!"

"What about the dead in the water?"

Olson chewed on his lips and shook his head. "TIGHTEN IT UP!" he said again, just as a flaming houseboat broke loose from the firestorm and drifted into the circle of defenders, Jits in silhouette standing on the burning deck arm in arm, singing hymns.

And the weapons sang along, picking them off the deck, trying to selectively drive them back into their own fires so they could save the fuel it would take to burn them.

"Cat!" Jan yelled. "I've got Abdullah!"

Olson dropped his bullhorn and squeezed past Jerry Joe to get aft. Nodding, he grabbed the gear away from Jan and put it on.

"Abdullah?" he said, and the static made the man seem millions of miles away.

"What do you want with me?"

"Where are the balloons?"

Abdullah's response was lost in a gigantic explosion as the fuel tank on one of the Jit boats went up, sending a ball of fire high into the night sky.

"Say again!" Olson yelled. "Say again!"

"We do not know where the balloons are!" came the response. "Majid has taken the command balloon back to New Mecca to find out what happened to the replacements."

"Can't you radio them?"

Another explosion sent a shower of debris falling on Olson like a summer rain. He crouched low, covering up.

"We get nothing on the radio. We fear something's happened!"

"Then we can't expect the balloons?"

"I am truly sorry."

"Yeah," Olson said, and pulled off the headset, handing it to Jan. "Use it to call any other radios tuned to us. Tell them to clear the river area."

The man narrowed his eyes, his cheeks corked black where they showed beneath his helmet. "What are you going to do?"

"Not a whole lot of choice," Olson returned, and he was staring at the monstrous black hulk of the Arabian tanker in the distance.

*   *   *

Majid could see the flashes of gunfire before he could hear
the sounds. On the walls, within the compound, a battle was
raging. He used the radio to talk to the pilot in the back.

"Take us slowly over the garrison," he said.

He turned to the crew, all handpicked, his most vicious
fighters. He was glad that the Elite who had been running the
balloon had stayed behind in Orleans with Abdullah.

"Turn out the cabin lights," he said, and after the lights
went down, he spoke. "No noise or firing when we go over the
compound. I want you to observe. I want you to observe what is
happening to your brothers."

They cleared the balloon field and reached the walls,
staying high enough to hopefully avoid detection. There were
audible gasps as they got above the courtyard.

There was fighting going on, Arab against Arab, and many
small fires burning. Majid saw the remnants of the caravan
wagons and put the scenario together in his mind. Those who
hadn't indulged in the caravan's wares tried to kill all those who
had. The fires were for burning the bodies. No wonder they
hadn't used the radio. They feared that someone would come in
and kill all of them. They were right.

"Take us back over the landing field," he said quietly into
the mike, and the balloon executed a long, slow turn.

A terrible sadness overcame Majid when he realized what
he must do. He had come friendless to the Western Sector many
years before and made it his home. He loved his new land; he
loved the people in it. And now he was going to have to consign
it to the flames.

"I want two volunteers," he said. "Two men who aren't
afraid to die."

To their credit, many stepped forward. He chose the two
senior men and had the balloon set down at the edge of the field,
near his secret passage.

"You two arm yourselves," he told the volunteers. "You
will kill anyone we meet, be it your brother or your best friend.
They are all Jits now. The rest of you, scuttle the balloons.
Untether them, but drain the power on the lasers first. If we do
not return by the time you are finished, go back to Orleans and
tell Abdullah what has happened."

Majid went in to the radio table and came out with a big
cigar, which he stuck in the side of his mouth right next to his
gold teeth.

"Let's go," he said, and walked out of the balloon.

*   *   *

Olson sat alone in what had been Rennie's downtown Agri office. The desk he sat behind was cold steel, the walls were painted an obscene blood red. A small box containing a single toggle switch sat before him. His finger gently caressed the small silver switch.

"I've killed Jits," he said aloud to the specter that hung in the air of his imagination, "in cold blood and without provocation, just like you said I would. And now I'm going to do the same to the people I swore to protect. Funny, huh?"

He released his feather touch on the toggle and sat back in Rennie's well-broken-in chair. All of Mr. Elwood's words came back to him, and he knew now why the man had always looked so tired all the time.

The switch was Rennie's plan, the dynamite planted by his people. Olson had killed Rennie because of it, and now was getting ready to use it himself. Funny.

It would be a firebreak this time, would hopefully save at least half the city and its inhabitants; but it would also kill half of them—cold-bloodedly, without provocation. And it was his decision to make.

There was no decision about it. That was the funny part. He had to do it, contrary to everything he felt or believed. And just as the Director had said, he just had to know that he was doing better than anybody else could do.

He sat up straight. He did believe that. He did know it. And the hand that reached out to flip the toggle was the hand of duty, the instrument of the inevitable.

He pushed the switch, and immediately heard the rumbling of distant explosions as he literally tore the city in two. And he cried, but didn't have the time to cry for long. He had to get back to the river.

Arab men do not show emotion publicly over what could generally be termed "acts of God." It is an insult to the wisdom and planning of Allah. So perhaps it was the influence of the Western Sector that made Majid weep continually as he took steps to destroy New Mecca. Or perhaps he didn't feel that Allah had much to do at all with the turn events had taken.

"Hurry," one of his volunteers called from the door of the armory as he rigged the detonator, jamming the contacts into the ring of plastic explosive by the powder magazine.

The armory was large and Majid had the only key. It held twenty thousand rifles and handguns, lined up in racks and crated up. Hundreds of thousands of pounds of ammo and explosives were stacked against the walls, plus huge drums of dynamite and casings for self-loading in case they were ever cut off from supplies. It would make for a hell of an explosion.

There was gunfire in the hall, his volunteers driving back their Arab brothers.

"No Jits," they kept calling down the halls. "Clean. Clean."

"Majid," one of the men called into him, and his eyes were red, too.

"Don't listen to them," Majid said, his own eyes blurring as he set ten minutes on the small red metal timer.

"I think they're all right," the man called.

"No!" Majid said around his cigar, and when he pushed the plunger to start the timer, he bit the cigar in half, nearly sending himself up with the explosives.

Kicking the still-burning cigar away, he spit out the part in his mouth and ran to the door.

"Quickly," he said, pulling the hand laser out of his belt. "Lay down covering fire."

The men looked at him.

"Do it or join them," Majid said, his hands shaking.

The men began firing automatics down the long dark cinderblock hallway.

"No!" came the voices. "No Jits. We hid here. Let us join you!"

"Majid," the man said again.

"Keep firing!"

"Shareef!" a voice called. "It's me, Khalid. Please, listen to me!"

The rifle faltered, and Majid realized that this was the first time he had even heard either of the men's names. "Shoot to kill," he said, "or I'll kill you."

Shareef raised his rifle and began firing again.

Majid pulled the heavy iron door closed, locking it with the six-inch key. Then he dropped the key on the floor and used the laser, melting it in a glob on the ground.

The firing set up a continual rumbling echo in the hall. "We have ten minutes," Majid yelled. "Run!"

They took off in the opposite direction down the hall, and as they turned a corner, Majid could hear shouting coming from the armory as the Jits tried to break the door down. He had personally oversaw its installation himself and knew they'd not succeed.

He ran for all he was worth, up the stairs and through the headquarters building. He ran hard, not so much to avoid the detonation, for that didn't affect his thinking at all, but more to release the tension that had built to an overload within him.

Everything rushed past him in a blur as he took the steps to the second floor of Administration. He could hear footsteps behind him as he ran, and assumed that his volunteers had decided that discretion was the better part of valor.

A man was blocking the hallway upstairs. It was Yassur, his administrative assistant, who smiled wide, a smoking pistol in his hand, and raised the other arm to wave. Majid ripped a laser line straight up his abdomen without breaking stride, and vaulted the body before it had even settled on the floor.

He was into the end room and through the passage, minutes later exiting at the end of the field. He climbed into star-filled night, hundreds of balloons rising all around, floating to the Northeast with the prevailing breezes.

The command balloon was waiting where it left him, some of his men running back to it after dispensing with the dirigibles. He turned back to the garrison, saw the front gates slowly opening.

Climbing into the gondola, he ran to the radio table and contacted the pilot. "Take it up," he said.

"But we're still waiting for—"

"Now!" Majid screamed, and checked the charge on the laser. He was only down a third.

The balloon rose slowly, Shareef cursing, dangling from the doorframe from outside while others yelled and waved for them to come back down.

"To your stations!" he yelled at those already inside, and men moved to fill the window slots.

He stuck his head out a window, watched Arabs charging out of the gates, trying to escape. He heard a scream, and figured that Shareef must have lost his grip on the door.

"Fire on anything that comes out the gate," he said, but no one fired. Bracing his arm on the ledge, he opened up the laser and raked the gates, several men going down, small and alone in the distance.

"Fire!" he yelled, and they finally did, probably more out of fear of him than anything. "Don't let any escape!"

And they pounded the structure for several minutes, Majid mentally bracing himself for what was to come. When it did come, Arizona night turned into an afternoon in Hell. There was a vision-filling ball of light, then a sound like a billion books being slammed on the floor all at once, then a concussion that knocked them all over and blew the dirigible with gale-force winds for over fifteen miles. From that moment on, the area would be known as the New Mecca Crater.

When Majid picked himself up off the floor, he looked Eastward, refusing to ever look back the way he had come. He had one piece of business left to take care of.

The deck of the tanker was flat and wide like a big pasture and glowed eerie orange from the light of the distant night fires at the mouth of the harbor. Olson stood and supervised from there as his people opened all the valves to all the separate tanks and began pumping too hundred and fifty thousand tons of fuel into the Mississippi.

He hated the thought of what he was getting ready to do, but there was no other way to keep from losing the whole city if he didn't. He would burn the Jits here, burn them like yellow jackets in a ground hive. Then he could concentrate on the gates.

He was standing atop a powder keg, standing atop one of the greatest explosions the world would ever see. One match, one cinder from the fighting farther upriver would send everything up. But somehow, it didn't bother him. Death, he figured, was the least of his problems at the moment.

Using his fieldglasses, he checked the fighting. It looked bad. The semicircle was getting wider and wider, expanding to deal with all the boats that were getting through. Trouble was, the wider the circle became, the more gaps between the links. He couldn't put it off any longer.

He picked up the bullhorn. "OKAY! LET'S GET THE HELL OUT OF HERE! THEY'RE GETTING IN!"

Men began scurrying down ladders, getting to their boats. Olson ran across the deck, feet slapping hollowly, clanging. Coming to the edge, he gazed down into the sticky black water and knew that changes had already occurred that could never be made right. Maybe Majid was right. Maybe it was a question of extinction.

"C'mon!" Jerry Joe was waving, calling through cupped hands. "Hurry!" He was pointing upriver.

Olson looked. A large Jit steamboat had broken through all the barriers and was drifting with the current. The thing burned bright crimson, wood crackling. Olson held up the glasses. Dead Jits lay all over the double decks. The thing was unmanned, out of control. And it looked to be only a matter of minutes away from blazing into the middle of all that fuel.

Without a thought, Olson jumped the eighty feet into the river. He held his breath going in and hoped that he would come up where Jerry Joe could fish him out. He went way down, doubling over to try to keep from going any farther under. It was a long, dark, quiet pull back to the surface. When he broke water, the man with the leather face already had a hand out.

Jerry Joe got him up only far enough to get his own handhold; then he ran back to the controls and throttled them forward, nearly losing Olson before he could get up in the boat.

"You all right?" he called over his shoulder.

"Just go on. Go on!" Olson yelled, as he got an oil-slippery leg up over the rail and fell back onto the deck.

He rolled up onto his knees, his exo covered with sticky goo, and looked back at the steamer. It was edging closer to the oil spill, everyone in the harbor now in a flight for his life.

Jerry Joe bounced them over the small breakers, and it was obvious that not all of them were going to make it. Olson stood on shaky legs and looked over the side. It was as he had feared: the oil was not only filling the river, but was joining the flood pool of the city. The whole place would go up when the steamer grounded out.

Olson dragged himself up to groan into the seat next to Jerry Joe. The man was hyped up, shaking and talking a thousand miles an hour.

"Oh God, it's gonna be somethin'," he kept saying. "God, God, God."

"We're going to lose most of those people," Olson said, looking back at all the other craft, and he had a twinge of conscience when he realized that they had the only motor. "Can't they hurry?"

"God, God," Jerry Joe said. "We're gonna lose most everything. Fuck those assholes. Valuska mostly sent Rennie's people out here anyway. God, it's gonna be somethin'!"

At the mouth of the harbor, Jits were pouring in unrestricted as the steamer got right up on the oil spill. Jerry Joe reached the dock area, all of which was underwater. He went over the banks along with the river and hustled the city streets. And Olson turned around in time to see the world coming to an end.

The steamer hit the oil, and the whole river went up in a monstrous wall of fire, taller than the city walls. The tanker blew up first, spewing more burning debris hundreds of feet into the air. There was probably screaming mixed in with the fire, but the whoosh of the flames drowned out everything else. Nature was having its way.

And the fire overspilled the river and licked through the city, burning the streets with watery flame, as Jerry Joe kept talking and goosing them to stay ahead of it. They were passing others now, Engies mostly, who filled the streets, trying to outrun the fire. The bodies of Engies floated everywhere because the real people wouldn't let them in the buildings.

The smell began to permeate everything, the petroleum smell of the burning oil, Faisel's smell throwing a blanket over them all.

And the day became night as an incredible black oil cloud rose majestically into the sky, seeping over everything, covering everything. Black rain began falling from the black cloud, sticky rain.

They turned corners, got some distance, and when Olson looked back again, they had finally reached calm waters. But it wouldn't stay that way for long. Even now, plumes of black smoke were curling up the streets and overhead, the black rain falling now in all parts of the city and surrounding countryside, covering everything in dark goo.

They couldn't see much behind them through the cover of smoke, and Olson thought that was just as well. They'd lost that part of the city. Through the dark curtain, he could still see orange fire blazing an inferno. It looked as if the whole sky, the whole world, was burning. And he knew, really knew, that there was no other choice; to think otherwise would have caused madness.

* * *

*And strike for them the similitude of
    the present life:
it is as water that We send down
out of heaven, and the plants of
the earth mingle with it; and in
the morning it is straw the winds
scatter; and God is omnipotent over
    everything.*

> —The Koran
> XVIII. The Cave

LV

LOW Building, Orleans, Ninetieth Floor

Olson and Gret stood with their arms around one another and watched the city burn. They were in the living room of what had once been Mr. Elwood's apartment, but that now belonged to someone named Director Catanine. Daylight of the last day was just beginning to creep in around the edges of the dark clouds, making the smoke haze that had settled on the whole city a little brighter. Wexler lay huddled on the floor beside them, asleep, his sleep breath setting a soothing metronome cadence.

"You did the only thing you could do," Gret said quietly. "Don't blame yourself."

"Who should I blame then?" Olson returned.

"Everything is transient."

Olson fixed his eyes on the burning towers on the other side of the firebreak. "Apparently some things are more transient than others."

She looked up at him. "You made the decision," she said. "Feeling sorry for yourself won't do anyone any good."

"I'm not feeling sorry for myself," he returned, "I'm mourning."

"Yeah," she said, hugging herself closer to him. "Me too."

"Mr. Elwood told me once how I'd understand someday what it felt like," he said.

"What do you mean?"

"This. All of it. Doing your best and still coming away a loser."

Gret stood away from him. She started laughing, laughing loudly. "You're the loser? You? You clawed your way to the top, you cared about your people, you did what you knew—KNEW—was right. And because a miracle didn't happen you're suddenly a loser. Hey, dumb shit. We'd have all had the Jitterbug by now if it weren't for you. You're a fucking hero."

He thought about that, wanted to believe it; and since all reality is simply a matter of choice, he did believe it.

"You're right, by God!" he bellowed. "We're still alive, we're still clean. What more should I expect?"

"Exactly."

Moving away from her, he turned from the window and walked into the guts of the apartment, his apartment. It was his, he had inherited it fair and square. The Jits were at the gate, the fire threatened the city and the available oxygen, the rain still came—but he could put that aside for the moment. This was the spoils of war, and if it was only for five minutes, he was going to enjoy it.

He sat on a rich wood chair and pulled his boots off, feeling the deep pile of the carpet on his bare feet. Hell, Valuska knew where he was and could get in touch with him if necessary. Smiling, he began snapping out of his exo.

Gret turned to him. "What are you doing?"

He ripped off the chest plate and threw it on the floor. "I'm the Director of the South/Central Region and, by God, I'm going to start acting like it."

Sitting on the floor, he slid the plasteel leggings off, then shinnied out of the overalls he wore beneath. Then, naked and giggling, he rolled on the floor like the cat that he was supposed to be.

Gret ran over to him and she was laughing, too. "You're a crazy man!" she yelled. "A maniac!"

"A happy maniac!" he returned, and executed a rolling block into her legs, knocking her atop him. "That's why you love me."

They knotted in a bundle on the floor. "What makes you think I love you?" she said, pulling a handful of the loose, curly hair that she had cut so many lifetimes before. "You might be just another Exec to me."

He stopped rolling, looked into her eyes. "I'm not an Exec," he said, voice strained. "I'm a little boy lost in the woods, and you're the mother of all the Earth. Oh, God, I love you, Gret."

"You've made me real," she said, "as real as my feelings for you. I'd die for you, vagabond."

He shook his head. "Don't you dare."

They made love then, sweet gentle fingers of commitment playing on the piano keys of sharing, and for Gret this time there were no brass bands and no short-circuiting electric wires shooting fireworks into the night sky of her psyche.

It was much deeper than that.

If they hadn't gotten the computer-room door open for him quickly enough, Abdullah ibn Faisel Al Sa'ud would have run right into it, he was moving so fast.

"Where?" he said, as he passed through the door, but moved past the man before he could even point.

Two green-suits held a frightened looking man in check before a computer console. He was struggling lamely, the kind of struggle someone puts up when he knows it won't do him any good.

Abdullah hurried over to them, took one look at the balding man, then cast his eyes to the green-suits. "Tell me," he said.

"He broke in a little while ago," said a corporal with a twitch in his right eye that pulled on his entire cheekbone. "When he fired up the machine, we moved in."

Abdullah nodded. "What is your name?" he asked the man.

The man just stared up at him with dark, frightened eyes. He had the look of a cornered rabbit. He said nothing.

Reaching into his bandolier, Abdullah pulled the laser. "Hold his hand up," he ordered.

The green-suits jerked the man's arm out straight, grabbing

his hand at the wrist to hold it steady. Abdullah laid the barrel of the laser right on the man's thumb and pulled the trigger. He screamed as it burned away his thumb, leaving a charred, smoking stump.

They let him have his arm back, and he doubled over, holding it to him.

"An ear goes next," Abdullah said. "Then your nose. Tell me your name."

"Baggins," the man choked out. "Paul-Paul Baggins."

"What are you doing here?"

"Nothing, I . . ."

"Hold his head up," Abdullah said.

"No . . . wait!" Baggins said, looking up. "I was stealing from the stores."

"Why?"

"There's a new city, a new land . . . in Wichita. I was promised a high position if I would steal from the Orleans stores and ship it there."

"Who promised? Who?"

The man shook his head. "I . . . I don't know."

"Lift up his head."

The man was crying, shaking his head. "I don't know!" he shouted. "I was given codes . . . and promises. They had no reason to give me a name."

That satisfied Abdullah. "Where did the orders come from?"

"LOW Arabia, the Corporate offices."

"Faisel?"

"I've been doing this for five years," the man said. "Why would the man who has everything look for some more?"

"That's a question I've been asking myself," Abdullah replied.

"Look," the twitchy-eyed corporal said, pointing to the screen on a far wall.

Abdullah turned his face to the screen. The new day's broadcast was beginning. He hurried over to it, turning up the sound. Faisel's face filled the screen. He began talking.

"My regrets to the people of Orleans," he said. "You have shown your utter disdain for the authority of LOW by your failure to assist my brother in reaching a satisfactory conclusion to our fiscal problems. It grieves me to destroy you, but you

leave me no choice. I cannot let you stand as a bad example
to the rest of the empire. Sorry.

"To my brother, Abdullah. You have thirty minutes from
the time of this broadcast to use your Jitterbug key. If you
fail to do so, not only will you die, but your wife, my
hostage, will unfortunately have to die with you. These are
difficult times for all of us, but the power must remain
intact."

With that, transmission ended.

Abdullah turned from the screen and looked at the man who
could have at least come a day earlier. His hand crept unconsciously
to his chest and felt the key there. Nura. Nura. Worth more than
a hundred cities and all the Nasrani on the planet. He couldn't let
her die.

He moved back to the console and spoke to the soldiers. "I
have a balloon waiting on the roof," he said. "If you go up now
without telling anyone, we may escape together."

"What about him?" the corporal asked, nodding at Paul-
Paul Baggins.

Abdullah made the sign of the evil eye. "Tie him to his
machine," he said. "Let him know, slowly, what it is that he has
done."

With that, he strode out of the computer room to find a
hallway full of Elite waiting for him.

Olson sat on the edge of the long couch and snapped his
leggings back into place, day fully arrived, Faisel's tv message
still fresh.

"What are you going to do?" Gret asked as she pulled the
simple shift over her head to flutter gently onto her slender
frame.

"Stop him somehow," Olson said. "I know Abdullah
enough to know what he'll do."

"Because it's what you'd do?"

"Maybe."

She ran to him, put her arms around his shoulders.
"Don't go," she pleaded. "If we are to die, let's be together."

Olson shrugged her off. "We're not dead yet," he said, and
pulled his boots back on.

Wexler was up, rubbing his eyes and stumbling sleepily

around. "When will the fire go out?" he asked from across the room.

Olson stood up, settling into the boots. "When all the bad stuff has burned away," he said. Turning, he hugged Gret, but couldn't feel her through the exo. "Stay here. I'll be back."

She just stared at him, brows knit.

He moved to Wexler, knelt down to hug him. "You be good," he said. "And mind Gret."

The little man with the lopsided head nodded slowly up and down. "You come back?" he asked innocently.

"Sure," Olson choked out, and kissed him on the forehead.

Standing, he turned once to stare at Gret across the expanse of room. They locked eyes but shared no message. Then he grabbed his M-16 and bandolier and hurried out of the apartment.

Gret stood for several minutes staring at the closed door, hoping that he would open it and come back to her. When he didn't, she hated him for it, then hated herself for being so selfish.

Then she cried.

"Awww," came a voice behind her. "Ain't that touching."

She flared around to see Rennie, black with soot and red with cuts, staring fire at her. He was a mess, torn and dirty, his exo cracked and dented beneath the tattered con-tam suit, his wrist lasers shorted and smoking.

"Wh-what do you want?" she said, edging toward the door.

"Well, first I want to have a little talk," he cooed. "Just like last time. Then I'm going to go and cut your boyfriend up into little pieces."

She backed across the floor slowly, the door merely a quick run away. "We have nothing to talk about," she said.

He smiled. "Sure we do. We can talk about how much sex a Houris can stand before she goes crazy or her heart bursts right in her chest. We can talk about who Mr. Cat really is and how much you know about him . . ."

She bolted for the door, charging headlong, but Rennie wasn't about to be denied that easily. He charged the door, blocking it just as she got there. Grabbing her roughly, he picked her up and carried her back to the bedroom, Wexler running after them, banging his little fists against the man's legs.

She flailed away at him as he walked her into Mr. Elwood's bedroom and dumped her on the bed. She kicked at him as he reached for her, and he buried an elbow in her stomach, doubling her over.

"Leave her alone!" Wexler screamed. "Leave my mother alone!"

Rennie laughed. "Mother!" he said. "What a pair. She's gutted, hollowed out and filled with wires, and you're just a toy made out of scrap pieces."

"No!" Wexler screamed, tears streaming from his big brown eyes.

Rennie's laugh turned sour and he swung out, catching Wexler across the face, sending him across the room to bang into the wall, where he slid down and lay very, very still.

"You bastard!" Gret screamed, and tried to get up, but he knocked her down again. Reaching out large hands, he ripped her dress off, then held a viselike grip on her throat as he tore at his own clothes.

Naked, he forced her legs apart and climbed between. "You know what you're good for, don't you, honey?" he said, and began massaging her breasts.

She fought it for a minute, then lay back, head rolling from side to side. "Yesss," she sighed, and reached down for his already rigid penis.

"That's right," he said. "You know what to do."

Her hand went down, bypassing his penis. She grabbed his testicles, and squeezed as hard as she could, jerking them.

He screamed, loud and painful, somehow wresting himself away from her to roll in a ball on the floor.

"I'll pull them out next time!" she yelled and made a run for the door.

Somehow, he got up on hands and knees and grabbed her ankle, tripping her. She fell hard against the wall, hot white pain shooting through her head. She crumpled, groggy, and he crawled toward her, his face still twisted in agony.

"You want it the hard way?" he rasped, doubling over again. "It'll be my pleasure."

And as she slipped out of consciousness, she saw him looming over her.

*   *   *

Abdullah stood in the LOW lobby, sandbags totally covering the outside windows and doors, keeping out the rain, keeping out the light. The Elite stood with him, somber, watchful.

"You will need to draw a balloon here," he told the captain, "so that we may try to make an escape after we do the job."

"Arrangements are already being made," the man returned, and Abdullah nodded, but his eyes were on the open elevator and the man who stood against the door, keeping it open.

Abdullah walked casually with the captain toward the elevator.

"You must do it now," the man said.

Abdullah stopped before the open door, smiling at the Elite who held it. "How much time do we have?"

The captain reached into his robes and pulled out a large gold pocket watch. He flicked his eyes downward to read the time, and Abdullah made his move.

Grabbing the man by the door, he flung him at the captain and jumped through the entry, punching up the roof. Several of them tried to jump in, but his laser flashed and burned three of them.

The doors closed and he was on his way up. If he had to do this thing, he would take the Elite with it. It was the least he could do.

Everyone was out on the wall, so it was a straight trip up. He leaned against the wall, watching the numbers light on the panel, trying not to think about the death of a city, perhaps the death of a people.

When the door slid open again, he thought he'd be on the roof. He wasn't. He was on the ninetieth floor, staring at Cat.

The man screamed loud and jumped in the car, pushing Abdullah to slam against the wall.

They went down, the door closing on them, Abdullah's laser clattering to the floor. They fought, wordlessly, viciously, both of them trying to keep the other down and get to a weapon at the same time.

They both wore exos without masks, their faces the only unprotected area of their bodies. They pounded and rolled, trading blows, reveling in pain, for it made them feel useful.

It went on, the implications obvious to both, and as they wore on, it was only natural that one of them would have to end it. It was an elbow, an unintentional elbow that caught Olson in the eye, that made the difference. When he rolled to protect the eye, Abdullah stunned him with a blow behind the ear, following it with hard right-hands all over the man's face.

Olson rolled, groggy, and Abdullah knocked him down again, blood flowing thickly from numerous cuts to the face. He rolled, tried to rise again.

"Give it up," Abdullah said, gasping with the exertion and the pain in the stitched-up fist. Blood was beginning to seep through the white bandages.

"No," Olson choked around a mouthful of blood. "I can't."

Reaching back, Abdullah hit him with everything he had, knocking the man hard against the side of the elevator. Olson went down again, tried to rise again.

"Come with me," Abdullah said. "We'll escape this together."

"There ... is ... no escape," Olson said, and tried to rise again.

"Please, no," Abdullah said, and hit him again, the man's face nearly unrecognizable. Pain was shooting up his arm as blood began to ooze through the bandages to drip onto the floor.

It wasn't enough. Olson somehow got to his knees, his eyes swollen shut, and fumbled for Abdullah's laser.

The Arab looked to the heavens, pleading silently, then hit his friend again, knocking him to the floor in the cramped space.

Olson was coughing blood, spitting teeth, and still he tried to rise.

"Why?" Abdullah asked.

The man tried to focus on him through slits for eyes, his face lying in a puddle of blood on the elevator floor. "D-duty," he managed to say, and Abdullah hit him again.

Scooting away from Olson, Abdullah picked up his laser and struggled to his feet, pointing the thing at his friend's head.

Majid watched clinically as they unstacked the flying carpets in the cargo hold of the command balloon and prepared them for flight. There were ten men left on the dirigible with him, including the pilot, and they all seemed to be moving quietly and steadily, either out of determination or shock.

As they checked the controls and the power train of the various carpets, he spoke to them.

"I will not ask you to come with me in search of Milander. Neither will I harbor ill will toward you if you do not. Our people treasure our lives above all things save Allah, and those of you who choose to preserve that life may do so with my blessing. I cannot do that.''

He looked at them for reaction. Finding none, he continued. ''We know that Milander is in the old boneyard of auts near Orleans. We cannot hope to take the balloon there because of his lasers. The carpets hold our destiny. Our task is simple: we will go in and kill the devil and probably die in the doing. It is a task worthy of Mohammed himself.''

Walking to the big cargo door, he slid it open to rumbling clouds and sputtering rain. Then he dragged a carpet up right in front of the opening. They would be within range in less than an hour.

''I will go out first,'' he said. ''I will not look back to see who follows. Whoever chooses to go with me, remember that the Jitterbug is a slow and painful death. Save a bullet for yourself.''

*　　*　　*

The West can teach the East how to get a living, but the East must eventually be asked to show the West how to live.
　　　　　　　　—Chinese Proverb

LVI
Allahu Akbar, Arabia

Misha'al's hands were shaking as he tried to fit the key into the lock of the door to life support, and he didn't know if it was out of excitement or fear or both. This was it, the culmination of years of planning and Faisel's abuse. In a matter of hours he would be free.

Getting rid of the Elite who guarded his door had been easier than he thought it would be. They answered the evening call to prayer in the LOW mosque, and when everyone prostrated to Mecca, he had slipped into his sandals and simply walked away. They'd be looking for him soon, but hopefully he'd be long gone.

The door creaked loudly open, but there was no one to hear it, everyone participating in the evening prayers. He walked into life support, the huge machines spinning their life cycles, their motors whining out the electric heartbeat. Hurrying through the grinding heart of LOW, he went to the door of the extra room, stopping only long enough to retrieve the small stainless-steel box from behind one of the storage tanks where he had hidden it days before.

He walked into the large, empty room, Nura standing ready at the bars on the other side. Once in, he ran to the cell.

"We must hurry," he said, pulling her gown out from under his robes. He handed the clothes through the bars and fumbled with the keys to open the cell. "They will check the monitors when they return from prayers."

"Is everything ready?" she asked as she slipped the linen robes over her head.

"I certainly hope so," he returned, and pulled the door open. "My neck is lying squarely on the chopping block."

She adjusted the robes and brought the veil around to cover her face. "Any word of my husband?"

He knelt on the floor and adjusted the box. "No," he answered. "But it can only do him good to have you away from here."

"I am ready," she said, and stepped out of the cell.

He stood. "Then let us both bid farewell to the Light of the World."

He closed the cell door, then bent down, reaching out a hand to flick the toggle and turn on the hologram machine. It hummed to life, then faded-in a life-sized image of a naked Nura that slowly paced the small cell.

"It's so . . . real," she said, embarrassed more in retrospect of her nakedness than at the time.

"This should throw them off for quite a while," Misha'al said, studying the gram. "The caravan awaits."

They broke into a trot, hurrying from the room. As they climbed out of the subbasement, the hallways were filled with people returning from prayers. They casually joined the flow.

Misha'al had found the secret exit ten years earlier during one of his forays through the computer. It was a secret that Faisel guarded very carefully, and the computer knew about it only because it was set to warn Faisel if anyone used it but him. Misha'al had already taken care of that little problem.

They traveled through the lower levels for several minutes until the ulema stopped before a door marked MALE EXCRETION.

Nura's eyes widened behind the veil, but she didn't say anything. Misha'al shrugged.

"Let me check for occupancy first," he said, and went in.

The room was foul-smelling and dirty, filled with the kind of toilets that Faisel had been impressed with in the Western Sector, but which his Arab workers didn't know how to use. They were lined up, forty of them, against a dirty tile wall. Only one was occupied, by a man who had his robes hiked up and his feet on the seat as he squatted over the thing, an illegal cigarette in his mouth.

"Your unit chief is searching all over for you," Misha'al said.

The man's face went slack as his foot slipped off the seat and he went crashing to the floor. Jumping up, he ran out, leaving the cigarette behind. The prophet picked it up and stuck it in his mouth.

Misha'al went back to the door and saw Nura staring down the hallway at the man who had run away.

"Quickly," he said, and she slipped in the door when no one was watching.

Moving to a section of blank wall done in yellow and blue tile, he searched around until he found the tile that popped out. Behind it was a red button. He pushed the button and that section of wall slid open, revealing a metal cave behind.

Misha'al threw his cigarette in one of the toilets and they entered without hesitation to find Bandar and thirty men waiting a short distance away.

"Why so many men?" Misha'al asked. "They might get suspicious at the air base."

Bandar was smiling at Nura. "Are you . . . unhurt?" he asked, and she knew the nature of his question.

"All is well," she said, and put an uncharacteristic hand on his arm for just a second. "Thank you for coming for me in the name of my husband."

"It was our duty and our pleasure," he responded.

Bandar walked back a few paces to the door to close it. "We must go now," he said.

"Don't do that," Bandar said as the man reached for the button to close the door.

Misha'al turned to him, eyebrow arched. "What?"

"We are going in," Bandar said.

"We just escaped!" Misha'al said.

"We have a murder to avenge," Ahmad said, walking up next to Bandar.

"The devil you say," Misha'al replied, and reached again for the button.

He stopped when he heard Bandar cock his .45. He turned back around. "We had an agreement."

"We will keep the agreement," Bandar said evenly, keeping the gun trained on the man. "It will just take a little longer than you had anticipated."

"There are thousands of people in there," Misha'al said, exasperated. "You don't have a chance."

Bandar shrugged. "Allah will steady our aim. Now, please move away from the door."

Misha'al was just smart enough to know when to keep his mouth shut. Taking a deep breath, he moved away from the opening and the button.

* * *

Charity is a duty unto every Moslem. He who hath not the means thereto, let him do a good act or abstain from an evil one. That is his charity.

—The Prophet Mohammed

He has not faith who fulfills not his trust, and he has no religion who fulfills not his promise.

—The Prophet Mohammed

LVII
The Elevator

Abdullah stood looking down at Olson, and his fingers turned to mush, unable to pull the trigger. He tried to picture

Nura being tortured, anything to keep his resolve firm, but it couldn't work and it didn't work.

"Oh hell," he said finally, and slid down into a sitting position on the floor and laid the pistol next to him. His hand was throbbing terribly. Pulling it to his chest, he held the wrist tightly.

Olson moaned beside him, tried to get up. "Give me a . . . hand . . . would you?"

Reaching out, Abdullah helped his friend to sit also. Sticking a finger into his mouth, Olson fished out a broken tooth and dropped it on the floor. "You knocked holy shit out of me, you know that?" he said.

"It's because you're so hardheaded, friend Cat," Abdullah replied.

"Name's Olson."

"What?"

"Olson. It's my real name."

Abdullah nodded absently. "Oh."

Olson shook his head, but it didn't help to clear it. "So what happens now?" he asked.

Abdullah pulled off his ghutra, stuffing the aghal into his bandolier. He tossed it to Olson, who began wiping the blood off his face. "My wife dies," he said. "Your city probably dies anyway. I guarantee you that my brother will certainly die."

"Everything dies," Olson said.

"In its time."

The elevator jerked, started moving.

"The Elite are bringing it down," Abdullah said, and then he thought about something. "Why does the power still work in this building when it went off everywhere else when the fighting started?"

Olson tried to narrow his eyes, but it hurt too much. "All LOW buildings are self-contained," he replied. "The computer controls life support, so it doesn't need human assistance."

Abdullah looked up at the light panel. They were on the seventy-fourth floor and still traveling downward. "Could the Corporate offices work the same way?"

Olson nodded and groaned. "Mr. Elwood told me once that LOW Corporate was the model for all the branches. He said that Faisel didn't trust anyone enough to control his life support, so it was entirely under computer control."

"That is my brother," Abdullah said.

And they reached the fiftieth floor.

"They will be waiting in the lobby," Abdullah said. "How can we get to the computer room without being seen?"

Olson stood on shaky legs and moved his jaw around, grimacing. "I believe I can help you out," he said, and pressed the elevator button marked "Z." "We'll get out on two and climb down the shaft when they take it up. Why do we want to go to the computer room?"

"It's a matter of honor," Abdullah returned, his voice grave. He stood himself, picking up the laser and holstering it.

Olson looked at him, admiring his decency but not mentioning it. A man like Abdullah would never want to be commended for doing the right thing.

They made the ride in silence, each lost in his own thoughts, and it wasn't until the elevator jerked to a stop on the second floor that they returned to the business at hand.

They got out, Olson picking up his M-16 by the strap before the door slid shut. There were windows on either side of the hall by the elevator. Olson ran to the fire side and peered out.

"God, it's getting past the firebreak," he said. The smoke haze was extremely thick, nearly impenetrable, but the orange flashing through it was a lot closer than it had been before.

The elevator doors shut, and the machine went down. Olson thought about Gret up on ninety, but couldn't see any way to get back to her until he had helped Abdullah. His face hurt and was throbbing horribly. One eye was swollen shut and the other was blurring.

"I can hear the machine," Abdullah said, his ear to the doors. "It's moving again."

"Back away," Olson said, "in case it opens here."

They flattened themselves against the wall on either side of the elevator doors. The rumble of the elevator got louder, then, by degrees, softer.

"It's going up," Abdullah said.

Olson came around and tried to pry the doors open with his fingers. They wouldn't budge.

"Use a lever," Abdullah said.

Olson pulled the rifle off his shoulder, jamming the barrel into the crack between the doors. Grunting, he pried enough for Abdullah to get his big hands in and force them apart.

They were staring at a brick-lined shaft. Below, everything was swallowed in darkness.

"Are there handholds?" Abdullah asked.

"One way to find out," Olson said, and climbed into the shaft.

Bricks jutted on the inside. It wasn't much, but was enough for the men to scrabble down the shaft. Reaching bottom, they pried open the basement doors and found themselves in the computer-room hallway.

Abdullah took off running, Olson right behind. Getting into the wide open room, they found Paul-Paul Baggins whimpering at the console he had been tied to.

"Oh, thank you," he said, when he saw them. "I knew you wouldn't just leave me here to die."

Abdullah moved right up to him, drew his laser, and put it to the man's temple. "Are you going to tell me the truth and do everything I say?"

The man nodded dumbly, eyes and mouth wide.

"Untie him," he told Olson.

Fumbling with the knots, he began to loosen the hasty job that the green-suits had done.

"You have access codes to the LOW Corporate computer?" Abdullah asked.

The man nodded again.

"Does that mean you have access to all computer files?"

"Y-yes . . . I think so."

Olson got his hands untied and went to work on his waist, which was tied to the chair.

"Get into the LOW computer," Abdullah ordered.

The man's hands literally flew across the keys, giving code and countercode until he had split the skin of LOW and was staring at the pulsating innards.

"I'm in," Baggins said, his nearly bald head glistening with sweat.

Abdullah looked at Olson, nearly smiled. "Overload life support," he said.

"I don't understand," the man returned.

"Screw it up," Olson said, grinning. "Increase the power, blow out the system."

The man stared from one of them to the other. "But that will . . ."

"We know," Abdullah said. "Do it now."

Baggins looked once at the barrel of the laser and went to work on the Corporate computer. "You understand," he said while he worked, "that if we make that system self-destruct, it will destroy the net to the rest of the empire. There will be no contact..." He looked back up at them. "There will be no empire."

"We understand perfectly," Olson said.

Baggins shrugged and continued working, the keys clicking quickly. Then he stopped.

"That's it," he said. "When we press the ENTER key, it all happens. Are you sure?"

Abdullah smiled for real this time. "Let me press it," he said, reaching.

"Your thirty minutes is up," came a voice from the doorway, and they looked up to see the Elite captain holding his pocketwatch up, letting it dangle back and forth on the chain.

He moved into the room and the rest of the Elite poured through the doorway, taking up positions within the room.

"My orders," the captain said, "are to kill you if you don't do your duty, and then release the Jitterbug myself."

"I am doing my duty," Abdullah said, and pushed the ENTER key with a throbbing, bloody finger.

The captain looked back and forth at his men in position. "All right," he said smoothly. "Kill them."

And he walked out of the room.

*   *   *

> *O believers, when you marry believing women*
> *and then divorce them before you touch them,*
> *you have no period to reckon against them;*
> *so make provision for them, and set them free*
> *   with kindliness.*

—The Koran
XXXIII. Confederates

> *The greatest monarch on the proudest throne*
> *is obliged to sit upon his own arse.*

—Poor Richard
Old World Wisdom

Be on your guard against envying others, for
verily, it eats up goodness as fire eats of
fuel.

—The Prophet Mohammed

LVIII
Desert Dreams

Faisel sat in front of the big board and watched the Orleans light burning straight and hard, no flicker, no waver. The board showed the world, all the Jit-dome locations in the world. The Orleans light should have gone out.

It didn't.

His thirty-minute timer went off, a soft bass hum, and still the light burned. That meant that Abdullah didn't follow his orders and was even now being killed by the Elite. Good, but what of Nura?

He had a gown tightly clutched in his left hand, a gown that wasn't Nura's but could be. Reconstructed through the hypnosis-enhanced memories of all those who had seen her, it was as close to the genuine article as he could get.

His eyes wandered from the board to the gown. He had her now, legally had her, his dreams as close to fulfillment as a walk to the subbasement. But he wouldn't take her. He couldn't.

He cried then, and wiped the tears on the gown. In the world, the whole world that was his to own, he couldn't own this woman. He could possess her body, but never crack through its titanium shell to the spirit beneath. He could never steal or buy or pillage the emotion that was hers to control. He could never beg the love he so desperately needed. And so he would release her. He would release her and watch his own life drain slowly away through simple erosion. He knew what he'd never have now, and the knowledge was maddening.

The radio on the console buzzed, and he bent absently to the pole mike, his finger on the toggle. "Yes," he said.

The voice came back excited. "We have intruders on level four! A squad of Bedouin has engaged our security force!"

"How many?" he asked, and looked down at the dress.

"We don't know. There's too much confusion."

"Keep me posted."

"There's something else . . . Misha'al has disappeared. We cannot locate him anywhere."

Abdullah nodded and clicked off. There was a personal-effects cabinet on the wall opposite the board that contained an exo for emergency situations. He absently went and got it out, putting it on even though it was far too small for him.

He walked into the tiny boots, his mind in a fog, Nura's face mixing with the burning face in the dream. He would free her now, at least expiate the dream demon from his brain.

He walked out through the large archway and into the halls, the gown dangling from his fingers. If only she could understand how much he loved her, but maybe, if she understood, she wouldn't be half the woman she was.

There was a smell in the hallway. Smoke, burning circuitry. He looked up and saw light gray smoke drifting out of the hall ventilators.

Odd.

He'd give her an escort back to her camp, at least show her that he could lose gracefully. He'd give her the respect she should have gotten from the beginning.

There was a rumbling sound and the hallway shook, knocking him against a wall. Others in the hall fell, yelling, as the smoke in the hallway got a lot thicker.

People were up, running all around him. There was another rumble, then another, and the lights were flashing on and off as the hallway rolled and buckled. And the wall beside him blew out, an overpressured water line bursting, sending white, frothy liquid pouring into the hallway.

People were screaming as the smoke filled the hallway and the building shook. Faisel stood, his back against the wall, as the confusion reigned all around him. It was all coming down, every bit of it. He had to get to Nura.

He walked again, moving in the direction of the subbasement, his ghutra pulled around his mouth. The lights flashed violently in and out again, finally going out completely as the electricity overloaded and blew out the burned-up motors.

He kept walking, the emergency dry cells coming on, bathing the hall in a pale red light, making the acrid smoke billow like bloody fog. And he was in a dream, his dream, and he was the dream and the dreamer.

He moved around a corner and could hear the fighting

farther down the hall, could smell the gunpowder mixing with the melted wires.

Going down the subbasement stairs, he moved to the heavy door. It didn't need to be locked; it was blown off, twisted off the hinges.

He stepped inside life support, filled with thick, choking smoke. Small fires burned in various parts of the room, threatening the storage tanks.

It was a surreal landscape of bloody fog and crackling light that he wandered through to get to Nura. The exo was beginning to cut into him, to pinch him painfully. It was cutting off his circulation. He walked into billowing white smoke, and it was cold, freezing, ruptured cooling lines shooting Freon into the subbasement.

Getting through it, he opened the door and walked into Nura's quarters. The room was smoky red, the walls wet with running water from the burst water pipes. He looked through the fog to her cell. She was standing, pacing, as if nothing was wrong.

"Nura!" he called to her, stumbling across the wet floor, sliding, trying to walk. "Nura!"

She looked in his direction, but right through him as if he weren't there. She was a wraith, a spirit, moving in a world removed from him.

He hurried to the cell, unlocked the bars, and opened them. "Nura," he whispered, but she ignored him.

She was smiling at something. He went to her, arms outstretched, but he couldn't hold her. She was a spirit!

And the water ran down the cell wall, reaching the hologram box, shorting it out.

Smoke poured through the spirit of Nura, dark smoke. And Faisel backed away in horror. Then the box caught fire, flames licking the figure, who laughed through it all.

She was burning, burning!

"No!" he yelled, backing away, arm up to protect him from the flames.

And as the machine shorted out, it caught itself in a time groove, playing and replaying the same image of Nura over and over. She had bent over somewhat, then straightened, bent, straightened, and it looked to the whole world as if she were laughing.

Laughing!

He slipped backward through the cell, falling in the water that rushed through the room. He scooted backward through the water on his hands and knees, the cell disappearing in the smoke, Nura's burning specter floating in the gray-white fog.

He got up, fell again. The water was rising rapidly as he sloshed through it, up to his knees. He got into the boiler room, burning machines floating as the water kept rising. It had reached his waist by the time he got out the door and up the subbasement stairs.

The hall was full of Bedouin.

He climbed into their midst, circling madly, looking for his own people. What was going on? They were staring at him, wrapped in their camel-stinking mishlas and their wind scarfs.

"Where are my Elite?" he screamed. "To arms!"

The one called Bandar walked up to him.

"What do you want with me?" Faisel demanded.

Bandar leveled his pistol. "We have come to exact the justice of Allah," the man said, and pulled the trigger, the force of the bullet knocking Faisel to the floor, the exo deflecting the shot.

"I am the King of the World," Faisel told them.

"You murdered Thamir," Bandar said, and pointed the gun at his unprotected head.

"Wait," Faisel said, holding out a hand. "Before you . . . is the woman safe?"

"She is with us."

"Hurry and get her out of here. The fires will reach the storage tanks soon."

Bandar nodded. "As you say."

Faisel looked into the barrel of the gun and tried to make some kind of sense out of everything that had happened.

*   *   *

> *Say: "If you love God, follow me, and God*
> *will love you, and forgive you your sins;*
> *God is All-forgiving, All-compassionate."*
> *Say: "Obey God, and the Messenger." But*
> *if they turn their backs, God loves not*
> *the unbelievers.*

—The Koran
III. House of Imran

LIX

The Computer Room

The Elite charged.

They attacked as they lived—silently. Black robes billowing like dark clouds, they jumped the consoles and chairs and threw themselves into battle.

Olson and Abdullah took cover, weapons out, firing. And the Elite were all over them. In the cramped spaces, they were there in the blink of an eye.

Olson was firing wildly on automatic, spinning a semicircle, black robes exploding red, falling, more behind to take their place. In flashes he saw Abdullah's laser cutting a blurry swath through their ranks, while Baggins fell over, chair and all, a knife buried up to the handle in his chest.

They were on them, Olson swinging his rifle like a club, connecting with flesh, with bone, no steel under the black, just men. But so many. Abdullah had an Elite in his hands, raising him above his head, while three of them tackled him around the waist, knocking him back over a console, the Elite in his arms falling on his head and audibly snapping his neck.

They had Olson, looking for vital organs. He came down with the rifle butt on a head, but felt the gun being stripped from him just as he lost his balance and went down.

He flashed then, flashed in slow motion on the knife poised high above an Elite head ready to gut him, and he knew, was absolutely convinced for the first time in his life, that he was going to die.

The Elite grunted, began to bring the knife down—when his head exploded in red pieces. The man was gone from the nose up. The veil fell, attached to nothing, and drifted to the floor as the headless man's mouth fell open and he toppled over.

Everything stopped.

Another head exploded with a loud pop, and the Elite backed away from the fight, looking at one another.

Abdullah was up on his feet, looking, as another head popped, then another.

"Faisel's dead!" Abdullah said. "They will all die."

The remaining Elite got down on their knees, bowing toward Mecca, their heads popping one after another, filling the room with splattering gore. And they all died silently.

They all popped but one. The man stood there and looked at his compatriots. There was silence for a time; then he turned and ran from the room, his head popping no sooner than he got through the door.

A radio transmitter sat by the television screen. Olson ran to it and keyed in his emergency frequency. He got Valuska after a moment.

"Cat!" the man yelled. "Where are you?"

"What's it like out there?"

"The whole place is going up!" he returned. "The fire's made it to the LOW building."

"You're going to have to get out of there!" Olson yelled.

"What?"

"Evacuate the city for God's sake. Go overland!"

"But we've never—"

"Just do it! Send the message on all frequencies! Blow a hole through the wall and go!"

"Cat—"

"Go!"

"I've got a balloon on the roof," Abdullah said.

"Let's get up there," Olson said, taking a last look around the room. "I'll grab Gret and Wexler on the way up."

They ran into the hall, taking the elevator up. The ride was interminable, the walls and floor of the thing hot, nearly burning to the touch.

They finally stopped on ninety, Olson jumping out as soon as the doors slid open. He couldn't see anything but thick smoke through the side windows.

"You get the balloon ready," he said. "We'll be right up!"

The man nodded and the doors closed. Olson ran down the hall and turned the corner to Mr. Elwood's door. Rennie was sitting at a table blocking the hallway. He had a gun pointed at Olson. Behind him was Mr. Elwood's large matching screen.

"Had a feeling you'd show up here." He smiled. "Couldn't stay away from your little Houris, could you?"

Olson started walking, made to go right past him.

"No!" Rennie screamed, standing up, the gun stiff-armed out in front of him. "It's not going to be that easy."

"What have you done with them?" Olson said, low.

"We've just been . . . visiting," Rennie returned. "They're in there now . . . waiting for you to go past me."

"You know the building's on fire," Olson said, itching for a way around the man.

"I know a lot of things."

Olson made to move around him again. "Let's just get out of here," he said, "and straighten this out later."

Rennie blocked him off, sticking the gun right on his forehead. "You don't get it, do you? We had a match going before; it got interrupted. We're going to finish it right now and prove who the real man is."

"There's no time."

"And you keep wasting it."

Olson looked in his eyes, saw the madness and determination there. "I'll match with you," he said, "but let Gret and Wexler go. They're not a part of this."

"Why, they're the stakes, Catty old boy, the Christmas bonus—winner take all."

"You son of a . . ."

"You're wasting time."

Olson walked to the table and sat down, sticking the alpha ring on his forehead. "Let's go," he said softly.

Rennie smiled and sat down, putting on his own alpha ring while keeping the gun trained on Olson. "Looks like you took a bit of a beating," he said.

Olson's eyes flicked to the apartment door behind the screen. "Gret!" he yelled.

"She won't answer," Rennie said. "She's . . . indisposed."

He could see part of the apartment windows. Flames were curling up, just licking the glass.

"It's my turn to pick," Olson said.

"Be my guest."

Rennie pushed the transmission control in Olson's direction and reached his finger to the center toggle, the gun still pointing at Olson.

He flicked the switch. . . .

Olson was standing, naked, in a deep forest. The trees were thick and close-packed and stretched incredibly high, their spreading branches practically blocking out the Sun. Heavy vines tangled through the branches, drooping low, covered with purple blossoms. Ivy buried the ground and rotten logs full of spiders, while animal sounds pierced the windless stillness of the claustrophobic landscape.

Rennie stood a distance from him. Also naked, he was partially hidden by trees. Olson moved toward him.

"My territory," he called into the brush. "My terms."

They charged one another, their bodies slapping loudly, savagely there in the middle of the primal forest. There would be no interruptions this time, no coffee breaks.

Majid pushed the control lever and the carpet slipped out of the hold and into the rain-filled sky. The Orleans fire burned as a beacon in the distance, drawing him.

He could hear others behind him but, true to his word, he didn't turn to see. It was time for individual decisions.

The wind and the rain beat against his face, making him squint, making his robes whip around him; and the trees so far below formed a lush green carpet beneath him.

And in his way, he said good-bye to all that he had come to know and love, good-bye to the land of differences that he had grown to call home.

The junkyard loomed in front of him, a land of metal stretching several square miles all around. It was rust-colored with splashes of bright color mixed in like bluebells in a turnip patch. As he closed in, he could see Jits moving through the dreamlike landscape like ants around their hill.

With a laser in one hand and his controls in the other, Majid dived into the fray.

Abdullah climbed out on roof level, and already the flames were climbing all the way up the structure, playing peekaboo over the top ledge.

He moved toward the balloon, finding the dead Elite captain, his head popped, lying next to the gold dome, his own dome key in his hand. Two more Elite lay by the balloon, one half in and half out the gondola door, the other at the bottom of the stairs leading up to the thing.

The green-suits who had captured Baggins were poking their heads, wide-eyed, out the window spaces.

"Who can fly this?" Abdullah called.

One of them stuck a hand out of the window. "I can," he said.

"Get it ready. We'll leave in five minutes!"

Olson jumped off the limb right on top of Rennie, knocking them both to the ground. They were battered and weary from fighting, worn to a single thread, their hatred the only fuel that powered them. The man rolled away from him, getting to his feet. Moving backward, he stepped on something, bouncing on one foot while grabbing the other.

Scrambling to his feet, Olson threw himself at the man, knocking him back against a tree, hearing ribs crack.

Rennie went down, hand to his back, his face twisted in agony.

Olson staggered up, moved toward the man. "So, what are you without your exo?" he said, and his face was throbbing again, bleeding from several of the old cuts. Even here the wounds transferred.

Rennie got painfully to his feet. "You're a freebooter," he said, finally figuring it out. "You're no Exec."

"I'm Exec enough to retire you," Olson returned, and bent to pick up a sturdy limb lying beside him.

Rennie backed away, trying to keep an eye on Olson and the terrain. "You have no right to live with decent people," he said.

"Yeah?" Olson said, raising the limb. "Show me one."

He made to swing out with the limb, but Rennie chucked a large rock that bounced off his face, knocking him back. Then the man threw himself at Olson, both going down again.

Rennie got his hands around Olson's throat, choking. They rolled that way in the fallen leaves and the rotted spider stumps. Olson used his fists, pounding Du'camp's broken ribs until the man bled from the mouth and released his hold on Olson's neck.

He rolled away, moaning with the pain. Olson rose, retrieving his limb, and stalked Rennie.

"It's time for a long vacation, VeePee," he said as Du'camp tried unsuccessfully to stand upright. The man doubled over, limping off.

He whacked him with the club, and Du'camp went down to his knees. Bringing it back full, he swung around hard, clipping Rennie by the right ear and knocking him out spread-eagled on the rich black earth.

Setting his jaw, Olson went in for the kill.

* * *

Abdullah watched the fire rage all around the building as he dragged an Elite body off the ramp to the gondola. The streets below were full of citizens moving insanely in all directions. There was no place left to run, so they ran aimlessly, the instinct to survive driving them blindly on. There was some organization by the front gates, high-riding auts and skiffs manned by heavily armed Execs preparing to make a break for it.

Where was Olson? He should have been up here by now.

"We must go!" one of the green-suits shouted from the balloon, and Abdullah looked up to see fire reaching dangerously close to the balloon.

"Wait here!" Abdullah ordered, and he turned and ran back for Olson.

Getting into the elevator, he took it the one floor down. It was burning in there, like an oven; he had to hold his breath for the one-story ride.

The door opened and he hurried out, feeling the skin of his face prickling with the heat.

"Cat!" he called. "Olson!"

He charged down the hall, rounding the corner to see Olson, naked on the mind-match screen, pounding the long-dead image of Rennie Du'camp in a forest somewhere. He brought a club up and down methodically, pounding, pounding.

Du'camp lay dead across the table, a pistol lying inches from his clenched fists. Olson still sat on his chair, his head lolled back, his eyes rapidly blinking. Behind them, the raging fire had totally consumed the apartment and was moving down the hall.

"Olson!" Abdullah screamed, and ran to the man, shaking him. "Stop! He's dead, he's dead!"

He grabbed the ring off the man's head and shook him by the shoulders, eyes gradually focusing.

"Come on. We've got to get out of here!"

"Wh-what?"

"The fire! The fire!"

Olson shook his head and turned toward the apartment.

"No!" he yelled when he saw the fire, and jumped up, trying to pull the table out of the way.

"It's too late!" Abdullah yelled, grabbing his arm. The heat seared his face, making him flinch as fire gutted the hallway.

Olson shook him off. "They're in there. I've got to go to them!"

He pulled on the table, Rennie's body sliding off to crumple to the floor. He tried to edge around the table to rush into the searing heat and suffocating smoke.

"It's suicide!" Abdullah yelled, grabbing his arm again.

Olson jerked violently against him. "Let me go!"

Reaching out, Abdullah grabbed Rennie's pistol off the table. With a grimace, he brought it back and slammed the butt of the thing on the back of Olson's head.

The man collapsed against him. Grunting, Abdullah got him up on his shoulder and stumble-carried him to the elevator, where he scorched his finger pushing the panel button.

The elevator screamed for one floor, whining like a dying animal, moving upward in jerks. It stopped before making it all the way up, Abdullah having to climb half the length of the door, then reach back in to drag Olson out too.

As he got him up on the roof, the elevator screamed again, then died, plummeting ninety stories straight down. All the electricity went after that as sections of the building began to crumble and fall.

Majid went in low, just over the tops of the auts, to make himself a harder target. Other carpets buzzed around, crisscrossing his path, laying trails of napalm and laser fire.

He picked his targets selectively, going for the men with the balloon lasers strapped on their backs, and looking, always looking, for Milander.

And then he saw the bus.

The graveyard Jits were rallying around the bus, surrounding it with what weapons they had, and Majid knew he had found Milander's headquarters.

He turned a wide circle around it and began drawing fire. There was only one way to go in.

Taking the carpet way down, he got it down in one of the aisles, walls of piled-up auts all around him, and he ran the aisle. He wound it out fast, barely sneaking through as jagged rusty metal rushed past him as streaks of color. And suddenly Jits were blocking the path!

Instinctively they dived for cover and he just cleared them, homing on the bus and the crowd farther down the corridor. He took it to chest level and screamed in, laser opened up, burning a hole through their midst.

A man was bent over, one of the big lasers on his back as another fired a wide pink line at Majid. He had a second to see the right side of his carpet melt away, taking part of his leg with it, before he crashed into the Jits, the whole world tumbling crazily.

He came down hard in the center of them, bones breaking. But he still had a hold on his laser. They were on top of him, but he rolled over painfully and opened up, burning them backward.

He struggled to his feet, using the side of the bus for support. The Jits had moved back somewhat. He kept the laser on them and edged toward the door, the side of the bus the only thing keeping him on his feet.

They were aiming the big laser at him again from the end of the bus. He flared around, taking the head of the laser operator and the arm of the man carrying it. They went down.

The pain was deep in Majid, touching vital places. He had to hurry, to keep moving. He reached the open door of the bus, and the crowd surged at him again. He raked the laser through their midst, driving them back once more, and then managed to get himself up the bus stairs.

He swung the door closed with the long metal arm, and leaned against the handhold, the Jits moving up to the doors, trying unsuccessfully to force them open.

He looked down the aisle. A young man was sitting in one of the seats, looking at him, and there in the back aisle, a man on a stretcher was propped up against the back door.

"You're Milander," Majid said, and was surprised at how weak his voice was.

"Welcome, my son," the man said, and smiled with half his face. "You've come to end my suffering."

"I've come to end everyone's suffering," Majid said, and he coughed, shooting pain all through his body.

"That's quite a task," Milander said. "The best way to do that is to join us. You look like a good man to me. Be one with us. You know that Mohammed was an epileptic; it's a holy sign. The disease doesn't frighten you?"

"I'm beyond that," Majid said, and raised the laser. "I don't have the time for this."

The young man was up out of his seat, limping toward Majid, blocking him from Milander.

Majid fired, killing the boy. "Maybe human beings aren't ready to be replaced," he said, and aimed at Milander again.

"Where have you seen humanity?" the man asked him. "I've looked for it my whole life."

"You're already dead," Majid said, "you and your people. Why must you kill us?"

Milander's eyes softened, the good side of his face quivering. "You cannot kill that which is dead already," he said, using Majid's words. "Your kind must move aside for the rebirth of this world. We are God's own pestilence, come to save life. We all came on our own; no one summoned us. We share the vision in common. We persevere."

Majid pulled the trigger. Nothing happened. He looked at the gauge; the charge was depleted. Throwing the gun down, he moved toward Milander, using the seats to hold himself up. He had no feeling in his charred and smoking right leg and he knew there was spinal damage that he was aggravating with movement.

"I welcome you, sweet friend," Milander said. "Come and kiss me."

Majid reached him as the Jits poured into the bus. He got his hands around Milander's throat, the man offering no resistance. The others grabbed him, tugging and falling, and all at once the emergency door swung open and they all tumbled out onto the ground.

Incredible pain shot through Majid, but he didn't release his hold on Milander. There were people all around, grabbing, but they seemed removed from the struggle. Milander was using his good arm to pull them across the dirt toward the fallen laser.

He reached it, Majid still choking the life from him, and with his last breath he managed to turn the barrel of the thing toward the golden dome that just barely shone through the curtain of smoke drawn around the city. He died, his finger locked on the trigger, as Majid watched the wave of Jits wash over him, closing him in blessed darkness.

Abdullah staggered toward the balloon with a groaning Olson over his shoulder, green-suits rushing down the ramp to help him. Then a laser line flashed by him after severing the Jit dome from its base.

Abdullah turned, horrified, and watched the huge ball rock back and forth on its mooring. The green-suits took Olson from him.

"Get him into the balloon!" Abdullah yelled through the flames and smoke and creaking dome.

And the golden ball fell, crashing heavily on the roof and rolling with a terrible rumbling sound. It rolled to the end of the roof, crashed through the retaining wall, and fell ninety stories into the crowds below.

Abdullah rushed to the end of the building and looked down. The ball was floating down the street, a huge gash ripped through it, infesting the Mississippi floodwaters and everyone in them.

He hurried back to the balloon and ran up the gangplank. "Take it up!" he yelled when he got inside.

*   *   *

> *That person is not a perfect Moslem who eateth*
> *his fill, and leaveth his neighbors hungry.*
> —The Prophet Mohammed

XL
The Empty Quarter

They moved off slowly in the dark, off across the dunes, the slowly shifting sculptures of Allah. Behind them, a pillar of fire rose high in the air, many miles distant.

"It is the end of many things," Bandar said to Nura across the distance of their camels.

She nodded and turned to look at Misha'al, who rode with his head turned to look back at what they had left behind.

"Endings mean beginnings," she returned. "Perhaps the new roads will lead us to better places."

"Perhaps," Bandar said, but his voice sounded unsure. "At least Faisel will not be a part of it."

Nura looked at him thoughtfully. "He could have been different," she said. "I really believe that. He had many of Abdullah's good points. I could almost see the good in him."

Bandar smiled at her. "It is proper to speak well of the

dead," he said. "You never know whom you will meet later on."

And they moved off into the black velvet night, uncountable stars bathing them in pale light. They moved toward the oasis South of Riyadh, where they would camp until Abdullah came back to them or they knew he was dead.

* * *

How many a beast that bears not its own
provision, but God provides for it and you!
He is the All-hearer, the All-knower.
　　　　　　　—The Koran
　　　　　　　XXIX. The Spider

Ah, Love! could thou and I with Fate conspire
To grasp this sorry Scheme of Things entire,
Would not we scatter it to bits—and then
Remold it nearer to the Heart's Desire!
　　　　　　　—Omar Khayyam
　　　　　　　Rubayyat

LXI
Death and Life

They had been aloft for less than thirty minutes when Olson came around completely. He stood up, a hand on the back of his neck, and joined Abdullah at the window.

Far in the distance, Orleans burned out of control, and Olson watched his hopes burn with it.

"I'm sorry I hit you so hard," Abdullah said.

Olson waved it off. "You had no choice," he replied. "Are we all that's left?"

"No," Abdullah said. "Not really." He pointed to the East. "A column escaped the walls and fought their way through the Jits. I've been watching them the whole time. I think they're clean."

Olson looked, and saw several thousand people moving through the frontier. His evacuation force.

"How far away are they?"

"A few miles," Abdullah said. "We've stayed close. I thought you might be interested . . ."

Olson looked at him, then turned once more toward the city. Gret was gone; there was nothing he could do about it. He looked toward the column. "Would you mind dropping me off?" he asked.

Abdullah smiled. "I expected it," he said, and moved to the radio to give the order.

Fifteen minutes later, they caught up to the evacuation. It was an even division of citizens and Engies, surrounded by a protective force of Execs in auts, the Execs covering the auts, hoods and tops, the big machine guns mounted on the aut tops.

They brought the balloon to gently touch down right in front of the advancing column. The force halted, several of the auts breaking away to approach the balloon.

Olson opened the door and stepped out, Abdullah right behind him. The auts roared up, screeching to a halt by the balloons.

York and Valuska jumped out of the first one, running with smiling faces toward Olson. They ran up, grabbing him, hugging.

"Thought we'd never see your ass again," York said. "This is a hell of a deal."

"Tell him what happened," Valuska urged.

"What?" Olson asked.

"Damnedest thing," York said. "When we went to make a break, they needed somebody in charge. Guess what?"

Olson smiled and pointed to the man. "You," he said.

"I had the most seniority," York answered. "Can you believe that shit? I'm sure glad you're here to take this off my hands."

"Don't I even rate a hello?" came a voice behind Olson.

He turned to find Gret standing behind him, Wexler in her arms.

He grabbed them, words totally gone, and hugged them with all his strength, Wexler giggling like a crazy man and crying at the same time, Gret and Olson just crying.

"I thought . . ." he said, wetting her cheek with tears and kisses. "I thought . . . Rennie . . ."

"Rennie?" she returned. "The last time I saw Rennie he was laid out on the apartment floor after Wexler knocked him on the head with a lamp."

Olson pulled away. "You mean . . . you weren't there when the fire . . ."

Gret looked puzzled. "We got out of there after Wexler bopped him. I didn't know where you were. We went down on the streets, and the fire came, and we found Junex York and stuck with him."

Olson smiled, nodding. "You two are never getting out of my sight again."

"That sounds great to me," Gret returned, her eyes sparkling like fresh water in a mountain brook.

"What about when we sleep?" Wexler asked. "What about when we bathe? What happens when two of us have different things to do at the same time? What happens when three of us have different things to do at the same time? I have lots of things to do, you know, and not all of them can be done with you watching me all the—"

"Okay!" Olson laughed. "We'll talk about it later."

Jerry Joe and Jan walked over from the other aut, shaking hands all around.

"Well, here we are," Valuska said, his long face frowning. "Now what the hell do we do?"

"We survive," Olson said.

"Outside?" Jerry Joe said.

"Stranger things have happened," Olson said.

"There's another possibility," Abdullah said, and they all looked at him.

He pointed. "To the North," he said, "lies Wichita. It should be quite a place, judging from what I've learned from it, and I should say that they are probably in need of settlement. I'll wager there's no Jitterbug dome, either."

"Wichita," Jan said.

"Sounds good to me," York said.

Olson smiled and looked at Gret. She nodded. "Why not?" he said, and they all cheered.

And Olson realized that he had another chance, a chance to do it right. Perhaps none of it was wasted. Perhaps all of them—Execs, and Engies, and citizens—could make a better world out of the chaos of the old. Perhaps Mr. Elwood's faith in him, and his faith in himself, could yet be recaptured and realized. Wichita. It had a good ring to it.

He turned to thank Abdullah, but the man was already getting back on the balloon. He closed the door behind him.

Olson ran to the gondola as Abdullah poked his head out a window. "Come with us," Olson said.

"That is your path, my friend, not mine."

Olson nodded. "Good luck to you."

"And to you," Abdullah said. "I will not forget you."

"We will meet again," Olson said. "Of that I'm convinced."

Abdullah smiled a sad smile. "The paths wind," he said, "and cross often." The balloon began to rise. "Take some advice," he called out the window. "Live for love."

The balloon rose into the sky, and the rain was dissipating, breaking up, patches of pure blue showing through the gray. Abdullah gave the order and they turned the balloon to the East—to Nura.

Glossary

Aghal The double head cord worn on top of the Arabian cloth headdress.

Al Literally, "of the." A term of respect for Arab leaders.

Al Sa'ud Of the House of Sa'ud.

Alky A person addicted to fermented juices.

Allah The God of all, who made heaven and earth.

Allahu Akbar The daily call to prayer. "God is great."

Arm of Allah Name for the black-hooded enforcer of LOW rules.

Aut A four-wheeled motorized carriage.

Aziz, Abdul Patriarch of the House of Sa'ud, conqueror of the Arabian Peninsula in the early twentieth century.

Bashball The major spectator sport of the Western Sector, played with genetic mutations.

Bay'ah An oath of allegiance.

Bedouin Arabian nomads, desert dwellers.

Breeder Genetic mutation capable of breeding with any number of genetic codes. An adaptable, passive gene base capable of reproducing offspring of a kind of the breeding partner.

Bug Any of various kinds of clandestine listening devices.

Byat Home.

Caliph Literally, "successor" (to the Prophet Mohammed). The title was adopted by leaders of the Moslem community after the Prophet's death and was appropriated by the Ottoman Turks in the sixteenth century and used by the sultans until 1924.

Cardamom The aromatic seeds of either of two Asian plants of the ginger family. Used for making coffee.

Cause Célèbre In legal terms, a celebrated or notorious case.

Citizen The populace that works for the various LOW branches in a semislavelike atmosphere.

Con-tam Highly illegal "clean" suits that offer an amount of protection against the Jitterbug virus.

Corporate The word used to refer to the LOW Headquarters and its leadership in Arabia.

Dirigible A large passenger-carrying helium balloon.

Dome Refers to the gold sphere that sits atop each LOW Branch Headquarters and contains the Jitterbug virus.

Eastern Region That area of land encompassing all of Asia and the Middle East.

Eed al Adha The feast celebrating the end of the Pilgrimage and marking the day on which the pilgrims offer sacrifices in Mecca.

Elite The personal guard of the King of the World.

Emir A commander. The word can designate the governor of a town or province. Male members of the House of Sa'ud are known as "emirs," and this is usually translated as "prince." The English word "admiral" comes from the Arabic "emir al Bahr," "Commander of the Sea."

Encephalomyelitis An inflammation of the brain and spinal cord.

Engy A genetically created human, literally an "engineered" human.

Epileptic Person subject to seizure activity. There may be convulsive movements, and motor, sensory, and psychic dysfunction.

Erg A unit of electrical energy.

Eunuch A neuter Engy bred without sex organs or sex drive.

Exec One of the ruling class in LOW society.

Exo A form-fitting protective shell, a type of armor.

Fireman A lower-management Exec whose job it is to burn the remains of those infected with the Jitterbug virus (*see* Jit).

Freebooter Someone living outside the direct control of LOW.

Fuzztop (or **Fuzz**) Citizens in charge of law enforcement within the walls of each branch. Subject totally to the control of Corporate Execs.

Gaters Miniature Engies who control passage in and out of the city walls through the gate.

Ghutra Arabian cloth headdress, usually in red and white check.

Green Card Allows passage back into the city during times of crisis.

Guild Departmental structure of citizens having no power.

Hadhar The Arabian word for settled folk, as opposed to nomads. Hadhar derive their living from farming and trading.

Harem Collective word for the wives and concubines of Arab men.

Herpes medeaii The Jitterbug virus, named for an epileptic cat.

Holmes Air Base Located near the LOW Headquarters in Arabia, named for an Englishman, known as the Father of Modern Arabia for his introduction of the Arabs to petroleum.

Holo A three-dimensional projection.

Hooka A water pipe.

Hornies The word used by Houris to describe a state of sexual frustration.

Houris A female electrically altered at birth to sustain a physical addiction to the sex act. Traditionally, the sultry Nymphs that accompany the good Moslem in Paradise.

Ibn (sometimes **bin**) Son of.

Infidels Those not of the Moslem faith.

Insh'allah As God wills.

Islam The Moslem religion.

Jaluwa Exile.

Jihad Holy war.

Jit One infected with the Jitterbug virus (see appendix).

Junex A lower-management bureaucrat (*see* Exec).

Karma A belief in the law of cause and effect.

Kevlar Durable synthetic fabric tightly knit to provide tensile strength. Kevlar clothing is strong enough to prevent penetration from small arms fire and hand wielded blades.

Koran The Holy Book of Mohammed.

LOW Acronym for Light of the World.

Magne-carpet Airborne platform that is powered by the magnetic field of the earth itself.

Majlis Reception or sitting room, from the Arabic *yajlis*, "he sits down."

Mecca The holiest city of Islam.

Melters Old machines that are melted down to make bullets.

Minaret A high, slender tower attached to a Moslem mosque and surrounded by balconies, from which a muezzin calls the Allahu Akbar.

Mind Match A form of competitive recreation in which creative intelligence is tested by opponents on a cathode screen.

Mishla The traditional Arabian outer robe or cloak, usually black, brown, or cream and trimmed with gold thread.

Mohammed   Author of the Koran, progenitor of the religion of Islam.

Mosque   Moslem place of worship (*see* Minaret).

Mover   Someone who received unusually rapid promotion within the Corporate structure of LOW.

Mu'mim   A believer.

Musak   Official music of LOW, atonal and innocuous.

Nakull   Let's eat.

Nasrani   Literally, "a follower of Christ." A general term applied to all citizens of the Western Sector.

New Mecca   LOW garrison in the Arizona desert.

Nirooh   Let's go.

OB   Literally, "office boy." An Exec trainee.

Ordnance   A general term applied to ammunition and explosives.

Plasteel   A malleable, yet tough plastic; lightweight, yet containing an extremely dense concentration of molecules. The material used in making an exo (*see* Exo).

Plastic   Official currency of LOW, made from precious petroleum products.

Promotion   Upward movement through the LOW ranks, usually attained by assassination or backbiting.

Qadi   A judge.

Regional Director   The highest Exec position attainable for a non-Moslem.

Retirement   The end of usefulness, usually severing the retiree from further LOW connections.

Rounder   A small, point-scoring animal (*See* Bashball).

Safe   A building on neutral territory, unknown to your enemies. Used for troop bivouac.

Salaam   The traditional Arab greeting. "Peace be upon you."

Scimitar   Sword with a curved blade.

Scone   A small cake or loaf of bread.

Senior VeePee   The highest upper-management ranking below Branch Manager.

Seniority   The system of life, decides Exec ranking in natural order of succession.

Shariah   The law of God—Islamic law.

Shooters   Point-scoring Engies in bashball (*see also* Rounder).

Sifre, wahhed, etnayn   One, two, three.

SOP   Standard Operating Procedure. The rules that govern the LOW Corporate.

Symby Partner Defining a symbiotic relationship between two or more Engies that couldn't exist well on their own.

Thobe A long shirtlike garment worn by Arabian men. In the summer it is usually white and made of thin material. In winter, heavier material is used, and the thobe may well be dark or striped.

Transie Freebooter who drifts, nomadlike, without roots.

Tribute The payment that a LOW branch office must make to Corporate in order to survive.

Ulema Religious scholar.

Vacation An abrupt form of retirement.

VeePee LOW upper management.

Wa alaykum as Salaam Response to "Salaam." "And upon you be peace."

Wahhab Strict, severe qadi, revered by the House of Sa'ud and the basis for strict Moslem practice.

Wallahi! "By God!" a common Arabian exclamation.

Wallers Bashball defensive players (*see* Rounder, *also* Shooters).

Western Sector Roughly defined by the Continent of North America.

Yid Traditional enemy of the Arab.

Appendix 1

Brief History of the World
Use Restricted
Upper-Management Execs Only

570 Year of the Elephant. The Prophet Mohammed is born.

622 Year of Mohammed's Hijrah migration to Medina, and the beginning of the Moslem era.

630 Mohammed conquers Mecca.

632 The Prophet dies with the words "No, the friend, the highest in Paradise."

1703 The birth of Mohammed ibn Abdul Wahhab.

1744 Alliance formed between the strict faith of Wahhab and the House of Sa'ud, marking the historical beginnings of the world to come.

1876 Modern history begins with the birth of Abdul Aziz and the beginning of the House of Sa'ud.

1902 16 January, Abdul Aziz captures Riyadh, marking the end of Turkish rule of Arabia and the start of Sa'ud rule.

1922 Major Frank Holmes introduces Abdul Aziz to the possibilities of Arabian oil.

1949 Arabia begins to nationalize its oil holdings.

1960 OPEC is formed.

1974 OPEC demonstrates its control over world energy for the first time.

1997 Is'al Dim ibn Fahad begins installation of the Jitterbug domes in every major city in the world.

2005 Installation of the domes is completed without mishap due in large measure to Is'al's creation of an elite corps of engineers and builders whose bywords were silence and secrecy. This cadre of electronically controlled men later formed the root of the House of Sa'ud's personal bodyguards, the Elite.

September 23, 2005   Is'al Dim ibn Fahad makes historic "Temple of God" speech to the world, detailing his plans for restructuring the nations of the world into an Arab state.

September 24, 2005   The Jitterbug virus is released through the domes in the Australian cities of Melbourne, Sydney, and Broome and spreads rapidly over the entire continent. Before anyone appreciates the danger, the disease is spread to New Zealand, Tasmania, New Guinea, Java, Singapore, Malaysia, and the Philippines. Other nations wisely ban flights and seagoing vessels bound from Australia. There is much ado as Australian small craft trying to escape the growing peril are shot on sight on the high seas.

September 25, 2005   The nations of the world threaten Arabia with nuclear retribution if the domes are not dismantled. The House of Sa'ud refuses, accepting the one obvious fact about nuclear warfare: it spells suicide for the countries that use it.

October 3, 2005   The Union of Soviet Socialist Republics storms and takes the buildings in Russia containing domes and accidentally releases the virus. As its citizens try to escape, they are repelled by a large standing army on the borders of China.

November 1, 2005   Australia becomes the first continent to be declared officially uninhabitable; others follow.

Nobember 15, 2005   The House of Sa'ud cuts off all oil shipments to the world to speed up compliance.

December 1, 2005   The House of Sa'ud pulls its considerably large holdings out of every bank in the world, marking the collapse of Earth's monetary systems and bringing on worldwide depression immediately.

January 14, 2006   The USSR is the largest country to be declared uninhabitable, as its bordering countries mount major conflicts to keep the Russians out of their borders.

February 1, 2006   The world in chaos, the LOW Corporate is officially formed, offering financial and energy aid to those countries who voluntarily comply with the Arab restructuring.

2010   Istanbul, Turkey, becomes the first city to complete its surrounding wall and be made an official LOW branch office. It serves as the model for the rest of the world.

2012   The nuclear arsenals of the world are dismantled.

2024   The restructuring is complete with an estimated 90 percent of the world either under LOW control or uninhabitable. The remaining 10 percent contain small pockets of survivors in remote sections. When it is no longer cost-effective to hunt them down, they are officially characterized as "freebooters" and trade with them becomes unlawful.

2026 The Compact of Mecca is signed, which delineates the death penalty for the crimes of unauthorized energy production, scientific research, and education.

2030 Plastic is introduced as the new monetary unit, replacing in some instances simple barter, though barter remains the chief form of commerce.

2033 The Exec system is officially sanctioned.

2034 A dome is accidentally opened in Nagasaki, Japan, and the entire population of that country commits mass suicide to avoid the degradation of the virus.

2057 Engy labor is introduced for the first time in the London branch.

2063 A fission reactor in a freebooter stronghold in the Western Sector melts down, causing a massive disruption in the San Andreas Fault and triggering major earthquakes throughout the Western Sector, reforming the topography of much of this area.

2065 Is'al Dim ibn Fahad Al Sa'ud dies at the age of 103, his funeral is viewed on the television by an estimated two billion people.

2066—2071 The Black Years of succession. A series of wars fought by Is'al Dim's children and grandchildren over control of the LOW Corporate, ending in February 2071 with an Engy war that placed Is'al's grandson Ma'atsam ibn Naif at the Board Chair.

2075 The LOW Headquarters in the Rub al Khali is dedicated.

2099 Africa is declared uninhabitable.

2118 Ma'atsam ibn Naif dies and is succeeded by his son Faisel ibn Ma'atsam after a bloody purge of close relatives.

2132 The territory of Canada is declared uninhabitable.

2135 Greenland is declared uninhabitable.

2142 The Mexican and Central American branches are declared uninhabitable.

2151 Faisel ibn Ma'atsam dies by his own hand and is succeeded in a bloodless coup by his son Faisel ibn Faisel, who also bears the name Al Sa'ud.

Appendix 2

MEMO

To: LOW Administrative, Orleans
From: Computer Research

JITTERBUG: REPORT TO LOW MEDICAL ASSOCIATION

Jitterbug is a lethal form of encephalomyelitis. The term encephalomyelitis refers to an inflammation of the brain and spinal cord. This disease is frequently fatal, and survivors are usually subject to serious sequelae, ranging from grand-mal seizures to impaired respiration, sensory deficits, and, invariably, impotence in males, due to damage to the spinal cord.

The viral agent responsible for the disease process is known as Herpes medeaii. Dr. Joan Thorgeson, the virologist who first isolated this microorganism, reportedly named this virus for her pet cat, who was epileptic.

Different forms of the Herpes virus have haunted man through the centuries. They have caused harmless fever blisters on the mouth, very painful venereal diseases, shingles, and chickenpox. The virus itself seems to have mutated into more serious forms. This particular Herpes strain may be an adaptation of what was known as the Herpes simplex virus, the agent causing oral fever blisters and venereal disease. Even in the twentieth century, the disease was known to possibly have a type of encephalitis as sequelae.

EPIDEMIOLOGY

The patient with Jitterbug may be of any age or race. It has been noted in epidemiological studies that some groups are slightly more predisposed than others to survival of the disease. Patients in lower socioeconomic groups seem to have slightly better chances with survival of Jitterbug than do middle- to high-income groups.

As with most disease processes, infants and the elderly are in the highest-risk group for this disease. People aged

415

thirty to forty-five have the best chance of survival, but, even at best, those chances are marginal. Patients with strains of Negro ancestry appear to be most protected from this virus.

Herpes medeaii is spread via droplets through the air much as the common cold is spread. It is *extremely* contagious. As soon as a person is known to be infected with this virus, he *must* be isolated from the rest of society and encouraged in self-immolation. This cannot be stressed enough. This virus seems to have mutated so completely that it can circumvent the human's normal immunological mechanisms. Only a minority of victims have demonstrated ability to produce any amount of antibodies against this disease.

PATHOLOGY

Herpes medeaii is a neurotropic virus: it has a special affinity for damaging nervous tissue. Cerebral edema (swelling and fluid retention of brain) invariably occurs. Numerous petechial hemorrhages (minute, spiderlike hemorrhages) are scattered throughout the brain's hemispheres, the brainstem, cerebellum, and spinal cord. Areas of neuron necrosis (dead nerve cells) are found in the brain on postmortem examination.

Perivenous demyelinating lesions characteristically are found scattered on the spinal cord (lesions around veins where there is damage to and destruction of the myelin sheath, or white matter, the protective and insulating coating around the gray nerve cells).

The meninges (protective coating around brain and spinal cord) and perivascular spaces of brain (areas around blood vessels) are intensely infiltrated with polymorphonuclear leukocytes (a type of white blood cell).

Invasion of vessel walls by neutrophils and leukocytes (blood cells) may result in thrombosis (clot formation) with resultant small infarcts (blockages of circulation).

ASSESSMENT

When assessing the patient, note any prodromal (initial, vague) symptoms. A detailed health history must be taken. Of critical importance is whether the patient has been outside city walls. Question the patient as to when, location, and length of time spent on outside. Exposure to "Jits" must be noted also. The health-care professional should try to assess whether the patient has been subject to memory lapses, strange dreams, and any other mental aberrations. Any change in behavior patterns should be noted. Memory lapses of a few minutes are common. Question about their personal contacts, so those contacts can be examined.

Males should be examined as to whether a penile erection is possible, as erection is always impossible with this disease process. A Houris may be utilized for this test.

Head and neck stiffness, coordination of body movements, and level of consciousness must all be carefully evaluated. Note the patient's speech patterns.

Electroencephalogram may or may not show aberrant wave patterns. It is too inconclusive to be recommended.

Lumbar puncture and other invasive diagnostic tests *should not* be attempted. Until Jitterbug is ruled out, the patient must be treated as contagious. Invasive procedures, which technically help the diagnosis, may also act to spread the disease further, especially to the health-care workers performing the tests.

All examinations should be conducted in a dry environment under laminar flow. The health-care professional and the patient each should wear disposable gown, gloves, and mask. The health-care professional should wear a decontamination suit if available. If Jitterbug is suspected, the examination should be thorough but as brief as possible. The disposable clothing worn (but not the decontamination suit) should be burned as soon as contact with the patient is discontinued.

Identification of Jits is a delicate process. In the beginning stages it is not a clear-cut diagnosis, but it is highly contagious. Once diagnosed, the patient will be isolated from all known civilization and then eliminated, so it is important to accurately assess this patient.

There will be some cases which are hard to diagnose accurately. The Light of the World Medical Committee recommends that, in these cases, society should be given the benefit of the doubt. The patient should be isolated and encouraged in self-immolation. Allah's justice and mercy decree that patients should not be unnecessarily eliminated, but if there is suspicion, society must be protected from that individual.

SIGNS AND SYMPTOMS

There is often an incubation period of seven days before signs and symptoms appear, but the incubation period may be shorter or longer. The patient is himself contagious within two days after exposure, although symptoms may not appear for another five. A patient may be contagious without even knowing that he has been exposed to the virus.

For the first two days, the symptoms are generally of a prodromal nature. They include fever, chills, drowsiness, malaise, anorexia. The patient may present an unexplained weight loss. There may be mild to severe gastrointestinal distress, ranging from mild nausea to severe vomiting and diarrhea. Headaches are generally present and are mild for the first two days but increase in severity. Rhinorrhea (runny nose) may be present.

The patient may demonstrate alterations in his level of consciousness. He may show signs of progressive dementia and may become disoriented. Hallucinations are often visual and auditory in nature, and they appear to be of a "religious" nature. Patients frequently report, by the third day of the onset of symptoms, that they have seen "God and his angels" and claim to be recipients of direct messages.

Males invariably become impotent with this disease. There may be some degree of urinary and fecal incontinence also, due to spinal-cord damage.

Damage to areas of the cerebral cortex may cause alterations in speech, sight, hearing, and other sensory areas, depending on the areas of the cortex damaged.

Meningeal irritation can be seen with nuchal rigidity (head and neck stiffness). The deep tendon reflexes may or may not be impaired.

Brainstem damage usually results in some respiratory depression, which may become severe, possibly fatal. There may be impairment of the gag reflex: the patient cannot eat or drink without aspirating the substance into his lungs. The patient then chokes to death or dies of pneumonia.

A swaggering gait indicates cerebellar disease.

The patient is subject to seizure activity, usually within three days of the onset of symptoms. Seizures may be grand mal, petit mal, Jacksonian, and psychomotor. Status epilepticus may occur. This is a state in which there is a succession (two or more) of generalized seizures with no recovery of consciousness between them. Exhaustion and acidosis may prove fatal.

Seizure refers to clinical manifestations, including disturbances in sensation, alterations in perception and/or coordination, loss of consciousness, convulsive movements, or a combination of any of the above. The clinical manifestations are caused by the erratic, synchronous discharging neurons. It is believed that Herpes medeaii interferes with GABA synthesis at the synapse, producing a shift of the normal excitatory-inhibitory balance, resulting in a seizure. Compromised circulation due to Herpes-induced cerebral thrombosis may lead to seizure activity.

The grand-mal seizure is the classic epileptic seizure in which the patient suffers convulsions. Petit-mal seizures are characterized by short lapses of consciousness. In psychomotor seizures there may be sudden recollection of past events, hallucinations (visual and olfactory are common), forgetfulness, word-finding difficulty, personality changes, and inappropriate moodiness.

TREATMENT AND PROGNOSIS

There is no known treatment for the Herpes medeaii virus. Jitterbug is highly contagious and almost always fatal. Treatment must be directed at protection of society.

The patient should be removed from society—immediately. He should be encouraged in self-immolation. Medications should be given to allay the patient's pain and anxiety regarding self-immolation. Any clothing and personal effects must also be burned without delay. The patient's personal contacts should be examined, as they may have been exposed to this disease.

It is estimated that 93 percent of patients die within two weeks of exposure to this virus. Statistics are unavailable on the outlawed survivors. However, it is known that they are subject to all manner of seizure and movement disorders. There are reports that Jitterbug survivors frequently hallucinate and falsely believe themselves holy. The males permanently lose the ability to attain a penile erection. And, most importantly, these people always are carriers of this dreaded disease. When discovered, they must be eliminated. This is what Allah, in his infinite compassion and mercy, decrees.

Appendix 3

CHAIN OF COMMAND
LOW CORPORATE

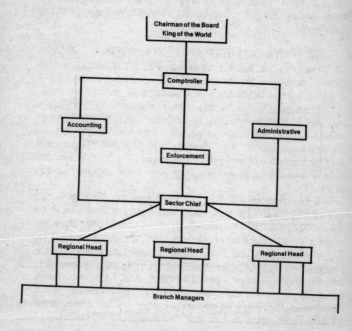

Note: The positions from Board Chair to Sector Chief must be filled by pure-blood Arabs. The Regional Head is usually the Branch Manager of his residence branch.

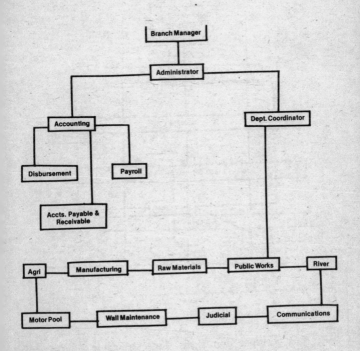

BRANCH ADMINISTRATION

Note: Not all departments are listed.

INTER-DEPARTMENTAL

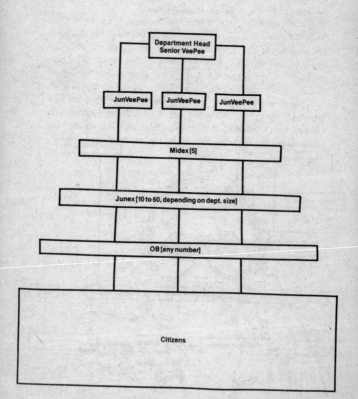

ABOUT THE AUTHOR

Mike McQuay began his writing career in 1975 while a production line worker at a tire plant. He turned to writing as an escape from the creeping dehumanization he saw in the factory, and gradually worked himself out of Blue Collarland and into Poor-but-happy-starving writerism.

His first novel, *Lifekeeper*, was published in 1980. Since then, he has published eleven others, ranging from juveniles to mainstream horror, with the emphasis on s/f.

Jitterbug is his sixth novel with Bantam, following *Escape from New York* and four books of the Mathew Swain detective series. *Jitterbug* is by far his most ambitious effort. The idea began several years ago as an "Ivanhoe in glass towers" concept, gradually evolving into the larger ideas expressed herein. Hard research and writing on the project took over a year and a half.

McQuay is thirty-five years old, and lives in Oklahoma City with his wife and three children. He is an Artist in Residence at Central State University in Edmond, Oklahoma. He watches too much television and adamantly refuses to eat fried okra.

Mel White
9/5/82

"TRULY A BRAVURA PERFORMANCE. I PREDICT THAT ITS POPULARITY WILL RIVAL *DUNE*, TO WHICH I CONSIDER IT SUPERIOR AS A TOTALLY REALIZED EXTRAPOLATION."
—Thomas N. Scortia

"HARRISON'S BEST BOOK IN YEARS. INVENTIVE, EN-GROSSING, AND SOLIDLY BASED ON WHAT MIGHT HAVE BEEN."
—Ben Bova

WEST
of
EDEN

by
Harry Harrison

Sixty-five million years ago, a disastrous cataclysm exterminated three-quarters of all species on earth. Overnight, the age of the dinosaurs was ended; the age of the mammals had begun. But if that disaster had never happened and the dinosaurs had survived to fulfill their evolutionary destiny, this is what the world might have been. The world WEST OF EDEN.

A fascinating and deeply moving saga of two cultures fated to struggle for control of the earth, WEST OF EDEN is a remarkable odyssey, a scientifically accurate projection of what could have been the true history of our world.

Buy WEST OF EDEN, on sale now wherever Bantam hardcovers are sold, or use the handy coupon below for ordering: